Someone to Daydream About

Someone to Daydream About

SYDNEY LANGFORD

Farrar Straus Giroux
New York

Content warning: This book contains light references to a deceased parent, financial insecurity, sexist comments (challenged), and online harassment (challenged).

Farrar Straus Giroux Books for Young Readers
An imprint of Macmillan Publishing Group, LLC
120 Broadway, New York, NY 10271 • fiercereads.com

EU representative: Macmillan Publishers Ireland Ltd, 1st Floor, The Liffey Trust Centre, 117–126 Sheriff Street Upper, Dublin 1, D01 YC43

Library of Congress Cataloging-in-Publication Data is available.

First edition, 2026
Book design by Julia Bianchi
Emojis designed by Julia Bianchi and by OpenMoji—the open-source emoji and icon project. License: CC BY-SA 4.0
Printed in the United States of America

ISBN 978-0-374-39365-6
10 9 8 7 6 5 4 3 2 1

For the dreamers who chase their stars,
even when the world tells you the sky isn't yours

Content Note

Sign language, like all languages, is rich and layered.

While multiple variations of signing exist, in SOMEONE TO DAYDREAM ABOUT, ASL (American Sign Language) and SimCom (simultaneous communication—speaking and signing at the same time) are used.

ASL is a visual language that has different grammar rules from English, thus, any author representing it on-page has tricky creative choices to make. In SOMEONE TO DAYDREAM ABOUT:

- ⋆ Pure ("voices-off") ASL is *italicized.* This is typically an interpretation of what's being signed (not an exact translation), using English syntax.

- ⋆ SimCom is written in standard text.

- ⋆ For clarity, ***bolded and italicized*** words do not relate to ASL; these are emphasized English words.

It's also important to note deafness exists on a wide spectrum, from mildly Hard of Hearing to virtually no hearing. Natalie, the main character, is medically Hard of Hearing but identifies as Deaf. This reflects her cultural and personal connection to the Deaf community and is unrelated to her level of hearing. "Big D" Deaf typically refers to those who identify with Deaf culture, while "little d" deaf represents the medical/physical condition of profound hearing loss.

Other D/deaf authors may portray deafness and ASL/SimCom differently, and those creative choices are also valid!

Chapter One

Dare to Dream

Seattle, June 7

"*Is anyone confused? Have any questions?*" I ask in American Sign Language as I wrap up the Beginner ASL class I'm teaching.

From the front of one of the run-down classrooms at the Nielsen Family Deaf Center, I scan my students' faces, searching for any hint of uncertainty. They all look mildly confused, but nobody raises their hand. "*OK-OK. We're finished. See you next week!*" I dismiss them.

As everyone trickles into the hallway, I turn to the whiteboard behind me. My forced smile disappears, and I let my forehead thunk against the board in exasperation. I pull back and stretch my neck and roll my shoulders, the muscles sore and tense, and swallow the sour feeling that always bubbles up after teaching this class.

When my dad taught it, all twenty-five seats were full. He'd share colorful stories, his face twisting and contorting in perfect combination with his signs, hands flying smoothly through the air. His students were captivated and laughed along even if they didn't understand everything. He knew how to capture people's attention. He knew how to teach people in a way that didn't ***feel*** like teaching and could coax even the most reluctant learners out of their shells.

I've been trying to fill his shoes at our small, family-owned Deaf Center these last two years, but evidently I can't teach half as passionately as him. I'm lucky if twelve students show up.

I force the all-too-familiar pang of grief down and glance at my service dog, who's in a down-stay underneath my desk, oblivious to my woes.

"Ging, am I a good teacher? Be honest." Ginger doesn't stir. I nudge her with my foot, and the yellow lab simply stretches and yawns. She's not the best conversationalist.

I startle when someone taps my shoulder. I whip around and see two students, Sabrina and her grandfather, Frank. Sabrina dons an apologetic smile. "*Excuse me . . .*" she signs. Great, they caught me asking my dog about my teaching competency. That's not embarrassing at all.

"*Hi. What's up?*" I ask after regaining my composure.

"*Do you teach . . .*" She frowns, not having the right signs for what she's trying to ask. She looks to Frank, but he doesn't know, either. "*Alone lessons?*"

"*Private,*" I supply the correct sign. "*Yes.*"

"Oh, great!" she exclaims, then clamps her mouth shut, adhering to my "voices-off during class" rule. "*Sorry.*"

"It's okay. Class is over," I say while signing at the same time—simultaneous communication, or SimCom for short.

"*Grandpa made a new friend* at his retirement home," Sabrina explains, half-speaking, half-signing. She nudges Frank playfully.

"IT'S HARD FOR HER TO TRAVEL," Frank yells. Sabrina plugs her ears. "SHE'S IN A WHEELCHAIR."

It takes everything in me to not burst into laughter. Frank's adjusting to his hearing loss and screams all the time. Personally, I think it's adorable, but I'm also Deaf. Yelling doesn't really faze me.

I quell my amusement before turning back to Sabrina. "My rates for private lessons are a little higher. With gas prices and everythi—"

"HER NAME IS JANET!" Frank interrupts. "DOESN'T LOOK A DAY OVER SIXTY!"

Against my will, a laugh breaks free, and I cough to cover it. While he rambles on about their Bingo Night meet-cute, I catch a glimpse of the clock hanging on the classroom wall: 4:37 p.m. Damn it.

My little sister, Jo, is coming home for the summer from deaf residential school, and I'm supposed to pick her up at the bus station in twenty minutes.

"I'm so sorry, but I'm late for something. You can email me for private rates," I explain, rushing to gather my backpack and my dog. Sabrina gives a thumbs-up as I head into the hallway. Ginger obediently trots alongside me.

In the lobby, Mom is reorganizing our display of incredibly outdated assistive technology. Her steel-gray eyes flick away from the shelves and land on me. Her harsh expression, accentuated by the furrowed lines etched between her brows, could probably curdle milk. "*You're late,*" she accuses, adjusting her glasses with a clipped movement.

"*I'm going now. Two students haven't left yet—can you lock up the Center when they leave?*"

"*Fine.*" She jerks her head toward the doors.

I push outside, buckle Ginger into her doggy seat belt, and climb into my dingy 2007 TOYOTA Corolla, resigning myself to the fate of sitting in Seattle's bumper-to-bumper rush hour traffic.

"*I thought you abandoned me!*" Jo laments as soon as I get out of my car at the bus station pickup spot.

"*I texted you I was running late. You're worst-dramatic.*" She sticks her tongue out at me, but our annoyance quickly morphs into sprawling grins.

"*I missed you. I'm happy you're home for the summer,*" I tell her.

She circles her sternum with a claw-shaped hand. "*Make-me-disgusted!*" She feigns a look of revulsion but yanks me into a hug.

We originally went to the same residential school, but when our dad got sick, I decided to attend mainstream school in Seattle (with the assistance of an interpreter) so I could help Mom with the Center and Dad.

A memory of thirteen-year-old Jo and fourteen-year-old me bickering during the three-hour bus ride home about who got to hug Mom and Dad first flashes through my mind. Now ***I'm*** the one greeting her at the station. It's strange how life . . . goes on. Shifting so suddenly and without mercy, leaving you to mourn pieces of a world that doesn't exist anymore.

When she pulls away, I study her. The orange Camp Half-Blood shirt she shamelessly stole from me a few months ago is French tucked into a black miniskirt. Her hazel eyes, which we both inherited from Dad, gleam in the evening sunlight. She looks at me closely, too. And ever-so-kindly remarks, "*You need better concealer. It doesn't hide your eye bags. Or you can borrow some of my R-E-T-I-N-O-L cream."*

I instinctively touch my dark, puffy eye bags and sigh. I guess that's the consequence of getting less than four hours of sleep a night for two years.

"*What did Mom say about our new Deaf Center ideas?*" she asks, then loads her luggage into my trunk.

I avoid answering by getting into the driver's seat.

"*You didn't tell her?!*" Jo accuses me when she buckles in. I shrug.

For years, Jo and I have been brainstorming new ideas to improve the Center. It's not falling apart or anything—except for the only-slightly-leaky roof—but it's outdated. The world evolved, but the Center didn't. We agreed to start Project Revamp while she's home for summer break, but I was supposed to lay the groundwork with Mom beforehand, since she's been stubborn about modernizing the Center ever since Dad died.

"*I know, I know!*" I tap flattened fingers to my temple. "*But sharing our new ideas will be easier now that you're here! She'll be happy to see you after such a long time. You're her baby.*"

Mom's favoritism for Jo has always been painfully obvious. I might as well use it to my advantage.

"*You're annoying. And I'm not a baby.*" She flicks my arm. "*And it's only fair Mom loves me more. You were Dad's favorite. Don't get greedy.*"

I roll my eyes. Technically, Dad never played favorites. But he and I were in a similar boat, being the medically Hard of Hearing half of the family, and there were certain experiences that only we shared; people incorrectly assuming we had no issue following conversations just because we were comfortable voicing, or how overwhelming the background noise of the world could get. We knew what each other was going through. We never needed to explain it.

Mom and Jo share a connection like that, being medically deaf, and ***I'll*** never fully know their experience.

The only difference is that I no longer have a family member who understands mine.

"But I'm right." I flash her a grin. *"I'm the smartest sister. True biz."* I stick my key into the ignition and start the trek to Ballard—the part of Seattle we call home.

"We'll tell her tonight, then," Jo replies as I stop at a red light.

I shake my head and sign one-handedly, *"She'll react better if we let her have a nice, peaceful night and do it tomorrow."* Jo sticks her hand in front of me and signs an affirmative *"OK"* since I can't look at her while driving.

Good. Hopefully tonight will go smoothly, then.

I have everything perfectly planned. The Center barely makes enough to cover the mortgage and our monthly payments on Dad's outstanding medical bills, but over the past year I've squirreled away some of what I made from private ASL lessons and my senior-year-lunchtime-side-hustle: Algebra Tutoring for Cash.

I mean, yeah, I've been teetering on the very edge of Poor Kid Burnout, but my lack of a work-life balance has yielded $3,232.77 for my slush fund. Worth it.

And since I've spent my precious few spare moments coaching Jo on how to be an ASL tutor, she can get her own clients this summer and add to that fund. Primary speakers or users of a language aren't automatically good at teaching it, but Jo has a knack for it, like Dad. Sure, this money won't be enough for all the building upgrades, educational resources, and community outreach we eventually want to implement, but it's enough to get us started on redecorating and designing a new website while we fundraise for the rest.

When Dad was still in the hospital, Jo and I would squeeze into his bed and brainstorm ideas for the Center while I drew design concepts in my sketch pad. This will be a step toward bringing the place back to life and bridging the gaps between the Deaf and Hearing worlds, like we dreamed with Dad.

All that's left is to convince Mom . . .

After we pull into our driveway, I turn to Jo and sign, "*Remember, we'll bring it up tomorrow. OK?*"

She gives a hesitant nod, her attention on our house. It looks like it's in its pre-HGTV makeover stage, with brown paint chipping off the panels, a huge crack in the driveway, and moss covering the roof, but it's home to us.

Inside, Jo leaves her sandals strewn next to the door, and I place both my thrifted Carhartt boots and the sandals on our shared shoe rack. My eyes land on the rack next to Jo's and mine—Mom's shoes take up one half, while the other half is empty. I can still vividly picture Dad's work boots, beat-up sneakers, and flip-flops being there. We finally mustered the courage to donate most of his stuff a year ago, but Mom's never put her shoes on his side or her clothes in his dresser drawers.

I've walked past these racks every day for a year, but tonight, it sends a shock of grief through me, and I have to force a deep breath into my lungs.

No matter how much time passes, or how much I've grown used to living with only memories of their overflowing shoe rack, I can't grow used to the empty spaces in our house and our hearts.

I pull myself out of it as Mom comes into the entryway and wraps Jo in a hug. After she steps back, her face lights up with a type of joy I've never been on the receiving end of. "*How are you? You're taller now! I'm making a nice dinner to celebrate you coming home for summer and Natalie graduating high school.*"

She smiles at both of us, and I cheer internally. I knew this family dinner to celebrate Mom's Golden Child being home from school (and my graduation) would put her in a good mood! We'll have a nice evening and discuss the Center tomorr—

"*We have tons of new ideas for the Center!*" Jo announces, beaming.

Shit. There goes that plan.

"*Mom, our new ideas are KissFist! We'll redecorate, and I'll make social media posts. We have plans for summer camps, game nights! It's exciting!*" She does jazz hands, trying to get Mom to match her enthusiasm, but it falls flat as Mom shoots me a withering glare.

"*I wanted one nice night with my daughters, but you HAD to mention the Deaf Center, didn't you?*" Her signs are laced with frustration. "*Act like an adult! We don't have money for new ideas.*"

"*I didn't mention the Center!*" I gesture toward Jo. "*But . . . I've saved up some money, and now we can afford small changes. It'll be good for the Center! Good for the Deaf community!*"

"The Center is fine. Conversation finished." She flips both hands away from her body, fingers splayed, and storms into the kitchen. Jo grabs my wrist and drags me along as she follows her. Mom angrily fills a pot with hot water and snatches gluten-free pasta out of the pantry.

"She has great ideas. Let her tell you!" Jo pushes me forward and encourages me to share.

Well, I guess it's now or never.

"Mom . . . updating the Center will make life easier for so many deaf kids. Most deaf centers in the whole country are old, outdated. If we make a good, modern center in Seattle, maybe it'll inspire other centers! More deaf kids, all around the US, would have better resources."

This strikes a chord with her. Mom didn't grow up proud of her Deaf identity or her language. Unlike Jo and me (until I left residential school), she attended mainstream, Hearing schools where she was ridiculed, harassed, and called "deaf and dumb" by students and teachers alike. I'll do anything I can to prevent other D/deaf kids from experiencing that. I can't understand why she wouldn't want the same.

Mom takes off her glasses and scrubs hands over her face. *"We don't have money. No."*

"We do! I saved up. Now that I'm done with high school, I have more time and I can fundraise for more." Before I can stop myself, I add, *"Dad wanted this."*

"Don't guilt-trip me with Dad!" she snaps.

"I'm not 'guilt-tripping'! Mom, you're being unreasonable! Give me one good reason why we can't upgrade!"

"*Conversation finished!*" She gives one last, resolute sign, anger burning in her eyes. "*You ruined tonight. Good job.*" She stalks out of the kitchen and slams her bedroom door so forcefully I feel the vibrations. A half-filled pot of water sits abandoned by the sink, uncooked noodles spilling out of the box and onto the floor.

The sudden stillness in the room feels like it's mocking me, amplifying every emotion I'm trying to suppress. I slump onto one of the stools at the kitchen island, the weight of her anger pressing down on me like a stone.

Jo sits beside me and squeezes my hand—a small, grounding gesture—but it's not enough to stop the accusation replaying in my mind of a celebration tarnished by a conversation I didn't even start.

In moments like this—when I'm exhausted from twelve-hour days or weekends with no breaks or Mom's blown up to the point of storming off—I question whether this is the hill I'm willing to die on. Is it worth all this to keep Dad's vision alive, even when it'd be easier to let go?

But then I remember the Center I dream about—the ***world*** I dream about. A place where everyone is welcome, where respect isn't a luxury but a given. Where D/deaf kids who've faced language deprivation and feeling less-than can thrive. Where parents can learn how to raise a D/deaf child with love and confidence. Where Hearing people can unlearn the ableism deeply ingrained in our society and grow into better allies.

It's a vision bursting with hope and possibility, and it deserves to exist.

We'll never have enough money to make all our dreams come

true, but we have enough to ***try***. And we have to. Because this isn't just about me—it's about the kids and families who will walk through those doors one day. It's about creating a future I can be proud of. One Mom might not believe in yet, but I do.

If she wants me to act like an adult, I ***will***.

Chapter Two

The Return of Felix Song

Seattle, June 8

I was hoping Mom would've slightly cooled off by the next day, but to my dismay, she remains adamant about giving me the silent (or should I say signless) treatment—a Mom specialty.

Thankfully, a distraction comes in the form of a private lesson with the Songs, some of my favorite long-term clients. Shortly after I ring the bell, the door flings open, and I'm enthusiastically greeted by Ava.

"*Hi!*" The twelve-year-old's shiny baby blue hearing aids stand out against her long black hair. She sports a CELINE T-shirt and teal yoga pants.

"*Hey, A-V-A.*" I use her sign name, which is just a lexicalized version of her name.

I started working for the Songs two years ago, shortly after Ava was diagnosed with degenerative hearing loss. Initially, it was a weekly lesson with Ava, her parents, and her older brother, Felix—when he bothered to show up, that is.

It wasn't long before she was signing circles around her family. So, to keep up with her enthusiasm, we added an extra weekly private lesson for her. We also incorporated regular outings to put her skills to use in real-world situations. For instance, Deaf events, Broadway plays with interpreters, or hanging out at the Center.

The more time I spent with Ava, the more I grew attached to her. These days, she feels more like a bonus little sister than a client. (Though, honestly, she's much less annoying than my actual sister.)

"*Why are you so perky today?*" I ask with a chuckle, noting she's somehow more cheerful than ever.

Her expression briefly turns mischievous. "*Just excited for today's lesson,*" she explains, and scampers into the kitchen.

As I step inside the sprawling house (like, chandeliers-in-nearly-every-room-and-a-guesthouse-in-the-backyard ***sprawling***), a massive, signed poster of Felix Song and his bandmates instantly greets me.

I can't help but make eye contact with poster-Felix as I untie my boots. When his boy band, DAYDREAM, moved to LA eight months ago and exploded onto the music scene with almost as much velocity as One Direction, Mrs. Song started proudly displaying the band's photos on the fireplace mantel and fridge doors. But this gigantic poster in the entryway is new—and looks comically out of place hanging with the up-to-interpretation, avant-garde art pieces the opulent home is decorated with.

I make my way over to the kitchen island, where Ava is sitting with her parents, and put Ginger in a down-stay before taking a seat facing the entryway.

"*Are you OK, sweetie?*" Mrs. Song asks me in ASL. She basically pressed copy and paste on both her children, with her black-brown eyes and sharp jawline an exact match for Felix's, and her thick, shiny hair and tan skin mirroring Ava's. Even her "athleisure" fashion matches Ava's style: yoga pants that probably came from an MLM company and a Ralph Lauren top. "*You look tired.*" Her kind eyes rove over my face.

"*My sister came home from school yesterday. It was a busy day,*" I tell a half-truth. "*Anyway, we're doing conversation practice today.*" I grab the folders with lesson materials from my backpack and set them on the marble countertop. Mr. Song nervously rakes fingers through his cropped salt-and-pepper hair and messes with his necktie. It's an eclectic range of clothing, but on brand for Mr. and Mrs. Song's careers—CEO of a tech conglomerate and a women's empowerment coach.

"*You'll do great!*" I assure him.

Mr. and Mrs. Song are well-versed in ASL but struggle with complex sentences. Their son was the only problem I have ever faced when tutoring them—with how he'd goof off and never do his homework—but since he moved, lessons have been a lot smoother.

We get into our usual groove, and the first fifteen minutes of our lesson fly by.

"*Perfect!*" I thrust an F-shaped hand toward Mrs. Song when she aces a hard phrase. Ava applauds her mother with jazz hands.

"*OK-OK, your turn,*" I tell Mr. Song, scanning my list of sentences for an easier one. He's the least conversant but makes a sincere effort.

Right as I'm about to give him a phrase, Ginger's nose squishes against my leg—the action she does when she hears a sound she's trained to alert me to. I peer at my phone on the counter, but nobody is calling and I have no new texts.

Before I can ask her to show me where the sound is coming from, Mrs. Song inadvertently fills in the blank. "*Doorbell,*" she signs to Ava.

In a flash of movement, she crosses the room and yanks the door open, beaming. My jaw unhinges.

You have to be kidding me.

I stare in wide-eyed surprise as Felix Song casually strolls in, hands full carrying a cardboard drink holder.

My reaction is likely the exact opposite to most other teenagers. Any mention of him is usually followed by ear-piercing squeals. I hate sounding like "I'm not like other girls," but I've seen him in the real world, when the spotlight is off and he's back to being a Trust Fund Baby.

A stark contrast to the teenage heartthrob everyone else is obsessed with.

Honestly, I'm not sure this week could get worse. First, I have a big fight with Mom, and now Felix Song is interrupting my lesson?

I watch with a small frown as he takes off his hideous plaid BURBERRY trench coat; tucks shoulder-length, bleached-white-blond hair behind his ears; and casually kicks off his costs-more-than-my-car designer sneakers.

I'm half tempted to steal the shoes and auction them off on eBay. I bet they'd fetch a pretty penny.

I glance at their parents and find Mrs. Song wearing a wide grin similar to Ava's, but Mr. Song's brows are knit and his jaw is locked, his body language tense and almost unwelcoming. Maybe I'm not the only one taken aback by the surprise appearance.

Ava taps an "N" above her heart, my sign name, and jerks her head toward the kitchen. I freeze as Felix's dark eyes land on me. The corners of his lips tip into a sunny smile before he looks at Ava.

"How ya goin', Aves?" he asks. "Sorry I'm late. The line— — coffee shop— —long— —" I only catch a few words here and there. Part of it's probably that his New Zealand accent is almost impossible to lipread and that he talks faster than an auctioneer, but also he's still a whole room away and the sound doesn't carry well.

Ava readjusts her hearing aids. "*What?*" she shakes a flattened hand in front of her. It's weirdly reassuring to know that Ava doesn't fully understand him, either. At least I'm not alone in that.

His brows knit, and his fingers wiggle in the air as he tries to form a response. Ava takes his hand and tugs him into the kitchen, taking charge of the situation.

Felix stays focused on me. I fix my posture as he pulls away from his sister and heads for me with missile-like precision. He stops at the island and flashes a too-sweet, too-wide grin. His teeth are so white they almost glow. He slides an iced coffee across the island, and it skids to a stop right in front of me.

"Hiya, Nat. Still drinkin' Americanos, yeah?"

"*N-A-T-A-L-I-E*," I fingerspell.

Exhibit A of him being as annoying as an unskippable YouTube ad: I've literally never said he could call me "Nat." But he does anyway.

I turn to Mr. and Mrs. Song.. "I should get going. You guys probably want to catch up?" I ask using SimCom. I haphazardly shove lesson materials into my backpack, but I'm distracted when Felix waves his hand in my face to get my attention. I raise a brow at him.

"I like— —it's cute— —"

I blink slowly, trying to decipher what he said.

I sigh in frustration. "I didn't catch that," I reply using SimCom.

He rubs a fist on his chest. "*Sorry. Your . . . hair . . . different,*" he makes a clunky attempt at signing. "You look cute."

I stare at him blankly, messing with my freshly dyed bubblegum-pink waves. He's wasting his time. His ingratiating flirting won't work on me. Because A: I'm demiromantic, and flirting only affects me if I have a deep connection with someone, and he hasn't even come close to earning that. And B: I have a stellar Bullshit Detector, and weirdly, it goes off whenever he's around.

In lieu of a response, I sling my backpack over my shoulder.

"*Wait! You can't leave!*" Ava peers up at her brother, a conspiratorial glint in her eye. A glint that anyone who has a younger sibling knows means there's a scheme involved somehow.

"Why don't you stick around?" Mrs. Song encourages using SimCom; her Kiwi accent is even thicker than her son's. Hearing her speak briefly catches me off guard—of course, I ***know*** she's a first-generation New Zealand citizen, but since she obliges my "voices-off during lessons" rule, I sort of forgot. And before Ava chose to exclusively sign, she had a subdued version of the accent. Probably because she was so young when they moved from Auckland to Seattle.

I do wonder, though, if Felix exaggerates his pronunciation at times to score fangirl points. Aren't Kiwi accents supposed to be sexy or something?

"Stay! Please?" Ava flashes me sad, puppy dog eyes, then points to the empty barstool I was sitting on.

My gut is telling me to get out of here before I can be roped into something I don't want to be roped into, but Ava is well aware of my soft spot for her, and I sit back down, dropping my backpack.

"My doctors are saying my hearing loss is progressing faster now," she admits. *"Six months before I'm fully deaf."*

When I started tutoring the Songs, the doctors thought she'd be in high school before that happened. *"I bet that's a hard development,"* I reply, carefully avoiding "I'm sorry," since my mindset is about Deaf Gain—an idea that reframes deafness not as an impairment or deficit to be overcome, but as a unique kind of diversity that challenges ableist, phonocentric cultural norms and contributes to the greater good. Regardless, I know this is difficult news for her.

Ava exchanges another look with her brother. *"Because I don't like voicing since I can't hear myself very well now, I really want him to learn sign."*

My focus flickers to him, and my frown deepens. "Did you fly all the way to Seattle for a lesson? That's not going to do much." I can't help how sharp my tone is or how my signs are brimming with frustration.

Maybe it's the older sister in me, but I suddenly feel protective of Ava. Even if ***she's*** not upset at Felix for not prioritizing ASL for her all along, it doesn't mean ***I'm*** not upset.

"Nat," he starts, "I really wanna make this work." He flashes me a glittery grin. A grin I'm sure he thinks I'm going to melt for, like everyone else seems to. Instead, it upsets me more. If he had paid attention during lessons or found a tutor in LA, he wouldn't need me to swoop in and speed teach him.

"*I have a proposal,*" Ava chimes in. "*Do you promise to stay until I finish?*"

I gulp but reluctantly reply, "*Promise.*"

She sets up her laptop on the kitchen island. A PowerPoint slide appears on the screen, and an ugly, barking seal laugh tears out of me before I can stop it.

Why Natalie Should Go on Tour & Teach Felix ASL

On the next slide, bullet points list all the reasons I should accept the offer—ranging from ASL is the only way we'll be able to communicate to you're the best teacher in the world (ILYSM!!).

The presentation isn't very impressive, but to be fair, she's only twelve.

Finally, she gets to the last slide, which reads: Questions? I have more questions than I've ever had in my entire life, but my hands are frozen in midair and the words rattling around my brain refuse to form cohesive sentences. Out of all the potential things I thought this could be about, Ava suggesting I become her brother's personal, on-the-road ASL tutor didn't make the list.

Felix doesn't leave the room silent for long. "Tour starts— —few days— —Aves' hearing— —I hired someone— —now you're the only option— —and— —" Words spew out of his mouth at lightning speed.

I try to talk myself off the mental ledge this conversation put me on. What, so now he thinks he can simply pick up where he left off? That I'll drop everything to teach him since he's suddenly deemed it urgent?

"Please? I want L-I-X to learn ASL more than anything!" Ava retakes control of the conversation. She's determined; I'll give her that. She looks at me and juts her lower lip, shamelessly guilting me. She rubs a flat palm in circles on her sternum, *"Please, please, please?"*

I knew I shouldn't have stayed. This definitely counts as roping me into something way above my pay grade.

"I . . . I can't. I have other clients and important projects this summer. And besides, who would teach you guys?" I ask Mr. and Mrs. Song, my hands and voice both stuttering. Then I look at Ava and sign, *"And we have outings planned for the next three weeks! Who would take you?"*

Even if Felix Song didn't make my Top Five Most Annoying People list, I have too many plans. Organizing fundraisers, emailing potential private donors, and overhauling the Center. There's no way I can do it all myself once Jo heads back to school, and I don't want to wait another year. It has to be this summer.

"Could your sister fill in?" Mrs. Song asks. "We all think— —great opportunity for Felix to learn sign, and— —very important to Ava, so we'd love to work this out."

Ava nods enthusiastically. *"J-O is cool! I wouldn't mind getting to know her more."* They met at the Center's Christmas party last year and got along really well. Almost ***too*** well. They ganged up on me quite a few times.

I blink at her, then Mrs. Song. I love working with the Songs (with one obvious exception), but I can't help but feel a little ambushed. They're sort of backing me into a corner.

A million potential responses run through my head. All eyes are on me, but I stay silent, half convinced I'm about to wake up from a very bizarre dream.

"I'm sorry. I . . . I have to go." I stand up, grab my backpack, and pick up Ginger's leash from the ground. She yawns but obediently steps into a heel.

"Wait, Nat!" Felix blurts. "Please stay. We should really talk about this."

"I'm really busy today."

It's another lie. My next lesson isn't for hours, but this is a lot. I can't even form proper sentences right now, much less try to process.

He pauses, staring me down while a ghost of a frown crosses his features, but he quickly hides it. "No biggie. See ya soon."

I give Ava a quick hug goodbye, grab the half-melted iced Americano Felix brought for me (I'll never turn down free caffeine, pride be damned), and rush toward the foyer, kneeling underneath the huge DAYDREAM poster while pulling on my boots.

Mr. Song is speaking to his son in terse Korean, his face stony. Mrs. Song attempts to sign for Ava's sake, but she's not paying attention, content with being tucked under her brother's arm.

And Felix . . . is staring at me . . .

He responds to his dad in monosyllables, eyes firmly fixated on me. As desperate as I am to leave, something about his intense stare manages to make me lose sight of what I'm doing—

Tying my shoes! I'm tying my shoes. Yes. Right.

I tighten the laces and rush toward the entrance. One foot out the door, Felix calls out, loud enough for me to hear, "Chat soon, Nat!"

I turn on my heel. "My name is Natalie."

Chapter Three

Gallivanting Is Not on the To-Do List

Seattle, June 8

When I get back to the Deaf Center, Mom's teaching an Intermediate ASL class in the front room. I quickly dart into the hall before she sees me through the small glass window in the door.

Mom is Medusa-like, except instead of turning me to stone if I make eye contact, she takes it as an invitation to start arguing. Her fuse isn't short; it's microscopic.

I lead Ginger down the fluorescent-lit hallway. We pass cringey motivational posters with cats dangling from trees that read HANG IN THERE!, three more classrooms with long-unused chairs and tables, and a second office we don't have employees for anymore.

When I was a kid, this place was full of life. There were always people around, laughing and learning. It was chaotic in the best way—proof that the world didn't have to leave Deaf people behind. Here, we were understood, celebrated, connected. And now . . .

Now it feels hollow. Stacks of unpaid bills sit precariously on the front desk, a visual reminder that this space, once a haven, is on its last legs. The once colorful walls are faded and chipped and only emphasize the emptiness. It's like the Center is holding its breath, waiting for the inevitable.

The silence presses down on me, a quiet indictment of everything we've lost and everything I can't seem to fix.

When I enter the main office, I flip the light on and off to alert Jo to my presence. She peers up from the chunky desktop computer that overheats if you use it for longer than thirty minutes.

"*How's the website design going?*" I ask. Jo is redesigning the Center's website and starting social media pages to help boost visibility, while I manage the budget, write blog posts, and fundraise. (I'm the brains of this operation, let's be honest.)

"*We need a better resources page.*"

"*OK-OK. I'll send you links. Now, come on. I want to show you my ideas!*" I grab a clipboard and a piece of paper, then motion to the hallway. Jo pops out of her chair.

Our first stop is the small classroom near the office that's mostly used for storage. "*If we move the bookshelf, I'll paint a mural on the wall. The budget for this room is $500.*" With L-shaped fingers, I frame the area and grin. I can already picture it as a room for grades K–5.

If we can get local bookstores to donate some diverse children's books, we'll be able to host Sign Language Storytimes. Parents of D/deaf kids can see how incredibly beneficial interacting with the Deaf community from an early age is, and kids who go to mainstream schools will have a refuge from auditory fatigue they face during the day.

"*KissFist!*" Jo signs.

Next, we step into the second-largest space, which I've already claimed in my heart as the middle-through-high-school hangout.

Standing in here fills me with bubbling excitement, and I can almost see the finished version in my mind: cozy beanbags, desks painted vibrant colors, and laughter echoing in the air. My hands move quickly as I let my enthusiasm spill out. "*If we get a projector, we can have movie nigh—*"

The lights rapidly turn on and off, cutting me off mid-thought. Jo and I whip around to see Mom in the doorway, using the lights to get our attention. Her eyes burn with a similar fire as last night. I glance at the time on my phone and see her class ended two minutes ago. Shit. I thought she'd be preoccupied longer.

"*What are you discussing?*" she asks, her fingers moving through the air in frustrated, choppy movements. Based on her expression, it's a rhetorical question.

I take a deep breath, sensing another argument on the horizon. "*Mom, please give us ONE reason why you don't want us to revamp. It's my money, not yours. Why are you so opposed?*"

She directs another withering glare at me, her muscles tensing. "*I told you NO. I'm sick of you bringing this up! STOP.*"

Always needing to have the final word, she turns on her heel and leaves, slamming the door even harder than last night.

☆ ☆ ☆

I'm suddenly thrust back into reality when Jo flicks my arm. "*Sorry,*" I sign. We came to the park during our lunch break so we can catch up and give Mom some time to calm down, but I keep zoning out.

Mom's somewhat easy to ignore since I've spent eighteen years of my life walking on eggshells around her, so my mind keeps drifting. Ava, Felix, the weight of everything lately—it's like my brain is juggling too much at once.

Jo flaps her hand in my face. Damn it, I zoned out again.

She chews a bite of her homemade bologna sandwich. *"You'll get wrinkles if you frown that hard."*

I ignore her. It's not my fault I have RBF, or more like TBF—Thinking Bitch Face.

"Your face has been doing this"—her expression rapidly changes from an overexaggerated frown to contemplatively chewing her lip to a death glare—*"for ten minutes. It has to be something other than Mom."*

I scratch Ginger's chin while she sunbathes and aimlessly pick at blades of grass. Eventually, Jo flicks me again. Curiosity is painted across her face. *"What are you hiding? Your face is doing gymnastics again! Tell me!"* she urges.

I decide there's no use lying. She'll keep pestering me. *"You remember F-E-L-I-X?"*

"Duh. You brought him up constantly!"

"No, I didn't!"

She shoots me a look.

It wasn't constantly! Just . . . you know . . . sometimes . . .

But it's only because in Felix's pre-fame days, she was the one I complained to when he didn't do his homework, talked during voices-off lessons, or arrived late wielding an excuse like "our bassist plugged his bass in with wet hands and electrocuted himself."

"He showed up during the ASL lesson today." I brace myself for her commentary.

"You're kidding!" Her jaw is on the ground.

"True biz," I sign, focusing on a very interesting blade of grass.

She pokes my leg to grab my attention again. "*Are you still mad he moved to LA and doesn't know sign?*" My sister is like a damn mind reader. "*I think you're overreacting.*"

I scoff. "*How would you feel if I was Hearing and didn't learn sign for you, and we couldn't communicate?*"

"*That's different.*"

"*No, it's not! But suddenly he can learn ASL now that his family's forcing him? Now that A-V-A is begging him?*"

"*What do you mean? 'He can learn now'?*"

Shit.

"*Nothing. Conversation finished,*" I snap. Oh god. I'm turning into Mom.

Jo doesn't stop staring, disbelief painted across her pale features.

When I can't take it anymore, I groan and admit, "A-V-A *wants me to go on tour with him. Her hearing loss is progressing faster now, and she wants me to teach him sign.*"

"WHAT?!" she wildly shakes both upturned hands in front of her. "*I hope you said yes! The* S-O-N-G-S *are so rich we could probably upgrade the whole Center. Did you ask how much they'll pay you?*"

"*No, I didn't ask! I told them no. Even if he weren't basically the worst, you and I have plans!*"

"*I thought you were the smartest sister! Say yes! When would you get to tour with a famous band ever again? Plus, it's good money, hot guys, and you'd be helping* A-V-A*!*"

"*Are you kidding?! Mom's already pissed at me, but if I did* THIS, *she'd never talk to me again!*" I poke every conceivable hole in Jo's plan.

"*I can handle Mom. She might listen to me. And, if you let me borrow your car, I'll cover your private lessons and the Center classes."*

"*I doubt even YOU could get her to be cool with this.*" Mom's favoritism only goes so far. And besides, Jo's way oversimplifying this. This is why I'm the brains. It's not only about covering my clients or facing Mom's eternal wrath . . . It's also about the dozens of things on my ever-growing to-do list that I couldn't possibly accomplish if I'm gallivanting around with the Prince of Bubblegum Pop.

"No," I sign. "*I need to paint, plan fundraisers, find sponsors . . .*" I list everything Jo didn't mention, ticking each item off on my fingers. "*Going on tour is impossible. We have enough money to get started. I'm staying in Seattle.*"

@daydream영원히 4h ago

I'm coming from Seoul to Seattle for the last show!!! Any tips about where to stay or DREAMERs who want to meet up? I'd love to make friends and share the experience with others!! ✈♫

#DAYDREAMtour #InternationalDREAMER

@glitterfrog99 3h ago

cries in broke portuguese fan SOOO JEALOUS! i NEED them to come to the eu next tour! have fun and blow mateo a kiss for me ☹

@FelixSongUpdates 22m ago

Hotels in downtown Seattle are $$$ during summer so check Airbnb. I'd be down to meet up! What section are you in? I got VIP barricade tickets for pit 3!

Chapter Four

Pawns in the Game

Seattle, June 10

I was wrong. My week can, and ***does***, get worse.

When Ginger and I exit the main classroom after teaching Advanced ASL on Monday morning, the first thing I see is Felix. He's standing in the middle of the lobby, randomly wiggling his fingers in the air as if he's performing a magic trick.

From where she stands behind the front desk, Jo holds her own against Felix's fashion statement in her white tube top and pink floral maxi skirt. He's wearing a black T-shirt under his beloved plaid trench coat, a crossbody PRADA fanny pack, loose-fitting black pants with a thin GUCCI belt, and black sneakers. His long platinum hair is in a half-up ponytail; two strands frame his face and hide his chiseled jawline.

Ava's beside him, and her outfit is also straight from a BURBERRY ad—a white knee-length dress with a Peter Pan collar in that same awful plaid fabric.

I value practicality over being fashion forward, but an unexpected self-consciousness overtakes me, and I smooth the wrinkles out of my gray crop top with bleach stains on the bottom hem.

My eyes flit to the extremely intimidating person with sunglasses and a tough frown standing behind Felix. Ava watches his "signing," exchanging an amused look with Jo.

"Oh! Hiya, Nat!" he chirps enthusiastically when he notices me.

I stare at him a beat too long, my mouth slightly ajar. Everything about him clashes with the cramped lobby of my shabby Deaf Center, and I'm suddenly hyperaware of the sagging furniture and the mismatched chairs in the waiting area. The peeling linoleum floor seems even more noticeable with him here, as if his very presence is highlighting every imperfection.

As my last student leaves, I glance through the glass front door and into the parking lot. A sleek metallic blue MERCEDES-BENZ sticks out like a sore thumb, practically glowing next to the faded parking stripes. But even worse, a small crowd is forming—presumably fans who've somehow caught wind of where Felix has wandered off to.

My stomach churns with a strange mix of protectiveness and discomfort. This is my space, and it's run-down, sure, but it's ***mine***. The idea of gawking strangers peering in, making this place feel even smaller, makes me bristle.

Felix follows my line of sight, and a fleeting frown crosses his features. He motions toward the parking lot, and the Sunglasses Person heads outside, firmly shepherding fans away from the building.

"*You OK?*" he points to me, then flicks an "*O*" into a "*K*." At least he's retained that much.

"*Yes,*" I sign in a rush. "*Fine. Great.*"

"*Wow, his ASL is god-awful,*" Jo interrupts with a snort, not even trying to hide her amusement. My focus flickers to Felix, but the confusion on his face tells me he didn't understand her. "*But DAMN is he gorgeous. He's single, yeah?*"

I choke on spit and clear my throat. "*Shut up!*"

Ava knocks a balled fist in the air, "*Yes, he's single.*" She waggles her brows, and Jo laughs.

I very pointedly ignore them. "Why are you guys here?" I ask using SimCom.

Felix stares at my hands while I sign—which is considered rude, but since he's a beginner, he has more leeway—and his neatly trimmed brows tug downward in intense focus.

Jo props her elbows against the front desk and watches us while mimicking eating popcorn. Felix shifts uncomfortably. "Can we chat?" he asks me.

I nod, waiting for him to continue.

"Er . . ." He eyes Jo. "I meant privately."

I interpret for Jo and Ava, which leads Jo to make kissy faces. Ava laughs. Felix's ears turn bright red. I shoot her an "I'm going to hurt you" look, and she feigns innocence.

I gesture for him and Ava to follow me down the hall of cringey cat posters. At the end, I hold open the door to the future K–5 zone.

I'm about to close the door when Sunglasses slips in. Up close, I see them eyeing me suspiciously.

"What's up with Sunglasses?" I ask Felix.

He whips around from where he's browsing the dusty bookshelves. "Ah, she's my bodyguard," he says straight-faced, like that's a totally normal thing for an eighteen-year-old boy to have. God, it must be weird to be rich and famous.

Felix asks Sunglasses to wait outside, and she obliges.

"Um. So. What'd you want to talk about?" I ask using SimCom. "I have a class in twenty minutes, and I need to prep."

"Hey, don't shoot the messenger." He holds his hands up in faux defense and gestures toward Ava. "Aves dragged me here to convince you. I am but a mere pawn in her game."

"Really?" I stare him down, hoping he'll take ownership for once.

Silence engulfs the room. Ava's eyes flicker between us, assessing the tense atmosphere, before she rushes toward me and takes one of my hands, signing with her other.

"If I'm fully deaf in six months, I can't hear him and we can't talk! He needs to learn ASL. You're our only hope! Please?" She gives me those damned puppy dog eyes again, and she looks especially cute today with her hair in two French braids decorated by blue butterfly clips that match her hearing aids. Felix might have been right (and this is the only time I'll ***ever*** admit that): We're simply pawns in Ava's game. The kid knows how to play the system.

"We'll be touring until August, then— —taking a break," Felix chimes in. "I'm gonna— —and then— —Aves— —so, whaddya say? Will you come?"

"You could set a world record for fastest talker." I sigh, massaging my temples. "Slow down. It's hard to understand you."

"*Sorry*," he signs. "After the tour, I'm staying in Seattle for a while before I have to go back to LA to record our second album. I wanna be conversant in ASL before then since Aves probably won't have much hearing left."

"Pfft!" He's making this seem so casual! Like he's not asking me to clear my schedule for the whole summer. "And why exactly does it have to be me? Surely you have the resources to hire someone else."

"I did. But he had a family emergency four days ago, and nobody else is available on such short notice. I'm desperate," he explains.

"*It was my idea to ask you. You're the best!*" Ava smiles.

I exhale sharply. "How about remote lessons? That way you can learn ASL, and I can stay in Seattle," I suggest.

Felix bites his lip and shakes his head; loose pieces of hair fall in his eyes. "I need you with me. Basically 24/7."

"Whoa, buddy. Laying it on a bit thick."

This earns a small chuckle. "Yeah, nah, I just mean my schedule is gonna be hectic. Interviews, meet and greets, filming a music video, sound checks. It'll be different every day. I'll need to squeeze in ASL whenever we have a spare moment."

"Look, even if I ***could*** go," I emphasize, using SimCom, "there's way too many logistics to sort out on such short notice."

"*Ask him your questions!*" Ava encourages. "*You'll feel better if you have more information!*" Before I can reiterate that me going isn't even a possibility, she pulls out her phone and plops onto the floor, leaving us to have our Q&A. She mutes her hearing aids so she can fully tune us out.

To appease Ava—and not because I'm considering going in the ***slightest***, of course—I sigh, unlock my phone, and open my Notes app, ready to jot down his answers to my impromptu questions. "Fine. First, what's your actual tour schedule?"

"Uhh . . . I dunno, exactly. You can find the dates for the shows on DAYDREAM's Instagram, or, like, Ticketmaster or something."

I type: Felix doesn't know anything!! Ava is his adorable puppet master!!!!

"What's the transportation situation?" I ask.

"There's a few flights, but mostly the tour bus." He must notice my apprehension, because he adds, "Ah, I'll pay for your flights and hotel rooms."

Hotels/flights = covered. But I'm not going so it DOESN'T MATTER

He continues. "But sometimes we'll be sleeping on the bus. You'll get your own bunk, of course. It'll be us, my mates, and a bodyguard. Or two. Three, max." He pauses, wiggling his fingers in midair as he thinks. "Oh! *Bus!* That's bus, yeah?" He slides a flattened H-shaped hand over a second flat H shape, beaming with pride since he thinks he remembered the sign.

The way his eyes light up almost makes me not want to break the news that he actually signed "train." ***Almost.***

"That's train," I correct him. "*B-U-S*," I show him the lexicalized version of the sign.

His excitement fades, replaced by a flicker of embarrassment. "Ah."

We stare at each other for a beat too long while I try to think of more questions. I clear my throat and check my notes, which are unhelpful, to be honest. "To recap: Basically, you want me to spend an unknown portion of my summer trapped in a bus with your band and an undetermined number of bodyguards?"

"Only on travel days. Otherwise, you'll be trapped in Green Rooms and hotels," he jokes. "But don't worry; I'll keep you company."

"Wow! This deal keeps getting better!"

"Obviously, I'd pay you," he changes the subject, ignoring my snarky comment. "D'you reckon $12,000 is reasonable?" he asks, head tilted to one side like Ginger when she's puzzled.

My eyes bug out. Oh my god, this is officially the most ridiculous thing he's ever done. The BURBERRY trench coat is a little outlandish, but ***this*** is a whole new level.

The sticker shock worms its way deep inside my brain. Twelve grand—even taking the loss of my planned summer side hustles into account—could put a nice dent in our bills ***and*** leave at least a couple of grand for Project Revamp . . .

No! Nooope. I can't let myself be sucked into Felix's fairy-tale celebrity bubble or allow his diabolically symmetrical, GQ magazine–worthy face and monetary offer tempt me. I have responsibilities! In what world would I be able to drop everything and accompany Felix on tou—

"$17,000?" he offers.

Okay, well. Maybe in a world where I'd be getting paid $17,000.

"Look, Nat," he continues, "I admit I've been a bit of a dickhead by not keeping up with my ASL and thinking I could pick it back up later, but there isn't a later anymore. I need to learn now. But if you won't do it for me—"

"I wouldn't," I mumble.

"—then do it for Aves. Please?"

I take a deep breath and pet Ginger's head. Running my palm across her soft, golden fur grounds me.

"Take time to think about it," he says. "But, y'know, not too much time. We have to fly to LA on the thirteenth."

"Wha—isn't that Thursday?"

"Yup."

"Like, in three days, Thursday?!"

"Yup."

I bark another disbelieving laugh, but I don't get a chance to reply before Ava pops up, tucks her phone into her pocket, and turns up her hearing aid volume. *"Did you say yes?!"*

"I need to think about it," I reply.

Wait—why did I tell her that? I'm not going. It's a firm ***no***. Very firm! Like, a slab of stone ***firm***.

Ava wraps me in a hug. Over the top of her head, I watch Felix. Joy is evident on his face, his eyes crinkling at the corners.

Ava skips into the hall after thanking me profusely for considering the offer, but Felix stops in the doorway. "See ya later, Nat." He winks.

As he disappears into the hallway, I glare at the empty doorway as if I can still burn a hole through his smug little wink.

DAYDREAM Wiki Member Profile

FULL NAME: Felix Ye Joon (예준) Song

AGE: 18

HEIGHT: 6'2" (188 cm)

HOMETOWN: Auckland, NZ

FELIX FACTS:

- His hobbies include learning new instruments (he knows 5—violin, piano, guitar, bass, and harmonica—all self-taught besides childhood violin lessons), watching cheesy rom-coms, and playing board games
- His role models are his little sister, Conan Gray, and Jonghyun from SHINee
- His Korean name (Ye Joon/예준) means someone who's gifted and has an undeniable allure. *Ye*/예 captures the essence of creativity and artistry; *Joon*/준 adds an aura of charm and attractiveness
- His dad's from Gwangju, SK, and his mom's from Auckland, NZ. His family moved to Seattle when he was 14 because his dad was hired as the CEO of a major tech company
- His life motto is "When wishes are infused with passion and purpose, they become unstoppable forces of creation"
- If he weren't in DAYDREAM, he said he'd explore fashion (modeling and/or designing)

Chapter Five

Hot Girls Commit Federal Crimes

Seattle, June 10

"*Why'd he show up? Was it about the tour?!*" Jo bombards me as soon as I finish my second ASL lesson of the morning. She was forced to wait ***an entire hour*** to interrogate me because I had to start class immediately after Felix and Ava left. Poor thing.

I scan the lobby for Mom but don't see her. She must be in the office.

"*I told him no. Again. He's so annoying! And presumptuous! And just the worst!*" I exclude the part of the conversation where I foolishly told Ava I'd think about it. It was but a moment of human weakness.

"*Did you ask about the money?*" she pries.

I press my lips into a thin line and keep my hands planted by my sides, refusing to answer.

"*Tell me! How much?!*"

"*$17,000,*" I admit, avoiding eye contact.

Horror colors her features. "*Go say yes, RIGHT NOW! What the fuck!*" Her signing is frantic, like the money will literally disappear if I don't accept the offer in the next five seconds.

"I already told you, I'm too busy to—"

"Hey!" Mom waves her hand wildly, appearing in the lobby so suddenly it's almost like she teleported. *"What about $17,000?"* she asks in bewilderment.

I scrub hands over my face. Damn it.

"Is this about the tall boy who came in with A-V-A?" Mom asks, her eyes narrowing. Medusa Mode: activated. *"Who is he? Did he give you money? We don't need charity!"*

I choose not to argue the fact that, actually, we ***could*** use some charitable donations.

"He's . . . my client." It's technically not a lie.

"And what did J-O mean about the $17,000?" she presses.

Jo adopts an impish-youngest-child smirk. *"Natalie got a job offer."*

I reach for her hands to shut her up, but before I can physically restrain her, she shelters behind the front desk and elaborates. *"He's* A-V-A's *brother. He's a famous singer, and he wants her to teach him* ASL. *If she goes on tour with his band, he'll pay her* $17,000!"

I study Mom in anticipation. But to my ultimate surprise, she's measured. Composed. The only movement is her brows tilting into a contemplative frown.

What the hell? I exchange glances with Jo, who seems equally puzzled why Mom didn't immediately launch into a fit of rage—her usual reaction to . . . well, most things.

My curiosity outweighs my fear of setting Mom off, and I hazard, *"Why aren't you mad?"*

Her fingers twitch, a reply dancing on the tips, but she changes what she started to sign. *"What did you tell him?"*

"No."

She considers me for one of the longest moments of my life. "*But do you want to go?*"

"*What? No. It's good money, but I'm busy and he's annoying.*" A deep, baffled frown crosses my face, and I stare into Mom's piercing gray eyes. "*Wait . . . do you WANT me to go?*"

She shrugs. "*It's your choice. You're an adult now.*"

Okay, now I'm less confused and more concerned that my mother was abducted by an alien overlord and the woman standing in front of me is some cybernetic clone. Unless . . . she's trying to get rid of me, isn't she? I huff. ***That*** seems more like Mom. If I go on tour with Felix, Project Revamp would practically come to a screeching halt. (Not to mention, she could spend a lovely, tranquil summer with her Golden Child if I were out of the picture.)

I bite the inside of my cheek and take a beat to center myself. "*OK-OK. If it's my choice . . . I'll stay in Seattle and revamp the Center this summer.*"

"*Stop! No revamp talk. Conversation finished. Finished!*" she finally snaps. ***There's*** the Mom I know.

"*You tell me to 'act like an adult,' but when I make a choice, you tell me no,*" I shoot back. "*Tell me why I can't revamp, Mom! Tell me ONE good reason!*" I beg. "*If you're going to be this adamant, I think we at least deserve an explanation!*"

But I don't get my answer. Mom's expression darkens before she storms toward the exit.

That afternoon, after the students from my last Monday class leave, my Teacher Mode smile slips from my face. I plop onto the floor behind the front desk and heave a defeated sigh.

Ginger blinks her big brown eyes at me. I pat my legs, and she curls up on my lap and nuzzles me. I lean down and bury my face in her fur, in desperate need of some dog cuddles.

Everything that's happened over the past few days plays in a loop in my head. The arguments with Mom; Ava begging me to teach her brother; and most unfortunately, Felix's gratingly brilliant smile and his bottomless, son-of-a-tech-CEO and global-musical-sensation pockets.

I thought this was going to be the first summer in three years I could simply ***enjoy***.

Three summers ago, Dad got sick.

Two summers ago . . . he died.

Last summer, I was still too numbed by the ache of grief to do anything except survive.

But this year? This was supposed to be the summer when my dreams started coming true. But with the days in June ticking away, and the fights with Mom growing more heated, I'm starting to think I've been full of false hope all along.

"Excuse me?" a loud voice calls out.

Startled, I rip my head away from where I'm suffocating in Ginger's fur and look up. A mail courier peers over the front desk. I awkwardly chuckle and nudge Ginger off my lap. Some of her fur is tangled in my mascara-coated eyelashes and glued to my glossy lips, and I inelegantly pick them off while standing up.

"Hi. How can I help you?" I ask.

They extend a clipboard toward me. "This is signature-required," they explain, gesturing to the manila envelope in their other hand.

That's weird. We never get any mail that's even remotely important enough for all this. I scrawl my name on the clipboard and thank the courier.

My confusion mounts when I see the envelope is from our bank and is marked with a bright red high-priority label. It's also addressed to Mom, which means I should absolutely ***not*** open it. Legally, I can only open mail addressed to The Nielsens or The Nielsen Family Deaf Center.

I glance at Ginger. "Should I open it?" She boofs in disapproval. "I know, I know! But it's a victimless crime, Ging. I'll just take a peek . . ."

Who cares about a silly little federal crime!

Account in Arrears Demand Letter

This letter is to demand payment in full re: previous insufficient mortgage payments, in order to bring your loan current.

The total sum due, including late fees, must be received within four weeks from the date of this notice, or the bank has the right to foreclose on your property.

Total Due: $12,506.95

I read the letter three times. Six times. Ten times. My heart races and hands tremble more with each re-read. I can't breathe. Every bit of air is being squeezed from my lungs. How could this happen? How could we owe so much money? Mom's been paying the mortgage every month!

I scramble to grab the landline phone that has auto-captions and punch in the bank's number. The line rings for a few seconds before someone picks up.

"Hello? I'm calling about a . . . a demand letter I received." I choke out the words, forcing my voice to not wobble. "There has to be some kind of mistake. We pay our mortgage every month."

"I'll look you up and see what's going on," the person on the other end replies. I read the live captions on the screen attached to the phone while they speak. They ask a bunch of verification questions, but I can barely focus.

"Unfortunately, there's not a mistake, Ms. Nielsen. You owe the bank $12,506.95."

My heart thunders in my chest. Out of the corner of my eye, I see Jo enter the lobby. Her hand-me-down backpack is slung over one shoulder, indicating she's ready to go home. She stops dead in her tracks when she sees me. Panic must be written all over my face.

"*What's wrong?!*" Her signs are anxiety filled.

I don't have a chance to reply before the banker speaks again. "I can see monthly payments— —only $200— —and— —mortgage is $2,000. Those payments aren't enough." Their speech cuts out and the captioning technology isn't perfect, so I lose some of what they're saying.

I cover my mouth with my hand to block out the strangled gasp that escapes me. "You can't threaten to foreclose on us without any warning!"

"We've sent multiple warnings about insufficient payments over the past several months. They were all signed for."

I never signed for anything, and Jo's been at school . . .

Mom must've signed for them. My initial shock morphs into a hot, pulsing anger. My breathing quickens as the phone trembles in my hand.

It's bad enough Mom didn't tell me how far in debt we were with the bank—that we've been barely scraping by every month—but to not tell me we could lose the Center?!

It dawns on me that this must be why she's been so cagey about Jo's and my plans. She didn't want us to pour time and money into a sinking ship.

I wrack my brain for a solution. ***Think, Natalie. Think.***

"I can pay $2,000 right now. Would that give us more time?"

"Unfortunately, we need the full payment."

"How the hell am I supposed to make $12,000 in four weeks?!" I bite, finally losing my grip.

Calmly, the banker replies, "We need— —payment— —July. No exceptions."

I don't trust myself to not say something I'd regret to someone who's just doing their job, so I simply hang up.

Jo steps forward. "*What happened?*" she asks.

Anger burns inside me, and I can only point to the letter that lies on the desk. Jo picks it up, and her hazel eyes flit over the page.

"*What?! How!?*"

"*Mom didn't pay the mortgage,*" I explain. "*The bank needs the full payment in July or we'll lose the Center.*"

She gulps. "*Can we sell something?*"

I shake my head. The only thing I own that potentially has

value is my car—but the windows stopped rolling down months ago, and the check engine light has been on for two years. I'd be lucky to get a grand for it on Facebook Marketplace.

"We both know what can make that much money . . . F-E—" I push her hands down and cut her off, jaw clenched. I can't bring myself to think about ***that***. The very last thing I can devote brain cells to right now is Felix Song.

"We need to go home," I announce, stuffing the letter into my backpack. I have to talk to Mom.

Jo follows me into the parking lot. The empty expanse seems to emphasize the gravity of the situation. She climbs into the passenger's seat while I buckle Ginger into her doggy seat belt. Then, we're off.

While we're stuck in relentless Seattle traffic, I'm left to stew in my anger. Betrayed doesn't even begin to describe how I feel. A whole dictionary couldn't describe it. Mom has known for years how important updating the Center is to Jo and me, how we're keeping part of Dad alive with this project, yet she's been lying.

She's let me work day and night, blissfully unaware of the ticking time bomb under our feet. And now, here I am, finding out about it from some sterile papers instead of her.

I knew we were poor. I knew we had to ration groceries. I knew we had to use as little AC and heating as possible. But if she had told me the entire truth about our financial situation, I could have come up with a solution. But now that the truth is staring me in the face, it's too late to do anything about it.

As I park in our driveway, Jo gives my shoulder a comforting squeeze. With her small reassurance, I unload Ginger and we walk to the front door. My sheer rage has cooled to a slow, simmering burn, but I still need to take the longest, deepest breath I can before going in.

I enter the kitchen to find Mom cooking; her brows knit as she studies me. I slink farther into the room, unfold the letter, and hold it up for her to see. I don't sign anything, waiting to see what she'll do. How she's going to explain herself.

Mom drops the spoon she's holding. *"You opened my mail?"*

I scoff. *"THAT'S what you're worried about?!"* I crumple up the paper and toss it toward her. *"Why didn't you tell me!? If you told me about this months ago, I could've fixed it!"*

Indignation crawls across her face. *"You're not 'fixing' anything! I handle our finances. You're the kid; I'm the parent!"*

"And you think that means I don't deserve to know the truth? You've been shutting me out, making decisions for all of us, while we poured everything into plans you KNEW we'd never get to finish! Do you know how much that hurts?!"

She sucks in a breath. *"After Dad died, I had to grieve him while raising you two and running the Center!"*

"We grieved him, too, Mom!" Tears blur my vision. *"We want to revamp BECAUSE we miss him—because we want to make his dream happen."*

"Maybe letting go is what you need. Do you really want to be tied down here forever? Feel trapped by this place for the rest of your lives?" she asks, knocking the wind out of me. *"I'm doing the best I can for you girls!"*

"Well, it's not good enough!" I snap before I can stop myself. Tears spill freely from my puffy red eyes, and a sob bucks in my chest. *"The Center is all I have left of Dad! I can't lose it."* Every memory I have of the Center is tangled with memories of him.

Playing after-hours hide-and-seek with Jo and me, helping him teach little kids the fingerspelling alphabet during weekend day camps, or conspiring to splurge on take-out for dinner between sessions.

He and the Center are inextricable. Losing it is like losing him all over again.

And I don't think I'd survive that pain a second time.

Mom's face is a perfect mix of anguish and fury. Wetness forms in her own eyes. I recognize her pain, I understand the unspoken heartache that always follows us around better than anyone, but I can't provide any comfort when my own heart is breaking.

"I'll fix the mess you made. I'm not giving Dad up, even if you do," I tell her, my fingers flying in an enraged, jerky manner.

She raises her hands to reply, but I'm already speeding to my room. I pass Jo in the kitchen doorway, and she snags my wrist, but I yank it away.

Ginger runs into my room seconds before I slam the door and collapse onto my bed. I glance at the photo on my nightstand. The last one Dad and I took together, in Gas Works Park on my sixteenth birthday. Our grins are identical, our hazel eyes shimmer the same, and if it weren't for me having dyed my hair blue a few days prior, we'd have the same mud-brown locks.

I reach out and set the frame face down, unable to look at it any longer. Ginger hops onto my bed and drops her gross, slobber-encrusted stuffed duck on me to cheer me up. I run my fingers through her fur.

When I've calmed myself enough, I grab my phone. Jo's right. There's only one way I can make enough money to save the Center.

The last thing on earth I want to do this summer is be around Felix Song 24/7 . . . But my head isn't ***so*** far up my ass that I can't acknowledge his offer is my only option to get us out of this mess.

Mon, June 10, 8:03 PM

[Natalie]

Can you come by the center tomorrow at 12:30?

[Pretty Boy 🙃]

U already miss me? 🤭

[Natalie]

Strictly business. Can you come? Yes or no.

[Pretty Boy 🙃]

I'll be there!!! ♥

X

r/DAYDREAM 47 min ago

mateoluvr

ANYONE ELSE GOT MEET & GREET TICKETS??

The ones for NYC sold out SO fast! I barely managed to snag the LAST ticket and might actually pass out from meeting DAYDREAM in person 🥹 Are they really as nice as they seem in interviews?

TOP COMMENTS:

wanderlust_will 22 min ago

I randomly bumped into Will & Felix in a Burger King last week lmao & I was super worried I'd annoy them by saying hi but they were suuuper sweet! They took time to ask me questions & took a picture with me & everything!

fandomhopper69 12 sec ago

i met lachlan in erewhon and he seemed rly scary but after i said i was a fan he was v nice and bought my smoothie for me 💀

Chapter Six

The Post-It Note Promise

Seattle, June 11–12

Felix has four bandmates.

Calum, Will, Mateo, and . . . the other one. Lucas? Landon? I can't remember. (In my defense, he's hardly featured on DAYDREAM's Instagram account—home to a whopping nineteen million followers.)

Ahead of our meeting at 12:30 p.m., I plant myself on the floor of the office. Ginger naps next to me. Usually, I avoid the main office—a.k.a., Mom's evil lair—after a fight, but she didn't bother coming to the Center this morning. So I can cyberstalk in peace.

So far, my knowledge has greatly improved from the obvious: Felix Song is DAYDREAM's irksome lead singer-slash-frontman.

Their Instagram feed is mainly things they posted themselves, like cooking content from #ChefMateo, Calum playing his green guitar, or Will's gym rat selfies and artsy photography. But there are more professional posts, too, like the ad campaign Felix did for BURBERRY. (Why am I not surprised?)

I stop scrolling when I come across their tour announcement.

At the top of the sky-blue background with fluffy white clouds, the text reads: "DAYDREAM North American Tour." The names of twenty-two cities and corresponding dates are at the bottom. Felix stands front and center in a silky white V-neck button-up, flashing that dazzling grin of his. His arms are crossed, causing his biceps to bulge. The other boys are perfectly posed around him, wearing a spectrum of pastel shades.

Their Boston concert grabs my attention. Ellen, my dad's best friend-slash-Jo's and my godmother, has a D/deaf summer camp in Boston. I haven't seen her since Dad's funeral, and I wonder if I could work in a visit. It would be nice to see her and pick her brain about the Center.

I scroll to another post, and I recognize it instantly—it's the image from the signed poster the Songs proudly display. Like the tour-announcement photo, Felix is the center of attention, singing into a bedazzled mic while the other members are gently smiling beside him. The more photos I look at, the more that becomes a recurring theme. The other members almost seem like background models.

I zoom in on the members' faces and notice they all have light, dewy makeup on, really driving home the soft-boy brand their band name implies. They look unnaturally perfect.

As I zoom out, someone taps my shoulder. I jolt in surprise.

"*J-O—*" I pause my grumpy signing as I whip my head around to see Felix squatting behind me.

"*Sorry!*" he signs.

Ginger glances up from beside me, a string of drool dangling from her jowls. She harmlessly boofs at him, then goes back to ignoring him.

"You can't sneak up on people like that!" I gripe. "Turn lights on and off when entering a room." I motion to the light switch and awkwardly wave when I spot Sunglasses in the doorway. "It alerts deaf people someone is there."

"*Sorry*," he reiterates.

I check the time on my phone. 12:14 p.m. "You're early." I squint at him.

"I always leave thirty minutes early— —traffic, but it wasn't bad today. I stopped by— —coffee shop but— —line wasn't long— —cut down on travel time. Ah, and Jo told me— —back here. I didn't mean to scare you." His words come flying out before I have a chance to even ***try*** and lipread or fill in the blanks.

The way he talks is like a stream of consciousness.

He stands up and offers me a hand; the other holds an iced Americano. I reluctantly take his hand, and he pulls me to my feet. His lips curve upward when we make eye contact.

Felix is a lot taller up close. I'm a perfectly average five-five—no matter how much Jo (who's ***barely*** five-seven!) teases me about being short—but standing here with him, I feel like a little kid.

He's got to have eight or nine inches on me. This close it's hard not to notice his inky eyes, sparkly smile, and blemish-free, bronzed skin. It's like Felix won the genetics lottery.

He's gorgeous.

I hate it.

"So whaddya think? We look good together, don't we?"

"W-what?" I splutter. I look down at our hands and realize they're still tangled together, his long, tan fingers encasing my smaller, pale ones. I yank mine away and take three steps back, which is as much distance as this tiny office can provide.

His eyes crinkle as he laughs. "The boys and me." He points to my phone. "You were looking at our photo."

I ignore the heat rising in my face. The last thing Felix needed to see was me lurking on the band's profile. Although, in the context of us holding hands and gazing into each other's eyes, I'm grateful he was referencing my cyberstalking.

"I guess." I pull my best neutral face. "Kind of looks like a unicorn threw up on you, though. With all the pastels and sparkles."

From the doorway, Sunglasses snickers. Felix looks at her, startled by her display of human emotion, and her face returns to a blank slate. He sighs and hands me the iced Americano he's clutching.

I accept with a frown. "You didn't get a coffee?"

"Yeah, nah. Caffeine makes me extra hyper."

It's hard to imagine him even more hyper. I take a swig as he casually leans against the wall, one leg crossed over the other. He stares at me, waiting for me to lead the conversation. I lean against the desk, mirroring his posture.

"I'm willing to give you ***one*** chance," I enunciate. "I'm going to be honest: I don't believe you're committed to this. You've never given me any reason to trust you'll actually do the work to learn ASL."

He flashes a comically kicked-puppy frown, alongside a momentary crease in his brow. If I didn't know better, I might suspect some hurt behind the façade. "I've tried my hardest."

I tsk. "Your hardest was skipping lessons for band practice? Never reading the ASL grammar books I gave you? Making me reteach you the fingerspelling alphabet every week?"

He opens his mouth to reply, but he decides against it, instead hazarding a timid "*sorry*" by rubbing a fist on his sternum.

"Don't even try to half-ass it," I continue.

His Adam's apple bobs as he gulps. "Nat, in the past I wasn't able . . . it was really hard because . . . well, I . . . never mind." He stops wracking his brain for excuses and forces a tight-lipped smile. "I'm committed this time. I promise."

I search his face for any hint of deceit but find his expression to be open and honest. Maybe . . . vulnerable?

It's almost painful to accept the offer and resign myself to a summer of being Felix Song's hired help—but not nearly as painful as losing the Deaf Center.

"Okay, good," I say.

"Sweet as!" He claps his hands together. "So I'll see you—"

"Whoa, buddy, hold on. I have some conditions," I continue. "I'd like to have a day off from 24/7-Felix duty in Boston. My godmother runs a Deaf summer camp, and I want to visit her."

He chuckles. "Sure. No biggie. I'll double-check with my manager"—the corners of his lips twitch in a nearly imperceptible grimace—"about the schedule, but that should be fine. Is that all?"

"No, actually." Now's as good a time as any to tell him about how situational my hearing can be. "My hearing ability varies depending on the circumstances. Right now, it's quiet, we're close together, and I have a clear view of your lips, so I can pick up a fair amount. But throw in things like background noise, low lighting, soft voices, accents, or ***fast talking***"—I can't help the way I emphasize his bad habit—"and it's way harder to follow a verbal conversation. So please be patient if I need you to repeat yourself or slow down. Okay?"

"Alrighty." He nods thoughtfully. "Maybe we can just be patient with each other, yeah?"

His tone is good-natured, but I bristle. Is he ***already*** giving himself a free pass for slacking off?

I press on. "Now, let's talk about the fact that you're lowballing me."

This triggers a loud laugh. "I'm sorry?"

"$17,000 for the sixty-six days I'd be on call is $32.20 an hour, based on an eight-hour workday. But you need me to be available 24/7. That math isn't mathing."

He's the son of a businessman. He should know how to negotiate proper compensation.

He opens his mouth, makes a loud "uhhh" sound, then closes it. "Does that mean you want more money?" His face is scrunched up, like he's using his muscles to think.

I guess business sense isn't a genetic trait.

Before I have a chance to teach him the art of the deal, he says, "Name your price."

I freeze. I didn't expect him to fold so quickly. Luckily, though, I crunched the numbers last night. Besides what we owe the bank, we'll need enough to continue making monthly payments until I get back and can start my fundraising in earnest. If I include our mortgage payments for the rest of the year, thirty thousand total would be ideal—and leave my slush fund untouched so we'd have money for the revamping and eventual roof repairs.

I fall back on every ounce of business knowledge I have and start higher than what I'm aiming for so we can negotiate down.

"$40,000," I say.

"Alrighty."

“Then how about—wait, ***what***?!” I gape at him. He . . . agreed. To my first number?! “‘Alrighty’? Like, yes? You’re saying ‘alrighty’ to paying me forty grand?” I clarify.

“Yup.”

“Oh . . . kay.” I swallow. Then, since I’ll need enough to pay the mortgage while I’m gone, I add, “Um. I need $16,500 of it up front. You can pay me the rest after.”

He does a curious-puppy head tilt. “$16,500? Not twenty-five percent? Half? That’s oddly specific . . .” His dark eyes rove over my face. “Ah. Are you in debt with a mafia boss?”

“Oh no. You’ve discovered my secret,” I deadpan.

“Russian or Italian? Makes all the difference.”

“Yakuza, actually. Joke’s on you.”

“Well, then you’re fucked.” Playfulness gleams in his eyes, and he wets his plump lips before breaking into another cheeky grin. We hold each other’s gaze for far too long before he walks over to my desk and roots through his PRADA fanny pack. I move away when I catch a hint of his weird, eau de wet dog cologne and feel his warmth radiating too close for comfort.

He discards tissues, a fancy French hand cream, and a luxury black credit card on my desk before pulling out a pad of Post-it notes.

“I’ll give you the money to escape your mob boss up front. My accountant will call this afternoon to work it out,” he says. He snags a pen from the jar on my desk and jots something onto a Post-it note. He straightens from being hunched over the desk, peels the note off the pad, and extends it toward me. Scrawled across the paper, in what has to be the messiest penmanship I’ve ever seen, is:

A sound halfway between a laugh and an incredulous gasp works its way out of my throat. "What's this supposed to be?" I blink at the note, bewildered, as he thrusts it toward me again. Fed up with my refusal to accept his offering, he slaps the note onto my forehead.

I peel it off as he says, "If you feel like I'm goofing off, you can leave at any time. Hand me this IOU, and I'll send you what I owe. No strings attached. Unless you wanna attach strings . . ."

"Um. I'm sorry . . . You can't hand me a ***sticky note*** with an IOU for ***twenty-three thousand dollars***! That's not something people just . . . do!" I exclaim.

"I wanna prove to you that I'm committed. You can leave if I'm not taking it seriously." He sticks his pinkie finger toward me. "Pinkie swear."

I fight an eye roll, but he doesn't retract his finger and, instead, stares me down. I heave a sigh and, on the exhale, hook my pinkie around his.

I get a wire transfer for $16,501 with the note "the extra $1 is a treat" at 4:00 p.m. on Wednesday, and by 4:30 p.m., the bank has sent me confirmation that they're processing my $12,506.95 payment for the Center. We're not out of the danger zone, but we're not going to be foreclosed on. It's a win.

I exit out of email and refocus on cramming my clothes, sketchbook, laptop, some books, and my wallet into my backpack. It's a tight fit, but I manage to successfully zip it in the end.

Jo lets herself into my bedroom. I sigh when I see she's wearing the embroidered District 12 hoodie ***she*** bought me for ***my*** birthday. She hands over the suitcase she uses to transport her belongings to and from residential school.

She's letting me borrow it to haul Ginger's supplies. Packing my things was easy; I basically only have four outfits, and my two forms of entertainment are reading and drawing. Packing for ***Ginger*** is the problem.

She needs bowls, food, grooming tools, poop bags, toys . . . Her list is longer than mine.

And I can only fit a few days' supply of kibble in the suitcase, so I'll have to track down a pet store that carries her brand of food at our first tour stop.

Jo sits with me as I arrange Ginger's things like an elaborate jigsaw puzzle. She pokes me to get my attention.

"*You nervous?*" she asks.

The one time I've been out of the country was when I drove three hours to Vancouver, British Columbia, for a book signing by my favorite author, but I've never been on a plane. Sure, I'm a little nervous, but with Ginger by my side and all travel expenses being paid by someone else, I feel oddly prepared to venture outside my bubble. Despite my initial resistance, maybe even a touch excited.

"I'm mostly sad I can't spend all summer with you." I pull her into a side-hug, and she rests her head on my shoulder, sliding a Y-shaped hand between us—the sign for "*same.*"

After a few seconds, she scoots away and smirks. *"Can you bring me a signed album?"*

"What would you do with an album? You can't hear, remember?"

"Wow! Funny!" She reaches out to smack my arm, and I dodge her with a laugh. *"People buy signed DAYDREAM albums for, like, $1,500."*

My eyes widen. I'd rather stub my toe every day for a year than ask Felix for a signed album and, god forbid, for him to think I'm a ***fan***, but evidently, there's a lot I'd do for money. I can put my pride on the back burner to make an extra $1,500.

"OK-OK. I'll try."

"Posters are good, too. Maybe a life-size C-A-R-D-B-O-A-R-D cutout. The F-E-L-I-X ones sell best, but M-A-T-E-O is the cutest."

I flash her an appalled look. Why do they have life-size cardboard cutouts?!

She laughs, then asks, *"Have you told Mom?"*

My abject horror at the concept of Felix being immortalized in the form of a cardboard cutout shifts to irritation at the mention of Mom.

Since our latest blowup, she hasn't so much as glanced in my direction. Honestly, though, I prefer the signless treatment over our never-ending cycle of arguments. Usually, I'll be the bigger person and smooth things over, but I've never been this hurt before. I can hardly even think about her without that deep, cutting feeling of betrayal rearing its head.

"You're not allowed to give me shit for being a procrastinator anymore. You have to tell her!"

"*I know, I know!*" Then I continue, "*I'll tell her! Mind your business.*"

"*Just make sure she doesn't blame* ME *for any of it.*" Her nose scrunches in displeasure, likely not wanting to be caught in the middle. "*You'll text me when you land?*"

I choose not to argue that she is ***absolutely*** to blame for some of it. "*I have to finish packing.*" I lift my index finger, pinkie, and thumb in the air and shove it in Jo's face, "*I love you.*"

She shakes another Y-shaped hand between us.

Thirty minutes later, I successfully zip the overflowing suitcase and catch my breath. Packing this thing was a full-body workout.

"You're lucky you're cute," I grumble at Ginger, and she replies by squeaking her obnoxiously loud duck toy. I stage my backpack and suitcase near the front door, then peer down the hall. My eyes land on Mom's bedroom door, and I tense up. I briefly debated writing a letter and dipping, but that's not exactly a ***mature*** response.

I mentally run through what I'll tell her. It's one quick conversation. I can do this.

Before I talk myself out of it, I head straight toward her room and open the door.

She glances away from the book she's reading in bed, her face blank. I take a breath.

"*I accepted the S-O-N-G-S' offer. I'll be gone before you get up tomorrow,*" I explain from the doorway. Her gray eyes shoot daggers at me though her glasses, but her expression doesn't waver. "*I paid the bank,*" I continue.

Her attention flickers back to her book, and an indignant scoff escapes me. I vigorously flap my hand until she looks up again. "*You're not even going to acknowledge me?*" A fresh wave of anger washes over me. She practically has a PhD in giving me the cold shoulder, but she's never ignored me quite like this before. "*Mom?*"

I stare at her, waiting for a response. For acknowledgment. For something.

Instead, she wordlessly returns to her book, delivering a final, devastating blow to our fractured relationship.

Is DAYDREAM's Will a Teen Dad?

Will, a member of heartthrob boy band DAYDREAM, faces a paternity scandal after photos surfaced of him with a toddler who bears a striking resemblance to the 19-year-old star. The images, sourced from his grandmother's Facebook page, sparked a frenzy.

The band's representatives have issued a statement saying it's Will's nephew. But the world is left wondering if that's a convenient excuse since the scandal comes at a crucial time for DAYDREAM, who embark on their debut tour in mere days.

Chapter Seven

Main Character Energy

Seattle + Los Angeles, June 13

Call it cliché, but I feel like I'm having my Main Character Moment as I speed across the bridge linking mainland Seattle to Mercer Island the next morning.

How else could I describe it? I'm driving to a ***pop star's*** house at the crack of dawn to accompany him on ***tour***, with a ***not-even-slightly-legally-binding*** Post-it note as the only evidence of our arrangement. It's a scene right out of a rom-com.

My dashboard reads 4:42 a.m. I catch sight of all the private docks lining the backyard beaches. Above us, the sky lightens to a dusty blue with purple streaks as the morning sun glints off the water.

"You'll always love me, right? Even though I've gone off the deep end?" I glance at Ginger through my rearview mirror. She gives me the evil eye, which isn't even slightly evil, since she's the dog equivalent of cotton candy.

I turn on the radio and flip to the Local Seattle Musicians channel. I crank the volume and move to the beat of a heavy metal song that definitely doesn't fit the vibe of an early-morning commute.

Minutes away from the Songs' house, the radio host says something I interpret as a bunch of garbling noises. I catch the tail end: ". . . This is 'Daydreamin' of You' by DAYDREAM!"

You've got to be kidding me.

I've refused to listen to their music on principle, but seeing as I caved and accepted Felix's offer, there's not a lot of principle left to stand on. Soon, singing blasts through my speakers. I try to decipher the lyrics, but the overlapping voices make it nearly impossible. The only part I understand is "can't stop daydreamin' 'bout you" being sung over and over.

The song ends right as I park across the street from the Song residence.

Mrs. Song is standing outside their opulent home, her mouth moving rapidly as she cups her son's cheek; Ava clings to her brother. Mr. Song silently observes, several steps away. His brows are twisted into another taut frown, mouth pressed into a line.

I unbuckle Ginger, grab the suitcase and backpack, and cross the street.

Ava lights up as I approach. *"You're teaching him? True biz?"* she asks, like she can't believe I said yes. (Not that I can blame her for being shocked . . .)

"True biz," I reply.

Felix taps her shoulder and scrunches his face as he considers his signs. *"I'll . . . learn . . . sign. I'll try . . . hard . . . now. Promise."*

If I didn't know better, I'd almost think his clumsy signing was oddly charming. ***Almost.***

Felix kneels on the driveway and wraps Ava in a tight hug. "I'll be a better brother. Pinkie swear." He offers an outstretched finger that she eagerly catches with her own. "I won't let you down again."

She beams from ear to ear and plants a kiss on his cheek. "*You're the best brother. I love you so much*," she signs. Mrs. Song interprets so he can fully understand Ava's sentiments.

He forms the ubiquitous "*I love you*" sign but spins his index finger, "*I'll always love you*."

Okay, that was kind of sweet. Slightly. When he stands up, I hurriedly look away.

I turn to Mrs. Song and hand her my car keys. "*When my sister tutors on Saturday, you'll give her my keys, right?*" I confirm the plan I sent last night.

"*Yes. We'll miss you!*" She gives me a hug. On instinct, I tense up. I can't remember the last time my mom hugged me. Years ago, probably. The maternal warmth she extends to my sister is always cold by the time it gets to me. As foreign as Mrs. Song's hug feels, it's also loving. Motherly. I find myself sinking into it, but she releases me as Felix taps my shoulder.

"*Airplane now*," he signs, eyes bright like a little kid.

Mrs. Song and Ava both drag him into another embrace; Mr. Song offers him a curt nod and nothing else. I kneel and change Ginger into her pink service dog vest that coincidentally matches my hair.

I boop her nose before straightening. Felix smiles and waves an ASL letter "*U*" in the air. "Ready?" he asks out loud.

I cross my middle finger over my index, an "*R*," and shake it, "*Ready*."

"See, I was close, though. Progress!"

He grabs my suitcase and his GUCCI duffel bag and trots toward the black SUV parked in front of the house. Sunglasses opens the door, lets him inside, then puts the bags in the far back.

Once we're on the road, Felix turns to me with an inquisitive look. "Did you get into Harvard?" he asks, motioning to my red crop top that has HARVARD printed on it.

The way he asks it so casually makes me unexpectedly self-conscious. Of course the first thing that would occur to him is that I have the means to attend an Ivy League. That's his reality. Really, I bought this shirt for four dollars at Goodwill.

I button the gray-and-black flannel I'm wearing on top of the shirt, hiding the logo. "Um. No," I squeak out.

The car goes quiet. Through my peripheral vision, I catch Felix staring at me. When I look his way, he pretends to be scrolling through his phone, but his screen is turned off. What a dork. Finally, as Sunglasses gets on the bridge connecting to Seattle, I break the silence.

"What are your bandmates like?"

Committed to his casual act, he cocks his head toward me like he didn't catch what I said. He presses his phone's Power button to "turn it off" but actually turns it on. His lockscreen is him and Ava, pre-fame days. I snort as the tips of his ears tint red.

"Your bandmates," I repeat. "What are they like?"

"Ah. They're . . ." His face scrunches in deep thought. "Er . . . nice."

"Usually when people are nice, it doesn't take thirty seconds to say it."

The corners of his rosebud lips tip upward. "They're . . . a lot. Especially as roommates. You'll like 'em, though. They're cool."

While Sunglasses parks at the airport, Felix pulls a black

hoodie over his purple-and-white-striped sweater, throws on a pair of sunglasses, and dons a black surgical face mask.

"Fair warning," he says, turning toward me, "we're gonna have to move quickly."

I don't have a chance to reply before Sunglasses ushers us out. The pandemonium hits me immediately—flashing cameras and an indecipherable wall of sound that makes my ears buzz. With assistance from police officers, we're rushed to a first-class lounge.

As I perch myself on a chair, clutching my backpack like a lifeline, Felix sheds his hoodie, glasses, and mask. He grabs a green juice from one of the mini fridges, then hesitates. His gaze shifts to me, and without a word, he picks up a cold brew and hands it over. He sinks into the leather couch opposite me like this is just another day in the life. For him, I guess it is.

Still, he pauses mid-sip. "That was a lot. I'm sorry."

I glance at the coffee in my hands, the chill grounding me. "Fans even showed up to the Deaf Center. That's . . . dedication."

He smiles faintly. "It can be overwhelming, but their hearts are in the right place."

While we wait, I hand Felix the ASL grammar study guide I brought him. "Some of our lessons will be structured around chapters in this book, so you'll need to read it," I explain.

He runs his fingers along the cover before slowly turning his head toward me; his Adam's apple dips as he gulps. "Are you sure? I'm not really, er, a book person."

"Is this what you being 'committed' to learning ASL looks like? Making more excuses for not doing homework?"

It comes out harsher than intended.

His brows and lips tug into a weary frown. "It's not an excuse.

I . . ." He hesitates, nervously messing with the hem of his sweater. "Never mind. I'll read it."

"Good," I say. "Our first lesson is based around chapter one, so read that on the plane."

"Actually, I was hoping we could practice some key signs and phrases on the flight," he admits.

I like my lessons to be very structured, but this situation is unique. The whole point of me being here is to teach him whenever he has time. We should use this flight to our benefit. "Okay. But you still have to read the book. No cop-outs."

As promised, for part of the flight, I teach him some basic signs and phrases. During the second half, he reads while I tweak our lesson plans.

Out of the corner of my eye, I see him intensely studying the book. His index finger traces each word, and he silently mouths them as he reads, concentration painted across his features. Good! He's focusing.

Soon enough, we've landed and Felix puts his sunglasses and mask back on. The instant we disembark, screams and cheers fill the terminal. There are double the number of police officers, and they do crowd control as Sunglasses guides Felix and me through the airport. I stumble when the crowd jostles us and nearly fall behind, but Felix grabs my hand and pulls me back to him. I trade his hand for the strap on his GUCCI bag and grip it until we make it to another SUV.

I exhale a long breath as Sunglasses starts to drive. After an hour spent stuck in traffic, we park in front of a luxury apartment building. Felix steps out and waits for me.

I struggle to slide across the bench with Ginger at my feet. I peer out my window and see cars whizzing by, making his side my only exit.

"*Need help?*" he signs.

"*Yes. Thank you,*" I lower a flat hand from my chin.

"C'mere, dog." He timidly pats his leg. Ginger doesn't budge. She looks at me, and I could swear she's judging him. Valid.

"Hold on. She's trained better than to obey random people while she's working," I explain. "Okay! Go." I say her release word, and Felix leans away as she jumps out. "Are you scared of dogs?" I ask after getting out.

"I'm a cat person. They're smarter."

"Then why can't they be service animals?"

"Because humans serve cats. They keep ya humble," he jokes as the building's doorman lets us in.

"Pfft." I laugh. "Yeah, I get real humble vibes from you."

"I never said ***I*** have a cat."

We load into the elevator with Sunglasses, and Felix presses the button for the top floor. ***Oh god, they live in a penthouse, don't they?***

As he unlocks the last door at the end of a long hallway, I brace myself to be smacked in the face by grandeur.

And I am. Sort of.

The apartment is massive, with floor-to-ceiling windows showcasing a bird's-eye view of LA. Sleek modern furniture fills the space, but any illusion of luxury is disrupted by sheer chaos. There are crumbs scattered across the floor, random socks and underwear abandoned in corners, and several half-built LEGO sets on the kitchen island.

It makes sense, though. Give five teen boys free rein and this is probably the result.

The place is also alive with movement. Staff members bustle around, carrying garment bags, checking lists, and taking phone calls. It's like a command center for the impending tour.

My eyes land on a velvety L-shaped sectional couch bigger than my entire living room, where the other members of DAYDREAM are sprawled out.

The boys zone out as a short, stocky white person in a navy blue dress shirt and black necktie paces. Necktie reads from a piece of paper, brows furrowed.

One of the members spots us standing in the entryway.

"Will, focus," Necktie snaps at the Black guy with light blue locs.

"Mornin'! How ya goin'?" Felix interrupts, stepping into the living room. He flashes Necktie a sarcastic smile. "Wow, he looks great, doesn't he!" he says to his bandmates before turning back to Necktie. "Did ya get a haircut?"

They hold a collective laugh as Necktie touches his brown quiff styled with so much gel it could double as a skating ramp.

Felix motions me into the room. I take a small step toward him and wave nervously, feeling like a piece of meat hurled into a cage of hungry lions.

"Nat, this is Andrew— —*charming* manager," he enunciates, gesturing toward Necktie, then to his suddenly alert bandmates. "And Mateo Vazquez García, Lachlan McCarthy, Calum Evans, and Will."

"Just 'Will'?" I eye the blue-haired boy.

He nods. "Just Will."

"Who exactly is this?" Necktie demands, looking me up and down before turning to Felix.

"My ASL tutor."

"Your ASL tutor," Necktie parrots, "is supposed to— —forty-year-old man named Leonard." He sucks on his teeth. "A word." He drags him out of the room.

I teeter awkwardly in the living room. The teenage celebrities study me before Mateo—a boy with fluffy brown curls, green eyes, and smooth, tan skin—waves.

"Hi, I'm Mateo," he greets shyly.

"I know," I reply. The ghostly pale, dirty blond mystery boy is the only one who's hardly shown on DAYDREAM's accounts . . . oh crap.

I've already forgotten what Felix called him. Logan? Lincoln? The most memorable thing about him is the spiky eyebrow piercing he's wearing now but didn't have in any of his Instagram photos.

He takes my staring as an invitation to approach. "Nice to meet you," he says.

"You too . . ." I trail off, hoping he'll fill in the blanks.

"Lachlan," he supplies with a chuckle.

His ocean-blue eyes carefully scan me, but not suspiciously—unlike Will, who's staring me down like he's trying to identify a robbery suspect.

"Wait . . . you're Ava's— —aren't you?" Lachlan's question blurs slightly.

The room is loud, chatter bouncing off the walls, and it's taking a herculean effort to follow conversation. It's like trying to put together a puzzle with half the pieces missing. I don't have the opportunity to ask him to repeat himself before he continues: "You seem young for a teacher."

Ah. He must've asked if I'm Ava's teacher.

"I mean, I don't have a degree, but my dad did," I explain. "He taught me, well, how to teach. My family and I are Deaf, so teaching ASL just . . . fits."

Understanding flashes across his face. *"I took it throughout high school. But I'm . . . rusty."* His signing is clunky but better than Felix's. I stare at him in shock. The last thing I expected was for one of his bandmates to know more sign than him.

"Can— —pet— —your— —" Will interrupts. I turn to face him, eyes trained on his lips, but I'm still lost. "Or is— —working?" His eyes land on Ginger, and the context clues suddenly combine in my head. He's asking to pet her.

It's obvious she's working, with her vest covered in I'M WORKING! patches. But I've been known to make exceptions for petting. Mostly cute little kids, not teenage superstars, but I appreciate Will asking for permission. Most people don't.

I say her release word, and Ginger trots over to him. His face lights up as he scratches her head.

"That's a bad idea, bro," Calum warns from where he's melted into the couch, munching on a family-size bag of Flamin' Hot Cheetos. He's wearing nothing but a pair of Ninja Turtle boxers; his shaggy dark brown hair is tied into a ponytail that resembles a unicorn horn in the middle of his scalp.

Will ignores Calum, but forty seconds later he's sneezing, and Calum shakes his head in disapproval. He pats the couch, inviting me to sit.

"Nice— —meet you, Nat."

I sigh. ***Of course*** Felix has only called me Nat. God forbid that boy use my government name. "Ignore whatever Felix told you. My name is Natalie."

Lachlan smiles amusedly. "I take it— —not Lix's biggest fan?"

"I mean, I wouldn't categorize myself as a fan at all, but it's not like I poke needles into a Felix voodoo doll every day, either. I took this job for Ava. He's a client."

"That's refreshing." Lachlan chuckles.

From my seat on the couch, I have a view of the outdoor patio, where Felix is getting chewed out by an angry Necktie.

"So you're deaf." Calum changes the subject and studies me closely, licking Cheeto dust off his fingers. "But— —can hear us? Or are you really good— —lipreading? Do you have— —brain-implant thingies?"

Everyone's attention snaps to him. Lachlan face-palms, Mateo cringes, and Will's watery eyes bug out of his head.

"Cal, shut the hell up!" Will scolds.

"It's fine," I jump in. "I would probably recommend posing questions more . . . elegantly . . . in the future, but I don't mind answering."

I engage Teacher Mode and explain, "Deaf identities are a spectrum, but typically, 'big D' Deaf refers to someone who identifies with the Deaf community and culture. 'Little d' deaf is essentially just a medical diagnosis. In my case, I'm medically Hard of Hearing, but culturally, or 'big D,' Deaf. While not all deaf or Hard of Hearing people lipread, I do. But it's exhausting and not always accurate. And no, I don't use cochlear implants or hearing aids."

I leave it at that. He doesn't need the long-winded backstory about how I wore hearing aids until I was six but ***hated*** them. Dad always found his hearing aids incredibly helpful, but I would get horrible tinnitus and feedback that sounded like a tiny, angry banshee wailing in my ears—no matter what adjustments the audiologist made.

Calum takes a beat to process the information, then after ten seconds, he gives a thumbs-up. "Cool. Thanks for explaining."

"Is there anything— —do to help?" Mateo chimes in, looking at me thoughtfully.

I smile. "Actually, yeah. Thanks. Can you all slow down a bit and face me when you speak? It's hard to keep up in all this . . ." I gesture vaguely toward the chaos.

"You're not from Mercer Island, right?" Calum abruptly changes the subject, though, thankfully, he talks slower. He seems like a goldfish. But a cute goldfish.

"No," I breathe. "Do I give off broke vibes or something?"

He laughs. "I didn't mean it like that. You seem down-to-earth, that's all. Mercer Island vibes— —different. Privileged."

Will looks up from his snuggle session with my dog and quirks a brow. "You say, as a privileged Mercer Island kid."

"Dude, did I insinuate I'm not? We're all in— —same boat. Except for you." Calum glances at Mateo.

Suddenly, Necktie and Felix re-enter, and Necktie pushes Felix toward the couch. He lands on the cushion next to me, his muscular thigh pressing against mine.

He looks down at me, a soft smile gracing his features. I look away as his manager starts walking the length of the room.

After pacing for a few seconds, he says, "This tour is extremely important. Depending on how successful— —North American tour is— —DAYDREAM might— —world tour next year, and I— —promoted— —full-time manager. Nobody is going to get in the way of that." He gives me a pointed look.

"Why would we ever want you— —our full-time manager?" Lachlan mumbles just loud enough for me to hear. The boys laugh.

"Lachlan, so help me god, if you don't—" Necktie's interrupted by his phone loudly ringing. His voice drops to a low grumble as he answers the phone with his back to us, so I can't lipread. However, his body language is tense, muscles locked up.

He ends the call. "Change of plans. We're flying— —Miami tomorrow, not today. ROLLING STONE wants an interview in the morning."

Calum leans forward, suddenly alert. "Holy shit. We've made it, boys!" He laughs raucously and high-fives his bandmates.

"Don't feel too special. Taylor Swift had— —last-minute schedule conflict. You guys are— —backup," Necktie explains.

They don't seem to care. Rapid, unintelligible speech fills the room as the boys all talk over one another, their enthusiasm overthrowing the bored atmosphere I walked into.

Over the excitement, Mateo timidly raises his hand. "Does this— —we get today off?" He's soft-spoken and it's hard for me to pick up everything he says, so my mind has to fill in the blanks.

"No. But it does mean you have time— —film some LA shots for— —tour music video." The sounds of excitement morph into groans, but their manager silences them with another scowl. He's good at those. "And marketing wants— —TikToks using 'Lovely Girl' and 'Daydreamin' of You'— —film those, too."

He motions over a tall staff member, who is one of the most stunning people I've ever seen. Which is saying a lot since I'm surrounded by a bunch of Professional Pretty Boys right now.

I catch sight of a THEY/THEM badge pinned to their black sleeveless turtleneck, which is tucked into high-waisted forest-green pants. Their waist-length, thick black hair is in a very Katniss Everdeen–like braid.

"Help them film," Necktie commands.

The staffer laughs in his face. "I'm— —hair and makeup artist, not— —videographer."

"The videos must seem like different days. Their hairstyles— —outfits should be different. Surely— —can handle that," he bites. "Oh, and Lachlan? Try to be interesting. Pretend you have— —personality, would you?"

Lachlan tries to appear unfazed by the comment, but his jaw locks up and lines crease his forehead in a subtle frown. Mateo comfortingly pats his shoulder, but Lachlan pushes his hand away.

As Necktie leaves, I look around at the carefully curated chaos and wonder how long anyone could survive this pressure without breaking.

r/DAYDREAM 5 days ago

shesintodrummers

MATEO + LACHLAN RE: OTHER MEMBERS

AJSDHAJGFAJK when Mateo & Lachlan were livestreaming I asked how they'd describe the others in 1 word & they SAW MY COMMENT!! Here's what they said~ (≧◡≦) ♡

Mateo:	**Lachlan:**
Felix is chaotic	Felix is captivating
Calum is goofy	Calum is weird
Will is clever	Will is dependable
Lachlan is determined	Mateo is cute

TOP COMMENTS:

d.reamer2011 5 days ago

mateo getting all shy when lachlan said that was adorable! i squealed!! i want to put him in my pocket

shesintodrummers 4 days ago

~~HE'S SUCH A CUTIE PIE!!! Lachlan was so real for saying that!! \(^ワ^)/

Chapter Eight

Adonis by Day, Annoyance by Night

Los Angeles, June 13–14

"I'm Bhavani," the stunning staff member introduces themself, and extends a hand to shake mine. "You're Nat, right?" Bhavani continues.

"Natalie."

They smirk. "Felix told me about you."

He told them about ***me***? What could he possibly have to say? All he knows is I'm Deaf, I corrupted my integrity for $40,000, and I have pink hair—and he only recently learned two of those things.

"I told them about Aves! You were . . . incidental," Felix rushes. "Nat's my ASL tutor."

Bhavani casts a suspicious glance in his direction. "Well, it's nice— —meet you, Nat . . . alie."

Bhavani guides Calum into a chair and starts slathering sunscreen onto his suntanned, olive-toned face and neck. "Felix, Will, your outfits— —always fire. Lachlan, Mateo, you need to change— —something more DAYDREAM-y. And bring Cal clothes, please!" Bhavani calls as the pair obediently slink down the hall.

Part of me knows celebrity images are curated, but seeing it in real life feels like I'm being let in on an industry secret. Nothing is inherently wrong with Lachlan's vintage David Bowie T-shirt and black skinny jeans or Mateo's shirt with a cartoon drum kit that reads IF YOU HIT MY DRUMS THERE'LL BE REPERCUSSIONS, but they're definitely a departure from the boyish, and usually designer, outfits DAYDREAM are pictured in online.

"What music video are you filming?" I ask.

"We're taking— —bunch of clips— —different cities— —make a tour montage as a thank-you to our fans," Felix answers. "Dunno what song we'll use yet."

"Hopefully a new one, if— —approves!" Calum singsongs.

"That's cool. But you guys don't have a social media manager?" I ask.

"The label offers 'suggestions,' but we film— —upload everything ourselves. We're basically singers, models, brand ambassadors— —influencers," Felix explains with a frown.

"That's . . . a lot," I say.

"You're telling me," Will chimes in, dabbing dog drool off his white-and-black-striped button-up shirt. "Two months ago, they wouldn't— —release our new single, 'Cloud 9,' until— —ten different videos with over a million likes using— —sound bite."

Before I can reply, Lachlan and Mateo reappear in different outfits. Lachlan throws a pair of long jean shorts and a green GIVENCHY T-shirt at Calum.

"You had to pick the *jorts*?" he groans in protest, then disappears into what I assume to be a bathroom to change.

Lachlan sits down and opens his Notes app. "Let's make today efficient. What videos— —popular right now?"

The way he's taking charge and organizing everyone, it feels like he could be DAYDREAM's manager, rather than Necktie. Lachlan gives me Dad Friend vibes, someone who knows how to handle each of the boys.

Their speech fades into background noise as they discuss day-in-the-life videos. A dull headache thumps against my skull, and I recognize it as oncoming auditory fatigue—debilitating exhaustion that stems from listening for long stretches.

The only time I had to deal with auditory fatigue before was during mainstream high school. It wasn't often, since I focused on my interpreter instead of trying to understand speech. But after an early flight, the airport mobs, and spending the morning in an apartment filled with Hearing people and auditory overload, it was bound to happen.

I zone out and stare at a corner of the living room where nine guitars, an electric keyboard, and red drums are placed underneath a low-quality, framed picture of the band onstage at a high school dance. They're in terribly uncoordinated grunge outfits, holding instruments or microphones, and barefaced with pimples and sad, teenager stubble. Beside the setup, a small tank houses two orange goldfish oblivious to the mayhem around them.

"Why do you guys have nine guitars?" I ask, unable to contain my curiosity.

Immediately, all the boys' eyes land on me, and I freeze, under the impression I asked something horribly offensive.

Felix chuckles. "Six of 'em— —Cal's basses. But don't call a bass a guitar around him. Ever."

"What does that even mean?"

"Just trust me. No guitar talk with Cal, *OK?*" he signs the last word, and I flash an "*OK*" back, still confused.

I spend a few more minutes spaced out, but I'm drawn out of it when Felix finishes getting beautified and gently places a hand on my shoulder. "*What's wrong?*" he signs, concern etched on his features.

"*I'm overwhelmed,*" I admit.

He repeats the sign, arcing both hands over his head. He flicks an index finger by his ear and shakes his head, "*I don't understand.*"

"*O-V-E-R-W-H-E-L-M-E-D,*" I form each letter slowly.

"*Sorry. I don't understand,*" he repeats before hanging his head. Long, blond locks fall in front of his face and hide his embarrassment.

Before I can re-engage him, we're being herded down to the parking garage by three bodyguards, including Sunglasses.

Our group is split between two SUVs. Lachlan, Felix, Ginger, and I are in one, the other members in another. Sunglasses and a second bodyguard sit in the front of our vehicle; I sit in the middle of the back seat, Felix on my right and Lachlan on my left. I place my backpack on my lap and move my feet to create room for Ginger.

Sunglasses pulls out of the parking garage, and I have to shield my eyes. The bright sun is decidedly unhelpful for my growing headache.

Lachlan extends a pair of DOLCE & GABBANA sunglasses toward me. "*Thanks,*" I sign.

While we're stuck in traffic, I Google pet stores in Miami so I can buy dog food there. Felix glances at my screen before rooting around in his fanny pack and eventually emerges with

Post-it notes. He scribbles something mostly unintelligible, but I make out "dog" before he shoves the pad back in.

After fifteen minutes, he pokes my knee. "*ASL . . . I learn . . . A-V-A . . .*" he fumbles the signs. "*If I learn ASL signs . . .* damn it," he bites, frustration coloring his usually upbeat tone.

"*You can voice*," I sign slowly. The car is quiet and we're so close, having a verbal conversation will be easier.

"There are some specific things I wanna learn. Like how to tell Aves about my music stuff and ask her how her tennis tournaments go or what school drama is happening. I dunno. Conversational stuff."

"My first suggestion is to never get involved in middle school drama," I reply using SimCom. He laughs. "But sure. I can tailor your lessons to include relevant topics. You actually remembered quite a bit, so we can skip straight to Lesson Four, so read up to chapter three. We'll focus on fingerspelling first."

Even when he attended the occasional lesson with his family, his fingerspelling was abysmal, but he's clearly in need of a refresher.

"You're reading an ASL book?" Lachlan interjects. "Isn't that hard with your—"

"No, no, it's no biggie," Felix cuts him off. "Don't worry about it."

"But you really stru—"

"It's ***fine***, Lach," Felix enunciates in a voice more forceful than I've heard from him, shutting the conversation down.

The energy becomes uncomfortably tense. My focus shifts between them, curious about why Felix snapped and why Lachlan turned away from us, choosing to stare out the window, frustration visible on his face.

The interaction leaves my mind as we park at a beach. Outside, Calum immediately strips out of his shirt. Bhavani rushes after him, shoves his discarded shirt into their backpack, and fixes his tousled hair.

"You and the dog can hang here." Felix places a towel on the sand for me before joining his bandmates by a beach volleyball net.

I sit on the towel, and Ginger suspiciously noses the sand and glances at me, eyes alight with curiosity. I reach over and remove her vest so she can enjoy the beach off-duty. Neither of us has been to a beach like this before. Most beaches back home are full of rocks rather than the soft, sandy ones in movies. She starts rolling around, and sand sticks to her fur. I chuckle when I imagine getting sand all over their penthouse when I brush her later.

While Ginger happily digs holes, I grab my sketchbook. My pencil moves across an empty page, and soon a rough sketch of the tranquil waves and fluffy clouds appear in my book. Pops of red and yellow from towels and swimsuits and strokes of green from lively palm trees beautifully complement the array of blues.

I've always been drawn to art. Maybe it's because Deaf culture is rich in artistic expression or because my first language is a visual one, rooted in movement and physical storytelling. Either way, my sketchbook is an escape for me. My happy place.

While shading a wave, I glance to where the boys are filming with a GoPro. They're laughing and running around while playing a game of beach volleyball that seems to be driving Calum up a wall, since nobody follows the rules he's shouting at them.

After the game, the boys pull new swim trunks over their current pairs, and Bhavani changes their hairstyles.

In the sand, Calum shows Felix how to distribute his body weight on a surfboard. Will squats, stands on his toes, and even lies down to get the perfect angle as he films them on his phone, presumably for one of the TikToks.

If I didn't know otherwise (and if we're ignoring the fans who've surrounded them and the bodyguards keeping them away), I would've never guessed these guys were stars. As they squabble like best friends, film goofy clips of themselves, and splash seawater on each other, they seem like completely normal boys. Well, as normal as teenage boys can be.

My eyes flicker between them and my page as I continue to draw, but I pause when Felix takes off his shirt for "Day Three." The sun cuts through the sky like a spotlight, tracing every line of his six-pack, and a slight sheen of sweat catches in the light. He looks like an effin' marble statue. An Adonis-like figure whom entire temples would be built for. Good lord.

Unfortunately, being demiromantic doesn't make me immune to thinking some people are absurdly hot. Which means my carnal meatloaf brain is more than happy to remind me that someone—even as insufferable as Felix—can be an aesthetic masterpiece.

It's horrible. He's horrible.

Distracted, I press down on my pencil a little too hard, and it leaves a smudge where a seagull is supposed to be. For my sanity's sake, I pry my eyes away from him and refocus. He's not a work of art. He's a work of irritation. My brain just needs to catch up.

I finish the sketch right as it's time to leave. We were at the beach for only an hour, but it soon proves to be the most relaxing part of the day.

The rest of the day is a whirlwind of going from location to location—the grocery store to fetch ingredients for #ChefMateo's cooking video, a café for a staged songwriting session between Lachlan and Felix, a pond where Will snaps pictures of baby ducks with a red Nikon.

The boys switch shirts, Bhavani slightly changes their appearances, and they film dozens of clips on their phones that'll eventually be edited into five "Day in the Life of a Boy Band Member" videos, and several more on the GoPro for the music video.

When we get back to the apartment, we're all exhausted. The boys from creating content, and me from being on the brink of total auditory overload most of the day. Spending this much time around people who almost exclusively voice is more challenging than I thought it would be, and all I want is to lie down and not be vertical again for at least eight hours.

Will is the cameraman while Mateo cranks out a final video of him cooking chicken tikka masala for dinner. When dinner is ready, everyone, save Felix, takes plates to their rooms, completely done with human interaction.

After I give Ginger her kibble, Felix and I sit on the couch to eat.

"I'm sorry today was so hectic," he apologizes, followed by circling a fist on his chest. "I promise we'll practice soon. I'm not making excuses."

"I know, I know." I stifle a yawn. I might not trust his commitment yet, but I trust him in this moment. Today was

unexpectedly busy. Though, I suppose tomorrow will be, too. With two back-to-back interviews, then a flight.

"Oh, I forgot to ask, you alright sleeping here tonight? It's nothing much but . . ." He trails off, gesturing to the plush couch.

"As opposed to what? Sleeping with you?" I only realize my innuendo when I notice the pretty crimson color blossoming on his face and spreading to his ears. "Uh . . . yeah. I'm fine," I choke out. The sectional is both comfy and massive, bigger than my twin bed at home anyway.

We eat the rest of dinner in silence. When we finish, I'm half asleep, and Felix takes my plate and cleans it. He disappears into the hall, and I start to settle in for the night, only for him to reappear a minute later with a pillow and fluffy pink blanket. He hands me the pillow, then gently drapes the blanket over me. To my horror, an enormous, blown-up version of Felix's face smiles up at me from the fabric.

"Do you . . . sleep with a blanket that has your own face on it?" I balk.

"'Course not." He chuckles. "But we have a bunch of different ones in our hall closet. Figured you'd prefer mine, for ***obvious*** reasons"—he winks—"but I'd be happy to supply you with a different member. Cal's is pretty cute."

"It's okay." I sigh. "It's just surprising, and sometimes disturbing, how many things have your face on them."

"Wait 'til you see the bobbleheads," he says, and I can't tell if he's joking. "G'night, Nat."

"My name is Na—" I cut myself off. He's already halfway down the hallway. "Goodnight, Felix," I mumble, watching him close the door to his bedroom as I snuggle underneath the blanket.

☆ ☆ ☆

"Nat? Hey, Nat?"

I wake up with a jolt, nearly punching whoever was gently shaking me awake. Luckily, Felix reacts quickly and stumbles away as I swing my arm.

My brain takes a minute to adjust to my environment. While asleep, I forgot I crashed in America's Sweetheart's living room. From the other end of the L-shaped couch, Calum laughs in between mouthfuls of a PB&J.

"We have to head to the label in thirty minutes," Felix explains. He hands me a cup of coffee. I have to suppress a genuine moan as I breathe in the steam.

It's an early call time but makes sense considering the circus of prep I witnessed yesterday, and that was only to film social media content. ROLLING STONE is much higher stakes.

"How'd you sleep?" he asks.

"Decently. It was a little hard to get comfortable," I reply before downing the coffee.

"Ah, really? It seems like you were sleeping pretty deeply."

Calum snorts, then adds, "And by 'sleeping deeply,' he means you snore like a car revving."

Felix shoots him a look and makes a cutting motion by his neck. I snore?! My jaw drops. I had literally no way of knowing that. I live with Deaf people!

My attention is torn away from the realization when I notice Ginger pacing in front of the door. She lets out a long whine.

"Morning, Ging. Do you need to go outside?" I hook a leash to her collar and slip on my boots. Once we're outside, and I miraculously track down a spot where a seventy-pound dog can pee in the middle of downtown LA, I grab my phone and text Jo.

Fri, June 14, 7:52 AM

[Natalie]

Sorry I forgot to text yesterday! Popstars are really busy apparently. How are you?

[Jo]

i thought u died! already planned ur funeral

[Natalie]

You're so funny and clever and I wish I had your sense of humor

[Jo]

u wish u were me 💁‍♀️

i'm ok. mom ignore me when i mentioned u but i
can tell shes MAAAD so i can't be spy sorry <3
i don't want her mad at ME! i'm innocent!

[Natalie]

She didn't even reply when I told her I was leaving. If she's going to give me the silent treatment, fine. Two can play that game

[Jo]

girlll thats a little petty

[Natalie]

MOM'S being petty!

[Jo]

whatever. is mateo as cute irl? felix still "the worst"? you get me signed album yet?? 👀

[Natalie]

It's been less than 24hrs! I haven't gotten it! And I'm NOT answering cuteness questions

Ugh gtg. The guys have an interview

[Jo]

OOH!! have fun! 🤩

On our way to the record label, Felix and I work in some casual ASL practice. I know DAYDREAM is signed to a major label, but the sheer size of the building takes me aback. It's got to be at least ten stories.

Necktie is waiting for the boys right inside the doors. He doesn't offer so much as a "good morning" before handing four pages of paper to each member. "The first page— —prep— —call-in interview with Y100 Miami; the others are questions— —ROLLING STONE. Give some thought— —answers so— —don't embarrass yourself or the label." He speed walks down the hall, and the boys follow him in a single file line.

Felix stares at the paper, mouthing the words and tracking the sentences with his finger, like he did with the book I gave him.

He only manages to read half a page by the time we reach a small room where staff members are rushing around, pulling together outfits, and setting up makeup stations.

Without any warning, the boys are whisked away to get ready. Felix sits in front of Bhavani, and they apply a light coat of BB cream and sweep his hair into a half-up ponytail while a stylist puts dangly gold earrings in his ears.

I try to move closer so we can continue the ASL practice we started on the commute, but staffers push me aside, and Felix is preoccupied with trying to read his list of questions.

I can't help but be suspicious of how meticulously he's poring over the pages. Maybe it's a clever ruse he came up with to avoid ASL practice.

After an hour of the boys getting glamorized, Necktie barks, "Let's go! Y100 Miami is patching you in in five minutes!"

DAYDREAM lines up behind him with militaristic precision, looking every bit as dreamy as the name implies, with their array of pastel clothing and makeup.

Deviating from the lineup, Felix approaches me. His light pink sweater matches my hair and Ginger's vest. "*We'll . . . practice . . . soon. Promise. Sorry, sorry!*" He's pulled away by Necktie.

He glances back, casting me one last apologetic look, before he and the band disappear into the hallway, heading off to fulfill the duties of stars.

Y100 Miami Ft. Musical Guest DAYDREAM

[HOST]: How's the adjustment to fame been?

[FELIX]: A whirlwind! We went from begging small venues to let us perform and uploading videos for 15,000 subscribers to selling out arenas and millions of people hearing our songs. We're deeply honored, but it can also be overwhelming.

[HOST]: How do you stay grounded?

[CALUM]: We flip each other so much [*bleep*]—am I allowed to say [*bleep*]? No? Sorry. Yeah, but nobody has a chance to get egotistical because we incessantly tease each other.

[HOST]: That's a great dynamic. Mateo, you're the only member in school. How do you think it'll feel to return after touring? That's a unique summer vacation!

[MATEO]: I'm . . . nervous. The transition is going to be weird. I hope my classmates don't treat me too differently. I'm still me, just with a pretty epic extracurricular activity.

[HOST]: Hey, maybe some of them will be fans. Do you guys see fan posts?

[FELIX]: Absolutely! The memes are hilarious and often

clock us so accurately it's a little scary. [*laughs*] We share memes and song covers to the band group chat.

[HOST]: Now I have to ask . . . what's the group chat called?

[WILL]: Bandemonium.

Chapter Nine

Hopped *on* a Plane at LAX

Los Angeles, June 14 / Miami, June 14–15

When we get to LAX later that afternoon, the band members instantly settle into the even fancier first-class lounge.

Except Mateo, who carefully sits on the edge of his seat, twirling drumsticks with a Mexican flag design. I inadvertently mirror his nervous fidgeting while we wait to board. We lock eyes for a fleeting second, and there's a momentary feeling of mutual understanding. Calum's comment about Mateo not being a Mercer Island kid sticks in my mind.

"Have you adjusted to this . . . lifestyle?" I ask him.

"Not yet. But I only joined the band a month before the label approached us. Maybe I'll adjust soon."

It's oddly comforting to know I'm not the only person here who doesn't come from an affluent family.

Once we hop on the plane, Felix and I finally practice some phrases like "how are you?" and "how's school going?" and he slogs through a few pages of his book while I scroll through r/DAYDREAM and start re-reading LEGENDBORN for the millionth time, but eventually I doze off.

The plane forcefully rumbles, and I jolt awake, death-gripping the nearest object, which, unfortunately for him, is Felix's leg. He loosens my iron grip on his thigh and holds my hand, but his skin goes from tan to white as I cut off blood circulation. He leans over and says something to me, breath ghosting over the skin behind my ear, but I can't hear over the airplane noise.

He pulls back to sign, "*Airplane . . . stop . . . now.*"

When it's time to disembark, the boys line up with bodyguards acting as bookends. I try to walk with them, but Necktie appears out of thin air and blocks my path.

"Don't even think— —got it, missy?" The patronizing nickname and his tone make me cringe. He starts walking with the band before I can reply.

Someone touches my arm while I shoot daggers at the back of Necktie's head. I turn and breathe a sigh of relief when I see Bhavani standing behind me. "You can walk with me!"

I brace myself as we get past security, preparing myself for the chaos Felix and I faced at the airport yesterday. As I expected, the band is instantly encircled by a horde of screaming fans, but this crowd is double the size. The members shield their eyes as cameras flash. Most fans keep their distance, but some attempt to rush toward the boys and are kept away by bodyguards.

The thought of facing thousands of shrieking fans every time you leave the house makes my skin crawl. One teen manages to grab a handful of Felix's purple-and-white-striped sweater. He stumbles backward, but the fan doesn't let go. Lachlan hooks his arm around Felix's waist and hauls him away as Sunglasses runs additional interference.

I watch Felix's chest rise and fall heavily, betraying how shaken he is from the interaction, but he manages to paste on a cheerful look for the cameras and wave to the boundary-respecting fans who hold signs and film on their phones. His mouth tips upward, but his eyes tell a different story.

Sunglasses protectively places her hand on his lower back. He peers over his shoulder, meets my eyes, and seems to find fleeting relief before he's loaded into a van with Necktie and the other boys.

I get into a car with Bhavani and four other staffers.

"Felix is a good guy, and I'm sure he'll take care of you"—I watch Bhavani's lips as they speak, and thankfully the car is quiet enough I can make out most of what they say—"but I've been— —hair and makeup artist for a few different singers, and tours— —sometimes overwhelming and lonely, even if you're a special guest. So I'm here for you."

"Thanks, Bhavani." I smile.

When we arrive at the hotel, Sunglasses opens my car door, and I'm a bit confused as she ushers Ginger and me inside. A concierge hands us glass bottles of sparkling water sourced from Swedish icebergs, and I do a double take at the elegance emitted by every part of this lobby.

The floor is a gleaming marble with gold streaks, a Titanic-esque grand staircase leads to the second floor, and a massive diamond chandelier hangs from the twenty-foot ceiling. It's like I teleported into THE GREAT GATSBY.

I tune back in as Sunglasses guides me toward the elevator Felix is propping open with his foot. I cram in with a tired DAYDREAM and agitated Necktie. Felix hands me a key card. "You're in 509."

When we reach the fifth floor, everyone goes their separate ways, but Felix insists on walking me to my room. He even rolls my suitcase for me.

"G'night, Nat. See ya in the mornin'," he says as I step into the room.

I turn around to complain about the nickname, but I'm met with a closed door. I shake my head with a tired smile, imagining him rejoining the group and being scolded by Necktie.

"Goodnight, Felix," I say to the door.

The next morning, I'm awoken by Ginger's wet nose squishing into my shoulder.

I peel open an eye and when I see her jump off the bed and sit by the door, I realize she's alerting me to the sound of a door knock. Jet lag is clearly affecting me more than her.

I stretch out in the crisp hotel sheets and yawn. Even after a full night's sleep, I'm exhausted. But at least I got to sleep in a bed last night.

"Good girl, Ging," I praise her while shuffling to the door. I scratch her head and yank the door open.

"Hiya!" Felix greets me with an abundance of energy. His hair is combed into a bun at the nape of his neck, and he wears a white V-neck tucked into awful plaid BURBERRY pants. "How'd you sleep? You look . . ." His eyes drag up and down my body, taking in my disheveled state. ". . . tired."

I fight an eye roll. Not everyone has a styling team to make them look like they've descended from the heavens as soon as they wake up!

"We're leaving in thirty," he continues. When he drops that bombshell, I'm suddenly wide awake.

"What?!" I grab his wrist and peer at his watch. 11:02 a.m. Damn it. I slept half the day away. "I thought we had to be at concert venues three hours before showtime. Don't your shows start at 7:00 p.m.?"

"*Yes,*" he knocks a fist in the air. "*But angry man*"—he mimics Necktie's body language and I stifle a laugh at the impression—"*wants . . . new . . . videos . . . we're leaving . . . now.*"

I process the signs. Necktie wants new videos . . . ? "*He wants to film the music video?*"

He repeats the sign for music, brows cinched in confusion.

"*M-U-S-I-C?*" I fingerspell slowly. "*Understand?*" I flick my index finger near my ear and raise both brows. Nothing.

I try two more times, but he remains lost. Apparently, the fingerspelling lesson we did on the plane didn't do him any good. He needs to pay more attention.

"Does he want more clips for the music video?" I use SimCom.

"*Yes!*" he knocks a fist.

I sigh. "I'll meet you in the lobby in a few minutes."

He gives me a thumbs-up and leaves. I haphazardly freshen my makeup, slip boots on, snag my backpack, and put Ginger's vest on her.

As the elevator doors slide open on the first floor, I wave to DAYDREAM as I lead Ginger outside. When we re-enter the lobby, Will materializes in front of me, holding a to-go cup of coffee. He extends it toward me with a hopeful expression.

"Can I say hi?" He points to Ginger.

I immediately accept the bribe and exchange my dog for coffee. He sits cross-legged in the middle of the lobby to give her scratches. Mateo joins him in giving Ginger a belly rub. Calum face-palms when Will starts sneezing and rubbing his irritated eyes.

"Get off the ground!" Necktie demands. He peers through the hotel's floor-to-ceiling windows, scanning for paparazzi.

Seriously? He can't risk his precious band being spotted playing with a dog?

"And you"—Necktie turns to me—"get lost."

"Nat's supposed to be with me 24/7 so she can tutor me," Felix jumps in, coming to stand next to me.

Necktie sucks his teeth. "Not on the first day of tour, Felix. I'm already getting calls about— —mystery girl with DAYDREAM— —airport. Just lay low for 24 hours." He jabs a finger to Felix's sternum, then refocuses on me. "Be a good girl— —follow instructions, would you?" With that, he walks off and starts berating a staffer.

My blood immediately boils. ***What the*** actual ***fuck?***

Before the anger triggered by his raging misogyny has a chance to sink in, Felix asks, "Are you alright?"

I exhale. "Yeah. Forty-something-year-old men with Napoleon complexes don't scare me."

He suppresses a laugh. "He's actually twenty-seven."

"***Twenty-se***—" I interrupt myself with a gasp. "Wow, that is a rough twenty-seven."

He smiles amusedly before continuing, "Anyway, I'm really *sorry*." He reaches out and gently touches my shoulder. "I'm worried if you come, he'll make the day a nightmare. Would you be *OK staying here today*?" he half-signs, half-speaks.

I sigh. I wonder if he's secretly relieved I've been uninvited so I'm not there to get on his case about half-assing ASL practice. I swallow my true emotions. "Yeah. I'll stay."

"I'll make sure you can always come along in the future, even if I have to fight Andrew. I'm really, really *sorry*," he reiterates, giving my shoulder a light squeeze. I glance at his hand, and he tucks it into his pocket. Warmth from his touch lingers.

"Break a leg," I mumble, absentmindedly touching the spot on my shoulder where his fingers rested moments ago.

He flashes a half-hearted smile and heads for his bandmates.

Will and Mateo reluctantly return my dog as Necktie practically drags them outside. Calum trails behind, muttering something to Lachlan, who's looking back at me. When we lock eyes, he signs, "*Have a good day!*"

After they leave, I set up an oceanside office on the private strip of beach our hotel boasts. Ginger digs around in the sand and whines at flamingos flying overhead—yes, actual flamingos. In the wild. I text Jo a video of them.

The sun is high, heat waves rippling off the water. It would be almost unbearably hot if not for the gentle breeze and shade from the palm tree next to my chaise lounge. After an hour of drafting a blog post for the Center's website, my phone buzzes on the side table. Ginger glances up at me from where she's licking a rock.

"I got it," I say before she gets up to alert.

Sat, June 15, 12:14 PM

[Pretty Boy 🙃]

://video.attachment//:

How long do we reckon until Andrew starts yelling at them 😂

I play the video and laugh as Mateo and Calum, joined by some young kids, chase Lachlan and Will around a beach, soaking them with water guns. In the background, a MIAMI BEACH sign stands next to a turquoise lifeguard tower.

[Natalie]

0.5 seconds lmao

[Pretty Boy 🙃]

Pretty acurate 😂

I return my attention to the blog. Once I finish, I start researching Seattle roofing companies, but only a few minutes into it, my phone buzzes with another text. This time it's selfies of Felix and Lachlan in front of colorful giant chicken statues, Lachlan's arm draped around Felix's shoulder, both of them grinning. The second is inside an equally colorful restaurant with a Cuban flag hanging on the wall behind them.

Sat, June 15, 1:07 PM

[Pretty Boy 🙃]

We're at calle ocho, the food here is sweet as!
U ever had a guava pastelito??
Its like if god personaly blessed a pastry

Have u eaten?

I send a selfie holding up a sad pack of almonds I got in the lobby.

[Pretty Boy 🙃]

U could go into almond modelling 😍
u make those nuts srsly photogenic

[Natalie]

Ha. Ha.

[Pretty Boy 🙃]

No really! I see it now—Nat Neilsen, almond queen of the year 🥜👑

[Natalie]

I don't think they give out crowns for "Most Disappointing Snack Choice."

[Pretty Boy ☺]

Fair enough. But pls eat something besides almonds! Order from the hotel restarant and charge it to the room!!

[Natalie]

Damn, I didn't realize you were the lunch police

[Pretty Boy ☺]

Hey! I'm a lunch royal gaurd, my almond queen

After a clip of the entire band on a small boat with a huge fan propelling it, the other boys laughing as Mateo clings to Felix's arm and looks seconds away from crying because of nearby alligators—my notifications are empty.

It's easier to work without the constant texts, but an unexpected wave of FOMO sets in, like I'm missing inside jokes or wild adventures only they'll remember later.

Another part of me almost thinks the updates were endearing, like Felix didn't want me to feel left out. ***Almost.***

The rest of my day is spent on the beach. The only time I leave is to order a forty-dollar, gluten-free burger (of which I text a picture to Felix as proof of nourishment) and to grab the bag of dog food I DoorDashed to the hotel. The fee was exorbitant, but less than taking an Uber and more convenient than having to lug kibble around Downtown Miami.

As I'm eating an overpriced salad for dinner, a text lights up my phone screen. It's a video of Felix documenting the pre-concert process while running around like a giant toddler who drank a Red Bull.

Sat, June 15, 6:36 PM

[Pretty Boy 🙃]

1st concert!!!! But what if nobody actualy came & its an empty stadium & its a massive prank

[Natalie]

I highly doubt that. Nosebleed seats are reselling for like $800

[Pretty Boy 🙃]

U looking at tickets? 😏 If u want one all ya gotta do is ask (nicely)

[Natalie]

I'm not above blocking you

[Pretty Boy 🙃]

Oops gotta blast!! Time to seranade my adoring fans

But a minute before they're set to take the stage, one last photo rolls in—a group selfie of the boys in sparkly makeup looks, fancy stage outfits, and in-ear devices that kind of resemble hearing aids. Felix is taking the photo, a toned arm extended in front of him. He's smiling so widely his eyes are nearly shut and all his teeth are showing.

Before I fully realize what I'm doing, I save the photo to my camera roll.

Chapter Ten

Sexy Dyslexic

Miami, June 15

I trade my oceanside office for my hotel room at 8:00 p.m. in the hopes of falling asleep early, but since my internal clock is operating on West Coast time, I'm still wide awake at 11:00 p.m. I finally give up and start sketching ideas for a mural I want to paint in the Deaf Center's lobby instead. Halfway through drawing an ASL "I love you" sign, Ginger sleepily nudges my thigh with her nose—another hearing alert.

"Show me," I tell her. She hops off the bed and sits in front of the door. Someone must've knocked. I peer through the peep-hole. Felix stands in the hall wearing tight gray sweatpants and his purple-striped sweater.

Wet hair is tucked behind his ears, showing off his bare face. I notice a mole on his cheek for the first time once I open the door. It must've always been there, but maybe I haven't stared at Felix's face long enough to notice . . .

Shit. I'm staring at Felix.

He quirks a brow as I snap back to reality.

"Whaddya say to dinner and a lesson?" he asks. He holds up a bag of take-out food from a restaurant called El Pollo Cubano.

"Shouldn't you be exhausted?"

"I am. But this is what commitment looks like, Nat," he says. "Ah, and is this the right brand? I saw you Googling." He gestures to another forty-pound bag of Ginger's food that's propped on the opposite hip. His muscles are flexed from supporting the weight, but he makes it seem effortless.

He . . . bought dog food?

My heart beats ever-so-slightly faster—***what the hell?***

I'm usually a huge fan of bursting his bubble, but for some godforsaken reason, I don't have the heart to tell him I bought a bag myself. So I widen the door and mumble, "Um . . . yeah, it is." He steps inside. A crumpled-up Post-it note falls out of his pocket, and I pick it up and unfurl it.

A touched smile threatens my lips, and I tuck the note into my pocket. "How was the show? Was the venue empty?" I ask.

"Yeah, nah. It was chocka. You were right." He starts setting various to-go containers on the bed.

"Wait!" I urge, and he startles, looking at me with concern shining in his eyes. "Say that last part again—I want to film you admitting I'm right."

"You're really funny," he deadpans, but his lips twitch with a hint of amusement. I chuckle and sit across from him. "I dunno what you like yet, so I hope these are alright," he says as he hands me two boxes. I open them to reveal some kind of grilled sandwich with ham, cheese, and pickles, and two flaky pastries filled with pink jam. "Those are the pastelitos I told you about!"

"Are these . . . gluten-free by any chance?" I ask.

He's about to take a bite of his own sandwich but pauses. "You can't eat gluten?"

"*No.*"

"Bugger. *Sorry*," he signs with pursed lips.

"You didn't know. I appreciate it anyway." I start peeling the ingredients off the bread and eating them separately, but it pains me to relinquish the pastelitos.

Once we finish eating, I grab my laptop and open his lesson materials, which include some key phrases he'll often use with Ava.

"*We'll practice now*," I sign. He copies my hand movements, but his brows are knit in confusion. "*P-R-A-C-T-I-C-E*," I fingerspell slowly, then repeat the sign.

His frown deepens. "*I don't understand.*"

"*OK-OK, we'll start with fingerspelling*," I sign slowly. "I'll spell a word, and you show me the sign for that word," I explain, using SimCom.

He gulps but sits up straighter and focuses. I search my document to find the list of practice words.

"*A-P-P-L-E*." Each letter is shown for several seconds to ensure he catches them. I repeat when he doesn't answer. He stares at my hands, carefully studying each letter, then spells it back to me.

"*You remember the* ASL *alphabet?*" Otherwise, he'll have no idea what English letters the handshapes equate to. I should've asked before starting.

"*Yes,*" he knocks a frustrated fist in the air.

"You can say it out loud; it's okay." I finally use SimCom after realizing he may not know the sign for "*apple.*"

Silence.

"You don't know what I spelled, do you?" I squint at him.

"Er . . ." He hesitates, awkwardly raking fingers through his damp hair. "I know the letters, but I can't combine them in my head." His gaze flicks away, then back, like he's weighing whether to say more. He takes a deep breath before admitting, "I'm . . . dyslexic and dysgraphic. Fingerspelling is nearly impossible for me. I've also got ADHD, but that's less of an issue." The barest hint of a wince crosses his features, vulnerability laid bare.

Bewildered, I gawk at him, my mouth slightly agape. "I've been criticizing your fingerspelling for almost two years, and you're only ***now*** telling me you're dyslexic?"

The corners of his lips tip upward. "Yeah. But, like, in a sexy way."

I hold back my laughter, but a snort manages to escape. He grins a wider, genuine smile. A light bulb flashes, and I think back to the tense conversation between Lachlan and Felix back in LA. "Wait, is this why Lachlan was confused about me giving you a book?" I ask.

He gulps. "I reckon. My mates know about it, but I don't tell many people. Back in New Zealand, I was bullied pretty ruthlessly. It got better when we moved to Seattle, but there was still teasing, and my dad would berate me for hours when I got low grades because of my bad handwriting and spelling. I've always felt stupid for it."

Damn. Now I feel like a jackass for accusing him of making excuses when he expressed he didn't want to read the study guide or assuming he wasn't practicing fingerspelling enough.

"I'm sorry," I breathe. I've always imagined him being the most popular boy in school—and now ***America***—and I never stopped to consider he might face his own difficulties. "I wish you'd told me sooner. I would never judge someone based on their disability; I would accommodate it."

He looks up from where he was focused on messing with the blanket on my bed, eyes wide. "I'm not disabled, Nat."

The way he says ***disabled*** makes me recoil. Like he's spitting it out, trying to get it as far away from himself as possible.

"***Disabled*** isn't a bad word," I bite, a wave of defensiveness washing over me.

He hesitates, thinking through his next words. "Right. *No*. No, it's not. *I'm sorry*. I meant that having issues with reading and writing isn't a big deal, compared to . . . er, some things"—he vaguely gestures toward me—"so I don't think calling myself disabled would be valid."

My initial, guarded reaction fades away. After a lifetime of dealing with ableism, it's easy to get defensive, but he didn't mean anything harmful.

It's probably just a sprinkle of internalized ableism, which is a unique and gnarly beast.

I gently pat his hand, but he takes it and gives it a squeeze. I tense up . . . But I don't pull away. "There's no disability that's more valid than another. I promise."

"*Thank you*," he lowers a slow, deliberate hand from his chin.

We stay frozen in the moment for a long stretch. Finally, he gives my hand one final squeeze.

"Er, while we're talking about this . . . I don't do well with structured lessons, either," he says. "I learn best with real-life application. Like when you sign while speaking. I should've told you earlier, but I was embarrassed."

"You learn . . . by having conversations while I use SimCom?" I confirm.

Eyes focused on my hands, he nods. "Yeah. Is that *OK?*" he asks in a voice almost too quiet for me to hear.

"Sure. My job as a teacher is to accommodate different learning styles. I'm sorry nobody else did that for you. But," I continue, "if I do that, it might be tougher to learn proper ASL later, because when I use SimCom, I'm signing using English syntax."

He frowns. "A-V-A . . . *understand . . . if I sign English . . . now?*"

"She will. But it's not technically ASL, so as long as that's okay with you . . ."

His shoulders relax, and his smile returns, soft and appreciative. "Nah, yeah. *Thank you*, Nat."

I recognize the beaten-down-but-wanting-to-be-strong glimmer in his eye, and I can't help but wonder how many times he's opened up only to have his needs dismissed. Been made to feel like he's lesser for it.

Carefully hidden beneath fame and fortune, maybe there are more layers to Felix than he lets on.

Chapter Eleven

Pretty Boy Felix Song

Miami, June 16 / New Orleans, June 18–19

Sun, June 16, 4:17 AM

[Pretty Boy 🙃]

Good morning! Hate to be the bearer of bad news since ur my biggest fan but we gotta leave for New Orleans in 20 😬
Andrew changed the schdule last min

Felix stayed in my room until 2:30 a.m., and I didn't even reach REM sleep before Ginger alerts me to my phone.

The night passed in a blur, and by the time Felix left, he already made more progress than he would've in Lesson One. I wouldn't have traded that progress for sleep, but right now I really wish we could've done it during daylight hours.

[Natalie]

I'm going to curse that horrible little man's bloodline for the next 47 years

The first thing I see when I get to the lobby is Necktie making a passionate phone call while pacing. The second thing is Felix. His hair is in a signature half-up ponytail, and he wears a light layer of makeup. He's in a lavender button-up with his PRADA fanny pack slung across his body, white skinny jeans, and boots that add unnecessary inches to his height.

"G'mornin'," he chirps, extending a cup of hotel coffee toward me. I snatch it with a concerning level of intensity and chug half of it before acting casual, like I didn't just reveal my caffeine addiction. He chuckles and hands me a piece of paper. "Thought I'd give you the new schedule since Andrew probably won't."

"The man who would dance on my grave if given the chance? Of course not." I peek at the schedule while leading Ginger outside. Somehow every spare millisecond of the next few days is full. He even penciled in an hour to shoot the music video after their New Orleans concert. If someone told me to do ***anything*** except sleep after I was jumping around and singing for two hours, I'd commit war crimes.

Back inside, the band seems photo shoot ready. Lachlan's eyebrow piercing is removed, Calum's in a light green polo shirt instead of shirtless, and Mateo's and Will's hair is neatly arranged.

"Why do you look so perfect this early?" I ask while plopping down next to Calum.

He digs around in the jumbo-size box of Scooby-Doo fruit snacks he's cradling and hands me several bags. "'DAYDREAM has an image to uphold,'" he says in a spot-on Necktie impression. Lachlan and Felix laugh.

I tear open a packet, and we peacefully eat the gummies—he trades his purple Shaggys for my orange Velmas—until Lachlan suddenly tosses aside the trashy celebrity-gossip magazine he was flipping through.

"Wha— —this time?" Calum asks, chewing. "Are you 'purportedly' dating a Kardashian-Jenner? Are we being accused— —lip-syncing?"

"Are those things people have actually written about you?" I ask.

He nods, swallowing. "At one point Felix and I were 'allegedly' in a secret gay relationship, until he broke my innocent little heart because he decided it was best for the band."

"I woke up to the breaking news that I was attacked by a shark yesterday," Will joins in. "That was fun to explain to my mom."

"C'mon, Lach, share with the class," Calum pries.

Lachlan's focus briefly snaps to Mateo and then back to Calum. "Forget it."

"It's about me?" Mateo tenses, his voice small. "Is it bad?" When Lachlan doesn't answer, he grabs the magazine.

"Mateo, it's nothing." Lachlan tries to take it from him, but Mateo's already found whatever he was looking for.

He deflates, a deep frown crossing his features. I mirror Lachlan's disgust as I get a glimpse.

JAILBAIT NO MORE!

T-Minus Four Months Until Baby-Faced DAYDREAM Member, Mateo Vazquez García, Turns 18! Housewives Everywhere Mark Their Calendars!

"Jesus Christ," Will mutters before throwing the magazine into a nearby trash can.

Felix slides onto the floor and puts his arm around Mateo's shoulders. "You alright, mate?"

Mateo shrugs, picking at threads on his distressed jeans.

It's so gross how the media preys on them. I have the sudden urge to track down the sorry excuse for a journalist who wrote the article and give them a piece of my mind.

I'm starting to think DAYDREAM's reality is extremely dramatized by media. I mean, so far, they've been herded around like cattle with barely a second to breathe. When would they even have time for secret children or love affairs? I can't imagine having this level of attention and public scrutiny.

"Let's go," Necktie barks as he storms over. "And smile. There are cameras."

They stand at attention like well-trained soldiers. Calum and Lachlan are on either side of Mateo, their arms linked with his.

Felix walks beside Ginger and me as we head for the doors. Necktie blocks my path.

"I don't need any more controversy about 'the mystery girl.' You're riding with the staff," he bites.

"My name is Natalie." I cross my arms defiantly.

Felix puts himself between us. He towers over his manager, who only has a couple of inches on me. "What's the problem?"

Necktie's eyes are ice blue, but right now they're much darker than Felix's. "***Natalie***," he enunciates my name, spite dripping from his tone, "is the problem. Everyone thinks she's your little plaything. That's no—"

"Excuse you?! Did you call her a ***fucking* '*playthi*—'"** Before Felix can finish, Lachlan interjects.

"Andrew, there's a simple solution. Get the word out that she's his ASL tutor," he says. "I'm sure the label can milk that for all sorts of PR."

Necktie's face is bright red, seconds away from combusting (which, honestly, would solve some problems). He turns toward me. "If you cause any drama or jeopardize their careers—or, more importantly, ***mine***—you're gone. Understood?"

"Fine." I grind my teeth, then walk outside.

The swampy Miami humidity glues clothing to my body as we're rushed by shouting paparazzi and fans snapping pictures. It's a chaotic roar of voices and movement. I squish Ginger between Felix and me for protection. Sunglasses guides us onto the tour bus, and the noise fades.

Ginger stays calm, but I pat her head reassuringly. A hand brushes my arm, and I look up, expecting Felix. Instead, I'm met with blue eyes and a placid smile. Lachlan. *"You OK?"*

"Fine," I lie, touching my thumb to my sternum, other fingers extended. *"You?"*

"I'm used to it, but this is brand new for you. Do you want to swap numbers? In case you need a friend." He extends his phone to me, a blank contact on-screen. I enter my info, then he adds his number to my phone.

"Reach out anytime," he says, his tone sincere.

DAYDREAM's New Orleans Green Room is nicer than a lot of apartments. There's a TV and gaming system, a towel warmer, and a wall of mirrors with tables and salon chairs in front. The real centerpiece is a snack table loaded with local cuisine, like muffulettas, pralines, and beignets.

While staffers bustle around, Will sneaks in some last-minute "leg day" squats, Mateo plays his green, white, and red drumsticks on the coffee table, Calum eats a third beignet, and Lachlan bravely scrolls through DAYDREAM AO3 fanfics.

I'm about to sit down when fingers gently graze my elbow. I turn to find a grinning Felix.

"Question for ya." His voice has a playful lilt. "D'you wanna watch tonight's show? I can get you a great seat, and you won't even have to pay eight hundred bucks."

"Pfft." I laugh. "No, thanks. Attending concerts for me is like . . . well, imagine trying to listen to music through a 2009 iPod Shuffle while surrounded by screaming people." I paint the picture. "I'm going to go out on a limb and assume there's also no ASL interpreter?"

"Er, no. But maybe for future . . ." He trails off as he locks onto something behind me.

Even before Necktie stops in front of us, I know it's him. I swear the hairs on my neck stand up and the room gets colder when he's around, like he's a ghost in THE SIXTH SENSE. "Felix, Mateo, Will, come get changed," he commands, then scowls at me. Because it's totally normal for a grown man to beef with a teenage girl.

While Bhavani straightens Lachlan's middle part, I wander over. "*Why did you want to learn ASL in high school?*" I ask.

"*It's a beautiful language. Very expressive.*" Lachlan smiles. "I'm glad Ava and Lix will be able to communicate. She's a good kid."

My face lights up, but before I reply, he points to the pins on the pocket of my flannel. "Do you mind me asking what flag that is?"

The pocket has a bunch—like an ASL slang pin, "Pah"; a Mockingjay symbol; the Space Needle—but the only flag is white, green, and gray with a sideways black triangle on the left.

"Demiromantic," I say, prepared to explain further, but understanding dawns on his face.

"Cool. I was in my school's Gay-Straight Alliance, so I vaguely recognized it but couldn't quite remember." We continue chatting in sign as Bhavani applies makeup. He's not anywhere close to fluent, but he has a solid base. He's in the middle of a story when Felix, Will, and Mateo re-enter and my focus immediately snaps to them.

I briefly glance at Mateo's pink cropped sweater and jeans with a butterfly design, and Will's pastel color-block jacket and white shorts—but Felix's outfit commands attention.

He wears a silky white deep V-neck that exposes his collarbone and part of his sternum, and tight (like, very tight, ***too*** tight), light-wash jeans. The ensemble is completed by dainty gold chains around his neck and dangly earrings hanging from his multiple piercings.

Felix heads for the salon chair in front of me. It takes a second to readjust to my surroundings after being put under his spell, and I realize Lachlan isn't here anymore. I spot him slinking out of the Green Room.

"Thoughts on filming in the French Quarter after the show?" Will asks as he sits beside Felix.

"Er . . . I was thinking of skipping the shoot tonight."

Will hikes a brow. "Pretty sure Andrew won't approve."

"That's why you should cover for me! He won't even know until it's too late." He flashes Will puppy dog eyes and pouts his lip. Will heaves a sigh. "I really gotta practice my ASL, mate," he explains, his tone more serious. A mixture of appreciation for prioritizing ASL and worry that this will make Necktie hate me even more takes root.

Calum approaches, chewing his fourth beignet. He uses his sleeve to wipe powdered sugar off his mouth, and Bhavani glares disapprovingly. "C'mon— —can't miss Bourbon Street— —iconic!"

"Next time." Felix shakes his head. "Take pictures!"

"Whatever. Be boring. But if Andrew gets mad, we're throwing your ass under— —bus," Calum says. "And— —not bringing you any souvenirs."

"No loyalty in this band, I swear."

Bhavani starts applying subtle highlighter to Felix's high cheekbones—just enough to make them shimmer in the light—and we hold eye contact through the mirror. His typical glittery superstar grin or cocky "everyone thinks I'm a goddamn National Treasure" smirk are nowhere to be seen; his current expression is similar to the gentle sincerity he displayed when telling me he was dyslexic. There's something softer, more comfortable about this version of him.

Shit. Did I think about him in a positive ***way?***

I snap out of it, but evidently not quickly enough. His smile is replaced with the aforementioned exasperating smirk. He caught me staring at him for the second time.

"Whatcha thinking 'bout?" There's a teasing lilt in his voice.

"Nothing!" I rush. "Just, uh, w-well, don't you look pretty." I scoff.

He squints. "That's . . . not the insult you think it is."

When it's finally showtime, I allow myself one look at him. We lock eyes, and I offer a small wave. He winks at me before leaving.

The room is peaceful after the band and most of the staff clear out. Only Bhavani, Ginger, and I are here. Bhavani pats a salon chair, and I accept the invitation. They start weaving pink strands into two short, delicate fishtail braids.

"Why's Andrew DAYDREAM's tour manager? Why haven't the boys fired him?" I ask after a few minutes, watching their lips in the mirror as they reply.

"They don't call the shots. They're the puppets, not the puppeteers. Everything about their lives, careers, and images are micromanaged."

I cock a brow. "You know that because . . . ?"

They smirk. "You'd be surprised how much tea is spilled in the makeup chair."

☆ ☆ ☆

The next morning, we load onto the bus bright and early, the engine's rumbling, and everyone's here—except Calum.

Felix and Mateo are on the couch while Mateo shows him something on his phone, Ginger wrestles with Will on the ground, and Lachlan is in his bunk. I'm tempted to steal his idea and go back to sleep.

"Where's Uncle Calum, pretty girl?" Will asks my dog.

"His concept of time is more abstract than Picasso's blue period," Mateo deadpans. I snort.

As if summoned by pure spite, the door swings open, and

Calum steps in with a triumphant grin, carrying a large to-go bag and a tray of Café Du Monde–branded cups.

"Beignets and chicory coffee," he announces proudly.

"Ah, your 'no souvenir' threat was worthless." Felix chuckles.

"What can I say? Chivalry isn't dead." I might've believed the chivalrous act if he didn't unceremoniously strip down to his Ninja Turtle underwear right after setting the food down.

"Can we at least get moving before you strip?" Will groans.

"My legs need to breathe."

"They really don't," Mateo argues.

As they bicker, I grab a coffee. The scent alone makes me sigh in relief. The first sip is bold and peppery, the flavor unlike anything I've ever had. It pains me to skip the beignets.

"The French Quarter was epic. Next time you guys are coming with us. No excuses!" Calum says.

"I was showing Lix pictures," Mateo chimes in.

He and Calum tilt their phone screens so I can see as they swipe through photos and tell us about last night's escapades.

There are selfies of the boys wearing colorful Mardi Gras beads in front of stucco buildings with arched windows and wrought iron balconies, inside a bakery and restaurant, and along the Mississippi river walk.

Videos of huge crowds holding massive drinks; jazz bands playing in open-air bars; neon lights from businesses glowing brilliantly; and picturesque riverboats. I feel overwhelmed simply from the pictures. I'm glad Felix and I practiced ASL instead.

"But the best part," Calum says, "was hands down the turtle soup and frog legs. The world needs to eat more amphibians."

DAYDREAM's Felix Wins Hearts by Learning ASL for Kid Sister!

Felix Song is being hailed as a role model after a generous gesture toward his Hard of Hearing 12-year-old sister. His label revealed he's taken on the inspirational task of learning ASL amid speculation about an unfamiliar young woman seen with Felix and his bandmates on multiple occasions. She is his ASL tutor.

»»»

@FelixSongUpdates 1h ago

Really don't like the vibes in the fandom today 😱 Felix is learning sign! Awesome! But he's not a saint JUST for accommodating his disabled sister?? Like that's just being a decent person?

–sincerely, a Deaf DREAMER

@DaydreamingOfMateo 43m ago

The ableist microaggressions are astounding!! & let's not give Felix a savior complex pls!! (I'm also disabled & I'm so embarrassed by the fandom rn)

@Dreamer02752 37m ago

y'all hate felix. admit it. he's so compassionate & sweet. he's going out of his way to help his sis when he doesn't have to! why are u downplaying that like wtf stop criticizing him? jfc

@FelixSongUpdates 12m ago

. . . READ THE ROOM? Where did I criticize him?? I love Felix so much and believe he's kind but praising him for "going out of his way" to learn sign when "he doesn't have to" is SO absurd. BFFR

Chapter Twelve

The Return of Renegade Wizard

Atlanta, June 21

Fri, June 21, 9:02 PM

[Pretty Boy 🙃]

Hiya! Ik we were gonna practise ASL tonite but could u pls join us in the lobby? 🥰

XX

[Pretty Boy 🙃]

(& wear smth discreet)

When the elevator doors open, I spot all five boys huddled in a corner. They're wearing grungier, streetwear fashion, heavy eyeliner, temporary tattoos, and either beanies, sunglasses, or spray-on hair dye to alter their appearances.

Oh, ***hell*** no. They're plotting something—and I'm willing to bet a Post-it note worth $23,500 that I do ***not*** want to be an accomplice.

I consider pretending I never saw the haphazardly disguised superstars and going back to my room, but Felix waves before I can.

So much for plausible deniability.

"Hiya," Felix chirps. His hair's been sprayed black and pulled into a low ponytail, and he's wearing Lachlan's Alien Ant Farm band tee and black super-skinny jeans.

Actually, I'm pretty sure everything they're wearing is Lachlan's. He's the only member I've seen proudly don mid-2000s emo-kid fashion when not in public.

"We're gonna go on an adventure! It'll be . . . *fun!*" Felix slides an H-shaped hand off his nose and lands it on another H-shaped hand. "We can also do some real-world ASL practice."

Though there's a high likelihood of getting in trouble by doing . . . whatever they're doing, I can't help but be a little curious. "Fine. But if this goes sideways, I'm blaming you guys."

"I'd recommend only blaming Felix," Calum says.

"I second that," Will chimes in.

Felix heaves an exasperated sigh. "Alright, I'll take full responsibility. Now, let's get this party started!"

☆ ☆ ☆

"Yo, are we almost there?" Calum whines as we wander the streets of Downtown Atlanta. Summer heat lingers in the air, even at 9:45 p.m. "My arms are getting tired." He pokes the mole on Felix's cheek and gestures to the guitar case he's lugging.

Felix swats Calum's hand away. "You're the one who insisted on bringing Tina."

"Your guitar's named 'Tina'?" I ask Calum, using SimCom

automatically—a habit I've picked up since Felix told me about his learning style.

Everyone's focus snaps to Calum, gauging his reaction. Felix meets my eyes, cringing, and signs "*guitar*," and I suddenly remember his warning. Shit. Maybe his mom was killed by a guitar or something.

"She's a bass, Natalie. A ***bass***. She has ***four strings*** and ***a longer neck*** and she's an ***octave lower*** than a standard guitar," he emphasizes every attribute. "And yes," he continues after calming down, "her name is Tina. Like Tina Weymouth."

"Who is that?"

Calum sucks in a pained breath. "Tina Weymouth, the bassist and cofounder of Talking Heads? You've never heard of her?"

"Nope. But until this tour, I'd never heard of Calum Evans, either."

Everyone besides Calum and me howl with laughter. "Whatever. But Tina's a bass. Capiche?"

"Uh . . . okay. Capiche," I confirm.

"Hey, Nat?" Felix says as he falls into step beside me. "Where's the dog?"

"You told me to be inconspicuous"—I gesture to my black crop top, black jeans, and gray-and-black flannel—"Ginger is the ***most*** conspicuous thing I own."

"Touché." He chuckles. "Well, if you need a Service Felix, I'm available. Does the job have 401k benefits?"

Despite myself, I laugh. The offer is sweet, even as a joke. "No offense, but Ginger is highly trained and attuned to my needs. Nobody can fill her role."

"What kinds of tasks does she do?" Will chimes in, ever

curious when it comes to my dog. "If you're comfortable sharing."

"She alerts me to sounds I don't always catch, especially if I'm in a different room or asleep, like doorbells, knocking, my phone ringing or buzzing. Also, oncoming traffic before I cross the street. She sort of becomes my ears in those situations and helps me feel more confident on my own."

He grins. "She's like a superhero."

"Are you implying I'm ***her*** sidekick?" I feign offense but crack a smile.

Two minutes later, we arrive at The Apache Café. A doorman stands outside, collecting entrance fees.

The boys are alive with excitement as Felix pays admission. Lachlan jots "Renegade Wizard" onto an all-ages open mic night sign-up sheet.

Will groans. "Lach, can we ***please*** not use that name? The one thing the label did right was changing that god-awful band name."

"Will's right. Time to admit it, bro," Calum adds, clapping Lachlan's shoulder.

Lachlan gives them a death glare. "Thanks to Renegade Wizard and ***me***, you assholes are famous. You can thank me any time."

Inside the café, the lights are dimmed, except by the small stage equipped with instruments, where they glow a bright red. Currently, they're shining on someone performing a soulful R&B song.

The lyrics are lost on me, but I find myself moving to the rhythm as it reverberates off the walls. Felix snags an empty table and pulls a chair out for me. I sit, and he scoots my chair in, then makes a move for the seat next to me, but Lachlan takes it. Felix eyes him curiously, but Lachlan stares ahead, toward the stage. Felix brushes it off and sits opposite me, between Will and Calum.

Mateo's to my left, and we're so close together that I can feel when his leg starts wildly bouncing under the table. Felix, Lachlan, and Will watch the performance while Calum messes with Tina's tuning pegs. No one else notices when Mateo pulls drumsticks out of his hoodie pocket and starts nervously twirling them.

I grab my phone and write a message: You good?

He uses my Notes app to respond: A lil anxious. I don't like crowds. I'll be ok once I'm behind the drums tho, always am. :)

I want to help distract him from his anxiety, and maybe make another friend on this tour, but as I'm typing, Felix flaps a hand and my attention snaps to him.

"*Do . . . you want to . . .*" He watches his hands as he attempts to piece the sentence together. "*Make out?*"

I freeze, my brain short-circuiting. He repeats the question. For a solid ten seconds I can't function, my cheeks heating up. What the ***fuck***?!

Then, completely oblivious to my internal crisis, he says, "They have decaf."

Oh my god.

Realization dawns like a cruel punch line. He meant to sign "*coffee*."

Relief and mortification all collide at once, and before I can stop myself, I bark a laugh, then immediately slap a hand over my mouth but another snort escapes. Everyone's focus lands on me—even the next table over glances my way.

Felix looks at me like I've grown a second head. "*What?*"

The other boys look away, save Lachlan, whose blue eyes float between Felix and me as I correct him. I form two fists, the bottom one remains still while the top fist circles in a clockwise motion—like the movement of an old-fashioned coffee bean grinder.

Felix tilts his head in confusion. *"I signed that!"*

"No, no. You signed"—I repeat the sign he used, crossing my wrists and bobbing my fists up and down in a way that resembles the heads of a couple making out. *"That means . . ."* I pause. Fingerspelling will be hard for him to understand, and I need to make sure he knows the ***crucial*** difference.

Fri, June 21, 10:12 PM

[Natalie]

You signed "do you want to make out?" not "do you want coffee?" They're similar signs but VERY different meanings!!

His eyes widen as he reads my message. Even in the dim lighting, I can see a furious red blush creep onto his cheeks and the tips of his ears. I choke back another laugh.

But he doesn't have time to dwell on his faux pas as the boys are called up. Felix's embarrassment starts to fade as they get on the stage.

The setup looks incredibly natural with Mateo behind the drums, Lachlan and Will holding electric guitars provided by the café, Calum's fingers wrapped around Tina's ***longer-than-a-standard-guitar's*** neck, and Felix in the very back, unassuming, behind a keyboard.

"Hey." Lachlan's gruff voice is amplified by a microphone,

and the crowd quiets. "We're Renegade Wizard, and this is an original song called 'Tomorrow Is Gone.' We haven't performed our music in a long time, so thank you for listening, even just for one night."

During his short intro, it hits me why the arrangement seems second nature. This is who they used to be, isn't it? Before their label started "suggesting" changes. They're performing as themselves, as Renegade Wizard (as truly awful as that name is).

Even just for one night.

These are the boys I saw in the picture hanging in their LA living room, boys who were over the moon to be performing at a high school dance.

When Felix starts playing the keyboard, the tune is surprisingly slow until Will cuts through with a jolt of electric guitar. From there, Mateo begins drumming, Calum expertly plucks the ***four strings*** of his beloved bass, and Lachlan belts out lyrics I can't catch.

In an instant, the doe-eyed, teenage dream boys from DAYDREAM transform into gritty rock legends. I haven't heard much of DAYDREAM's music, but their songs are sickly sweet and commercial. This Renegade Wizard song couldn't be any more different, with the sharp edge in all their voices.

As the heavy, angsty song rolls through the café, the crowd whoops, which makes it even harder to decipher the lyrics. The café is intimate, and the sound ricochets off the walls, creating powerful vibrations I can feel buzzing up from the floor and on the table beneath my fingertips.

Calum's hair gets messed up from headbanging; Will and Lachlan jump around while singing; Mateo exudes cool confidence as he destroys his drum solo; and Felix provides backup vocals at the far end of the stage, the farthest he could be from the spotlight.

When the song ends, the café erupts with cheers and wild clapping. DAYDREAM—no, ***Renegade Wizard*** thank the audience with sprawling grins. They stumble back to our table, drunk on the thrill of performing.

I stare at them in amazement as they plop into their seats.

"Holy shit," I finally speak between acts. "You guys were incredible."

Felix's grin widens. "Told you— —fun." A bead of black sweaty hair dye drips from his hairline, leaving a streak on his forehead.

I reach across the table, rubbing the black stain off his glistening skin. I pull my hand away after noticing his small, amused expression and how the other boys are staring at us. "Uh . . . you guys are a mess!" I awkwardly chuckle. To act casual, I also dab dye off Lachlan's face.

Luckily, I'm saved when the next act begins. We watch singer after singer with tired smiles and full hearts. I can't understand most of the lyrics, but the energy in the air is electric, each note pulling us closer. I've been invited into something rare and sacred, a glimpse of the boys' world beyond the spotlight. Being here with them, sharing this moment, makes me hopeful that we're not merely surviving this chaos—we're becoming friends.

DAYDREAM Wiki Member Profile

FULL NAME: Mateo Alexander Vazquez García

AGE: 17

HEIGHT: 5'7" (171 cm)

HOMETOWN: South Park, Washington, USA

MATEO FACTS:

- His hobbies include trying new recipes, reading historical fiction books, drumming (on anything), and watching historical C- and K-Dramas
- His role model is Ringo Starr
- He was only supposed to play four shows as a substitute drummer, but the band was offered a record deal during that time
- He's first-gen Mexican American, the oldest of four, and says his siblings inspire him to set a good example and have integrity
- If he weren't in DAYDREAM, he said he'd want to study archaeology and anthropology in college

Chapter Thirteen

A Highly Suspect Game of Go Fish

Atlanta, June 23

After loading onto the bus bright and early after the Atlanta concert, I get a few more hours of sleep and emerge to find Ginger curled up on the couch with her head on Will's lap.

In between sneezing fits, he plays with her ears and talks to Calum, who's eating a bowl of Lucky Charms Oatmeal. Mateo is air-drumming while wearing earbuds.

All the members are in their personal wardrobe rather than their soft-boy, DAYDREAM clothes. They still seem like the Renegade Wizard boys. More relaxed—more ***themselves***—than the personas they display in public.

"*Good morning,*" Lachlan signs one-handedly, and passes me a mug of coffee.

I drink half the cup in one long sip. When I look up, Lachlan laughs, his brilliant blue eyes shimmering in the sunlight.

"You're hardcore," he says. "Even I don't drink it black."

My response is interrupted by Felix waving from the table. He scoots over on the bench to make room for me, his laptop in front of him. I join him and beam when I see Ava on-screen.

"*Hey!*" I sign. "*How are you? Is my sister a good teacher?*"

"You're better. But she's cool! She also lets me do stuff my parents won't. And she taught me cuss words!" Ava gushes. I sigh. Because **of course**. That sounds exactly like my sister. *"How's L-I-X? Is he a good student?"* she continues.

I glance at Felix. He wears a lost frown, unable to keep up with our signing speed. *"Surprisingly, he's not bad. Annoying, sure, but not bad."*

"And are you two"—she looks between us a few times with a nearly imperceptible smirk—*"friends?"*

"He's tolerable. Sometimes."

"I'm so happy that he knows so much now! He's learning fast!" Her signing is slower now, her bright, toothy grin an exact match for Felix's.

I notice Felix repeating her movements underneath the table, and when he pieces together the gist, he blushes. *"Thank you,"* he signs, lowering a flat hand from his chin. *"I'm learning fast for you! Nat's teaching . . . many . . . new signs!"* He uses my sign name, but somehow, I know he means "Nat."

"I have to go," Ava announces, checking the time on her phone. *"I have tennis practice."* She waves the "I love you" sign at Felix and me. We both return it, and she hangs up.

"She's right. You're getting a lot better."

His blush deepens and his lips move, but I don't catch what he says.

"Again," I touch my right fingers to my left palm.

He repeats himself, and I stare at his full lips with intense focus, but his speech remains a mystery. I massage my temples and sigh. "Your accent makes my brain hurt."

"Whaddya mean?"

"For starters, your lips don't pucker on an 'O.' So, instead of 'no,' you say 'naur.'" I do my best to articulate the difference in pronunciation. "It makes lipreading extra hard."

Out of the corner of my eye, I see Calum and Will snickering.

Felix recoils. "I do not sound like that!"

"Bro, you totally do." Calum laughs.

His face sinks, but we all get distracted when Will breaks into an aggressive sneezing fit. Felix hurries to unzip his fanny pack and starts rooting around. It must have the same magic as Mary Poppins' bag because he keeps pulling things out of it. TOM FORD's "Fucking Fabulous" cologne, a jade facial roller, an Aero chocolate bar.

He discards the random items on the table before finding Zyrtec. He stands and shoves a pill into Will's mouth. Will gulps it down with a sip of coffee.

"Another solution is to stop sticking your face in dog fur, dumbass." Calum flicks Will's forehead.

He wipes his runny nose on his tie-dye Jimi Hendrix hoodie sleeve and trains his puffy red eyes on Calum. "I would die for this dog."

While they bicker like little kids, my phone buzzes in my pocket. Ginger tries to squirm out of Will's grasp to alert but can't. I laugh. "I got it," I tell her, and she returns to wrestling.

Sun, June 23, 9:37 AM

[Jo]

://image.attachment//:

what u want me to do with all this painting supplies??
some guy named manny dropped
them at center yesterday

[Natalie]

Omg I emailed Manny's Hardware Store to ask about discounted rates for revamp supplies but I'm happy he donated them instead! You can put them in the K-5 classroom for now

[Jo]

ok. also moms pissed again! manny
NOT my fault!! 😑 have u talked to her?

[Natalie]

I'm not talking to her if she doesn't talk to me

[Jo]

i didn't think you'll last THIS long! i think mom
feels bad abt everything. she's even mad at me
for stuff too. esp when I mention u

[Natalie]

Well, she's more than welcome to apologize to us!

[Jo]

ur putting me in middle!!! 🙃

[Natalie]

Omg, well, maybe you shouldn't meddle!

[Jo]

I'M TRYING TO HELP!!

[Natalie]

I know. I'm sorry. But I don't want to talk about her, okay? It's stressful being on tour but also nice to have a break from mom's unpredictability

[Jo]

ok. i'm sorry too. ily 🤟

(remember my signed album!!!)

[Natalie]

Stop teaching Ava bad words and I'll consider it!

(ily2 🙃 🤟)

My excitement over chatting with Ava and the donation turns into frustration. It's like every time I manage to momentarily forget about Mom's deceitfulness and start enjoying myself, the feeling of betrayal cuts right back through me.

I only realize I'm death-gripping my phone and grinding my teeth when Felix lays a hand on my knee. *"You OK?"*

I gulp. *"Yes."*

He motions for me to follow him. We pass through the sleeping quarters and enter the back room. He settles on the cushy leather couch, and I drop down next to him, careful to leave space between us.

"You sure you're alright?" he asks again. "You weren't very convincing."

I consider him—the concern on his face, brows tipped into a frown. It's the same openness he has when talking to Ava, the same gentle sincerity he's shown in dressing rooms and late-night study sessions. I guess there's no use lying. "Nope," I reply simply.

"D'you wanna talk?"

"Nope."

"Alrighty. But if you change your mind—"

"I won't."

"—I'm here." He watches me for a beat, and I can practically see the gears turning, then his expression switches to concentration. His fingers wiggle as he thinks. *"Last night . . . we didn't . . . practice. We practice more now?"* His choppy signing is equivalent to. Putting. A. Period. After. Every. Word. But for some reason, I find it strangely endearing.

Engaging Teacher Mode, I reply, "Actually, I have an idea." I lean over and open one of the cabinets stocked with board games and grab a deck of cards. "I know you don't do well with voices-off lessons, but I think you can handle this. You know enough ASL. Plus, playing games is something you can do with Ava."

He smirks. "Oh, you have no idea what you're getting into. I'm the king of card games. The only person who's ever beaten me is Aves."

I scoff. "We'll see, Pretty Boy. I mastered all sorts of games when my dad—" I cut myself off. ***When my dad was in the hospital*** is what I almost said. DVDs, cards, and board games were the only entertainment available, and most of the movies didn't have captions, so we played hours upon hours of games. ". . . when I was a kid." I swallow the resurgence of bittersweet memories and deal the cards.

He gives me another unconvinced look but thankfully drops it as we start a cutthroat game of Go Fish. Felix's focus continually shifts between examining his cards and studying my hands and face; his own expression is alight with intrigue, seemingly spellbound by the immersive lesson. He one-handedly copies my signs and absentmindedly commits them to memory. The fierce, competitive smirk on his face fades when I win the first round.

I laugh. "How about a bet?" I suggest. "Best out of five. Loser will owe the winner a favor."

"A favor?" He quirks a brow. "Can it be anything?" I swear when he asks that, it triggers my stomach to do a mini flip.

That's impossible, though. Because the only time I've gotten this weird, fluttery feeling was when I had a crush on my friend at residential school. My ***friend***. Because I don't get ***crushes*** on people I don't ***platonically like*** or have an ***emotional connection*** with.

And I ***sure as hell*** don't platonically like or have an emotional connection with Felix Song. If he has one hater, it's me. If he has no haters, I'm dead.

I decide the coffee isn't settling well with my empty stomach. That explains it.

I pull a poker face. "Within reason, I guess."

"You're on. As long as a handwritten note declaring yourself my biggest fan and saying I'm the most talented and handsome devil you know is 'within reason.'" That infernal smirk of his reappears, and I roll my eyes, which earns a laugh.

"Get ready to owe ***me*** a favor, Pretty Boy," I challenge him, my confidence at an all-time high.

It doesn't last long, though, because he wins the next three rounds. With no hope of winning, I toss my cards onto the table, scowling at his smugness.

"Well, well, well. Looks like someone owes me a letter," he singsongs.

"I want a rematch. You cheated."

"How did I cheat?!" He clasps a hand over his heart. "We can play a few more rounds, but no take backs on my letter."

He doesn't glance at the cards as he reshuffles the deck. Instead, his eyes rove over my face, a satisfied glint shining in them. I wonder how many girls would give up their firstborn child to have Felix look at them like this. Thousands, probably. But Felix isn't looking at one of those girls. He's looking at me.

I gulp. ***Get a grip, Natalie.*** He probably thinks that it's physically impossible for anyone to view him as anything besides the center of the goddamn universe and that I'll fall for his goofy charm like a total fangirl. Pfft. No freakin' way.

Chapter Fourteen

Stars in His Eyes

Nashville, June 24–25

When we walk into Nashville's biggest music radio station at 8:00 a.m. and enter the Artist Green Room, we're met with instant pandemonium. Surprise, surprise.

Lachlan and Will are whisked away to be accessorized while Calum, Mateo, and Felix get their makeup touched up. After a few minutes of trying to decipher conversations and sort through background noise, a dull headache descends. I make a desperate attempt to stave off the auditory fatigue by stepping into the hallway, away from the commotion.

Ginger and I stop in front of a wall filled with signed pictures of various bands and singers. Most are country singers—Kelsea Ballerini, Little Big Town, circa 2011 Taylor Swift—but there are other artists, too, like Olivia Rodrigo, 5 Seconds of Summer, and Cardi B.

I text a picture to Jo: How much do you think these would sell for on eBay? (Before you ask, NO I'm not stealing any!)

I startle when someone taps me. "*Sorry!*" Lachlan apologizes.

"*It's OK,*" I reply.

His ears have diamond studs in them, but his spiky eyebrow

piercing is gone. He's dressed in a sky-blue houndstooth sweater-vest layered over a long-sleeve white button-up, white slacks, and white sneakers.

"You look like an eighth-grade substitute English teacher," I say.

"That's . . . oddly specific." He huffs a laugh. "You're right, though. I keep telling the stylists I look like a grandpa. I mean, Mateo's 'thing' is crop tops, Lix's is long hair and being beautiful, and mine is ***sweater-vests***," he emphasizes.

I snort. He did kind of get the raw end of that deal. He shrugs it off and glances at the posters. "*Do you—*" He stops himself, frowning.

"*What?*" I nudge him. "*Tell me.*"

"*Do you listen to music?*" he signs, then says, "I'm sorry if that's an offensive question."

"Music isn't a huge thing for me," I answer, using SimCom, "but I liked the song you performed at The Apache Café. I couldn't really hear the lyrics, but you have a nice voice"—Lachlan lowers a thankful hand from his chin—"and I could feel the vibrations. I prefer songs with hard bass."

"So the exact opposite of DAYDREAM?" Lachlan and I whip around as a recognizable Kiwi voice speaks from right behind us. Felix looks at me expectantly, one filled-in brow raised as he comes to stand beside me.

"Can't say Knockoff One Direction is my vibe," I quip.

"You say that like it's a bad thing." He winks at me.

Lachlan indecipherably mumbles before walking away. Felix and I hold eye contact for a moment before he signs, "*You OK?*" Even with rings weighing down his fingers, his signs are much smoother than before.

"*A little tired. You?*"

"Tired of being in DAYDREAM mode, honestly," he says before his attention floats to a stylist at the end of the hall. Their mouth moves, but what they're saying doesn't register. He hears it, though, and gives a thumbs-up. "*Walk with me?*"

As we make our way to the stylist, I ask, "What do you mean by 'DAYDREAM mode'?"

He sighs. "The label made me the face of the band. Interview questions are mostly directed to me, and I have the most lines in our songs. I always have to be 'on,' y'know? My mates can relax a little more, but I don't get a break to be, well, me."

"I didn't realize it was like that. It sounds . . ."

"Suffocating?" he supplies. My focus flickers away from his lips and to his eyes.

"Yeah. I guess. I'm sorry you have to deal with that."

"*It's . . . fine.*" He pastes on a sunny smile. "I'm glad you're here, Nat," he says. For a second, I wonder if he's deflecting from the serious conversation we were on the brink of. His hand gently brushes mine, and I'm not entirely convinced it's on accident.

We reach the changing room before I can respond. (Not that I know how to respond to that.) Halfway into the room, Felix peers over his shoulder and grins at me.

I know ***this*** smile is genuine. A fleeting moment meant for my eyes only.

☆ ☆ ☆

When we return to the hotel that night, I have a headache so intense it feels like someone is using my brain as a stress ball. My head hits the pillow, and I'm dead to the world.

I'm barely entering REM sleep when Ginger headbutts me awake. I mutter a string of colorful expletives and push her away. She keeps jamming her nose into my thigh and giving irritated boofs.

"Fine! Show me," I command harsher than intended. She is doing her job, after all.

She hops off the bed and sits in front of the hotel room door, looking proud of herself. I check the alarm clock. 11:41 p.m.

With a groan, I stumble over. I peer through the peephole, then yank the door open.

"Do you know what time it is?" I bite.

Felix teeters nervously. "*Sorry*," he rubs a fist around his chest, crumpling the fabric of the black hoodie he's wearing. In fact, his entire outfit is black. Hoodie, jeans, fanny pack, and those infuriating boots with the three-inch heels. "Let's go on an adventure!"

"Helping you hide a dead body is going to cost at least an extra $50,000," I deadpan.

He laughs and hands me a second black hoodie and a ball-cap. "You can consider it me cashing in my favor, since I haven't received my letter," he says, grinning conspiratorially.

"What kind of adventure?" I raise a brow.

"Anything." He looks at me with an almost desperate look. "Let's have one night where we can be normal teenagers. No cameras flashing, no fans, no Andrew. Just us. Felix and Nat."

I consider him for a moment and recall our conversation at the radio station. I think he needs this—to feel normal. Plus, I foolishly promised him a favor. "*OK-OK*."

He helps me hide my pink hair under the hat after I change

into the hoodie. I kiss Ginger's snout and give her a bone before heading into the hall.

"Service Felix reporting for duty!" Felix salutes as I close my hotel door behind me. "Y'know, if the dog gets bones as compensation, it's only fair that I get little treats, too . . ."

"I need to see how you perform before we discuss benefits."

"Fair enough," he chuckles.

I head for the elevator, but he grabs my wrist and leads me the opposite way. We walk to the far end of the hall, and he opens the service elevator using a staff key card.

"How'd you get that?" I ask as we head to the ground floor.

"Anything is possible with a checkbook," he jokes.

I tense up. Right as I was starting to see a new down-to-earth side to him, he drops a Rich Boy comment without thinking twice. Though he meant it jokingly, it stings in a way only someone who's experienced poverty would understand, and I'm suddenly and jarringly reminded how wildly different our perspectives are.

He's never watched his parents agonize over whether they should buy groceries or pay bills, or had to start a GoFundMe to pay for a service dog. It's not his fault he was born into a wealthy family, or mine that I wasn't. But his joke hurts all the same.

I feel my walls go up, and I stay quiet for the remainder of the elevator ride.

We head for a back door to avoid detection, but before exiting, we both put on black surgical masks. Outside, the night air isn't cold by Seattle standards, but it's still a refreshing contrast to the muggy June heat from earlier today.

We walk in silence for ten minutes, the only sound coming

from Felix's phone as it feeds him directions. When we finally stop in front of a brightly lit storefront, he does excited jazz hands. I read the sign and discover it's a gluten-free bakery. My cold mood thaws as we enter, and the scent of buttery goodness wraps me in a warm hug. My stomach rumbles as we approach the display case. Basically, everything DAYDREAM eats contains wheat, so recently I've been on a diet of fruit and Lucky Charms Oatmeal—magically delicious ***and*** gluten-free.

My eyes float across everything, but the doughnuts grab my attention.

"I've never had a doughnut," Felix admits from beside me, tracking my line of sight.

I gape at him in wide-eyed shock. "How the hell have you gone eighteen years without eating a doughnut?"

"I dunno."

"Okay, we're fixing that," I declare. Felix chuckles when I take charge and peruse the display case, asking the employee about the different flavors and if they have recommendations, before selecting an assortment.

While the worker boxes them up, Felix digs around in his fanny pack. Eventually, he locates his wallet and whips out his black card. I look away and swallow another pang of bitterness. ***Why*** is this bothering me so much? I take a deep breath and remind myself that other people's success doesn't reflect my failure.

Felix holds the door open for me as we leave the bakery, and we set off into the night with a dozen doughnuts and infinite possibilities.

While making our way back to the hotel, we stroll along the

Nashville Riverfront. Moonlight ripples off the dark blue water, and stars twinkle in the pitch-black sky. He gazes at the river, only looking away to check his GPS. Under the cover of night, while he's too distracted to annoyingly flirt or make oblivious jokes, I notice Felix's energy is different. Blond hair tucked under his ballcap, his face softened by the glow of the moon, he radiates a quiet wonder. His presence feels grounded, vibrant in a way that feels tangible, almost magnetic.

I'm torn away from studying him when I trip on a loose brick. I brace myself to hit the ground, but a strong hand steadies me. I calm my racing heart and look into Felix's moonlit brown eyes.

"You alright?" His long, slender fingers are woven through mine. He precariously grips the doughnut box in the other hand.

I glance away from our intertwined hands. "I wasn't looking where I was going."

"Was the view distracting you?" he asks, a mischievous lilt in his voice.

I tug my hand out of his grasp and power walk away. He laughs heartily.

"I meant the river!" he calls out. "Nat, wait up!" He catches up to me in a few long strides. I'm suddenly glad the face mask is hiding my flushed cheeks.

We walk in silence the rest of the way to the hotel. I glance at Felix more than I'd like to admit, and each time his eyes crinkle as he beams, having been staring at me all along.

It's horrible.

We re-enter the hotel and slip into the staff elevator undetected. We take off our masks as Felix brings us to the top floor, where we take a flight of stairs and he uses the staff key card to unlock a door to the roof.

My jaw slackens in awe. The glow of car headlights and building lights contrast against the dark sky, scattering like a thousand fireflies. The river below flows steadily while a cool breeze swirls. Everything else feels perfectly still, as if the world is holding its breath, the sleepy city blending with the magic of the moment.

"Peaceful, isn't it?" he asks. It's easy to hear him up here. Just us, like he said.

He's nestled between huge metal pipes, sitting cross-legged on the dirty concrete. I attempt to scale them but can't get my leg over. He stands up to give me a hand.

"You are not lifting me over this," I protest.

He chuckles as I try to hoist myself over several times. Defeatedly, I wrap my arms around his neck. This close to him, I catch a clearer whiff of his pungent cologne. The scent washes over me as his arms curl around my torso and he effortlessly lifts me over. He sits down, sweeps dirt away from the spot across from him, and gestures for me to join him.

I open the box of doughnuts as Felix lowers his hood and removes his hat. I do the same.

"Whaddya recommend for a doughnut virgin?" he asks, motioning toward the box.

Probably taking his question too seriously, I peruse the options. We have bougie flavors like cranberry and mascarpone, and lavender, but also the classics: glazed, jelly-filled, Boston cream.

"Let's start simple." I hand him a chocolate-glazed doughnut and take the raspberry-filled for myself.

He nods after his first bite. "Wow. Doughnuts are sick!" He makes a clunky attempt to use one-handed SimCom but uses the "illness" sign for "sick."

"Told you so," I say before showing him a sign that's a better translation. He copies it, but his thumb is incorrectly tucked to his palm like the ASL letter "B."

I repeat the sign, which resembles high-fiving the air above my shoulders. He does it incorrectly again.

I scoot closer and take his hand, gently prying his thumb away from his palm. Then, with my hand wrapped around his larger one, I slowly form it into the proper sign.

When I look up at him, he's staring at me, his doe-eyes shining, lips slightly parted, and sharp cheekbones tinted a gorgeous crimson.

He closes his hand over mine, his gaze slipping to my mouth with an intensity that makes my heart race. He leans in so close that the warmth of his breath sends a shiver down my spine, strands of his hair brushing my cheek.

I freeze as the distance between us shrinks. My heart beats in my throat as Felix releases my hand and delicately swipes his thumb across my lower lip.

He pulls away with that horrible, awful goddamn smirk. "There was some jelly," he says, showing me raspberry jam smeared on his finger. I scowl at him, my face burning.

He laughs heartily, then licks it off while staring right into my eyes. Warmth rolls through my body in a steady wave, and I cough, breaking eye contact. What the ***fuck*** was that?

He changes the subject as if nothing happened. "So I'm

guessing, based on how you took over at the bakery, you're basically a doughnut connoisseur?"

I take another bite to buy time and pull myself together. "I know my way around. Before my dad died, every year for my birthday, we'd go get doughnuts and drive to Gas Works Park to watch the sunrise."

Felix frowns. "I'm sorry, Nat. I didn't know he passed. You've never talked about him."

Oh. It slipped out. Talking about my dad is almost impossible. Even the happiest memories hold traces of sadness, simply because he's gone. Because we'll never make another happy memory together. Because even though it's been two years, every morning on my birthday I expect Dad to take me to watch the sunrise. I stare at the pastry in my hand and force the memory away.

"Try this next," I blurt, handing him a lemon custard–filled doughnut as a diversionary tactic while I patch my walls that have temporarily cracked. I know he sees through my act, but he doesn't question it and instead focuses on the pastry. "When done right, the lemon balances out the sweet custard."

I ramble about flavor profiles and dough consistency as he takes a bite of every doughnut in the box. He occasionally says "oh, yup" or "sweet as" but clearly has no idea what I'm talking about. He's content sitting here listening to me, though.

"This one's the best," he declares after trying a double-fudge Nutella monstrosity. I fail at hiding my disapproval. So much for my TED Talk on the cranberry and mascarpone.

After we devour half the box, Felix lifts me back over the pipe, then steps over it in one try.

He walks to the edge of the roof, leans against the railing, and spreads his arms out like Rose from that iconic scene in TITANIC. I chuckle as the wind messes up his hair, and it flies around in front of his face. He inelegantly bats at it and wrestles it into a ponytail.

For the longest time, we peacefully stare at the glittery Nashville skyline.

"Look." He points to a white streak cutting through the night sky. When I look away from the shooting star and back to the pop star, his eyes are squeezed shut and his lips are pursed.

"Did you just make a wish?" I ask after his eyes flutter open. "Aren't you living your dream, Pretty Boy? Fame, fortune, fangirls."

This draws a laugh out of him. "Dreams and wishes are different." I blink at him, and he shakes his head in amusement before returning to a serious, wistful expression. "My dream is to make a difference with my music, share my experiences, help people feel heard, y'know?"

He turns to face me and ensures I can see his lips before continuing. "That's why I loved Renegade Wizard. The songs we wrote meant something to us. They came from our hearts. I never wanted to sing the mainstream songs DAYDREAM does or be the star of the show."

He looks back to the skyline; his lower lip wobbles, and his eyes turn glassy. "And now, I wish we could go back to the way things used to be—when I could express myself through my art and had some semblance of privacy." His voice wavers, and a solitary tear escapes. "It's like I'm not even a person anymore. I'm a product. Something to be marketed."

"Felix, does your family know you feel this way?"

He shakes his head solemnly. "I would sound so self-absorbed if I told them. I mean, Aves is in the middle of becoming deaf." His voice breaks. "How could I whinge about being in a massively successful band?"

"What about your bandmates? Can't you talk to them?"

He explains, "They're doing the best they can in this situation. I don't wanna make things worse for them by bringing it up . . . Especially since I'm the one who got us into this mess." Guilt drips from his voice, and my heart breaks just a little for him at the sound. "Our contract is so predatory. Lachlan wanted to have it reviewed by a lawyer, but I convinced him it was okay. I was scared to mess anything up because this was our big chance at making our dreams come true, and I thought we could trust the label."

Tears rush down his cheeks faster than he can swipe at them. He turns around and slides to the ground, his back pressed against the railing, and tucks his knees to his chest.

Unsure how to comfort him, I sit next to him and take his hand. He squeezes it tightly, and I squeeze back.

I hadn't considered the fact that Felix might not like DAYDREAM's image or thought about how much pressure being America's Sweetheart must be. I assumed he was basking in the thrill, not being suffocated by the weight of it all.

It's impossible to say how long we sit here in the cool night air, our hands tightly intertwined, before he lets go, wipes his face, and looks over at me.

"Sorry for being a buzzkill."

"You aren't," I insist. "Thank you for telling me."

"Thank you for listening." His tone betrays how drained he is.

Moving of its own accord, my hand finds its way to his knee.

He glances down and grabs it, then takes a slow breath, fully expanding his lungs, letting the heaviness of the moment evaporate with each exhale.

"*What's your dream?*" he signs, not-so-slyly changing the topic, but I'm distracted by the stars dancing in his dark eyes, making them shine.

"To revamp the Deaf Center," I reply. "I want it to be a place people ***want*** to go, especially kids and teens. New classrooms and updated tech and captioned-movie nights. My dad, sister, and I dreamed of bridging gaps between the Hearing and Deaf worlds; sharing our culture, easing language deprivation, stuff like that . . ." I stop before I get too animated. Jo tells me I'm like an annoying coworker who's always showing pictures of their cats even though nobody in the office cares.

I've spent so long dreaming about it, thinking through every minute detail, that it's easy for me to get carried away when people ask. I don't want to bore him.

But Felix doesn't seem to mind. When I don't continue, he knocks his shoulder into mine and says, "That sounds amazing, Nat. So how are you gonna do it?"

"If I'm going big picture . . . I'd like to set up centers countrywide, especially in underprivileged areas, so all deaf people have access to resources. But that'll never happen," I admit, deflating a bit. "We barely have money to fix our own center. Much less fund others."

His face falls, as if he's only now realizing not everyone has a multimillionaire father, but he quickly wipes the expression. "Ya got any more daydreams? Pardon the reference."

I stare at him, confused. "What? That wasn't enough?"

Felix feigns shock, pressing a hand to his heart. "C'mon, Nat. I have no doubt you'll accomplish that. Look at you!" he chides playfully, and I look away to cover up my blush. "You've gotta have some kinda pie-in-the-sky, probably-never-gonna-happen, huge dream that some might call delusional. Everyone does!"

I shrug. "Not me, I guess. I don't have time to—as you so eloquently put it—be delusional."

"You're tellin' me there's ***nothing*** outlandish you find yourself thinking about in quiet moments?"

An odd heaviness settles in my chest, and I frown. When you take everything day by day, always worried your credit card will be declined at the store or spending every spare second brainstorming new side hustles, you don't exactly have the luxury of daydreaming—but maybe I'll give it a try. Someday.

"Not right now," I answer simply.

After a long beat, he breathes, "Well, then I hope your dreams come true, Nat."

I glance at him. "I hope yours do, too, Felix."

I look back toward the dark cityscape, relishing a moment of peace with the boy who has stars in his eyes and an unsung song in his heart.

Rolling Stone

The Boys Behind the Band:
A Tell-All Interview with DAYDREAM

With chart-topping hits and a dedicated fan base, DAYDREAM has risen to meteoric success. In this exclusive interview, the members open up about their creative process, the close bond they share, and their hopes for the band.

YOUR DEBUT SINGLE, "DAYDREAMIN' OF YOU," REACHED #1 ON THE BILLBOARD HOT 100. WHEN RECORDING, DID YOU THINK IT WOULD BECOME A MEGAHIT?

FELIX: We worked on it for three months, fine-tuning every detail to make sure it was perfect. When we finally recorded it, the energy in the studio was incredibly high. We didn't know it would be so popular, but we knew it was special. The melody, the vibe—everything came together amazingly.

YOU WERE FRIENDS BEFORE FORMING THE BAND. HAS YOUR FRIENDSHIP EVOLVED POST-FAME?

WILL: We've always been close, but now there's a deeper level of understanding and support. Our busy schedules and the constant pressure can make it difficult to prioritize our friendship at times, but at the end of the day, we'll always have each other's backs.

DAYDREAM HAS RELEASED NINETEEN SONGS, BUT ONLY THREE HAVE SONGWRITING CREDITS FROM FELIX, LACHLAN, AND/OR CALUM. DO YOU DESIRE BEING MORE HANDS-ON?

LACHLAN: Frankly, if it were up to us, those numbers would look *very* different. Unfortunately, those decisions have been taken out of our hands.

CALUM adds: I think what he means is that songwriting is something we're really passionate about, and we see it as a unique way for DREAMERs to connect with our music. Hopefully, we'll have chances to contribute more often.

IN TEN YEARS, WHAT DO YOU WANT PEOPLE TO REMEMBER MOST ABOUT YOU AS A GROUP?

FELIX: I think we all hope that folks will remember how we made them feel. We want our music—and who we are as people—to be a safe space. Music has always been that for us, and if we're able to give someone that same sense of comfort or belonging, even briefly, then we'll have done something meaningful.

Chapter Fifteen

Please Step on Me, Felix

Washington, DC, July 1

The ROLLING STONE interview is published the day after Felix and my midnight rendezvous on the hotel rooftop, and to everyone's delight, it's a smash hit.

But right as he started opening up and the boy behind the superstar appeared in a small glimmer, like a ghost walking through walls, the band's already hectic schedule increases tenfold, with dozens of publications and shows requesting interviews now that DAYDREAM has been solidified as ***the*** hot new boy band.

During this wild new wave of popularity, our ASL practice suffers. But even with his packed schedule, Felix shows up at my door at 10:30 every night. Whether it's for a SimCom conversation or a card game thinly veiled as an ASL lesson, he's there—no matter how exhausted he is.

Luckily, it only takes a few days to get back on track. And today we'll be filming clips for the music video montage all over DC and squeezing in practice where we can.

When Mateo, Felix, Ginger, and I get out of the car at our second location, I stare up in slack-jawed awe. The Washington Monument stretches into the vast blue sky; in front of it is a sprawling pool nearly longer than the eye can see. Tourists surround the obelisk, taking pictures and admiring its glory.

"What's the significance of this again?" Felix asks.

Mateo and I whip our heads around at the speed of light, in disbelief.

"Come on, Lix," Mateo groans.

He throws his hands up in faux defense. "I'm Kiwi! I don't remember what all your tax-dollar-paid patriotic structures signify!"

Mateo face-palms, but before he can conduct an impromptu history lesson, the other members join us. Bhavani, four bodyguards, and another staffer trail behind them. Will brandishes a GoPro. "Let's film solo shots and then some group ones."

The next hour flies by as I help film Lachlan pretending to hold up the obelisk, Will and Mateo chasing each other around, and Calum and Felix skipping along the Reflecting Pool while holding hands.

Right as I finish filming Will doing squats while holding Lachlan bridal-style, Felix taps my shoulder. I turn around, but before I can say anything, he smacks a sticky note onto my forehead and takes off, running full speed toward the other end of the Reflecting Pool.

"Hey!" I shout as Sunglasses chases after him. I peel the note off and force myself not to laugh as I read it.

It's a really bad joke . . . But somehow, it's amusing knowing Felix deemed it important enough to write it down. I tuck it into my pocket.

When everyone finally catches up to Felix and Sunglasses on the other end, he flashes a goofy grin and I make a show of rolling my eyes. But I'm quickly distracted because right in front of us is the Lincoln Memorial. The white marble pillars are almost impossibly large, the statue of the president sitting dignified and imposing at the top of a massive staircase. Pictures don't do the National Mall justice—the architecture, the history living in the stone are striking.

"Whoa," Mateo says, his mesmerized look mirroring mine. We pull out our phones, snapping pictures of the monument. I'll send some to Jo later and use them as references for a sketch. Mateo turns to Felix. "Please tell me you at least know what this one is."

Felix theatrically gasps. "I'm not stupid; I'm just Kiwi!"

The other members seem ambivalent. The bodyguards form a loose circle around the boys as people start to notice them. Mateo turns toward his bandmates. "Are we seeing the same thing? Hello?" He motions to the memorial.

Calum shrugs. "We saw Abe in middle school. School field trip." Will and Lachlan nod.

Mateo and I glance at each other, seemingly thinking the same thing: ***Of course whichever bougie private middle school they attended did cross-country field trips***.

We're torn away from our moment of solidarity when Bhavani says, "I hate to rain on your parade, but we've got half an hour to film the rest before heading to the concert venue."

While Bhavani touches up Felix's ponytail, Will snaps pictures of the other boys in front of the memorial using his red Nikon. I grab my phone and take my own shots of him in photographer mode.

They're interrupted when a kid, roughly Ava's age, approaches. They're holding the latest issue of ROLLING STONE, DAYDREAM's picture on the cover. Sunglasses starts to block their path, but Calum nudges her away and greets the kid with obvious excitement.

"I'm really sorry— —bother you but . . . could you sign this?" they ask shyly, extending the magazine.

"Totally, dude!"

Felix roots through his fanny pack and finds a metallic gold Sharpie, then chucks it at Calum. It hits him smack in the forehead, and he starts to curse, but catches himself and instead flips Felix off behind his back.

After Calum signs, he hands the marker and magazine to Mateo.

"I liked your answer. I hope— —your own music— —someday," the fan tells Lachlan when it's his turn to autograph.

"Thanks. Me too." Lachlan gives them a tight-lipped smile. They run off and excitedly show the magazine with all five signatures to their family.

Lachlan's expression sours, and he slumps onto one of the steps, staring at the ground while grinding his teeth. Felix sits next to Lachlan. "I liked your answer, too."

Lachlan scoffs bitterly. "One of ***two*** answers of mine they bothered to put in the article?"

"It was good, though!"

"Oh, please. It made me look like an ungrateful asshole ***and*** made the label mad," he bites. "You, on the other hand, sounded eloquent . . . like America's motherfucking Sweetheart. And even if you didn't, the fans love you no matter what."

The atmosphere intensifies when Felix pats Lachlan's arm supportively, and Lachlan jerks away. Before anything else is said, Calum and Will exchange glances.

"Yo, anyone else getting hungry?" Calum says airily, trying to defuse the tension.

"Yeah, sure. Let's grab a bite on our way to the venue," Will suggests.

"I've had enough family-bonding time. Bye," Lachlan gripes before trudging off.

"At least they quoted you," Mateo says to Lachlan's back. "I'm not in there at all."

"So . . . what was that about?" I hazard. Sure, it's frustrating to only have two answers published in an article with twenty-five, but it feels like something bigger is at play here.

"Lach's a hot-and-cold type of guy," Will explains.

"With a short fuse," Calum adds.

"It's not personal. We give him space, and he calms down eventually."

Hah. Sounds like Mom. Although, if this is as bad as it gets, I'd rather deal with his fluctuating emotions. If there's one positive from being raised by the poster child for hot-and-cold, it's that I know how to handle unpredictability.

The interaction takes a back seat when Necktie calls to yell at everyone to get to the stadium. As we head back to the parking lot, Felix has a mischievous glow in his eyes. He adheres a second Post-it note to my forehead.

WHY WAS ABRAHAM LINCON
NEVER PUT IN JAIL?
BECUSE HE WAS IN A CENT

Unfortunately, Lachlan's still brooding when we get to Capital One Arena's Green Room. He avoids the other members and busies himself with vocal warm-ups.

After Felix's makeup is redone—with significantly more glitter—he joins Calum and me for a cutthroat game of gin rummy. The whole time, though, he's distracted by taking glimpses at Lachlan.

"Hah! Take that!" Calum cheers after besting both of us.

I reluctantly cough up the five Chupa Chups we wagered. "For the record, I went easy on you," I mumble. Felix wordlessly hands over his lollipops.

Satisfied, Calum pops one into his mouth before walking over to where Will is doing push-ups. Then Calum sits on his back, claiming "I'm helping!" when Will protests.

My focus flickers back to Felix. He's watching Lachlan, who's by the door, waiting to go do sound check. "Are you okay?" I ask. His eyes meet mine.

"It's . . . nothing. Don't worry about it," he says. "*I want you to watch* the show *tonight*. I got you a great seat."

I sigh. "I already told you—"

He reaches out, delicately touching my wrist. "Nat, please trust me."

The patch of skin his fingers ghosted over hums with electricity, and I absentmindedly rub it while considering his offer. "*OK-OK. Fine*," I agree.

"You won't regret it, promise."

Suddenly, Necktie bursts through the door like the Kool-Aid Man. "Let's go! Time for sound check!" he barks.

While Necktie creates a single file line, Felix hangs back and puts every single member between him and Lachlan.

It's nothing, my ass. Using three people as human shields to protect yourself from your best friend-slash-bandmate is ***not*** nothing.

After the band clears out, I rush to Bhavani's makeup station.

"Are you here for gossip? Or a hairstyle?" they ask with a teasing smirk.

"Both?" I smile sweetly. I sit down, and they start detangling my waves. "What's going on with Lachlan and Felix?"

Bhavani hurriedly gives me the condensed, SparkNotes version of events. "Lachlan started the band in freshman year, and Felix was— —backup singer and keyboardist. But then the label made Felix the lead singer instead of Lachlan. They thought he was more appealing since he's a natural in interviews— —kind of ethereal in general. Nobody dislikes Felix!"

My mind fills in the blanks and puzzle pieces click into place: how the boys were arranged at open-mic night in Atlanta, with Felix in the far back, and what he confessed on the Nashville rooftop a week ago . . . Felix was never supposed to be the star of the show. Lachlan was.

Sure, I can see how Felix stands out a bit more than Lachlan. But it feels wildly unfair that he was forcibly dethroned, and Felix was required to take his place. Especially since neither of them are happy with the arrangement.

Thirty minutes before showtime, Felix leads a stagehand over to me.

"Nat, this is Tori. She'll show you to your seat." I start to follow Tori, but Felix holds up a finger. *"One sec."*

I wait by the door and suspiciously eye him while he rummages through Will's backpack. Eventually, he pulls out a small pair of pink doggy headsets and walks over to me. "It'll probably be too loud for her," he explains. "They match her vest!"

That awful warm, sparkly feeling blooms in my chest, and I have to clench my teeth to suppress a smile. He bought Ginger headsets that ***match her vest***? Jesus Christ.

"Thank you."

After Ginger has her doggy headsets on, Tori, Ginger, and I head out. Felix practically vibrates with excitement as I catch a final glimpse of him as we enter the hall. He signs, *"Enjoy!"*

We walk for a while before emerging in one of Capital One Arena's lower bowls. The sound of eighteen thousand fans buzzing with anticipation and singing an acapella version of what I vaguely recognize as DAYDREAM's latest single, "Cloud 9," renders my ears one-hundred-percent useless.

Tori guides us to a seat at the front. From here, I have what I suspect is the best view in the whole stadium. I tuck Ginger underneath the seat using hand signals.

I choke on a laugh at the person next to me. Their face is covered in DAYDREAM temporary tattoos, and they're showing their PLEASE STEP ON ME FELIX sign to another fan. At least they're asking politely.

Soon, the group effort of singing DAYDREAM songs turns into screaming as the arena goes pitch black, until a single spotlight turns on and Mateo is lifted from under the stage, spinning a mic in his hand like a thick drumstick. The crowd goes wild.

Four members are revealed the same way, until there's only one dark spot left in the center. When the final spotlight turns on, Felix appears and the three monitors surrounding the stage display a live image of him with an innocent, boy-next-door pout that contradicts the flirtation in his eyes.

The corner of each monitor displays someone wearing an earpiece, their hands primed in midair. It doesn't click who they are until Felix raises his mic and shouts, "HELLO, DC!" and they repeat the greeting in ASL.

Holy shit.

There isn't enough time to process the surprise interpreter when the stage lights turn on, bathing the stadium in a baby-pink hue. "Lovely Girl" blares, and the boys launch into the performance. They command the stage effortlessly; each move they make is charismatic and timed to the beat. They radiate energy and draw the crowd in like a magnet.

But my eyes keep flicking back to the interpreter, who moves in sync with the music as if their hands are painting the lyrics in the air. The fluidity and precision of their signs are a perfect extension of the song itself.

When the song ends, I find myself cheering as loudly as the other fans. (What a plot twist.) Felix overtakes the main screen again and holds his index finger to his mouth. Instantly, the fans go silent. The power he holds is terrifying.

"Thank you, DC!" He blows a kiss to the crowd and beckons Will over. He gives Will his microphone, and he holds it to Felix's mouth, freeing Felix's hands. "Real quick," he says while using charmingly clunky SimCom, "I wanna dedicate this show to my biggest supporter and best friend, my little sister"—the fans cheer—"and my incredible ASL teacher, who's an angel for putting up with me. This one's for you guys."

It's probably impossible because of the stage lights shining in his eyes, but I swear Felix looks straight at me. Thousands and thousands of fans in this building, and he's staring at ***me***, lips tipped into a toothy grin.

My heart unexpectedly tumbles around my rib cage. And even though he's not going to see it, I sign, "*Thank you.*"

Chapter Sixteen

The Right Fireworks at the Wrong Time

Philadelphia, July 4

"Jesus!" I exclaim and jolt backward, slamming my elbow into the hotel doorframe. Standing roughly a foot away, Mateo cringes. Calum stands beside him.

My heart rate slows as I look between them. "Why are you lurking outside my door?"

Mateo awkwardly messes with the hem of a threadbare denim jacket. "We need your help."

This piques my interest, but Ginger is squirming at my feet, needing to go potty. "Walk with me," I tell them, and head for the elevator.

"Obviously you know what today is," Mateo starts once we're inside.

"Yeah. The Fourth of July," I answer.

They exchange a look.

"It's also Lix's nineteenth birthday," Calum supplies. He pulls his hair out of its unicorn-horn ponytail, and shaggy dark brown curls cover his face.

"W-what?" I splutter. Why wouldn't Felix mention that?

“We need your help to surprise him!” Mateo announces. “Can you skip the— —bakery— —and then— —decorate— —after show— —does that work?”

Wow. I’ve never heard Mateo talk so fast.

“I didn’t catch most of that,” I admit as we step into the lobby. “Can you text it to me?” I motion toward the phone in Mateo’s hand. He unlocks it and hands it to me. I make a contact for myself, open a new text string, and give it back. They wait by the elevators while I take Ginger outside.

By the time the text comes through, we’re heading back inside. I read the message as I walk, chuckling at the incredibly detailed plan for a surprise party. He even included a shopping list.

“Can you do it?” Mateo asks after Ginger and I rejoin them.

“Sure. But how am I supposed to get out of the concert tonight?”

“Say you’re on your period or something,” Calum suggests. “Lix can’t force you to come when your uterus is attacking.”

It’s not a bad excuse. What guy is going to pry into the details of a period? “Okay. I’ll get everything prepped tonight.”

“Yay! Thank you!” Mateo beams while holding his hand out to Calum. Calum looks at it for a second too long before confusedly taking his hand and lacing their fingers together. Mateo pulls his hand away and sighs. “Your credit card, Cal.”

“Oh,” he breathes, realization dawning. “That’s all I am to you? Your sugar daddy?” He gives me one of his many cards and tells me the pin is 1234. I try my best to not let judgment show on my face.

Since the businesses near our hotel are closed for the holiday, it takes Ginger and me an hour-long taxi ride to find an open party store. I couldn't bring myself to look at the fare. Even though I'm using Calum's card, fees with three numbers and no decimal point make me dizzy.

I head for the birthday aisle; Ginger trots beside me. Even here, most of the decorations are patriotic, which makes sense, it being the Fourth of July in Philadelphia—the birthplace of America.

While looking at some extremely nationalistic bald eagle and American flag confetti, Ginger's wet nose squishes against my exposed thigh. I don't ask her to show me what she hears, because I feel my phone buzzing. I wipe her snot off my leg and answer the video call.

Jo's sitting on the floor of the office. She tilts her phone to show a stack of revamp supplies behind her. Paint, kids' books, and an unassembled desk still in the box. *"How did you get this many donations?!"*

I tie Ginger's leash around my waist so I can hold my phone and one-handedly sign. I carefully maneuver my cart with my torso, only occasionally bumping into things. *"I'm worst-charming."* I wink.

"The donations are great, but they're making Mom upset."

"If she doesn't like it, she can leave."

"She also gets super upset if I mention you. And I catch her crying sometimes."

"I don't wan— "

"I know, you don't want to discuss her!" she interrupts. *"But have you talked with her? Even briefly?"*

I shake my head. I'm ***not*** going to be the first one to break and message her. Even though I can't help but wonder what's going on inside her head. We've never gone this long without communication.

Jo sighs. "*Maybe you should talk soon. I think you both hurt each other.*"

I flash a disapproving frown in lieu of a response.

"*Damn, don't get mad! I'm done!*" Jo urges. "*How's the tour?*"

"*The tour's . . . fine. It's F-E-L-I-X's birthday. I'm buying party decorations and a cake.*"

Her brows shoot into her hairline. "*You planned a party for him?*"

"*No, M-A-T—* "

"*You like him! You DO care about hot boys!*" Her jaw drops.

"*No! I don't!*" I sign a little too defensively. "*I'm not emotionally connected to him yet. He's worst-annoying!*"

"'*Yet*'?" Jo waggles her brows.

I roll my eyes. "*OK-OK, maybe . . . I don't DISLIKE him but . . .*" She quirks a brow. "*I'm neutral. Stop meddling, and focus on preparing lessons and managing the Center!*"

I mean, sure, there's nothing wrong with being emotionally connected or ***mildly*** attracted to your friendly neighborhood pop star, but I couldn't stand the humiliation, personally.

Not that I'm connected to or attracted to Felix Song! Just . . . you know, in general.

Smugness floods Jo's face. "*I have to go. I'm busy,*" I rush, desperately wanting this conversation to end.

"*Have fun!*" she signs teasingly.

I hang up the call and pick out the most outrageously American party supplies the store has. Throwing an American pride–themed birthday party for a Kiwi is too good an opportunity to pass up.

I order a taxi to a nearby bakery while the cashier rings us up. Ginger scoots closer to my leg from where she's sitting. I glance away from my screen and see an employee patting her head and making kissy faces.

"Please don't pet her," I say firmly. Not to the same level, but I'm starting to see crossover between owning a service dog and being famous. Everywhere we go, people stare, take pictures, and invade our personal space. The employee gives me a dirty look, like they have a right to be upset they can't touch my medical equipment, and storms away.

Ginger and I get back to the hotel right as the concert starts, which gives me two and a half hours to set everything up. I load the decorations and cake onto a luggage cart and carefully navigate it into the elevator.

When we reach Felix's room, I hesitate. I'm not technically breaking and entering since Calum scrounged up a key, but it feels like a violation of privacy. I unlock the door. The party must go on, right? Inside, the room is disheveled. Skin care products and vitamin bottles clutter the dresser. His suitcase is open on the floor, and the clothes are haphazardly crumpled inside. The only tidy thing is his go-to outfit, the striped sweater and black flowy pants, which are neatly folded on his unmade bed.

The room reminds me of the random mélange in his bottomless fanny pack.

Needing a place to put the cake, I tidy the dresser first. I notice three neon Post-it notes stuck to the mirror above the dresser. It takes me a second of staring at Felix's chicken-scratch handwriting to recognize the words.

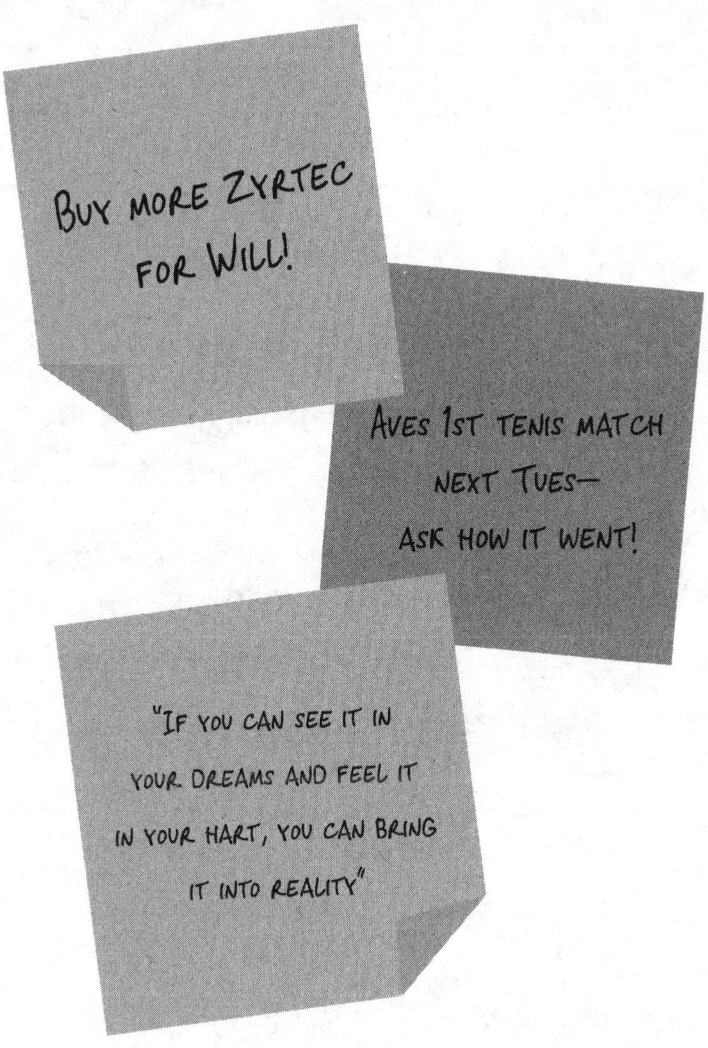

The notes spark curiosity, but I brush it off and continue the party prep. When I approach his bed, I see some glitter pens strewn around an open notebook. I pick up the book, and my eyes float over the mismatch of glittery rainbow scribbles.

UNTITLED

F.SONG 27/06

(VERSE 1) BORN IN A SUMMER BREEZE,
UNDER SKIES BRITE AND BLUE
I'D LIKE TO TRY ME AND YOU
EVERY GLANCE, EVERY SMILE, I'M FALLING DEEP
HER LESSONS HARD TO TEACH,
HER TOUCH JUST OUT OF REACH
DOES SHE EVEN NOTICE, DOES HER HART SKIP A BEAT?

(PRE-CORUS) DOES SHE FEEL THE SAME OR IS IT IN MY HEAD?
DOES SHE SEE A FREIND, A OPPORTUNEITY,
OR SOMETHING MORE INSTED?

(CORUS) SILENCE & SOUND, THE DIFFERNCE IN OUR LIFES
WALKING IN THE WIND, TEARING ME APART,
HIDDEN IN THE SHADOW OF MY DOUBT
THE STORY OF US WAITING TO BE WRITTEN

I slam the book shut the instant I realize what I'm reading.

This is Felix's songwriting book.

His filled-with-intimate-thoughts-and-feelings-that-I-have-no-business-reading-about songwriting book.

I toss it aside and stand up, my heart beating a million miles per hour. From the floor, Ginger watches with an incredible amount of judgment. "I didn't mean to snoop!" I exclaim. "It was lying there, completely open! He should've hidden it!"

She blinks at me.

My shoulders slump. "You're right. He left it open in his room, which I should ***not*** be in without permission. I have no excuse."

His lyrics ping-pong around my brain: ***Her lessons hard to teach . . . Does she see a friend, an opportunity, or something more instead? . . . The difference in our lives . . .*** The song isn't about me, right? That's impossible! Or . . . maybe it's not. A strange warmth unfurls within me, like his words are wrapping themselves around me, settling deep and steady.

Jesus. Pull yourself together, Natalie.

But the deep need to tell someone about this worms its way into my brain, and I decide I'll send one text to Jo before pretending I never saw it. A happy medium.

Thurs, July 4, 7:44 PM

[Natalie]

I think Felix wrote a love song about me?? He's horrible! I hate it here!

[Jo]

HELLO??????? ADJKADHJGK MARRY HIM!! SECURE THE BAG 🤑💰

[Natalie]

You're the worst

[Jo]

so im hearing FELIX isnt the worst anymore?

[Natalie]

Bold statement from someone who can't hear

[Jo]

ur ableism is sickening 😔

I put my phone away with a sigh. I don't know why I thought that was a good idea.

I force myself to focus on putting everything on the bed in Felix's suitcase, then I transform the sleek, expensive hotel room into a red, white, and blue birthday wonderland.

The real showstopper is the "Happy Independence Day!" banner I hung above the bed. Except I crossed out the word ***independence*** and wrote ***birth*** in its place. My finest work of art to date.

I check the time on my phone and see a text from Felix, from ten minutes ago.

Thurs, July 4, 10:19 PM

[Pretty Boy 🙃]

Hiya 🥰 Heading back! Want me too buy u anything (pads/tampons, choclate, etc)?

XX

Feeling a tinge of guilt for lying about being on my period, I reply: I'm good. See you soon :)

Right after, a text from Mateo pops up at the top of my screen: Almost there! Get ready!!

I reach to turn off the lights when the door swings open and a cacophony of people yell "surprise!" from the hall, behind Felix. He stands in the doorway, slack-jawed. I guess "almost there" means "literally right outside" to Mateo.

The band members, Bhavani, and two other makeup artists squeeze around him. Bhavani blows an air kiss as they pass me. Felix steps inside and closes the door, then quietly watches everyone dig into the hotel snack bar and make themselves comfortable.

His eyes drift away from the DIY birthday banner and lock onto me, and everything else fades. He pulls me into a hug, the warmth of his arms enveloping me in a way that's both sudden and familiar. I'm hit with an unexpected wave of emotion as his heart beats against mine. I make no move to step back, and he doesn't pull away, either, as if he's trying to take in the weight of the surprise I pulled off, the joy in this simple, intimate moment.

When he finally releases me, a strange emptiness lingers in his place.

The thought leaves my mind when I spot Lachlan watching us from the side. His brows are ever-so-slightly furrowed, but it's enough to make me wonder what he's thinking.

Before I can dwell on it, Felix presses his hand into a fist and kisses the back of it, a playful grin tugging at his lips, "*KissFist!*"

"*Since when do you know* ASL *slang?*" I ask, feeling a little lighter, but my heart still flutters from the way he made me feel like the most important person in the room.

"A-V-A *taught me.*"

I smile. "Felix, I've seen how hard you're workin—" My rare compliment is interrupted when Lachlan comes over and takes Felix by the wrist.

"You're missing your own party, birthday boy," he says. His eyes float to me as he pulls Felix farther into the room. Calum places a party hat on top of his sweaty, post-show hair.

Will and Bhavani hand out cups filled with suspicious purple liquid. Lachlan quickly downs his drink, connects his phone to a Bluetooth speaker, plays music, and the party takes off.

After an hour of nonstop auditory stimuli and two cups of Will's mystery drink (which tastes like Kool-Aid and hand sanitizer), I sneak into the hallway.

The quiet is a welcome reprieve to the overwhelming buzz of the party. My head throbs, and it's hard to pinpoint if it's because I'm a lightweight, auditorily fatigued, or both. I wobble as I sit and lean my head against the wall. Ginger lies next to me, and her presence is grounding, but I can't quite shake the feeling that the walls are swaying. The door swings open a few minutes later, and Felix emerges.

"*Are you tired* . . . of the party?" he half-signs, half-speaks, sitting across from me so I can lipread.

"Yeah. I've never actually been to a ***party*** party," I admit. My hands and face tingle as I use SimCom. "My mom is kind of"—I'm interrupted by a hiccup. Felix laughs—"a helicopter parent."

"How'd she react to . . . *you coming* . . . *on tour?*"

"Pfft." I laugh dryly. "Before I left, we got into a massive fight, and we haven't talked since. If you flip to 'silent treatment' in the dictionary, her picture is in there."

"*I'm sorry.*"

"Sometimes I just wish I had a functional family. Like yours."

His brows knit, lips twisting downward. "My family's hardly perfect."

I raise a disbelieving brow. I think about all the DAYDREAM memorabilia proudly displayed by Mrs. Song and the family's excitement whenever he's home.

"My relationship with my dad is . . . rough." His expression is similar to when he told me about his learning disabilities. Anxious, vulnerable. "He's got a wicked IQ and was always the best in school, all the way from childhood to uni. I never got anything better than a C+, and that was unacceptable. Even after my diagnoses, he accused me of using them as an excuse. And when I came out as pansexual a few years ago, that was the final straw. He's made it abundantly clear I'm a huge disappointment."

"God. I'm so sorry. He's always seemed so understanding of Ava's hearing loss."

"That's what sucks most, actually. 'Course, I'm happy for Aves. She has a dad who accommodates and loves her wholeheartedly. But *I* never got that dad. It makes it feel like the problem was never him. It was me. Y'know?"

"I do," I breathe. He quirks his head curiously. "Not to the same extent, but my mom's always snapping at me. Sometimes it feels like . . . ugh, like I can't do anything right. I wonder if she even likes me."

The words spill out in a long, tangled string, and I'm not sure if they make sense, and I don't even know where I'm going with any of this, but I can't stop rambling.

"God, it sounds weird, but in a twisted way, I think it wouldn't hurt as much if she were a jerk to us both, right? But she's like a whole different person with Jo. Like, how can you have such a different childhood as your sibling yet be raised by the same people?" I stop, but my mind keeps running circles around itself. Felix nods like he gets it, and I don't know if he really does, but the warm hum in my veins makes it feel like it doesn't matter anyway.

Anger toward Mom rears its head, and every argument flashes through my mind like a compilation. Every time she's spent days on end ignoring me or condemned me for having dreams. And her moments with Jo—moments with far more patience, forgiveness, and love.

It felt like I was a side character in their story, looking in from the outside while Jo got the childhood I didn't.

When Felix takes my hand, his thumb rubbing comforting circles on my skin, I'm torn from my thoughts. I look at him and find my cheeks are wet. I paw at the unexpected tears and fight oncoming ones.

We sit in silence for what could be seconds or minutes, the stillness of the hall carrying the heaviness of our conversation. Eventually, the fog in my brain starts to lift, and I can focus a little better.

"It was brave to come out to your parents, though. I won't ever tell my mom I'm demi," I say.

He frowns. "Er, sorry . . . demi?"

"Oh, demiromantic. I don't form romantic feelings until I have an emotional bond with people, or, like, connect with their personality."

"Ah." He nods. "Mum and Aves are cool with my sexuality. It's only my dad who's not."

He takes a beat before standing and extending his hand to me. With the elegance of a newborn giraffe, I join him. The hall isn't spinning as much, but I'm still unsteady. His hand grips mine tightly, and it's oddly reassuring.

"D'you wanna get some fresh air?" he asks. "*Maybe being outside . . . would help?*"

I stumble a bit while dropping Ginger off in my room. Felix tucks me under his arm as we head for the elevator. During the ride to the rooftop, he keeps me pressed against his side.

"So what's the deal with the Post-it notes?" I break the silence. "I saw some in your room, and you keep giving them to me. Wouldn't your Notes app be easier?"

"The digital world is a black hole. Anything I wrote there would get lost." He laughs. "Having a physical reminder helps me remember important stuff."

"And presidential puns are 'important'?"

"You underestimate my dedication to tomfoolery." He winks as we step out of the elevator.

On the roof, summer heat lingers in the air, but a cool breeze hits my face. This rooftop is vastly different from the one in Nashville. It has a patio, chairs, and a bar.

Several guests sip drinks and watch the fireworks. We lean against a glass barrier in a remote corner. From here we have a clear view of bursts of light exploding above the Schuylkill. Red, blue, yellow, and purple fireworks dance across the river's dark water and fill Philadelphia's sky with a kaleidoscope of colors.

But I can't focus on the actual display. Felix is compressing his tall frame as he bends to rest his elbows on top of the glass wall; chin propped in his hands, full lips pressed into a pout. I watch fireworks burst through his intense gaze. Every second, a new color shines in his midnight eyes, reflecting like an oil spill.

"I never thanked you for the concert in DC," I say. "The interpreter."

He glances at me with a small frown. "Making our music accessible isn't something to thank me for, Nat. It's the bare minimum. I'm kinda embarrassed I didn't think of it myself."

He's right. Of course that's right. Accommodations ***are*** the bare minimum. So why would his statement trigger butterflies in my stomach? Why does watching the way his rosebud lips form words make my cheeks hot? Why am I pretty certain I like Felix "pain in my ass" Song when he's the last person on planet earth I would've ever thought I'd connect with?

"—the rest of the tour . . . Nat? Are you listening?" He waves his hand in front of my face.

"Huh? What? Oh! Yes, sorry," I stammer. I was totally listening. I wasn't staring at his face. Nope. Not even a little bit. "Um . . . what'd you say, though?"

"Famke, the interpreter, will be with us for the rest of the tour. She's already memorized the set list." His eyes twinkle in a wickedly addictive way before he turns back to the show. I wonder how many girls would fall instantly and irrevocably in love with him if he cracked a smile half as dazzling as that one.

His childlike wonder is so captivating that I open my camera app. The same mystical force that compelled me to save the backstage selfie he sent in Miami possesses me tonight.

I take a picture of him.

He looks over. "Did you just take a photo of me?"

"I . . ." ***Can't think of an excuse fast enough*** ". . . didn't think you'd notice."

His eyes crinkle, and his teeth show as he giggles. "Nat, phones make a sound when you take a photo with your ringer on."

My jaw drops. "What?!"

He clutches his stomach and howls with laughter. I turn my ringer off and hide my face in my hands. I've never been this mortified in my entire eighteen years of life. He gently grabs my shoulder.

"It's alright, pinkie swear," he soothes. "Just thought I'd be safe from paparazzi up here."

"You're so annoying, Felix Song," I grumble.

His lips curl into a smirk. "Oh? Well, you're cute, Nat Nielsen."

"Is that an insult?" I scoff.

"It's a fact."

My heart traitorously flips. I comb the deepest corners of my mind for a witty retort, but I'm rendered speechless by the galaxy in Felix's eyes. I find his hand on my shoulder, and before I even realize it, my fingers are threading through his. The simple pressure of his fingers squeezing mine sends a shiver down my spine, igniting something deep inside me, something beautiful and terrifying.

I take a step closer, my pulse pounding in my ears. Like the night in Nashville, my arms find their way around his neck. Felix's eyes drink me in, studying every detail of my face. Slowly, he reaches out and his thumb brushes gently over my cheek, and I gasp softly. His touch is so light, so delicate, the sensation barely registers, yet every spot he grazes ignites like one of the fireworks above us.

His gaze intensifies as he dips his head down, inching closer to mine. The simple, magnetic action sends a shock of heat coursing through my body that settles low in my gut.

His fingers thread through my hair, pulling me closer, tilting my head slightly. My breath catches as I lean into him, feeling the heat of his skin, the warmth of his breath across my lips. My eyes flutter closed, every nerve in my body alight as his lips ghost over mine and—***Bzz bzz***.

I jump backward as my phone forcefully buzzes. He steps away from me and awkwardly teeters as I fumble with the device.

Thurs, July 4, 11:48 PM

[Lachlan]

Where did you two go?

"You OK?" Felix asks.

I open my mouth and prime my hands to respond, but once again, I'm at a loss for words. I rush forward, slide my hands underneath Felix's BURBERRY coat, and slip my arms around his waist.

I allow myself this one moment of weakness. His hands run up and down my back; his heart beats against my cheek when I bury my face in his chest; I breathe in the tang of post-concert sweat mixed with absurdly expensive TOM FORD cologne.

The alcohol in my veins has blurred the clear lines between us. And though my thoughts are muddled, I know we could never be more than what we are right now.

I'm learning that he's not who the world thinks he is, and I was wrong about his commitment to Ava, but I forcibly remind myself of the vast divide between our realities. He's so busy that we can barely fit in tutoring. He doesn't have time in his life for anything else. And neither do I.

I have to dedicate every free second to keeping the Center

afloat. My plans require time and energy—not to mention fund-raising—so we can stop merely ***surviving***. If I want my plans to come to fruition, I'll not only need to be totally focused, but I'll also need the money Felix owes me . . . If we take our relationship further and it ends badly, it puts everything I've worked for at risk.

My jaw locks up, and I exhale a sharp breath as the harsh reality sets in. I can't be that girl he wrote about in his songbook. I can only be his teacher. Nothing more, nothing less.

I pull away from his embrace. "We need to keep this professional." I hate how impersonal it sounds leaving my lips.

He puts distance between us, and his brows tug into a deep frown. Thirty seconds of painful silence pass before he swallows heavily, his shoulders sagging.

"I understand," he finally replies, trying to mask the hurt and confusion in his tone.

"Okay," I breathe. "I should go to bed."

"Okay," he parrots. "Goodnight, Natalie."

I stare at the ground while I walk away, but something akin to the Screenshotting Spirit stops me. "Felix?" I call out, halfway to the elevator.

He spins around, dark eyes filled with fireworks and hope.

"*Happy birthday*," I sign.

From across the rooftop, his smile hits me like a gut punch.

I've seen it before. When interview hosts tell unfunny jokes, when DAYDREAM is swarmed at the airport, or in promotional photos. The one that doesn't reach his eyes, his lips curved stiffly, just a façade. His "DAYDREAM mode" look.

A look I've never been on the receiving end of.

The Unplugged Podcast

SEASON 5 EP. 22

[HOST]: Lachlan, does it bother you that fans call you the "forgotten member"? Do you think you're a worthless addition?

[*tense silence*]

[LACHLAN]: I . . . yeah, who wouldn't hate hearing such negative comments? I mean . . . in any group, someone is bound to stand out, but that doesn't diminish anyone else's value.

[HOST]: Not sure the public agrees about your value, but speaking of public opinion, Will, you post a lot of workout content. Are you seeking validation?

[WILL]: Wha—? No. Usually when I'm not working, I'm at the gym, so I post it. It's a mental health thing for me. It puts me in a better headspace and helps me have stamina for concerts.

[HOST]: What's the max weight your girlfriend could be?

[WILL]: Wow. Um. Anyone who has "max weights" is a walking red flag and shouldn't be allowed to date. Or in public at all.

[HOST]: Interesting take. Moving on. The band was originally called Renegade Wizard. Why the change? What does DAYDREAM signify?

[FELIX]: We took a different direction sonically and aesthetically after signing to our label. Daydreaming is all about imagining endless possibilities. The goal is for our music to be like a soundtrack that allows fans to escape from reality and explore their own dreams and aspirations.

[HOST]: Damn, that was scripted! [*smug laugh*] Your image is "wholesome," but surely you aren't that pure. Are you all virgins?

[LACHLAN]: Do you have *actual* questions? What is this bull [*bleep*]?

[HOST]: Well, that certainly wasn't wholesome! How about you, Mateo? Have you taken advantage of your newfound fame?

[CALUM]: Dude, he's seventeen! Don't be a creep.

[HOST]: Geez! Then let me pose it to a legal member, if that's *so* important. Felix, have you hooked up with fans?

[FELIX]: I'm not answering that.

[HOST]: To all the disappointed fans, I'm sorry your burning questions are being ignored! A word of advice, boys: Don't be buzzkills. You won't be invited back!

[CALUM]: We don't *want* to be invited back.

Chapter Seventeen

Mile High-Jinks

Toronto, July 8

I pray I never have to take another flight after the tour's over. It's exhausting—especially at 5:00 a.m.

I yawn as I sink into the cushy armchair beside Felix's in Toronto Pearson's first-class lounge. He turns to me and jerks his head toward the snack station, where Necktie is trying (unsuccessfully) to eat a bagel while on a call.

"*You want anything?*" he asks. I shake my head. "Alrighty."

As he considers the multitude of green juice options, I frown. Since I left him high and dry on the rooftop in Philly, I've been waiting for him to have some reaction to my sudden friendzoning, but it's like nothing happened.

The morning after we almost kissed, he greeted me with iced coffee and a smile. On our flight to Toronto two days ago, we practiced signs about Ava's upcoming tennis season. Backstage last night, we played a round of poker with Calum and Will. (Which I won, taking home two packages of sour gummy worms, seven Slim Jims, and four bottles of Sprite.)

I'm confused by his refusal to acknowledge what happened, but also relieved. Denial is better than awkwardness.

After selecting a juice, Felix starts to return. Lachlan quickly relocates to the chair beside me. A fleeting frown crosses Felix's face, but he doesn't say anything and takes another empty seat.

Lachlan's hands are primed to sign, but he's cut off by Necktie, looking slightly less pissed than usual.

"There's been a change of plans," he announces. We all groan. "I'm sitting with Felix on the plane. Find a different seat, girlie." He shoots me a dirty look.

Felix straightens, muscles going rigid. "We're gonna practice. Besides, ***I'm*** the one who bought her ticket."

"Do I look like I care?" Necktie snaps. Then he explains, rapid-fire, "VERSACE invited you— —Milan Fashion Week. We have— —conference call when we land. Donatella wants to speak to you. The head of PR and I— —brief you on the flight."

Felix's face lights up like a kid on Christmas morning, all traces of indignation and anxiety instantly gone. "Really?!" His eyes nearly bug out of his head. Necktie nods curtly. "Holy shit!"

Necktie pulls out his phone and makes another call, heading back toward the snack counter.

Calum claps Felix's shoulder. "That's awesome, dude."

The others congratulate him, too, but when his focus shifts to me, he deflates slightly. "*I'm sorr—*"

"*It's okay,*" I interrupt. "*Congrats!*"

"You can sit with me and Cal. Our row isn't full," Lachlan says using SimCom. I glance at Calum, and he gives me a thumbs-up while slurping a Monster energy drink.

While we wait for boarding, Felix and I squeeze in some practice, but he's distracted. I don't hold it against him, though. If someone told me the Deaf Center won a once-in-a-lifetime renovation, I would be too thrilled to focus.

On the plane, Calum and Lachlan let me have the window seat and I tuck Ginger into the small footwell, but her tail spills over onto Lachlan's feet. I rub an apologetic fist on my chest, but he assures me it's fine, tapping his thumb, other fingers splayed, on his sternum.

Felix, Necktie, and the boys' PR person are across from us. Felix can't contain his joy while Necktie shows him an e-document I assume contains details of the VERSACE offer. I make out pictures of flashy runway outfits—they seem right up his alley.

I'm happy for him. Besides, this'll give me a chance to catnap before we land in New Jersey. Unfortunately, my dreams of relaxation come crashing down when the plane starts taxiing down the runway, the forceful rumbling causing my heart to thunder and my ears to hurt.

Out of pure instinct, I grab the hand of the boy next to me but release it immediately when I remember it's Lachlan, not Felix.

"*Sorry*," I sign, holding on to the armrest instead.

"*You scared of flying?*" he asks. When I don't reply, he holds his hand palm-out toward me, glancing at my iron grip on the armrest. I accept the offer and squeeze.

After what seems like an eternity, we're in the air, and my anxiety fades alongside the rumbling. Lachlan clunkily pats my shoulder when I release his hand. "Are you scared of flying?" he repeats.

"Takeoff and landing always freak me out a little. Thanks for your help."

"If you need to hold my hand during landing, you can." He flashes a supportive smile.

Calum leans forward in his aisle seat, and his brown eyes dart between us. He smirks, and Lachlan jabs him in the ribs. Calum only laughs. After putting his hair into a unicorn horn ponytail, he asks, "Natalie, what's ***bass*** in ASL?"

It's my turn to smirk. "You're not going to like it." He preemptively groans. I cup my left hand as if I'm holding the neck of the instrument and swipe an F-shaped hand in the air in front of my torso as if strumming with a pick, then I fingerspell ***bass***. "It's just guitar and then bass spelled out to clarify."

"There's not a separate sign?" He tsks. "That's bassism."

I stifle a laugh, and Lachlan face-palms before signing, "*Don't encourage him.*"

Calum doesn't dwell on the ***bassism*** for too long, and in true goldfish fashion, he suggests: "Let's play a game." He nudges Lachlan and looks at me hopefully.

"Aren't we a little old for games?" Lachlan deadpans.

"Lach, someday you're going— —be in a retirement home with memory loss because— —didn't keep your brain sharp in your youth— —you'll think, 'I should've played that damn game with Cal and Nat.'"

I bite back a grin. They interact like siblings. It reminds me of Jo and me and almost makes me wish I was at home bickering with her. ***Almost.*** "I'm down," I say.

"See? We'll age gracefully, but you'll be like— —potato left in the sun."

Lachlan pinches the bridge of his nose before reluctantly saying and signing, "Fine."

"Two truths and a lie?" Calum suggests.

"Hell no," I interject. "You've known each other over a decade! That's basically cheating."

"Okay, okay. How about Lach and I tell— —fact about a band member, and you have to guess who? If— —get three out of five correct, we give you our snacks. If you get ***less***— —three, you give me your snacks."

"That only benefits you," Lachlan argues.

"Do you really want— —extra bag of stale plane popcorn?" Lachlan doesn't reply. "Exactly."

They spend a few minutes whisper-conferring and write everything down on Calum's phone. When they emerge, Calum flips his phone toward me and presents the first question: Who memorized hangul—the Korean alphabet—and can sound out words but doesn't understand them since he doesn't actually know any Korean?

I was hoping their questions would be things I'd read online, but that was clearly naïve. I mentally run through everything I know about them. Will is smart, but so is Lachlan, plus he's Felix's best friend. I doubt Calum would dedicate precious brain cells to learning a different alphabet, and Mateo's only been in the group a year . . . "Lachlan?"

"Will."

Damn it.

"*Ready?*" Lachlan asks after Calum passes him his phone. I nod.

Who was the only member who took formal vocal lessons, pre-record deal?

Immediately, Felix comes to mind. He has an angelic voice.

The other boys are extremely talented, too, but I trust my gut instinct. "Felix?"

"No." Lachlan's lips twist in a lopsided frown. "Me."

I internally cringe. It was bad enough the label stripped him of his lead singer role, but when he was the only member who received actual lessons? That must've cut deep.

"For what it's worth, you have a great voice. I can tell you've worked really hard," I murmur, not sure what else to say.

"Thanks . . ." he breathes.

Calum quickly moves on to the next question, breaking through the lingering awkwardness: Whose first instrument was the glockenspiel?

"What the ***hell*** is a glockenspiel?" I ask, bewildered.

"I don't have to tell you. That wasn't in the terms and agreements."

I'm relieved when Lachlan grabs his own phone from the seat pocket in front of him and flips it toward me after a quick Google search. On the screen are photos of a vaguely triangle-shaped instrument with a wooden frame and metal bars laid out biggest to smallest. What catches my attention, though, are two wooden mallets I assume are used to strike the bars.

Based on the mallets alone, I guess, "Mateo?"

The hitting-glockenspiel-bars-to-hitting-drums pipeline seems plausible.

Calum heaves a disappointed sigh.

When I signal I'm ready, Lachlan flips Calum's phone toward me. Who had four hedgehogs as a kid that were named after the Teenage Mutant Ninja Turtles?

I'm taken aback by the sheer absurdity of this lore. How am I supposed to know who had childhood ***hedgehogs***? But then I remember the times I've seen Calum's Ninja Turtle boxers. It could be a coincidence, but I don't have a better guess. "Cal?"

Lachlan gives me a thumbs-up. Calum shows me the next question in his Notes app immediately. Possibly in an attempt to frazzle me.

Who volunteered at a dog shelter during middle and high school?

I freeze. Felix is the only member who hasn't been an answer, so by default, it should be him . . . But I can't imagine Mr. "cats are superior" at a dog shelter.

"It's one fact per member, right?" I clarify.

"Maybe, maybe not."

"What? You shouldn't repeat members!"

"I never said anything— —fact per member," Calum defends.

"This whole band is full of cheats and tricksters!" I cry. Lachlan chuckles.

"That's showbiz, baby." Calum winks.

I mentally remind myself to not play games with him again. Felix may be a suspected cheater, but at least he's not Rumpelstiltskin incarnate.

I've gotten two wrong and two right. The fate of my snacks hinges on this. "Will? It has to be Will."

A shit-eating grin creeps onto Calum's face. "Nope."

"Damn! Mateo?"

"Nope!" He cackles, then pokes Lachlan's cheek. "This guy."

"What?!" I exclaim louder than intended, and Felix peers

across the aisle with a concerned look. I rub a fist on my chest, then focus on Lachlan. "You're kidding."

"I started struggling with depression— —seventh grade, and my therapist suggested spending time with animals. So I volunteered— —weekends."

A flight attendant stops by our row and hands us each popcorn, a granola bar, and a fresh fruit cup. Calum extends his hand toward me. I give him my snacks with a defeated sigh. He pops in AirPods and opens Spotify.

"You don't strike me as an animal person. Maybe a fish person," I say, still shocked.

He hands me his fruit cup. "I love dogs."

"Really? You've never so much as glanced at Ginger."

"I'm not ***supposed*** to look at her," he says before taking a bite of his granola bar. I look at her vest, which, next to a large red STOP sign, says in bold embroidered letters: NO TALK, NO TOUCH, NO EYE CONTACT. Fair enough.

I squint suspiciously.

"I'm not lying!" he insists with a hearty laugh. I'm not sure I've seen him laugh like this. It's a direct juxtaposition to his typical stoicism. I like this side of him. "I try to not get too attached anymore. At— —shelter, they'd get adopted or put down, and either way, I'd never see them again. You can't break— —heart like that, Natalie."

"Well, we could see each other after the tour."

He lifts an eyebrow, his silver piercing rising with it. "Oh?"

My eyes dart across the aisle as Felix heads for the bathroom. Lachlan tracks my line of sight, and a muscle in his jaw leaps.

When he looks back to me, his lips are set in a hard line. I frown. There's the short fuse Calum and Will mentioned.

"We'd see each other because of you and Lix?" he asks.

"What? No. You're from Seattle, too. I don't know, I thought we could run into each other. Or you could come by my Deaf Center," I explain. "Or we could stay friends. I understand if you're too busy, but it's been nice getting to know you."

His Adam's apple dips as he swallows, considering me before signing, *"That'd be great."* He pauses, wheels turning, before asking, "So . . . how are things between you two? You never said where you disappeared to— —his birthday."

I hesitate—just long enough for his brows to furrow, suspicion creeping onto his face. Lachlan's become someone I trust, but this is . . . complicated. Unlike Jo or Bhavani, Lachlan has stakes at play, personal and professional. It's safer and smarter to keep the whole truth about Felix's and my . . . whatever-ship to myself.

"We went to the rooftop to get some fresh air and watch the fireworks," I lie by omission. "Things are fine. We're friends now."

He doesn't respond right away, simply stares at me as if he's trying to read between the lines. After a long beat, he simply signs, *"Good."*

His gaze shifts away a second later, but not before I catch the flicker of something behind his expression. Something a little too quiet, a little too knowing. I can't shake the feeling that my answer wasn't as "good" as he wants me to believe.

DAYDREAM Wiki Member Profile

FULL NAME: Calum Niall Evans

AGE: 18

HEIGHT: 5'10" (177 cm)

HOMETOWN: Boston, Massachusetts, USA

CALUM FACTS:

- His hobbies include trying new foods, surfing, and watching baseball games
- His role models are Tina Weymouth and Calum Hood (whom he wants to collab with and said it would be "the sexy bassist named Calum crossover you never knew you needed")
- He moved to Seattle when he was nine but remains an avid Red Sox fan
- His life motto is "ABS" (Always Be Snacking)
- He once admitted in an interview he didn't realize olive oil came from actual olives and not a region in Italy called "Olive" until he was 16
- If he weren't in DAYDREAM, he said he'd be in the MLB

Chapter Eighteen

The Thirty-Second Rival

New Jersey, July 9 / New York City, July 10

A warm New Jersey breeze swirls around us as we stroll down a walkway surrounded by cherry trees. The atmosphere is similar to one of Felix and my late-night tutoring sessions. No expectations, no heavy-handed managers, no façade. Just normal, everyday people.

Except it's not like one of those nights—one of ***our*** nights—because Will is here. And Sunglasses, ready to fend off fans or paparazzi. But there's free time before the show for once, so Felix suggested we explore.

We wander for a few minutes, and the boys take selfies together, then Will snaps some of Felix on his camera. Ever photogenic, Felix's poses look effortlessly chic, elegant yet approachable. The pictures seem candid. It's witchcraft.

After Will's done, I ask, "How'd you get into photography?" At this point, Ginger probably knows more about him than I do.

"One of my moms is an— —and she takes a lot of photos, so she taught me."

I blink at him, unable to decipher what he said. "She's a what?"

"Ornithologist." I ***hear*** the word this time, but I don't

understand the word. He laughs when he sees how lost I am. "A glorified bird-watcher. But Mama does it for fun; my mom is the breadwinner. She's a cardiovascular surgeon," Will explains, using more big words that take way too many brain cells to lipread.

"Do you want me to take some pictures of you? Since you took Felix's?" I ask.

"Oh, sure. Thanks. Let me show you how to use it real quick."

Felix and Sunglasses follow us while Will shows me how to adjust the exposure, teaches me the rule of thirds, and poses. My photos aren't perfect, but I'm pretty proud of the results. Some look like DAYDREAM promotional pictures. A pretty, blue-haired, dark-skinned boy against a backdrop of early-morning sky.

After a while, Felix steps between the camera and Will.

Will turns to me and squints, wracking his brain, before clunkily signing: "*Taking photos . . .* done?" he asks verbally.

I flip both hands away from my body, fingers splayed. If only he had shown his inclination for learning different languages before that (rigged) game with Calum. He repeats the sign multiple times, committing it to memory. I give him a thumbs-up before he rushes over to Sunglasses, who's wearing his backpack for him, and pulls out a tennis ball. He motions toward Ginger.

I hold back a laugh at his love for my dog and bend down to take off her vest. She wiggles excitedly, knowing that means she's off-duty. Will grabs her leash, and they take off, but as he passes Felix, I notice Will give him a subtle, encouraging nod. Oh god.

Dread washes over me as I realize this outing was all a ploy. Felix interrupting and Will walking away on cue? This shit was orchestrated!

"Don't worry; I gave him Zyrtec earlier," Felix says, as if ***that's*** what I'm worried about right now. "*Can we talk?*"

I swallow my nerves. "OK."

"About the other night—"

Right then, my phone starts ringing, and I scramble to grab it. Jo's picture is on my screen, and I've never been more relieved to get a call from her.

"It's Jo." I show him the screen to prove I'm not merely trying to get out of this conversation (okay, well, I totally am, but he doesn't need to know that). He jogs over to Will and Sunglasses as I answer.

"*Hey!*" Her face is illuminated by the light on my end, but otherwise she's in complete darkness. "*Any news? Gossip? Seattle's too boring.*"

"*You called for gossip? Really?*"

"*My life needs excitement. I only teach and redesign the website. There's nothing fun!*"

"*Sorry. Nothing new.*"

She seems unconvinced. "*How are you two? What happened with the love song?*"

Instinctively, my eyes dart away from her and locate Felix. He and Will are halfway across the park. Will throws the slobber-coated ball, and Felix reluctantly holds Ginger's leash while she chases after it.

"*We . . . almost kissed.*"

"*WHEN!?*" she signs so intensely I wouldn't be surprised if she hurt her wrist.

"*The Fourth of July.*"

"*WHAT?!*"

"*Stop yelling!*"

Her movements calm down. "*Why didn't you tell me?*"

I glance at Felix, and the details of that night come flooding back. How his lips felt when they brushed mine, the comfort of being wrapped in his arms, his fake smile as I walked away.

Finally, I look at Jo and sign, *"Even if I wanted to date him—and I don't—I can't. It's not a smart decision. He doesn't understand my life. He's rich and famous. Maybe he only likes me because I'm convenient right now. He'd get bored of me after the tour."*

"Even if it's not a smart choice, you're eighteen. You're allowed some bad choices!" I frown at her, unconvinced. *"Have you tried telling him how you feel? Communication is important. Wow. I'm kind of the smartest sister now,"* Jo insists.

Sure, maybe everyone deserves a few bad choices. But would Felix be the most beautiful decision I've made or my biggest mistake?

Maybe he'd end up being both.

I can't take that risk.

☆ ☆ ☆

On the bus the next morning, while the boys go back to sleep, I make myself a cup of watery instant coffee and curl up on the couch. Ginger jumps up and nuzzles me. I run my fingers through her thick fur and sip my coffee.

Relishing the peace, I flip through the pages of my sketchbook, which are mostly filled with drawings of Ginger and a few portraits of Jo, though a few DAYDREAM sketches have made their way in. I turn to the page with the unfinished mural. I get lost in my art until Felix steps out from the sleeping quarters in a skintight tank top and gray sweatpants.

"G'mornin'," he says, voice thick with sleep. He sits beside me.

I silently pray he doesn't try to bring up whatever Jo interrupted yesterday, but thankfully, he turns his attention to Necktie's latest schedule.

The rising sun bathes him in rays of orange and pink; his tan skin glows golden, his dark eyes brighten. I force myself to look away before I get sucked into his orbit. Never have I met someone with such an intense gravitational pull.

Already having read the schedule, I know it's another non-concert day Necktie's jam-packed with events. Starting with a TIME interview right after we get to New York.

He mouths every word and traces each line with his finger. After two minutes of re-reading the same line, I gingerly tap his shoulder. "*Can I help?*" I ask. He blinks at me a few times, hesitancy washing over his features, before handing it over.

"*At 8:30 there's an interview with T-I-M-E magazine. At noon, you're filming a video for G-L-A-M-O-U-R.*" He intently watches my hands. Whenever I fingerspell, I go slowly and allow him to form each letter with his own hand as well, which seems to aid in his understanding.

After we finish going over the itinerary, he looks at me fondly. A strand of hair falls in his eyes, and I instinctively reach out and tuck it behind his ear. My cheeks burn as I jerk my hand away. ***What is wrong with me?***

His smile wanes, and he pulls his hair into a low bun at the nape of his neck. "Er . . . I reckon we could do some ASL practice before we get to New York," he says while he scoots to the next cushion over, away from me. "D'you wanna hear how Lachlan broke my wrist? It's how we met, actually."

"Uh, sure. Tell me."

I settle into the couch and marvel at how smooth his SimCom

is getting. "It was the very first day of freshman year and we were playing volleyball in P.E. Well, Lach crashed right into me trying to spike the ball. I heard my wrist snap before I felt it . . . it was brutal." He winces at the thought.

"Damn. That's a memorable introduction to high school."

He chuckles. "He was super apologetic, though. Basically declared himself my personal nurse—he'd open doors and take notes for me in class since I couldn't write with my cast."

"Aw, that's sweet." The mental image of their freshman hijinks makes me smile.

Felix nods. "That's how he is—once he cares about someone, he's always got their back. We've been best mates ever since."

When we finally arrive in New York, we're taken straight to their TIME interview. Even at 8:00 a.m., a sea of fans scream for the boys. It's astonishing how their fame keeps skyrocketing. The crowds only grow bigger everywhere they go, a living, breathing testament to the boys' stardom. I spot someone wearing a FUTURE MRS. EVANS T-shirt crying when they see Calum. (I mean, hey, if Peeta Mellark walked up to me right now, I'd probably shit my pants. So I guess I can understand.)

Inside, Felix is whisked into the Green Room. With everyone rushing to get the boys ready, there's no time for small talk, so I plant myself in an empty corner and send emails to disability activists and outreach programs to see how they recommend I start a program of my own.

Finally, after they film a "friendship test" video for GLAMOUR, the boys are given what Necktie considers a lunch break: scarfing food down in the car on the way to the second fan meet and greet of the tour, which is being held in a rented hotel ballroom.

On our way, Felix rests his head on Lachlan's shoulder and catnaps, and I stare out the window and take in New York City.

It's nothing like the glorious city found in movies and romanticized descriptions in YA novels. Litter lines the streets, the sidewalk is packed with people pushing past one another, and traffic is at a dead standstill, but everyone is honking like the sound will turn a red light green.

A massive, circular building across from where our car is stuck grabs my attention. Displayed on a huge screen above the entrance is the picture the boys used to announce their tour, but instead of names of cities with dates, it says: DAYDREAM LIVE AT MADISON SQUARE GARDEN: JULY 11–12!

My jaw drops as I read the last part: SOLD OUT!

Not even a year after their debut, they're performing two sold-out shows at Madison Square Garden. It's not surprising, but still an incredible feat.

When we arrive at the hotel, Ginger and I follow the band inside through the staff entrance, and Felix peers at me over his shoulder like we're sharing a secret. The last time we used a back door like this was in Nashville. Are we thinking about the same thing? My heart flutters against my will.

Roughly two hundred fans erupt into cheers as the boys enter the ballroom. The number seems insignificant now that I know they sold out a twenty-thousand-seat arena two times over. As they make their way to the front of the room, Mateo is glued to Felix's side; his green eyes nervously scan the room. Felix places a comforting hand on his shoulder and only removes it when the members sit on stools in front of a white backdrop.

Bhavani and I sit in the far back.

At the front, people start taking pictures with them. Fans stand on a duct tape X on the floor and smile as a staffer takes a photo, then they're given a short, thirty-second window to interact with the boys. Some get starstruck and go speechless, others pass around an album to collect signatures.

Felix graciously accepts but struggles to get his signature down. It must be an incredible amount of pressure because of his dysgraphia. But it seems like the boys are enjoying themselves.

Halfway through, a fan around our age chooses to spend thirty seconds talking to Felix. Whatever they say earns his full, undivided attention. He takes their hands and flashes a smile so genuine it's like the sun has risen just for them. He's looking at them like they're the only person in the room.

It's how he used to look at me.

Time's up, I think, glaring at the wall clock. But no matter how quickly the moment passes, the pang in my chest lingers, sharp and sour.

Chapter Nineteen

Riding a Bike (Except There Are Knives on Your Feet and You Also Aren't on a Bike)

New York City, July 10–11

"We filmed at boring-ass places— —DC. Let's do something fun!" Calum pleads. "Pizza by the slice!"

"The theme of the music video— —iconic locations. We can get pizza anywhere." Mateo sighs.

"Italian ice? Street-corner hot dogs?"

"Wow, yeah— —really sold me with ***street-corner*** hot dogs," Mateo grumbles.

A headache thwacks my skull in steady beats, like my brain is a bird repeatedly flying into a window. I massage my temples from a couch in the hotel lobby. The meet and greet ended forty minutes ago, and for thirty-six of those minutes, the boys have been bickering about music video ideas.

Felix occupies an armchair across from me. He mimes choking Calum, one eye forcibly twitching. I snort.

I tune back in to the argument as Lachlan says in his assertive Dad Friend voice, "One way or another, we need— —choose before Andrew picks for us." Necktie is pacing at the far end of the lobby while on the phone. How many calls does this guy make every day?

"I vote Statue of Liberty— —Empire State Building," Mateo says.

"Boooo!" Calum calls.

"I'm with Mateo," Will declares.

"BOO!"

"Er, sorry for worsening— —problem, but I'd like to go— —Rockefeller Center," Felix interjects. "The Empire State Building is just a big building. We have those back home."

"And— —Statue of Liberty?" Mateo raises a brow.

"I'm from New Zealand. It's not my liberty."

"If you use that excuse one more ti—" He's cut off by Lachlan elbowing him.

Before the group-wide argument resumes, I chime in with, "Why don't you split up? That way everyone can do what they want."

Everyone's eyes land on me, unblinking.

"Oh," Lachlan mumbles.

☆ ☆ ☆

When I step out of a yellow cab in Rockefeller Center, I do a full turn, taking it all in. "Now this," Felix says beside me, "is gonna be so much more fun."

"And we even have statues and buildings of our own," I mutter, jerking my head toward the huge gold statue looming gloriously above an ice rink nestled between high-rises. "So what's the plan?" I ask.

He puts his BURBERRY trench coat on over the white-and-pink RAISE BOYS AND GIRLS THE SAME WAY T-shirt he's wearing, and

I shoot him a bewildered look because it's eighty degrees out. "We're gonna ice-skate!" he explains gleefully.

I pointedly look at Ginger. "Pretty sure the ADA doesn't cover dogs on ice."

"Could— —watch her for a sec?" he asks Sunglasses. She hesitates before curtly nodding. "If that's alright with you, Nat."

I'm not thrilled about leaving my service dog with someone else, but I guess Sunglasses is a safe choice given her entire career is protecting people.

After working our way through the crowd, Felix pays for two tickets, and we're handed skates. As he goes to put his wallet back in his fanny pack, a blue Post-it note falls out and is whisked away by the breeze before he can grab it.

"I hope— —wasn't too important," he says to himself.

We make our way to a bench; people stare and point at him, some kids wave from inside the rink. He politely waves back. After lacing our skates, he turns to me. "*Can you help film?*" I bob an affirmative fist.

I reluctantly hand Sunglasses Ginger's leash, and Ginger gives me a confused look. I plant a kiss on her head before Sunglasses positions herself by the rink's entrance, scanning the crowd. She gives us a thumbs-up.

I make my way onto the ice. The cold rink is a welcome change from the oppressive summer heat. It's been years since I went ice-skating, but it comes back to me immediately. Skating was another tradition for Dad and me. We'd go every Christmas Eve, just us, ever since Jo broke her arm when she was seven and never went near a rink again. A bittersweet haze clouds the memory, and I force a breath of chilly air into my lungs, grounding myself in the present moment.

"What shots—" I start, but when I turn around, Felix isn't behind me. He's still on the bench. "*You OK?*" I sign.

He nods uncertainly. When he gets up, I skate farther back, then press Record. Unfortunately, my plan for a perfect video of him stepping into the rink is ruined the nanosecond his first skate touches the ice. His long leg slips far in front of him, forcing him into the splits, one leg on ice and the other still outside the rink.

The howling laugh that escapes me is uncontrollable. "It's not funny!" he exclaims, trying to hoist himself up.

"No, Felix, it's ***so*** funny. Sweet Jesus." I keep the camera on him as his face turns tomato red, but I skillfully pull out my phone and snap a few pictures for my archive.

When he finally manages to get both blades on the ice, he stays frozen in place, his knees bent and arms extended in front of him for balance. I skate backward to fit his whole body in the frame, still laughing.

"Stop filming me!"

"You ***asked*** me to film you!"

He shoots me a dirty look. I take pity on him and stop recording. "Do you not know how to ice-skate?" I ask, gliding over to him. He swallows thickly. I fight more laughter. "Then why did you want to come here?"

"I dunno!" he cries. The tips of his ears burn red. "I thought it'd be easy! Like riding a bike!"

"Oh, right, because skates and bikes are super

interchangeable." I tuck the GoPro under my arm and take one of his hands. "Come on, I'll help you."

He grips the edge for extra stability as we move forward at a snail's pace. From outside the rink, Sunglasses trails us, her gaze constantly flicking between us and the cluster of onlookers, some snapping pictures, others whispering behind their hands.

I force it out of my head and teach Felix how to distribute his weight and use the backs of the blade to slow down. But the longer we spend on the ice, the more goose bumps pebble across my skin. After ten minutes, I start shivering.

Felix carefully stops. While in his hilarious half-squat stability pose, he takes off his trench coat and holds it out to me. Normally, I wouldn't be caught dead in this fugly thing, but warmth is the more pressing matter currently, so he helps me slip it on.

"*You look cute*," he muses, then looks to the GoPro and nods. I press Record.

Felix glances at his feet every few seconds and grips the edge so tightly his knuckles whiten. The cherry on top is his uneasy expression, betraying how much he's not enjoying this.

"Look alive, man!" I call out, then snap my mouth shut when I realize how much like Necktie that sounded.

Felix one-handedly signs, "*Then give me something to smile about*." His movements are oddly smooth given the circumstances.

My mind draws a blank. Making people smile on command isn't exactly an area of my expertise. But, almost like a prophetic vision, I suddenly remember some of my dad's favorite (and god-awful) jokes.

I double-check the angle on the GoPro before asking, "Have you heard the joke about the deaf guy?"

Felix closes his pointer, middle finger, and thumb together, "*No.*"

"Neither has he."

He stares at me blankly, head cocked in confusion, before understanding dawns. The corners of his mouth curve upward, eyes twinkling in the sunlight. "*That was bad.*"

"I'm only getting started, Pretty Boy." I smirk. "How do you speak sign language?"

"*How?*"

"You don't."

A laugh finally escapes, his shoulders shake, and his eyes crinkle at the corners. The jokes may be bad, but they're doing the trick. He hasn't looked at his feet once, and his expression is all confidence and glee.

I slow down and skate beside him to get a different angle. As I get closer, his mood lifts further. "What happened to the deaf woman who didn't show up for her court case?" I ask.

"I dunno. *What?*"

"She lost her hearing."

That earns me another cheery laugh. I mirror his grin, holding his gaze. With his attention locked on mine, it's as if the hundreds of people around us blur into the background—like someone pressed Pause on everything except us.

Gradually, his DAYDREAM mask slips, leaving something real and unguarded. One of those looks I find myself chasing after, despite my better judgment. Coldness radiating from the ice can't combat the butterflies thundering their wings in my gut or the warm blush I feel spreading across my cheeks.

"Oh my god, Felix!" someone squeals. Jarringly, the world

around us resumes. "I'm— —biggest fan! Literally, like, if you died, I would, too. Life— —have no meaning," they continue. "Can I get a picture? Please?!" They smooth their gingham dress and tuck long auburn hair behind their ears.

"Er, nah, yeah," he stammers, a little dazed, as he and the fan step off the ice. I make my way to Sunglasses and reclaim Ginger.

I've barely grabbed her leash when the fan shoves their phone at me. They immediately cozy up to Felix—getting much closer than I'd expect a total stranger to get to someone, famous or not, but Felix keeps his hands firmly clasped in front of him.

By the time the fan leaves, a dozen others have lined up, clamoring for photos or shouting declarations of love. He graciously takes selfies and thanks people for their support, then he looks to Sunglasses for backup. She shoos people away as we take off our skates.

"I'm sorry. We should go back to the hotel."

"That's fine. But are you OK?" I ask, concerned. He forces a nod, worrying his lip. I don't believe him one bit, but now's not the time.

However, "going back to the hotel" is easier said than done, because after we return the skates, Felix is swarmed again. Sunglasses keeps people under control as he scrawls his signature on random receipts, arms, and phone cases.

I keep myself and Ginger out of the way but keep track of Felix as the crowd swells. I study him as he interacts with fans. It's as if someone flipped a switch, and the Felix that mere moments ago was making my heart tumble in my rib cage, the boy so brilliant and bewitching that it can be disorienting, has vanished.

Replaced with a sensationalized clone, his tone considerate even when asked invasive questions.

Someone not unfathomably different, but not the boy I've come to know.

☆ ☆ ☆

"Hiya," Felix breathes as I open my hotel room door at midnight. He brandishes a pastry box. "Are you too tired for doughnuts?"

"Never." I widen the door and let him in, surprised to see him here. When we got back, he said he was exhausted and asked to take a rain check on ASL. (Honestly, I was relieved. I felt like I could sleep for three days straight.)

Ginger wags her tail from where she's sitting by the door. He acknowledges her with a nod and crosses the room. As he sits cross-legged on my bed, his exhaustion is clear in the slump of his shoulders, but his face softens as he gestures to the fuzzy pink Felix-branded blanket he draped over me in LA.

"I didn't peg you for a thief," he says, a joking lilt in his voice despite the weariness.

"What? I'm not! I borrowed it. You can have it back!" I rush, mortified.

He chuckles. "Yeah, nah. Keep it. It's just not a décor choice I would expect from you."

"It got cold earlier," I defend.

Comfortable silence envelops the room. I lean against the large, cushy headboard, and he sets the pastries between us. I grab a jelly-filled doughnut, and Felix picks chocolate-frosted.

"Team Peeta or Team Gale?" He motions to my well-loved copy of MOCKINGJAY on the bedside table.

"You've read THE HUNGER GAMES?"

"You do know they were made into films, yeah?"

I roll my eyes, and he laughs. "Peeta. Gale is a war criminal."

He goes quiet.

"Please tell me you aren't Team Gale," I groan.

"Nah, yeah, I am," he admits. "I reckon it's his unrequited love thing—liking a girl who feels impossible to make yours. It's a meaningful kinda romance." His intense, unwavering eye contact doesn't match the calmness of his expression, like the two halves of his face don't belong to the same person. I squirm, feeling like a starstruck fan from earlier meeting him for the first time.

I ***could*** argue that Peeta had an unrequited crush on Katniss before Gale did but . . . it doesn't feel like the right moment.

"Um . . . so . . . why are you here?" I change the subject. "You said you were too tired for a lesson tonight."

"I wanted to see you," he replies.

"What? Why? We were together all day."

"Not really." He sighs. "You've been with DAYDREAM's Felix. Not . . . me."

My eyes slowly drag up and down, taking in his current state. Icy blond hair in a messy ponytail, strands poking out in all directions, his skin speckled with small stress acne spots and dark undereye circles.

It's a stark contrast to the Felix who was interviewed by TIME this morning, and greeted fans for hours at a meet and greet, and Rockefeller Center this afternoon.

"Why can't those two co-exist?" I muse.

"Because nobody would like the real me." He gulps and licks chocolate off his lips. "This"—he motions to his entire being—"is real. What the public sees is mostly fake. My clothes, my image, my songs are chosen for me. DAYDREAM fans wouldn't like Renegade Wizard's Felix, but that's the real me."

His lips tug downward, and his brows crease, a storm of emotions swirling in his eyes.

"People like the real you," I assure him. "You're smart, like a true poetic genius with some of the lyrics and ideas you come up with; you're kind and thoughtful, and you genuinely care about others; you're probably the most annoying person on earth, but with you, I laugh more than I have in years. People like you, Felix. ***I*** like you."

I thought I'd uncovered unknown layers and depth to the Felix I knew from a year ago. But now I'm realizing that I, like so many others, had preconceived notions from the beginning, didn't I? Has he ever been a self-absorbed Rich Boy who prioritized fame over family, or did my assumptions make it impossible for me to see the starry-eyed boy who's been in front of me all along?

I scoot closer to him. Before I can stop myself, I take his hand, and his fingers curl around mine. Our hands fit together like they were made to be intertwined. His thumb traces circles on my skin.

"You make me feel human, y'know? Around you, I don't have to act like someone I'm not. I can be 'Felix from Seattle' or your pain in the ass but also incredibly attractive student." He theatrically winks at me.

Annoying joke aside, I'm tempted to push the doughnut box out of the way and hug him, like in Philadelphia. I start to lean in, but he jerks his hand away from mine and scoots away.

"Sorry," he murmurs. "You're not here to be my friend or my therapist; you're here to teach me. I forgot." His eyes are duller, but he straightens his posture and cracks his knuckles. His mask is back on, a saccharine fake smile overthrowing any trace of vulnerability. "Did I tell you about how I accidentally almost joined a cult?"

I blink. I was the one who put up this boundary and pushed him away . . . So why is there a heavy feeling settling over me? Why does the space between us feel like a gut punch, like . . . regret?

I bite the inside of my cheek and snap myself out of it. "Um. No," I say, sitting back and watching him tell his story with a lump in my throat.

r/DAYDREAM 5 hr ago

daydreambeliever
HOMEWRECKER!!
I'm sick to my stomach watching the videos of Felix and his "tutor" skating! There's DEFINITELY something going on. They were holding hands. HOLDING! HANDS! Felix is OURS and no random girl can swoop in like this! 🤮

TOP COMMENTS:

averagefangirl007 3 hr ago
Stop acting like you own these men?? Tbh I hope they ARE dating so you'll finally realize they wouldn't touch crusty losers like you with a ten foot pole 🤡

≫ ≫ ≫

@FelixSongUpdates 3m ago
That poor woman could save orphans from a burning building, and some of you would still vilify her for being within five feet of Felix. Touch grass.

Chapter Twenty

American Sweethearts (+ a Kiwi)

New York City, July 13

"Andrew was really going to make you face this death trap alone?" Bhavani asks as they stop the doors on the ancient elevator from closing on Ginger and me.

"Are you surprised?" I snort.

The main elevator leading to the studio where the boys are filming an acoustic rendition of "Cloud 9" for VARIETY was packed to the brim, and Necktie stuck me in this one that looks like it hasn't been used since the Reagan era.

"Well, if this thing goes down, at least we're together."

"Comforting," I mutter, but the corner of my mouth lifts despite myself. Our ascent is agonizingly slow, and the intermittent metallic groans are sheer nightmare fuel.

Bhavani studies me with a mischievous gleam. "So . . . what's up with you and Felix?"

"It's strictly business."

They hike up one thick brow. "I don't look at my strictly business acquaintances like I want— —smash my lips into theirs, but okay, girl. You do you."

My face burns as I whip my head around. "Shhh!"

"Girl, it's just us, your dog, and— —busted walls in here." They laugh. "But seriously, it's obvious. You have it baaad." Jo and Ava would get along with Bhavani.

"I'm starting to see a different side of him. He's not what I expected. But me being in his world is convenient for him. If he were in mine . . . he'd hate it. My life isn't fun."

"Natalie, that boy would move literal mountains for you. Do you maaaybe think you're self-sabotaging?"

"What?! No!" I blurt. "I have important things going on. I can't get distracted."

"Hmm. Okay. As the founder of— —#Natalix fan club, I'm rooting for you. Be careful so he doesn't get in trouble with— —label, but you'll figure it out. Being star-crossed lovers never hurt anyone."

"I think Romeo and Juliet would disagree," I mumble. "Wait . . . what do you mean about the label?"

Bhavani drops their playful demeanor. "There's a strict morality clause in their contract. No drinking, no partying, no . . . scandals. Dating isn't ***technically*** banned, but— —definitely frowned upon."

I have a million follow-up questions, but my brain is having a power outage, so all I manage to stutter is: "W-why?"

"Marketing. Fans can't fantasize about being with them if they're in relationships. Plus, DAYDREAM's whole brand— —being innocent and pure. Dating scandals don't fit that." They shrug. "I mean, it's been— —decade, and fans of Taylor Swift and Harry Styles still claim they're 'children of divorce.'"

What?! I knew the label was controlling, but in what universe is stripping a bunch of teenagers of their basic rights okay? Morally or lawfully.

"That's ridiculous," I choke out.

"Welcome to the entertainment industry." Bhavani clucks. "Look, I don't know what happens if they cross the line, but— —heard the label's 'conversations' are . . . intense. So don't get caught."

The elevator doors open, jolting me out of my thoughts.

I marvel at the studio. It takes up the entire top floor of the building, with light pouring in through floor-to-ceiling windows. A baby-pink backdrop dominates one corner, surrounded by sleek photography equipment and a small, bustling crew.

This is what I want to do with the Deaf Center. Take a rundown building and turn it into something modern, beautiful, and useful. I snap a picture for Jo.

A middle-aged person donning a pixie cut that looks like a horrible re-creation of Alice Cullen's marches up to me. "Get out of my studio! Get that beast out of here immediately!" They shoot daggers at Ginger.

My initial shock transforms into anger. Nobody messes with my dog. I pointedly motion to her vest, specifically the ACCESS REQUIRED BY LAW patch.

"She's a very good girl," Lachlan interjects, narrowing his eyes. "If you kick her out, we'll leave, too."

They gasp and—I could not make this up—clutch a pearl necklace. "I ***will*** be reimbursed if that creature destroys anything."

"I'd pay for it myself," Lachlan promises. They stalk off, and he turns to me. *"You OK?"*

"Yes. Thank you."

He smiles, but it's gone as soon as it came as Necktie storms toward him.

"What the hell is wrong with you?! I'm not babysitting you for five seconds and— —you ungrateful little— —" Necktie scolds Lachlan at the speed of light, and I don't catch most of it.

"Andrew, Lach was trying to—" Felix starts.

"I don't want to hear it. Ugh!" Necktie anger-grunts. "We'll talk later. We're already behind schedule."

When DAYDREAM is dragged away to change their clothes, Necktie flashes me the harshest scowl physically possible. I steel myself to be told off, but instead he points to an empty, dusty corner of the studio and commands, "Stay."

For once, I listen. Ginger and I sit in the corner, safe from the commotion. I try to focus on paying the Center's bills (I can't trust Mom to do it), but my mind keeps wandering.

After my conversations with Felix and Bhavani, I can't stop thinking about how much the label controls DAYDREAM. They've created this perfect, untouchable image while keeping their personal lives under wraps. It's hard not to wonder how much Felix is still truly ***himself*** under all those rules, especially now that it's growing increasingly harder to ignore how I feel about him.

I'm pulled from my thoughts when Felix walks toward the stools and mic stands. As usual, he's front and center. Mateo and Lachlan are to his left, Calum and Will on the right.

The director hands out acoustic guitars to Will, Calum, and Lachlan. "I'm a bassist," Calum says with a frown, handing it back. The others laugh, and I smile, being in on the joke.

After the cameras roll, the crew moves agilely around them, adjusting angles, while raw vocals fill the air. The pressure to be perfect must be crushing, knowing every minor detail will be scrutinized—from their pitch to their smiles to their group chemistry.

(Verse 3 - Mateo) Keep on floating, hold on tight
Living in a dream tonight

(Chorus - Felix, Will) We're so high in the sky
With you, baby, I can touch cloud 9, oh my!

After several more takes, I pull out my sketch pad. Before I've consciously decided what to draw, my freshly sharpened pencil drags along the paper. Soon, the outline of a body, then a face, appears. Four more follow it.

My focus flits between the paper and DAYDREAM as I sketch, instinctively capturing their positions. My art consumes me, and the world falls away while I shade Calum's dark brown curls and curve Will's lopsided smile.

As I draw, I can't help but think Felix was right—they're manufactured. Products.

Compared to the boys I know—who sneak out of hotels and sneeze into my dog's fur—they're practically strangers.

What kind of life is that?

I'm fully immersed until Felix sits beside me with a goofy grin. He pops a throat lozenge into his mouth. "That's sick!" he exclaims, peering at my drawing. "You're incredible. Not just the art, you."

His words linger between us, and I try to play it off by lowering a hand from my chin while avoiding eye contact. Theoretically, that should be easy since I lipread . . . But his eyes demand attention. I'm like a moth drawn to a flame, if the flame was inky black and ruthlessly, breathtakingly shiny. "Is filming done?"

"Not quite." He points to a fidgety Mateo, who's alone in

front of the backdrop. *"They're filming . . . C-U-T . . . A-W-A . . . Y shots."*

Felix is so close that the back of his hand occasionally brushes mine, and I'm plagued by the thought of grabbing it, weaving my fingers through his and savoring how our hands fit together—oh no. No! ***Damn it!***

I jerk my arm away when I realize my pinkie got adventurous and wrapped itself around his. From across the room, Lachlan watches us and works his jaw. When he notices me looking at him, he averts his gaze. I frown but shake it off and glance at Felix.

His posture is as stiff as when I tucked hair behind his ear or tried to hug him. He gathers his hands in his lap but stays beside me.

I debate whether I should say something. An apology? An "Oops! How did ***that*** happen? So random, omg!"? But I don't reach a conclusion before a phone starts blaring.

Ginger instantly perks up and nudges my leg with her nose—except it's not ***my*** phone ringing. Felix's ears burn red as he fumbles with his device. She's been trained to only alert to the specific ringtone I use to avoid situations like this, but apparently Felix uses the same obscure ringtone, so Ginger thinks it's for me. Seriously. What are the chances?

I huff a quiet laugh and scratch behind her ears. "False alarm."

All eyes on him, he shouts, "So sorry!" I catch a glimpse of the screen before he answers the incoming call: It's a selfie of him and Mrs. Song, with the contact name "Mumma." That's kind of cute; I can't lie.

I watch his rapidly fluctuating reactions as he whispers into the phone. He starts off with one of those annoyingly contagious smiles, then a frown, then he cringes. The interpretive dance on his face continues until he hangs up.

His thumbs dart across the screen, his forehead creased. By the time he's done typing, cameramen are getting close-ups of Lachlan.

"You OK?"

"Er . . . well . . ." Felix cringes again. "My parents'— —anniversary— —and I— —" He speaks inaudibly. Since lipreading isn't a perfect science, I don't quite understand him.

Noting my confusion, he holds up his index finger. *"One sec."* He types a message in his Notes app.

My parents 20th anniversery party is tmrw & I forgot. Obviosly I shouldn't have forgot bc I cleared this with Andrew months ago but its been a mess lately. I think the note I lost at rockfeller centre was about buying our tickets, so I did that now. Your coming too

I look up from his rambling and see his face flooded with guilt and stress. "Hey, it's okay. It'll all work out."

His expression softens. "I'll forward you— —tickets."

After the email shows up in my inbox, I glance at the details and sigh. Tickets from JFK to SeaTac, departing early tomorrow morning and returning to Boston Logan late that same night. Another travel day from hell, but at least we'll be in first class.

Forgoing further explanation, he stands and dusts off his white skinny jeans. *"My turn,"* he signs, jerking his head toward the director with the vampire haircut. "I hope you like hors d'oeuvres." He winks.

Chapter Twenty-One

First World Problems and Real-World Feelings

Seattle, July 14 / Boston, July 15

I do ***not*** like hors d'oeuvres.

"Why would you ruin a potato with fish eggs?" I ask Felix, my nose crinkled in disgust as I struggle to chew at the Songs' bougie anniversary party.

"Because it's fancy."

While caterers set up a spread, we check for poison by sampling each dish. So far nothing's been dangerous, but I do think caviar should be considered toxic.

He watches with amusement as I scrape the caviar onto my napkin. "D'you want me to tell you how much that costs or would you combust?"

I stare at the tiny, salty orbs. I'm probably holding close to a hundred dollars' worth of unborn fish in my palm, aren't I?

His focus jumps to the staircase before I can answer. His expression shifts from being entertained by my unsophisticated palate to pure joy as Ava barrels downstairs. He hands his fancy-people food to Sunglasses and rushes to his sister. I hurriedly feed my fish eggs to Ginger.

Ava laughs as he picks her up and spins in a circle.

"How ya goin', Aves?" he uses SimCom after putting her down. He runs fingers through her sleek black hair. *"Has summer break been fun?"* he signs perfectly.

She beams and wraps her arms around him for a second hug.

Mrs. and Mr. Song walk downstairs, arm in arm. Mr. Song remains neutral until his eyes fall on Felix, where a hardness sets in. Mrs. Song is just shy of euphoric as she watches her children catch up, her effervescence a direct contradiction to her husband's cool detachment.

The picture I'd painted for nearly two years of a loving, functional family feels shattered since Felix opened up—now, the cracks are clear as I see how closed off Mr. Song is around his son. I wonder if I had previously ignored the tension because I just didn't ***want*** to notice . . .

When Mrs. Song spots me, she hugs me tightly, and I allow myself to enjoy the fleeting moment of maternal warmth, closing my eyes and returning her kind embrace before she steps back. *"I didn't know you'd be coming! It's wonderful to see you."*

I freeze. Did Felix invite me without asking? *"I don't mean to intrude—"*

"No, no. You're always welcome. You're part of the family. I would have invited J-O, had F-E-L-I-X told me. I'm sure you miss her."

"Yes, but I'll see her soon." What I don't add is: I'm not sure Jo has the elegance or tact that the function requires. Besides, she's teaching three ASL classes tonight. We wouldn't have been able to see each other anyway.

"I see. You look beautiful, by the way!"

I shift uncomfortably. I don't own anything formal, and I stubbornly refused to let Felix buy me a dress when he offered, so my only option was a simple black romper. I thought it'd work, but now, seeing Felix's perfectly tailored suit and Mrs. Song's sapphire-blue evening gown, I realize how badly I miscalculated.

"You too." I force a smile. *"Happy anniversary!"*

She lowers a hand from her chin and walks toward Felix and encases him in her own hug. He instantly relaxes into her arms. Mama's boy.

Ava approaches me as their mom chatters to Felix in a blend of Korean, Kiwi-infused English, and ASL. It's pretty impressive.

"Thank you for teaching him. His ASL is so much better! He knows slang, too!" she gushes.

"You helped! You taught him KissFist." I wink.

She peers over her shoulder, and after confirming Felix is distracted, she turns back to me. *"I want to give him a sign name!"* She waggles her brows conspiratorially. *"What about this?"* She forms the letter "*F*" and pulls it away from the corner of her mouth with a flourish. *"Like the sign for 'singer' but with the letter 'F'?"*

I stifle a laugh and close my fingers into a no. Unbeknownst to Ava, signing "singer" with an F-shaped hand looks like "marijuana." I'm equal parts surprised and glad Jo hasn't taught her that.

"You want something music related?" I ask. She nods. After thinking, I present a one-handed version of the sign for "song" but alter my handshape to be an "*F*." It's a perfect homage to Felix's career ***and*** name. *"Do you like it?"*

She bounces excitedly, repeatedly signing KissFist. Her enthusiasm is contagious. She rushes over to where Mrs. Song is doting on Felix while Mr. Song watches from across the room with a glacial frown. Ava interrupts by tugging Felix's sleeve.

"Whoa, you look excited!" He laughs.

"I'm giving you a sign name! Natalie helped me come up with it." She glances at me, and Felix follows her line of sight.

"True biz?" he asks, face full of wonder.

"True biz," I reply, then motion to Ava, not wanting to steal her thunder.

Felix kneels like he's about to be knighted, and Ava shows him the sign name we came up with. He smiles wider than I've ever seen from him, which is an impressive feat for a guy who basically treats smiling as a full-time job. *"That sign means M-U-S . . . I-C or S . . . O-N-G, right?"* he checks the origin of the modified sign. Ava confirms. *"Thank you! KissFist!"*

His eyes flicker to me, and he lowers another flat hand from his chin.

Before too long, the house is flooded with Seattle socialites, and the Songs are busy tending to guests. It's like Felix's nineteenth birthday party, except instead of tacky Party City decorations and Will's vodka-infused Kool-Aid from hell, there's an ice sculpture and champagne with gold flakes in it.

I find the quietest corner I can and people-watch. Unfortunately, nearly every corner is filled with Hearing people chattering about yachts and the stock market.

While Ginger and I wander, several people mistake me for a server and ask for refills. I wonder what gives me away as an outsider. Is it my Ross Dress for Less romper or do I just have a lower-class aura?

We end up stationed by the kitchenette—a tiny kitchen attached to the main one. Because everyone needs a kitchen inside a kitchen. Obviously.

It's a little less overwhelming here. But my attention is soon caught by Felix and Mr. Song having a tense conversation near the stairwell.

Felix's posture is stick straight, muscles rigid. He stares at the floor while Mr. Song speaks. His dad's hands move around in angered jolts that definitely aren't ASL, and his face is twisted into a critical grimace.

Eventually, Felix reaches a breaking point and snaps back. He wildly gestures to the partygoers then points to himself, a vein in his neck bulging. Mr. Song scoffs and grabs his son's shoulder, but Felix storms away. Toward me.

I step forward to meet him and take his hand, worried. "Are you oka—"

"I wanna introduce— —some people," he interrupts. His brows are tugged in a frown, and I can feel his pulse racing through his wrist, but he doesn't acknowledge the argument as he leads me through the sea of guests.

As we enter the backyard, he snags a champagne flute from a server and downs half of it in one gulp. Lingering July heat sticks to my skin as we walk to the far end of the patio. We stop in front of two middle-aged guests. "Dr. and Mrs. Williams?" Felix says.

A white woman in a classy gray pantsuit with a blunt, strawberry blonde bob eyes me distrustfully, and a Black woman offers a familiar, lopsided smile. She wears a burnt orange cocktail dress, and a bird-patterned scarf keeps bouncy black coils in place atop her head.

"Felix!" The second woman hugs him. "How are you, dear?"

"I'm alright, thank you, Mrs. Williams," Felix says. His body relaxes, irritation fading. "This is Nat. My ASL tutor." He motions to me, and I wave. "Nat, these are Will's mums."

Suddenly, the bird scarf makes more sense.

Mrs. Williams hugs me, and Dr. Williams gives me a no-nonsense handshake.

"Nice to meet you!" I greet. "So why'd you name your son 'Will Williams'?" I ask, straight-faced.

Shocked, Felix sprays the champagne he was sipping. Luckily, he avoids hitting Dr. Williams by turning his head.

Ah. Right. ***These are Hearing people, Natalie. Don't be so blunt.***

"I mean, it's cool! Definitely unique!" I chuckle awkwardly.

Mrs. Williams laughs heartily. "His first name is Seymour," she explains. "But he decided that wasn't cool in middle school."

I take a second to formulate a response, since my first instinct is to question the name Seymour as well. "Oh. Nice. Is there, uh, a story behind that?"

I social bluff by occasionally nodding as Mrs. Williams yammers on about Dr. Williams' great-grandpa Seymour. I don't catch most of it, but I'm pretty sure he was a WWII pilot. Or something.

After that, she focuses on Felix. I politely exit the conversation as auditory fatigue starts to squeeze my brain. On my way inside, I bump into Ava, who also looks overwhelmed. Fleeting eye contact is all we need to know we're experiencing the same thing. I'm not happy she can relate to this very specific kind of exhaustion, but there's something comforting about the solidarity.

She takes my hand and guides Ginger and me upstairs. I've never seen this part of the Songs' house before, but it's on brand. Chic art hangs on the walls, a Turkish rug runs the length of the hall, and on the landing there's a leather armchair and bookshelves filled with classics. Austen, Park Wan-suh, Tolkien.

"*Are you and Felix dating?*" Ava springs the question on me.

She dons the same knowing smirk both Jo and Bhavani have shot me.

"No!" I rush. "*We're friends. Kinda. Maybe. He's . . . nice.*"

"OK," she signs, unconvinced. "*But whatever you're doing right now . . . don't stop. I haven't seen him this happy in a long time.*" His body language during that heated moment with Mr. Song flashes in my mind.

"*I'm going to the bathroom,*" she tells me. "*That room's quiet.*" She points to a door at the other end of the hall before disappearing.

Inside, I'm met with a cozy space. Lavender walls covered in music posters—Queen, Paramore, Conan Gray; a queen-size bed with a sage-green comforter is pushed into one corner; and the opposite corner displays three guitars, a microphone, and an electronic keyboard.

Wait . . . is this ***Felix's bedroom***?

Cautiously, I edge further inside and close the door, which exposes a mirror covered in Post-it notes. Most are nearly illegible, like he scribbled them down before the thoughts slipped away.

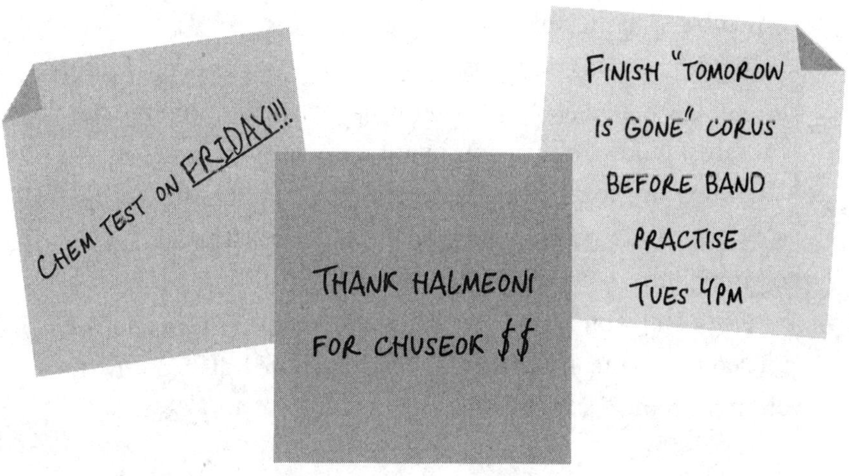

And then there are ASL notes with obvious thought put into them:

TIME + TOPIC + COMMENT = SINTAX

FINGERSPELING: SLOW DOWN, FOCUS ON CLARITY, NOT SPEED!

GOOD + MORNING + YOU + SLEEP + HOW?

Guilt churns in my stomach. These are from high school Felix. A boy whose sincerity I'd doubted and accused of making excuses. Yet here, stuck to his mirror like a badge of effort, was proof of how much he'd tried—and how unfair I've been.

I run my fingers over them, a knot in my chest. This version of Felix—one who struggled but still cared so deeply—feels closer to me now than the polished pop star.

I'm torn from my thoughts when the door swings open. I turn, expecting to find Ava, but instead Felix face-plants onto his bed. He grabs a pillow and screams into it.

Unsure how to react, I wait for him to sit up, but he remains face down like a corpse. "Are you okay?" When I speak, he sits bolt upright.

"Jesus, Nat! You scared me." His panic morphs into a chuckle as he considers me. He pats the spot next to him. I sit. "So why are you in my room?" He eyes me.

"Why are you screaming into your pillow?"

"Touché." He takes a second to collect his thoughts before ranting. "Mum keeps introducing me— —friends who want signatures for their kids. I know— —should be grateful she's proud of me but . . . I wanted to relax tonight, and instead I have to— —DAYDREAM mode. *Again*," he signs with a sigh.

"And my dad . . ." He pauses. "All night he's been saying— —embarrassing to tell his colleagues I'm a singer. He pulled strings— —got me a spot at South Korea's most prestigious university so I can 'do something meaningful someday,'" he vents, absentmindedly trying to fix his lavender necktie. "Like selling out arenas and being personally invited— —Donatella Versace and— —cover of VOGUE, TIME, and ROLLING STONE doesn't mean anything. Like being his ***son*** doesn't automatically imply I fucking mean something to him."

He scrubs hands over his face. "I'm sorry. Those are first world problems."

"Don't apologize," I urge. "You've given your all, you've been working so hard, and maybe sometimes it feels like too much but not enough all at once. And it seems like you're tired."

Defeatedly, his shoulders slump. "I reckon you're right."

When silence stretches, I reach over and gently remove his hands from the tie that's progressively looking worse. I fix it and tuck it back into his sleek black suit jacket.

His lips ever-so-slightly part, and his focus lazily drifts to my mouth. A dangerous warmth spreads through my body, and I'm suddenly keenly aware of how close we are—how ***alone*** in his ***bedroom*** we are.

No! Nooope.

"Will's moms are nice!" I blurt in a panic.

Very subtle, Natalie. Good lord.

He tears his eyes away from my lips. "Er, nah, yeah. They're sweet as. They were the first people I told when I figured out I was pan. Thought a couple of lesbians were the right place to start."

Warranted given his dad's reaction . . . It's not the same as coming out, of course, but when it comes to my desire to branch out, to bridge the gap between the Hearing and Deaf worlds, Dad always got it. He ***encouraged*** me. Mom has never supported my endeavors. She'd much prefer to stay in a bubble, where it's safe and familiar.

But remaining comfortable won't change the world. Risk-takers and rule breakers will change the world.

"Hey, Nat?" Felix draws me out of my thoughts. His thumb circles the back of my hand—wait, what?

Oh god. I did it again. Our hands are tangled together, fingers woven like thread.

Conflicting emotions stir as if Mom and Dad are sitting on my shoulders, bickering like a cartoon angel and devil. The utilitarian logic I inherited from her versus Dad's all-consuming emotions.

"Felix . . . ?" I murmur.

I hope he'll continue from there. That he'll do something that solidifies my friendzone choice.

He shifts, and for a fleeting moment, I think he'll pull me closer. Instead, he takes his phone out of his pocket and checks the time.

"We gotta go," he announces. "Can't miss our flight."

He heads for the hall but stops in the doorway. A heaviness

settles over him as his gaze sweeps over his childhood bedroom. He takes one last long look, his expression distant, as if trying to hold on to something he knows he can't keep.

I was naïve to think the universe would make this easy.

No. This is a choice I have to make for myself. A choice I ***already*** made.

But clearly, I didn't factor in my brain pulling me in one direction and my heart in the other.

After our flight touches down, Felix's mouth tips into a tired smile. "Cal's right. You snore," he teases softly.

I lightheartedly smack his shoulder as he pulls his hood over his head and puts on a mask, a small effort to fly under the radar, and offers me one. I do the same.

Sunglasses grabs his GUCCI duffel bag and my backpack from the overhead and we disembark. I brace myself for the horde of fans I've come to expect, but the only signs of human life in the airport are employees and some people waiting for red-eye flights.

We pile into an Uber, and Felix opens Instagram. I don't know how he's casually doomscrolling when it's—I peer at his phone—3:12 a.m. My whole body feels weighed down, and I struggle to stay awake.

"C'mere," he says, looking up. He scoots closer to me and pats his shoulder. "Rest."

Maybe clearheaded, didn't-take-two-flights-and-attend-a-party-in-one-day Natalie would decline the invitation, citing the friend-zone, but currently, I'm so tired I'm actually dizzy.

I rest my cheek on his shoulder. He sets his phone aside and cards fingers of his free hand through my hair. The action lulls me back to sleep.

When he wakes me up, we're at the hotel. He's usually careful to maintain distance while we're outside, but tonight he wraps an arm around my waist and supports me as I stumble into the lobby, half asleep. I prop myself against the front desk. Felix rings the little bell until a desk clerk finally appears.

"Two rooms under Song and Nielsen," he says.

A bit of typing, then, "You're in room 701, Mr. Song. Andrew Moore checked in for you, but I need to see your ID."

Felix roots around in his fanny pack. The endless stream of items—an unopened pack of glitter gel pens, a backstage pass from Madison Square Garden, and a mini tangerine—would be funny if it weren't yet another thing keeping me from sleep. He hands the desk clerk his Washington State driver's license when he tracks it down.

The desk clerk hands Felix a key card. "Miss Nielsen . . ." Their brows furrow. "I'm sorry, your reservation was given away. When— —didn't check in— —assumed you were a no-show."

The news perks me up. "What? Can I rebook?" If I'm not upstairs and in bed in the next fifteen minutes, I'll pass out in the middle of this ornate lobby.

"I'm sorry. We're full."

"Hey, Nat, it's alright," Felix soothes. He squeezes my shoulder. "You can sleep in my room."

"No," I mumble. "Boundaries."

He tilts his head. "What'd you say?"

"*Never mind!*" I sign with a burst of sleep-deprived frustration. I snatch the key card from Felix and head for the elevator.

Room 701 is right beside the elevators on the seventh floor. I unlock the door, swing it open, flick on the light, and . . . freeze.

Felix stands behind Ginger and me, bags in hand. "What's wrong?"

I crane my neck to look at him and dramatically gesture to the room. "There's only one bed."

"Oh, c'mon, Nat. There's plenty of room. We won't even touch. Unless you feel like having a cuddle," he teases with a mischievous smirk.

I unstick my feet from the invisible superglue in the doorway and enter. Ginger falls asleep on the floor after I take off her vest.

Felix's eyes twinkle playfully as I build a wall of pillows in the middle of the bed. "Stay on your own side, Pretty Boy," I grumble.

"Alrighty," he chirps. "But you do realize you already cuddled me during the flight—"

"Go to sleep!" I bite, and flop onto my side of the barrier.

"You're gonna sleep in your travel clothes?" He pulls a disgusted face. "Yuck." He tugs his sweatshirt over his head. "Fair warning, I'm gonna change my pants now." I close my eyes at the speed of light. After a moment, he says, "All clear."

I open my eyes right before he turns off the light, and to my horror, I find that he didn't put on another shirt. The bed shifts as he crawls in, and I tense up. Felix is shirtless. In the same bed as me. Inches away.

Suddenly, I'm wide awake as we lie here with only a half-assed pillow barrier separating us. There's no way I can ask him to put on a shirt, right? Right. Because that would mean explaining ***why*** it bothers me, and I'd rather have a toddler perform brain surgery on me than admit to Felix that his shirtlessness makes me ***feel things***.

After god knows how long, I roll to the very edge of the bed, as far away from him as I can get. I'm seconds away from falling asleep when he murmurs, almost too soft to hear, "G'night, Nat."

"Goodnight, Felix."

DAYDREAM Wiki Member Profile

FULL NAME: Seymour Hasaan Williams

AGE: 19

HEIGHT: 5'10" (177 cm)

HOMETOWN: Mercer Island, Washington, USA

WILL FACTS:

- His hobbies include watching nature documentaries, hiking, sudoku, solving Rubik's Cubes, and working out
- His role models are Jimi Hendrix, Hozier, and Jungkook
- His #1 bucket list item is going on a photography trip to the Galápagos
- He's allergic to all pet dander and has two goldfish, named Mermaid Man and Barnacle Boy
- If he weren't in DAYDREAM, he said he'd be a photographer and was accepted to several prestigious photography programs, but pursued music instead

Chapter Twenty-Two

Knock It Out of the Ballpark

Boston, July 15

Sunlight streams in through thin curtains, basking the room in a bright morning glow.

I flip over in an attempt to block the light and snuggle closer to the pillow I'm wrapped around, enjoying the warmth radiating off it. I bury my face deeper and breathe in its leathery scent as it snakes an arm around me.

My critical thinking skills are clouded by sleep deprivation, but it doesn't take a rocket scientist to figure out a pillow doesn't have arms. Or smell like TOM FORD cologne.

Shit.

My eyes shoot open, and I confirm my worst fear. My body is tangled up with Felix's. One of his toned arms is draped over the curve of my waist, and my head rests on the other.

I carefully unravel the knot of limbs we're tied in and slide out of his embrace. Holding up the arm that was laid across me, I reach for a pillow to act as a stand-in for my body, but he's using the only one on the bed. The others are strewn across the floor. Ginger has claimed two and is peacefully snoozing on them.

I bunch up the comforter to create a somewhat Natalie-shaped lump. Felix instantly pulls it closer and snuggles up. The small, sleepy curve of his lips; his thumb reflexively stroking the material as if it were my skin; and messy, platinum hair splayed on his pillow cause my heart rate to speed up.

I lean over and run fingers through his bed head. I wish I could excuse it as another instance of my hand moving of its own volition, but I'm fully aware of what I'm doing.

From a distance, Felix's hair looks healthy and sleek, but it's actually straw-like and full of split ends. When I withdraw, a sizable clump dislodges. My nose crinkles in disbelief.

"It's the bleach."

I startle when he speaks. He does a catlike stretch and yawns. "It's quite damaging. Especially since my roots have to be rebleached every month." His words are thick with sleep, and his deep, gravelly voice sends sensation rushing through my body. My mind wanders to many places, and none of them are the friendzone. Not even friendzone-adjacent.

I bite the inside of my cheek to ground myself. "Mm, right. That sucks," I choke out.

The look he flashes is somewhere between flirtatious and amused. I start to wonder if he's thinking the same things I am but force myself to stop. That's a dangerous question.

"I should go," I croak.

He wets his lips, which is decidedly unhelpful. "Alrighty. See ya."

I awkwardly set his strands of hair on the sheet, clamber out of bed, and haphazardly stuff my feet into my shoes like one of Cinderella's ugly stepsisters. I grab my backpack, put Ginger's leash on, then beeline for the door.

To my horror, when I open it, I'm greeted by the sight of

DAYDREAM's manager and the other band members. Necktie's in the middle, his fist raised like he's about to knock. Behind him, Will's and Mateo's eyes bug out, slack-jawed; Calum laughs; and Lachlan's forehead puckers in a tight frown, his lips thinned into a hard line.

Shit! I slam the door shut and flip the dead bolt, heart thundering.

"Your manager's here!" I whisper-yell to Felix.

He jumps out of bed, mirroring Will's and Mateo's flabbergasted expressions. "Bugger," he mutters. He pulls on a pink DAYDREAM-branded hoodie and walks over; his ears and cheeks burn red. "Deep breaths. I'll fix this."

I anxiously pet Ginger's head as he slides past me and opens the door.

Fire burns in Necktie's eyes. "What the hell is this?! You little— —" His speech quiets to an enraged murmur. He takes a step forward, but Felix shields me.

"It's not what it looks like—" Felix starts.

"You're out of here!" Necktie bites, pointing an accusatory finger at me.

"Her reservation was given away when ***someone*** didn't check in for her," Felix says, firmer this time.

"Don't you dare blame me for this!" Necktie scoffs. "It's not my job to handle your groupie. This is unacceptable! I want her gone!"

"What was she supposed to do? Sleep in the lobby?" Will chimes in.

Felix makes a cutting motion by his neck, urging Will to save himself. "Nat didn't do anything wrong," he says.

Steam practically comes out of Necktie's ears. He ***knows*** he's in the wrong. He shoots his signature daggers at me. "I'm watching you closer than a damn sniper, girlie. If ***anything*** like this happens again, you're on the next flight home."

"I am *so* back, baby!" Calum whoops as the band, staffers, and I are led outside one of Fenway Park's concourses, toward a sprawling baseball field. He squeezes his eyes shut, inhales dramatically, and exclaims on the exhale, "Smells like home!"

The other boys laugh as he runs ahead and onto the field, where he does a slow turn, drinking in his home stadium. He's in a navy blue Red Sox jersey, his shaggy dark brown curls tucked under a white baseball cap with a stylized, embroidered "B" on the front. Some of the people starting to filter in cheer for him from the stands.

I've never seen him this pumped, with energy practically radiating off him. The only moment that comes close was when he was headbanging in The Apache Café.

His unbridled joy is brought to a screeching halt when Necktie barks, "Get back here! We need shots of all of you walking on-field."

When he begrudgingly returns, three crews set up centerfield. DAYDREAM's tour photographer and someone filming on a GoPro for the music video, the Red Sox PR team, and a local news station. More reporters are staged on the sidelines.

Someone comes out from the concourse and greets the boys with a firm handshake. They're in a charcoal suit, their gray hair thinning. "I'm— —club PR manager. It's wonderful— —meet you!" They hand each member a custom white jersey with their last names printed on the back in bold red letters, then turn to

Calum. "We're honored you're throwing— —first pitch today." They give him another jersey, but this one is covered in signatures.

He's like a kid on Christmas morning. "No, ***I'm*** honored!" he says, clutching the jersey protectively.

Necktie signals for the boys to go onto the field, so they slip the jerseys over their heads and Bhavani tidies their hair.

"Can you hang on to this for me? *Please?*" Calum asks, signing the last word. He hands me his autographed jersey.

As DAYDREAM walks onto the field, photographers and the camera crews get pictures and videos from all angles.

The crowd has nearly doubled in a few short minutes, and the stadium roars to life as the boys wave, their blown-up selves displayed on the Jumbotron. I see signs in the stands that remind me of their concert—CALUM > A GRAND SLAM and BOSTON ♡'S DAYDREAM!—and folks wearing DAYDREAM merch. I wonder how many people are here because of them versus to watch the game.

The boys film their own clips for the music video on GoPros before the players join them centerfield and take pictures. The whole time Calum is grinning so widely his face might start cramping. He's really in his element.

My phone buzzes in my pocket.

Mon, July 15, 1:09 PM

[Pretty Boy 🙃]

U can head to our seats! We're gonna be down here for a bit w all the interveiws & national anthem

When I look up, Felix is smiling at me while they're being interviewed by a news station. I give him a thumbs-up, and a stadium employee guides me to our seats, which are in one of the private suites.

It reminds me of a Green Room, with its leather armchairs, beverage station, and TV broadcasting a live feed of the field. The walls are also literally green. Ginger lies on the carpet, and I take off her pink doggy headsets since it's much quieter here. I leave her and go sit on one of the barstools in an open-air part of the room.

From here, I have the perfect view of the boys down below, the swarms of people in the stands, and a huge green wall across the field with a manual scoreboard.

I grab some water and take my own pictures—mostly selfies to send to Jo—but tune back in when the loudspeaker goes off. "Please welcome— —DREAM— —performing— —national anthem!"

The applause is nearly as thunderous as one of their shows, which is impressive given it's an open-air stadium and half the crowd isn't even cheering and seems confused by the uproar. I wonder if Ginger will need her headsets after all, but she's twitching while she dreams.

The Jumbotron displays the boys in front of American flags waving in the breeze, and they have in-ear devices and hold microphones. "The Star-Spangled Banner" instrumental plays. I crank the volume on the in-suite monitor and turn on captions as Will starts the song off. When it's Felix's turn, he's given a solo shot on the screen. His long hair flows in the wind, his pearly teeth visible as he sings.

"Whose bright stripes and . . . bright . . . stars through the treachero—er, perilous fight."

I'm almost too distracted by how good he looks (and how funny seeing him against a backdrop of America's flag is) to notice he's flubbed the lyrics.

Rattled by his blunder, he incoherently mumbles in tune as he scrambles for the next few words. I instinctively sing the lyrics, trying to help him, but obviously it doesn't do anything.

Disaster strikes when he freezes and completely stops, but the music keeps going. His mouth is ajar, his eyes wide, with the microphone still primed in the air. I can see panic flooding his face and a humiliated blush coloring his cheeks. I reel with secondhand embarrassment.

He's saved, though, when another voice rings out. Picking up on the next line flawlessly, as if no lines were skipped, and during the ***hardest part***, for that matter. "The rockets' red glare"—pyrotechnics send streams of fire shooting up near the boys—"the bombs bursting in air"—fireworks explode.

The camera is switched to Lachlan. Even through the in-suite monitor, his voice sounds powerful and smooth. He truly is a brilliant singer.

Calum and Mateo successfully finish the performance. The crowd goes wild. You'd never know part of the minute-long piece wasn't even sung.

They wave to the audience then head off-field. On the sidelines, Lachlan gives Felix a consolatory hug. When Felix pulls back, he stares at the ground, his body language betraying his mortification. Will and Mateo give encouragements of their own, while Calum pats his shoulder.

Necktie speed walks over to them, anger evident even from up here. But what else is new? I don't get a good look at the interaction before the group disappears into the building. Assuming they're on the way to the suite, I go to the beverage station and pour hot water into a cup, then rifle through the tea assortment before selecting decaf throat comfort.

By the time it's steeped, four of the boys and Necktie enter the suite. Felix still has a pink blush on his face and the tips of his ears, but he's recovered his composure. I offer a supportive smile and hand him the tea.

Necktie plops into one of the armchairs and starts aggressively typing on his phone—though, pretty much everything he does is aggressive. He could be writing a love note for all I know.

Felix seems relieved he's distracted as he, Will, and Mateo settle onto the barstool seats while Lachlan makes his own cup of tea, his aura practically euphoric.

"Where's Cal?" I ask, approaching the barstool next to Felix.

"He's throwing the first pitch," Lachlan answers as he sets his tea on the stool I was about to take. He pulls out the one next to it and motions for me to sit. After I do, he pushes it in for me and sits beside Felix, putting himself between us.

Felix watches the whole thing with a puzzled frown, before it turns into something more appreciative. He knocks his shoulder into Lachlan's. "Thanks for saving me."

He grins. It's almost identical to the glee I saw when sitting with him and Calum on the flight from Toronto. "I'm sorry that happened, but also . . . I ***did*** crush it."

Felix laughs. I can't really blame Lachlan for being giddy about the mistake. I imagine it was satisfying to get his moment in the spotlight.

"All of you were amazing," I add.

We turn our attention to the field as Calum stands on a dirt mound in the middle of the diamond, a glove on one hand and a ball in the other. The Jumbotron displays the determination and concentration on his face. He winds up, standing on one leg, and throws the ball. It soars through the air in a nearly perfectly straight trajectory, and a Red Sox player squatting behind home plate easily catches it.

More applause erupts, but his bandmates cheer the loudest. They give him a standing ovation, whooping and catcalling. I laugh and do jazz hands.

Some of the slowest hours of my life pass during the game. Calum is completely enamored and continually explains rules to us or judges the umpire's decisions, but after the first twenty minutes, we all tune him out.

"You're not allowed— —complain about how 'boring' historical sites are anymore," Mateo grumbles to Calum.

Will swallows a bite of hot dog and adds, "This is taking years off my life."

I lean forward and peer at Felix. He's zoned out, staring at the water bottle in front of him, but underneath the table, his fingers move quickly, repeating the fingerspelling alphabet with both hands. Warmth spreads through me, delighted by the absent-minded practice.

Sitting back up, I glance at Lachlan's phone. He's been scrolling through social media for a while, and I don't mean to snoop, but I can't help noticing how his previous thrill fades as he flicks among apps.

His brows knit as he reads a long caption on a picture of the boys mid–national anthem, then moves to the comments. I can't see what they say, but his scowl worsens by the second, and every hint of elation is erased.

He reads several more posts, on multiple platforms, before shutting off his phone and standing up. He pushes his barstool in, and it hits the table with a clang. The other boys' attention snaps to him, but they don't pay him any mind as he stalks out of the suite. I guess they're used to it.

When he doesn't return after a few minutes, I go check on him.

I spot him standing by the red railing on our level. He works his jaw, hands tucked into the pockets of his jeans, as he blankly stares at the concourse below us.

"Hey. What's wrong?" I ask.

He doesn't acknowledge me for a long, tense beat. "The entire internet is talking about how shitty it was for me to 'steal' Felix's parts. Would it have been better if I'd let him flounder?" He scoffs. "I'm a villain for trying to help."

"I'm sorry," I say. "But we know the real you, and Felix knows your intentions. That's what matters, right?"

"No." His sharp gaze bores into me. "Because all people know about me is what— —label's released, which is nothing, because management doesn't like me. Everything else— —public opinion. But they're no better. I don't even know why I try anymore."

Sometimes simply ranting can help, so I don't reply, leaving space for him to vent.

"Did you know there was— —online poll asking who would care— —I wasn't in DAYDREAM? And— —majority— —wouldn't. ***Fifty thousand*** people said they wouldn't care if I left."

He scrubs hands over his face, then continues, "Maybe it makes me— —pompous asshole or self-absorbed, but I want to be recognized. I want to be cheered for. I don't even care if— —don't like me as much as the others, but I want— —at least care that I exist."

"You don't deserve to be treated like that," I finally speak. "How can I help?"

Lachlan turns toward me with darkened eyes. "You could tell me what's really going on between you and Felix."

I recoil, taken aback by the shift. "What?"

"You sure seemed like more than 'friends' this morning."

"***Nothing*** happened," I enunciate. Disbelief is painted on his features. Annoyance rises in me.

"Look, if you really want to help me, maybe . . . maybe you should keep your distance from him. He's my best friend, and I'd never— —but you don't know him like I do. I don't want— —get hurt, okay? I care about you . . . and Felix," he adds almost as an afterthought.

A muscle in my jaw leaps, and frustration pulses through me. Lachlan would never be an ***afterthought*** to Felix. And he'd never go behind his back to issue vague warnings like the Oracle of Delphi.

"You don't get to decide who I spend time with. And you definitely don't get to take shit out on me. I want to be a supportive friend, but I will ***not*** be your punching bag," I snap.

When I bite back, the irritation washes off his face. *"You're right. I'm sorry."* He gulps. "I'm just trying to look out for you."

I study his face but don't find any sign of deceptiveness or disingenuity. "*OK*." I'm still riled up from the sudden accusations, but I take his apology at face value. For now.

@Dreamer02752 58m ago
can yall finally admit that lachlans trying to capitalize off the other members talent?? like its painfully obvious how jealous of felix he is and stealing his spotlight today is concrete proof

> **@glitterfrog99** 52m ago
> FINALLY someone else who sees his bullshit! he has the *worst* vibes and he's such an attention whore!

⪢ ⪢ ⪢

@DaydreamOT4 33m ago
Lachlan's such a princess ohmygod he seriously can't let ANY-ONE have their own moment? ATP he's basically emotionally abusing them!! Poor babies 😭 😭 **#SaveFelix #DaydreamOT4 #LachlanIsCancelled**

⪢ ⪢ ⪢

r/DAYDREAM 27 min ago

> **daydreambeliever**
> LACHLAN IS A BULLY!
> I have a nagging feeling Lachlan is bullying the other members but especially Felix. During past TikTok and IG livestreams he's side eyed the boys or cracked "inside

jokes" they laugh at probably because they're scared of him. In some of their behind-the-scenes vlogs he's really quiet and broody. I genuinely worry for the boys' safety. IDK he just screams "narcissist"

Chapter Twenty-Three

The Hazards of Canoeing

Boston, July 16

Finally, the day I've been waiting for—my first visit to Camp SunSign, my godmother's D/deaf camp outside Boston. The front door of the main cabin swings open as Ginger and I approach, and my dad's best friend, Ellen, jogs toward us.

Her silvering hair is in a messy ponytail. She's in her late fifties, but moves with youthful energy and hauls me into a hug. Her hands are weathered and strong from years of work, but gentle.

"*How are you? How's your sister and mom?*" she asks after pulling back.

"*We're good. Mom's . . . fine. How are you? This camp is KissFist!*" Excitement spills out of me.

Ellen's face lights up. Her wrinkled fingers dart around as she tells me about her mission to enrich D/deaf youth. There's a vibrancy to her, a wisdom that comes from embracing the world as it changes around her. I deeply admire the way she's built a life that embraces both tradition and progress. I want to be Ellen when I grow up.

We walk around the cabin and into a large field; the grass is swaying in the breeze, and the sun is burning off the morning mist. Groups of children are scattered around with camp counselors.

Younger kids make DIY kites and jewelry; older ones weave baskets and construct birdhouses; and teens are learning canoe safety by the lake. The whole scene is a patchwork of enjoyment, busy hands, and learning.

I wish Camp SunSign existed when I was little. I would've loved spending my summers here.

"Ellen! Did you grab string?" An early-twenty-something counselor with a black faux-hawk and goatee asks from where they're helping adorable little kids make bracelets.

"I forgot! I'll go get it. Natalie, please help him." She nudges me toward him.

I put Ginger in a down-stay on the grass and sit with him. *"I'm D-A-V-I-D,"* he signs with a smile. *"My sign name:"* He taps a *"D"* over his heart like a name tag.

"I'm N-A-T-A-L-I-E. Natalie." I show him my sign name.

A Black kid wearing glasses with thick lenses that magnify their eyes approaches me. *"Help!"* the kid pulls a thumbs-up toward themselves, modifying the sign to be one-handed. Their other tiny hand clutches three mangled pieces of twine. I start carefully untangling.

"Is your dog nice?" The kid eyes Ginger, who's watching a ladybug crawl around on blades of grass in front of her nose.

"Very nice," I answer. *"She's my service dog."*

"I know, I know!" they sign with a huge amount of sass. It reminds me of Jo. *"I can read!"* They point to Ginger's vest. The questions about her set off a chain reaction, and the other campers start bombarding me, which is adorable but makes it hard to untangle. I can only do so many things with my hands at once.

I spend the next hour doing arts and crafts, including a personal favorite: gluing googly eyes on rocks.

The thing I've missed most about Seattle is my Deaf community. It's a whole world of shared experiences and pride—where you find the kind of understanding that only comes from folks who have walked similar paths. It's the comfort of a vibrant visual language and a sanctuary where your identity is celebrated, not questioned. It's history, resilience, and belonging all wrapped into one.

And while spending time with these kids, that sense of community and pride is stronger than ever. Some have hearing aids, a handful with cochlear implants, most have no hearing devices, but they're united through their Deaf identity.

This is the change I want to make in the world. This is what Dad, Jo, and I dreamed of.

"I'll be right back," I tell David. I leave Ginger in a down-stay near the blanket. I doubt anyone will run off with her.

I stop near the back of the main cabin, launch the Facebook app, and track down Camp SunSign's page. I share the page with Jo: Dad's friend Ellen runs this camp. I think we can do a day camp like this at the Center!

I'm about to power off my phone, but my eyes land on Mom's name right underneath my message string with Jo. The longer I stare at her name, the more pent-up frustration releases in me. All three of us could've been brainstorming ideas or asking Ellen questions. She could ***try***.

With a messy mixture of bitterness and baseless optimism that she'll actually try to see my perspective, I send Camp SunSign's page to Mom, too: I hope you'll look at this. This is what we're trying to do.

I anxiously stare at my phone for a whole minute until the Seen notification appears underneath the message. When the three typing dots pop up, I chew my bottom lip and hold my breath, but after a few seconds, the dots disappear and don't return.

The dejection washing over me doesn't have a chance to fully sink in before a hand flaps in my peripheral vision and I'm torn away from my unanswered olive branch. Expecting to find David or Ellen, I tuck my phone into my pocket and look up.

"*Sorry, I was texting my sist—*" My hands freeze in midair.

"Hiya," Felix greets.

He's in a yellow button-up shirt French-tucked into white board shorts; his hair blows in the gentle summer breeze and makes him look like a walking, talking L'ORÉAL commercial.

He resembles a literal ray of sunshine. It's horrifying.

"Nat?" He waves his hand in my face with a glittery, if not slightly puzzled, grin. "What's wrong?"

"Uh, nothing," I fib. I hardly want to talk about my mommy issues right now. I look for the other band members, but they aren't here. "What happened to Mateo's US history tour of Boston? And filming the music video?"

"I got a video in front of 'the Redcoats are coming!' guy's house and called it a day. Don't tell Mateo, but I agree with Cal—US history is boring as hell. You fight a war in the name of 'freedom,' claim you've won it even if you didn't, wait a few years, then rinse and repeat."

I laugh. "Okay, but how did you find the camp?"

"There's this magical thing called a GPS, and it tells you how to get places." I stare at him, unamused. "I Googled it," he explains. "There aren't many Deaf summer camps near Boston. Wild, I know."

"Why are you so sarcastic today?" I ask while we walk toward the kids. Felix trots beside me in a Ginger-like way, overflowing with energy.

"I accidentally had caffeinated green tea this morning," he says. "I warned ya it makes me hyper."

Remind me to never let him consume caffeine again. It's like his ADHD is on steroids.

When we reach the crafts area, most of the campers are running around the field and playing with their kites while David cleans up. His focus jumps to us as we stop in front of the blanket.

"*Who are you?*" He sizes up Felix.

Felix flashes a charming grin and salutes. "*I'm F . . . E . . . L . . .*" His ears turn red, and he looks at me helplessly.

"*He's my ASL student. F-E-L-I-X. Felix,*" I fingerspell his name, and then demonstrate his sign name. I go slowly for Felix's benefit but don't use SimCom. Today will be a good test of his comprehension.

"*Nice to meet you,*" David signs. "*Follow me.*" He stands and beckons Felix.

I tidy the crafting materials in his absence. While respooling twine, my focus drifts to the small dock where the teens take turns canoeing around the lake. Felix is standing on the outskirts of the group, watching their rapid signing with a slack-jawed frown.

I'm tempted to rescue him—this does feel like throwing him to the wolves—when a red-haired tween approaches him. It's hard to see what they're signing, but the kid goes slowly. I'm not sure if it's because they're still learning themselves or they recognize Felix is a beginner.

Pride swells in me at how well Felix communicates. I'm like a mom watching her baby take their first steps—wobbly and awkward, but a huge accomplishment nonetheless.

I look away when David returns. "*How long have you been dating?*" he asks. He motions toward Felix, who's getting geared up to go canoeing with the tween.

"*We're friends,*" I clarify.

"*True biz?*" David lifts a skeptical brow. "*You're cute together.*"

A blush spreads across my cheeks as I wrack my brain for a response.

"*Go help over there.*" He points to a counselor setting up a new activity table.

I make my way over; Ginger lazily walks beside me. The counselor and I set out thick charcoal wedges and paper, then we let the kids go wild. We compliment various stick figures and Picasso-reminiscent self-portraits.

After ten minutes, the counselor points to the art supplies and urges, "*Go ahead!*"

I guess my slight jealousy of the campers showed. Seeing them do charcoal sketches made me itchy to try. An artist can only stay away from art for so long.

I stare at the blank page in front of me for a long time, trying to figure out what to draw. Inspiration strikes when I see Felix and the tween rowing around the lake.

With each stroke of the paddle, Felix's biceps bulge. Though he hasn't mastered canoeing, he exudes confidence and continually peers over his shoulder to check on his partner.

I roughly sketch him in the tiny canoe with his wild hair flowing in the breeze. The charcoal is harder than I thought to control, and the drawing gets progressively messier, but it adds a certain charm.

I glance up to check the trees surrounding Camp SunSign in time to see their canoe capsize and the pair spill into the water.

My stomach clenches, panic flooding my veins. Before I even register it, my legs propel me forward, sprinting toward the lake. Am I yelling Felix's name? I can't tell—my pulse roars in my ears, my heart pounding in a drumbeat of terror.

The redheaded tween's head pops out from the murky water, and they swim toward shore with help from their life vest. Two worried counselors rush toward the edge and wait with towels and a first aid kit.

I'm seconds away from diving into the lake to drag Felix out myself when he bursts to the surface with a huge splash. My body relaxes when I realize he's not in danger, but relief quickly turns to frustration as he howls with laughter.

Here I was thinking he had drowned, and the first thing he does is ***laugh***?!

He darts through the water and catches up to the doggy-paddling tween in no time. They grab onto Felix's shoulder and are towed to shore.

The counselors fuss over them, and Felix signs "*not hurt*" over and over until they leave him alone. I storm toward him with a scowl.

"Why d'you look so upset?" he asks with a chuckle. His clothes are dripping water onto the ground, and wet hair sticks to his face and neck. It's all very sewer rat chic.

"Because I thought you . . . well . . . ugh! I don't know! I was worried, okay?"

"I was on a water polo team back in New Zealand. I'm alright. See, not even a scratch." He runs his hands over his arms.

I slow my breathing and calm my heart rate. He's okay. Everyone is okay.

"But y'know, if you're really ***that*** worried, I wouldn't be opposed to mouth-to-mouth," he teases with a smirk.

I smack his shoulder and roll my eyes. "You are the biggest pain in my ass, Felix Song."

"But, like, in a sexy way, yeah?"

Chapter Twenty-Four

Under the Spotlight

Detroit, July 19–20

"How was the concert?" I ask after the Detroit show.

Felix's eyes sparkle mischievously as he pulls a blue Post-it note out of his pocket. I instinctively dodge when he tries to stick it to my forehead, but he adheres it to my cheek instead.

☆ ☆ ☆

I only mildly panic as Felix ties a blindfold on me. Not being able to see anything is freaking me out more than I expected.

"Is it too tight?" His tone is laced with concern. I automatically turn my head toward the sound of his voice. It takes me a second to realize I can't lipread right now and have to depend on my unreliable hearing.

"No, it's fine—AAH!" I yelp when the Uber brakes abruptly. Felix's large, strong hand grips right above my knee. I snatch it.

Never mind. I am ***definitely*** panicking.

"I hate this!" I squeak out.

"You can take it off; it's alright," he soothes.

"No . . . I think I'm okay now," I murmur, tightening my grip on his hand. "I agreed to the blindfold."

"Yeah, but that doesn't mean you have to continue agreeing. That's kinda how consent works, Nat."

"I'm fine," I decide. "But . . . don't let go, okay?"

He squeezes my hand in lieu of a response.

When the car parks, Felix guides me out, slinks one arm around my waist, and carefully leads me into a building. A heavy door clangs behind us, and we walk up a set of stairs.

It's unnerving to be blindfolded and led to some mystery location in the dead of night, but something about how Felix's hand rests on my hip and my body is tucked against his is calming.

We go through another set of doors, walk straight, and go up a few more steps. Where ***are*** we?

My question is answered when he releases me and unties my blindfold. I blink a few times while adjusting to having sight again.

We're standing in the center of a stage; a bright spotlight shines down on us. On the ground on either side of the T-shaped stage that extends into a cavernous room there are small bits of confetti and DAYDREAM concert ticket stubs.

I do a slow turn to take it in but freeze when I notice a checkered blanket spread behind us. There's a picnic basket; a fancy charcuterie board with cheeses, meats, and crackers; an ice bucket with sparkling apple juice; and in the center, a vase of flowers. Small, battery-powered candles surround the onstage picnic.

"Surprise!" he announces. The sound echoes, ricocheting off the walls of what I now recognize as the arena where DAYDREAM performed. Then he tracks my line of sight to the candles and cringes. "Oh, er . . . I asked Bhavani for help setting this up and mentioned candles, as in, like, birthday candles . . . But I guess they misunderstood."

I snort. I highly doubt Bhavani misunderstood.

He sits and motions across from him, and I join him. He starts pouring sparkling juice into champagne flutes. "*Happy birthday!* Your birthday is tomorrow—er, technically today, yeah?"

My stomach drops. I never told him that. I didn't ***want*** to tell him.

"H-how did you know?"

"Aves told me. Jo mentioned it at their last lesson, and I wanted to do something special, like you did on my birthday. I'm sorry if I overstepped," he apologizes.

I stare out at the vast emptiness of the theater and bite my lip, willing myself not to cry. It doesn't work, though, because Felix sets aside the drinks, his focus shifting between my misty eyes and wobbly chin.

"You didn't." I take a deep breath. "But . . . well, I haven't really celebrated since . . ."

"Your dad," he finishes my sentence. "Your guys' doughnut tradition, yeah?"

"Yeah," I say on an exhale. "I'm sorry. I'm ruining your surprise."

"Don't apologize. You're not ruining anything." His hand finds mine. "What can I do to help?"

Nothing, I think. Because in these moments, when old wounds are split open and grief flows like fresh blood, the only thing that can help is the one thing I can't have: my dad.

Finally, a tear slips down my cheek, and Felix wraps both arms around me, encasing me in warmth and comfort, and it all comes spilling out.

He rocks me and rakes fingers through my hair as I cry. His calm breathing and the pressure of his embrace ease the heartache threatening to consume me.

When I pull away, the fabric of his hoodie is wet with a mixture of tears and snot.

He grabs a few napkins and hands them to me. I dry my eyes, loudly blow my nose, and awkwardly clean his hoodie. Not my sexiest moment.

The impromptu emotional breakdown was pretty cathartic, though. I've spent so long running away from my grief, instead of letting myself feel it, I never realized how healing it can be to cry. Maybe the good and the bad can co-exist.

"Can we press the reset button?" I ask. "I'd like to try this again."

Felix hops to his feet. He walks backward down the steps leading to the stage, then immediately walks back up. He looks out into the darkness, spreads his arms to either side, and calls out, "Surprise! Blame the candles on Bhavani."

I burst into laughter when I realize he's ***literally*** replaying the grand introduction he did.

When he sits down again, he hands me a flute of sparkling juice and quirks his head. "What's so funny?" he asks, pretending he doesn't recall cradling me while I cried.

"Nothing." I smile. "I appreciate you."

He raises his glass. "To fresh starts, friendship, and your nineteenth year being the best one yet!" I clink my glass against his and take a sip of the now-lukewarm juice. As we drink, demolish the charcuterie board, and share childhood stories, the theater fills with laughter.

While he yammers about his kindergarten boyfriend, he grabs a loaf of gluten-free bread, I Can't Believe It's Not Butter!, and a jar of round sprinkles from the basket. "Y'know, we never technically broke up . . . So does that count as my longest relationship?" he asks while covering a slice of buttered bread in sprinkles. He hands it to me.

Too preoccupied by the sprinkle-butter-bread, I don't answer his question. I hesitantly take it and crinkle my nose.

"It's fairy bread," he explains. "A New Zealand birthday tradition."

"I'm sorry, ***what***?! You can't have cupcakes or something?"

"Oh, don't whinge. Try it!"

Every time I think I've gotten used to his Kiwiness, he somehow baffles me.

I take a small bite. I can't say it'll become a new staple, but it's better than I thought.

Our conversation slowly becomes one-sided as Felix drones on about Kiwi traditions and . . . okay, I honestly have no idea what he's talking about. I'm not paying attention to his words. My focus is on the boy himself.

His crispy, overbleached hair is pulled into a half-up bun, and his chin bears a faint trace of patchy stubble; dark circles adorn his undereye area, and stress acne is lightly scattered around his cheeks.

He's onstage, quite literally under the spotlight, but he isn't acting. The charismatic, perfect lead singer isn't here; this boy isn't the star who fakes smiles on the red carpet and always worries about his image.

There's no glitz and glam, no smoke screen, no douchey manager with a terrible quiff yelling at him.

There's only Felix.

Felix whose heart is ten times the size of his bank account. Felix who holds me while I cry. Felix who buys Ginger dog food and me gluten-free snacks. Felix who cheats at card games. Felix who listens and learns and tries to do better. Felix who has an entire solar system in his inky eyes.

Felix from Seattle.

". . . Mum still won't tell me, though, so it—Nat?" Felix waves his hand in front of my face, and I snap back to reality. He quirks a brow. "You alright?"

The realization that I've been continuously misjudging him crashes into me like a wave, leaving my mind reeling, and all I can do is stare. A long moment of unwavering, hypnotic eye contact passes between us. My heart races, my breath catching in my lungs.

I try to organize my thoughts, but the longer I focus on Felix, the more jumbled they become. After a few more minutes, my brain fully stops computing and I inelegantly blurt, "You like me, right?"

Flabbergasted, he sprays the juice he was drinking ***all over me***. I recoil, liquid dripping down my face.

"What the hell!"

"I'm so sorry!" he rushes, shoving a handful of napkins toward me. "It's not like I was expecting you to ask that! Er . . . and why are you asking that, exactly?"

"Remember when I said we have to keep things professional and friendzoned you?" I sigh and dab my face dry. "Um. Well, funny story! I really like you, and I tried gaslighting myself into ***not*** liking you, but it's only made me like you more. Because you're lovely. And thoughtful, and a million other things, so unless I'm full of myself and super presumptuous, I think you like me in a more-than-a-strictly-business way, too, but—"

"Nat," he interrupts with a breathy laugh. "Jesus Christ, I like you in ***such*** an unprofessional way. Like, a 'someone get HR involved' way. I've never, not even once, liked you in a business way."

"W-why? I mean, I've sort of been an asshole to you."

"Yeah, you miiight wanna work on that—ow!" He winces when I slap his shoulder. "Kidding! You laugh with—and sometimes at—me, you accommodate me, and you make me wanna be a better person. You're wicked smart, and you've shown me new sides of myself and the world. I can trust you with anything. You're gonna change the world, Nat." He pauses, then, with a signature smirk, adds, "And you're really hot, too. But that's mostly a bonus."

"Felix . . ." I breathe.

Slowly, his lips tip into a half smile. "Nat?"

I open my mouth, but no words come. I can't drown out the part of me that wants to abandon all logic, ignore all the risks, and kiss Felix Song.

I just really, really, ***really*** want to kiss Felix Song.

So I do.

He flinches as I press my lips against his, and it briefly sparks doubt in me, but he snakes an arm around my waist and hauls me closer.

When our mouths reconnect, the kiss deepens with an urgency that steals my breath. His lips are soft but insistent as his tongue sweeps against mine, sending a shiver down my spine. I tangle my hands in his hair, and he responds with a low, guttural sound that sets my nerve endings alight. His hands slip lower, fingers brushing against the curve of my waist, and my skin tingles wherever he touches.

Eventually, he breaks away. He lays me back carefully, a hand behind my head to protect it from the hard stage. His weight presses against me, and I gasp softly. Heat pools low in my gut when his lips graze my neck.

His mouth is hot against my skin as he leaves a trail of open-mouthed kisses down to my collarbone. Each one is unhurried yet hungry, his lips and tongue tracing paths that make me ache.

Every minute our lips are connected, I'm reminded of how I could've had this all along if I hadn't been so goddamn stubborn. Not only the making out (however, that is a ***fantastic*** addition) but him. ***Us.***

These sparks could've been flying since his birthday. Maybe even longer. But I chose to keep denying my developing feelings. I believed the convoluted conclusions my silly meatloaf brain jumped to, and I forced myself to ignore what my heart was telling me.

I slip my free hand under his hoodie and run my fingers along his knobby spine and relish the way his back subtly arches into my touch.

He eventually pulls away, places a featherlight kiss on my cheek, and draws me into a sitting position; our heavy breathing syncs up, and I imagine our flushed faces and tousled hair match, too.

Felix tenderly tucks hair behind my ear. "You've had an, er, emotional night. I wanna make sure you aren't rushing this because there's a lot on your mind," he murmurs, using messy SimCom.

A deep ache still flows through me, but I consider his point and nod. My heart rate slowly returns to normal, my mind less clouded now that the heat of the moment has passed.

"It's late," he says. "How about we talk about this, us, later? That way we can approach it more . . . articulately."

The thought of talking about us—and the fact that there ***is*** an "us" now—freaks me out enough that I want to start drafting a list of talking points, but I take a deep breath and force the logical side of myself to shut up. I shouldn't be freaked out by the existence of us. This is a good thing. ***We're*** a good thing.

"Sure," I agree.

After we pack up the picnic, he stands, tidies his hair, and pulls me to my feet. He heads for the staircase leading offstage, but I stop him. "Felix?"

He turns, bottomless eyes shining under the spotlight.

I push onto my tiptoes and sling my arms around his neck. For the second time tonight, I press my lips to his. Unlike the first kiss, this one is slower, methodical, and drags on until my toes grow tired of supporting my weight.

"Thank you for everything," I whisper against his lips, too quietly for myself to hear.

Chapter Twenty-Five

The Little Things

Detroit, July 20

It's almost 4:00 a.m. when we get back to the hotel, and though I'm exhausted, I toss and turn, my thoughts running a million miles an hour. The picnic, the fairy bread, how Felix kissed me like it was his last day on earth.

I manage to fall asleep around 7:00 a.m., but soon after, Ginger starts bugging me, and I resign myself to sleep deprivation. Besides, hotel breakfast ends at 9:00 and it's 8:42. Going hungry on top of a sleepless night would be a bad combination.

After I run her outside, we head to the buffet. As the elevator doors slide closed, Jo video calls.

"*Happy birthday!*" She's in our neighborhood's park. Behind her, the sky remains dusky with hints of nighttime.

"*Thanks! But why are you in a park?*"

"*I jog now.*"

Home must be incredibly boring without me if she's started exercising. For fun.

"*Wait . . .*" I frown when I notice she's in the hand-me-down Seahawks shirt I got from Dad. "*Stop stealing my clothes, you parasite!*"

"You're not using them! Besides, I wouldn't be caught dead in most of your crusty dusty clothes. You don't have much to worry about." I stick my tongue out at her. *"Anyway, how are you? How's Felix?"* She waggles her brows.

I hesitate, fingers suspended in midair.

"*WHAT HAPPENED?!*" she signs with every ounce of energy left after her jog. *"TELL ME!"*

"We kissed," I admit.

Her euphoria skyrockets. She flails around like a limp spaghetti noodle. She tries to sign, but her fingers move so erratically that it's the ASL equivalent of a keyboard smash. The elevator doors open, and I walk toward the buffet.

"*WHEN?*" she finally manages.

"Last night. He surprised me with a picnic. It was worst-romantic."

"A-V-A *owes me twenty bucks.*" She smirks. *"I guessed you'd kiss before August. She thought it'd be later."*

I roll my eyes playfully. Leave it to them to place bets on our relationship.

"This is so exciting! So you like him? Was the kiss good?!" she continues.

I bite my bottom lip. Thinking about it transports me back to the stage, with his hands exploring my body, lips connected to mine. Kissing him felt warm and perfect and ***right***.

"KissFist," I admit with a buzz of nerves.

Jo's elation for me is written all over her face. *"Kiss him more! And have a fun birthday. Love you!"*

I don't have an opportunity to ask if Mom's mentioned anything about my Camp SunSign message, or how things are going with the Center, before she hangs up. My attention is caught by

Mateo motioning me over to where he sits with the boys at the far back of the dining area. The surrounding tables are occupied by bodyguards and staff.

I grab some food and head over. Mateo grabs a chair from another table as I approach. I put Ginger in a down-stay and sit.

"*Happy favorite!*" Mateo signs, beaming. I chuckle, assuming he meant "birthday," and supply the correct sign, which is similar. He repeats, "*Happy birthday!*" He pulls out a small envelope from his denim jacket and hands it to me.

I take the world's quickest glimpse at Felix, attempting to act casual, and he looks at me at that exact moment. We exchange a knowing look. A fresh jolt of electricity surges through me as his dark eyes are fixed on mine.

I feel my cheeks warming, then briefly meet Lachlan's gaze. His face is set in a glacial frown as his eyes flit from Felix to me. I force it out of my head and look back to the envelope. I open it and pull out a gift card to Charlie's Queer Books, a Seattle bookstore. "Thanks, Mateo." I smile.

"It's from all of us, but no problem. Are you tagging along for the concert tonight?" he asks.

"Probably not," Lachlan cuts in using SimCom. I flash him a puzzled look. "I figured you wouldn't want to spend your birthday stuck in a Green Room. Right?" His tone is just shy of honeyed, and there's a similar intensity to him as there was in Fenway Park.

I study him carefully but get frustrated when I can't get a read on him. The thing that bothers me most (besides his weird hot-and-cold thing) is sometimes I can't quite put my finger on what his intentions are.

His body language and tone are a melting pot of conflicting information, and I don't know how to begin sorting through it.

"You alright, mate?" Felix knocks his shoulder into Lachlan, who doesn't answer and opts for glaring at his half-eaten waffle. With a frown, Felix focuses on me. "Er, it's up to you if you wanna come or not."

"Uh, yeah, I'll come," I murmur.

We eat an awkward breakfast, with neither Felix nor Lachlan meeting my eyes for different reasons, until Necktie orders the boys to get ready. Knowing they'll take at least another half hour to get beautified, I stay behind to finish eating.

Halfway to the exit, Felix spins around. He flashes me a dazzling grin and signs, "*Happy birthday, beautiful.*"

☆ ☆ ☆

When I get back to the hotel after an uneventful evening in the Green Room, I pace around my room, eyes glued to the wall clock, waiting for Felix to reply to the text I sent asking if we're going to talk tonight.

My phone finally buzzes. "I got it. Good girl," I tell Ginger before she can alert. She seems miffed I interrupted her. My preemptive excitement disappears when I read the message.

Sat, July 20, 10:24 PM

[Mom]

Happy birthday.

I wait for typing bubbles or a second message with an apology or her version of an olive branch, but nothing comes. ***Seriously?*** She ghosted me for over a month, then waited until 10:30 p.m. to finally wish me a happy birthday? With a ***period*** at the end? Not even an exclamation mark? An emoji?

I don't know how to reply or even how to feel, so after a few more beats of anger-staring at the text, I throw my phone onto my bed. Right as I resume pacing, Ginger alerts to a knock. My feelings about Mom's text disperse at the thought of Felix's smiling face behind the door.

I quickly fix my hair before yanking the door open. To my surprise, instead of Felix waiting for me, there's a pink box with an envelope propped against it. I briefly debate calling the bomb squad—what if some territorial fan discovered my identity and planted this here?—but curiosity gets the better of me.

Luckily, inside are a dozen gourmet doughnuts. It takes an act of extreme self-control to shut the box and grab the envelope. I break the seal and pray there's not anthrax inside. You can never be too careful. Instead of a card or a letter, I find three sticky notes stuck together. I stifle a laugh. He's committed to the bit.

NAT,
HAPPY B-DAY!!! I WANTED TO TELL YOU HOW THANKFUL I AM FOR YOU. YOU BEING HERE & PUTTING UP W/ ME MEANS THE ~~WOLRD~~ WORLD. NO MATTER WHAT I WANT YOU IN MY LIFE. EVEN AS A ~~FREIND~~ FRIEND. WHATEVER YOU DECIDE IS

BEST FOR YOU IS OK. PROMISE!!!
COME TO MY ROOM WHEN/IF YOUR
READY TO TALK ♡

XXX
YOUR FELIX

P.S. I KNOW RASBERRY
DONUTS ARE YOUR
FAVOURITE BUT THEY
WERE OUT SO I HOPE
STRAWBERRY IS OK!

I re-read the notes, drinking in every messy, incorrectly spelled word scrawled in Felix's chicken-scratch penmanship.

I linger on the fact that he remembered my favorite doughnut flavor. It's such a little thing, a minor detail, but like the Grinch, it triggers my heart to swell three sizes, and I hug the Post-it notes to my chest.

Somehow in a cheesy, rom-com twist I thought only existed in books, the most annoying, gorgeous, sweet boy to grace planet earth has successfully wormed his way into my heart.

I put the doughnuts and notes on my bedside table, throw Ginger a chew toy to occupy her, and speed toward Felix's room at the far end of the hall.

I bang on the door. It feels like an eternity before it swings open. Standing in the doorway of his dimly lit room, Felix looks down at me with a faint trace of hope written across his features.

Not having the right words to say or sign how I feel, I opt to ***show*** him.

I step forward and connect our lips. He wraps his arms around me, and we stumble into his room, away from the potential exposure of the hallway. My back presses against the door as it shuts.

He hunches over, and I stand on my toes so we can reach each other. Kissing someone almost a foot taller than you is easier when you're sitting.

The passionate press of his lips deepens into something that feels as natural as breathing yet electric enough to make me lightheaded.

Felix's hands roam with reverence, each touch deliberate, like he's making a map of my body. His fingers glide along the planes of my chest, the curve of my waist. My pulse pounds as his teeth scrape against my jaw and collarbone. I can't suppress the quiet moan that slips out when he lingers at the hollow of my throat.

When he steps back, his breathing is ragged, chest rising and falling like it does after a concert. His dark, smoldering eyes rake over me with an intensity that's almost too much to bear.

"Nat . . . shouldn't we talk? I wanna make sure this is really what you want," he squeaks out. One of his strong, soft hands cups my jaw. He searches my face for any hesitancy.

I drag him into another slow, drawn-out kiss, savoring every second. "You're what I want. I don't need to talk about it right now. I just need you."

DAYDREAM Wiki Member Profile

FULL NAME: Lachlan Ian McCarthy

AGE: 19

HEIGHT: 6'0" (182 cm)

HOMETOWN: Mercer Island, Washington, USA

LACHLAN FACTS:

- His role model is Freddie Mercury
- His life motto is "Be a voice, not an echo"
- He has perfect pitch
- If he weren't in DAYDREAM, he said he'd be the lead singer in a different band

DISCLAIMER:

Profile will be updated as the public learns more about Lachlan

Chapter Twenty-Six

Dead Birds

Detroit + Chicago, July 21

Felix's tender embrace greets me in the morning.

He resembles a painting, as if each strand of hair and sweeping eyelash were created with the delicate stroke of a brush.

I lean in and place a kiss on his cutting jawline, breathing in the scent of the obnoxious cologne that always lingers on his skin.

"G'mornin'," he mumbles in that butterfly-inducing morning voice.

"Morning," I reply, softly running my fingers along his bare collarbone. "We should talk."

His face scrunches into a frown. "Or we could have a cuddle!" He drags me closer and kisses me, lingering as long as he can. Before I get distracted, I scoot away. Felix groans but hauls himself into a sitting position.

I want him. I want *us*. But that's never going to be an easy thing to have.

"Where do we go from here? Logistically this would be hard to maintain, and your label would be pissed. And what happens after this tour? You live in LA and I'm in Seatt—"

"Breathe, darling. Don't worry so much," he interrupts. "Now that the band's more established, I'll be visiting home more. I'm committed to spending time with my family and you."

I frown as seeds of doubt worm their way into my head.

"Trust me. I'm not missing any more of Aves' life—wait, did she tell you she has a crush on— —girl from tennis? I can't miss my baby sister's sexuality crisis!" I finally relax, and he kisses my forehead. "And I've gotta be there for you. I wanna see everything you do— —the Center. Plus, you've finally realized that I'm actually incredible, and talented, and hot as fu—"

"You're very humble, too," I grumble playfully.

He breaks into a cheeky grin before tilting my chin up with his thumb and locking eyes with me. "The tour will be over soon. For now, we have to lay low. Can you trust me, please?"

Tuning out my logical side goes against my very nature . . . But I'll try. Because Felix Song is worth every risk. Every. Single. One.

"*OK-OK*. I trust you."

"Good. We're doing this thing," he announces. I give him a quick peck before sliding out of bed. It's 6:05 a.m., but today is a travel day, which start bright and early.

He chuckles while I inelegantly put on last night's black romper. Nobody can look sexy while putting on a romper. ***Nobody.*** Before leaving, I peer through the peephole. Once I see the coast is clear, I slip out.

My delight immediately vanishes when I quite literally run into Lachlan as he's exiting Calum's and Will's room. I stumble backward, but Lachlan grips my shoulder and steadies me. I regain my footing and stare up at him.

Lachlan's forehead puckers in a frown. He leans down and snatches a gray sweater-vest off the floor. He must've dropped it when he grabbed my shoulder, because in his left hand, he holds a blue one.

"Good morning!" Calum says from the doorway. "Sleep well?" he asks, tone teasing. His brown eyes dart from Felix's door to me.

He knows. They know.

Shit.

"Oh, um . . . uh . . . we . . ." I scramble to string together an excuse, but nothing coherent comes out.

"Hey, dude. Snitches get stitches." He jabs Lachlan in the ribs when he doesn't piggyback off that. "Ahem. We didn't see anything, capiche?"

Lachlan's gaze pierces me. "Capiche," he says terribly unconvincingly.

"Thanks, Cal," I say.

"It's Bro Code." I start to leave, but he stops me. "Wait, Natalie, Lach's seeking sweater-vest opinions. Blue or gray?" He gestures toward the options. "Wardrobe's letting him pick his outfit since he's been such a good boy lately," he teases, pinching Lachlan's cheek.

I examine both. "Blue," I decide. "It complements your eyes. Makes them pop."

For a split second, I think he's going to thank me, maybe stop acting so weird, but instead, he holds up the gray. "I think I'm going with this one."

The action shouldn't sting so much, but his blatant disregard of my opinion feels symbolic of our friendship taking a hit.

Hurt and perplexed, I blink at him a few times and find his gaze distant, mouth tilted in a tight frown. Wordlessly, I head for my room.

☆ ☆ ☆

"Be back in the lobby in two hours," Necktie snaps as we arrive at the Field Museum of Natural History in Chicago. I rub my eyes and suppress a yawn, suddenly regretting playing games with Felix instead of squeezing in a four-hour nap between Detroit and here.

Will sets up his tripod and gets group photos in front of the museum's massive marble pillars—he even pulls me in for a few shots—then they take selfies and GoPro clips. Necktie sits on a bench and starts clacking on his laptop. The boys and I share a collective look of relief knowing he won't be breathing down our necks.

"There's nothing I love more than art. And looking at it. For hours," Calum grumbles as we pay admission.

"This isn't an art museum," Mateo corrects.

"Semantics. It's still ***boring***."

"There are dinosaurs."

"Oh shit, really?"

We crowd around Mateo while he looks at an exhibit map. Will declares he's going to the bird hall, and Mateo and Calum pair up for fossils.

Felix looks at me. "Where d'you wanna go?"

"You pick; we're here for your music video."

"*You sure?*" his pointer finger drops from his chin. I knock a fist. "The gem and jade halls sound cool."

Everyone disperses. But as Felix, Ginger, and I head for the jade hall, Lachlan follows.

I eye him. A few hours ago, he was acting standoffish and bizarre, so why is he hanging with us?

When we reach the jade hall, I gape at the mélange. Everything from ornate vases shaped like dragons to engraved tablets with Chinese characters to intricate necklaces are on proud display.

Felix's eyes light up as he takes it in. The walls are washed in a medley of greens and blues from the precious artifacts, and when he steps closer to a vitrine with cups and bowls, he glows green.

I record on the GoPro, getting candid shots of his awestruck smile. Lachlan enters the frame, and Felix points to something and speaks inaudibly, both of them laugh.

The routine continues when we reach the gem hall. Lavish jewelry and elaborate statues occupy glass cases. Colors dance on the walls, floors, and Felix and Lachlan as they explore.

I follow them around like a videographer and get an array of angles. Will would be proud.

After they look at the first two gem displays, Felix doubles back and walks beside me.

"I'm getting pretty good at GoPro-ing," I tell him. "I can add it to my résumé."

He chuckles, then quickly glances in every direction before his pinkie finger hooks around mine. We walk farther into the hall, and he intertwines our other fingers.

My heart beats faster. This is playing with fire.

The room is darkened to give the gems the spotlight, likely concealing us, but dozens of people surround us. Worst-case scenarios run through my head. What if someone sees? What if people are secretly recording?

The frenzy caused by innocent photos of us ice-skating spiraled out of control, turning harmless fun into conspiracy theories.

Yet . . . the danger sharpens the thrill. Tempting fate like this sends endorphins rushing through me, and instead of letting go, I squeeze his hand tighter.

Trying to act natural, I focus on a gold ring with a marble-size ruby encased in tiny diamonds. "This is a pretty exhibit," I say. Felix's grin nearly undoes me. There's a playful gleam in his eyes, like he's daring me to enjoy this dangerous little game as much as he clearly is.

"*Not as pretty as you.*" My insides start feeling as sparkly as the gemstones, and my cheeks flush.

Our fleeting moment of bliss expires when I see Lachlan out of the corner of my eye. His eyes are glued to our hands, and I quickly release Felix's.

"I'll get more clips of you," I say, motioning for him to walk ahead. He follows instructions, oblivious to Lachlan's glaring.

While he's focused on displays, Lachlan slinks past him and matches my stride. I automatically tense up, still sensing his weird aura from this morning. "*I saw you.*"

I don't reply, keeping my eyes forward.

"When did things change between you? Why didn't you tell me?" He grabs my wrist and stops me. "Please be honest."

"Why do you care? I don't expect you to tell me everything about your relationships."

His jaw tightens. "He's not right for you. You should explore other options."

Frustration bubbles up. Why is he so insistent on inserting himself into our . . . flirtationship? Relationship? We-confessed-our-feelings-but-technically-haven't-put-a-label-on-it-ship? Our ***thing***.

"I've thought through every pro and con. Every potential scenario," I respond. And I still chose Felix because I care about him so deeply it could consume me whole. We chose each other. "You don't get to dictate my personal life."

"I'm trying to look out for y—"

"Butt out, Lachlan!" I snap louder than intended.

His expression darkens, and he sucks his teeth, deep blue eyes roving over my face. His mouth is ajar, and hands primed to respond, but before he can, Felix approaches. "Everything alright?" He looks at Lachlan expectantly but is met with the cold shoulder as he storms out of the gem hall.

Felix watches him, confusion evident on his face. "What's going on?" he asks.

"I don't know. He's been acting weird lately."

If I tell him about this ongoing squabble with Lachlan, it would only stir the pot of tension soup these two are already cooking.

Although, if Lachlan doesn't address his attitude problem, it might be stirred anyway.

Felix decides to leave the conversation hanging in midair.

We speed run Ancient Egypt and Māori exhibitions, take NIGHT AT THE MUSEUM–inspired clips with a T. Rex skeleton, then head for the lobby. We beat the others, but before I celebrate getting here early, I spot Lachlan with Necktie. His hands move erratically as he whispers heatedly, his posture rigid.

Felix chatters about how he wants to be buried in a pyramid someday, clueless to their hushed conversation.

Necktie spots us, and instantaneously a fat purple vein on his forehead bulges. His sneer is unnerving, and his fists are balled.

Lachlan whips his head around and tracks his line of sight. He clams up when he sees us approaching and takes several steps away from Necktie.

Fortunately, Calum and Mateo show up, and shortly after Will enters from the opposite direction, potentially saving us from an outburst.

Instead, Necktie aggressively waves his printed schedule in the air. "Let's go. We have to be at— —thirty minutes."

"How was the bird hall?" Mateo asks as we leave the museum.

"I thought it was going to be an aviary." Will shakes his head solemnly. "They were all dead."

Chapter Twenty-Seven

Deep-Dish Drama

Chicago, July 21

The rest of the day, Necktie doesn't explode at Felix or me. But instead of feeling relieved, it deeply unsettles me. It isn't like him to stay calm; he's like a reactive dog. He's usually all bark, but I can feel the impending bite.

Ignoring the bad feeling in my gut, I chat with Felix while Bhavani does his concert makeup. I smile proudly as he strings together whole sentences using proper ASL grammar.

"Showtime!" Necktie's voice fills the Green Room.

The boys—save Lachlan, who still has an air of gloom about him—hype one another up as they filter into the hallway.

My uneasiness is finally proved right when Necktie orders the hair and makeup artists to leave, and when everyone is gone, he slams the door and barrels toward me. I can practically see steam coming out of his ears.

"Have something to tell me?" he booms inches away from my face.

My anxiety levels reach an all-time high, and I freeze, only able to shake my head.

“Don’t act coy with me, missy,” he hisses. “I know about Detroit.”

My stomach plummets, and my nerves go haywire. You don’t have to be Sherlock Holmes to figure out who the rat is. Like a scene in a movie, I picture Lachlan whispering to Necktie in the museum. ***Backstabbing asshole.***

I feign composure. “Felix and I practice ASL at nigh—”

“Do I look like I was born yesterday?!” he growls. “I warned you in Boston. You’re done!”

My breathing quickens. I’ve never been truly scared of Necktie before, but he’s also never screamed in my face while we’re ***alone***. I steady myself and choke out, “D-do you have proof of whatever you’re accusing me of?” I stare him down. “Without proof, you have no justification for sending me home.”

His expression is utter contempt. We both know he ***doesn’t*** have proof.

With a final scowl, he exits, leaving me shaky and forcing myself to take deep breaths. After a minute, my panic morphs into red, searing anger. The feeling of betrayal cuts through me, but not for myself. I can live with the temporary sting of being crossed by a new friend. My heart aches on Felix’s behalf. On the whole band’s behalf.

How can Lachlan so easily betray that bond? Crumple it up and toss it in the garbage? By putting Felix in Necktie’s crosshairs, he’s threatening DAYDREAM’s very existence. They could ***all*** suffer for this.

☆ ☆ ☆

The smells of melty cheese and pizza dough waft through a hole-in-the-wall deep-dish pizza parlor after the concert. Calum and

Will push two tables together to create space for the six of us. I stow Ginger underneath the table before sitting.

Felix is across from me, next to Lachlan. It takes everything in me to refrain from casting Lachlan the harshest glare humanly possible.

At the far end of the table, Calum looks at me and his lips move, but I can't make out more than two words over the din of the restaurant. "*Pizza*," he clunkily signs, like him randomly signing "pizza" while we're in a pizza parlor is supposed to clarify. I breathe a laugh.

Thankfully, Felix interprets: "*He's ordering now. What do you want?*"

I turn the menu toward Felix, tap the Hawaiian pizza, then the gluten-free option. His lips tilt downward in disgust, but he relays my request.

"*I can't . . . believe . . . you like fruit pizza!*" he exclaims after remembering the signs.

"*You eat pizza with tomato sauce?*"

"*Yes . . .*"

"*Tomatoes are fruit.*" His eyes roll into the back of his head.

When Calum returns, Felix gets swept into a conversation. I don't catch the specifics, but they're laughing and throwing around playful insults.

I'd be over the moon seeing them all so lighthearted and relaxed if it weren't for Lachlan. He's dramatically changed his tune and is bantering alongside the others, one arm slung over Felix's shoulders.

I almost prefer his brooding to this warmth. At least when he was acting like a mopey asshole, he was showing his true colors instead of being a fake friend.

For a brief second, Lachlan's and my eyes meet. His smile wanes as I glare at him. Finally reaching my breaking point, I stand up, and once Ginger moves, push my chair in a little too heatedly. It slams against the table.

Everyone goes quiet and watches as Ginger and I head for the hallway leading to the bathrooms. I slump against the wall and sigh. Ginger nuzzles my leg, and I bury my face in her golden fur.

Barely a minute passes before a hand grips my shoulder and gives reassuring squeezes. I peer up and see Felix squatting in front of me.

My anger starts to dissipate as he places a careful kiss on the top of my head. "*What's wrong, darling?*" he signs, sitting cross-legged on the floor.

With a gulp, I decide to tell him the truth. "Andrew confronted me during the show. He knows about us."

"W-what? *How?*"

I take his hand, wishing I could lessen the sting of what I'm about to say. "Lachlan ratted us out. He saw me leaving your room. He's been acting sketchy and keeps interrogating me about us. Like in Boston, he warned me about getting close to you, and this morning he said I should explore other options."

Confusion, pain, and frustration color his face in a mural of emotions. "What'd he—"

"Hey . . ." He's cut off when Lachlan speaks. He approaches us, hands shoved in the pockets of his vintage Alice in Chains hoodie. Felix pops up immediately.

"Did you narc on us?" he asks.

I stand, and Lachlan's focus darts between us. "I . . . Lix . . . damn it," he flounders, scrubbing hands over his face.

"I can't believe you." Felix's words are wobbly, drenched in hurt.

"I'm trying— —protect the band! It's too risky. We could lose everything!" Lachlan becomes animated.

"If you had— —problem, you should've come to me, not Andrew. You're supposed to be my best mate!"

"I a-am!" Lachlan chokes out. "That's why I'm doing this!"

"Yeah, nah, you clearly aren't! Best mates don't narc on each other." Then, "You think I don't know this— —risky? ***Of course*** I fucking know," he bites. "I'm well aware that me dating, me being happy, could ruin our career. You don't think— —feel guilty as hell for that? Scared that I'll screw this up for— —guys?" His voice is even shakier this time, betraying how deeply wounded he is.

"This relationship is a mistake, Felix."

"No. The only mistake was ever trusting you."

Their words blur together as they argue, and all I'm left with is body language. Lachlan's clenched jaw, tense shoulders, and fists balled by his sides tell their own story, and a light bulb goes off above my head as I think back to our conversation at Fenway Park and the museum.

After a lifetime of observing people, I've learned to recognize certain emotions with far less information, so how have I been so oblivious to his underlying motivation?

"Lachlan, are you . . . jealous?" I breathe in a rush.

They stop bickering, and their attention lands on me.

After a painfully long beat, Lachlan's eyes fixate on the floor. "How I feel abo—how I ***feel*** doesn't matter."

The discomfort is tangible, thick and cloying, and looms over our heads.

Finally, he looks up, takes a deep breath, and meets my eyes, his brows set in a troubled frown. "Someday you'll see that I'm right about this."

Chapter Twenty-Eight

Lights, Camera, Chaos

Chicago, July 23

Ever since Sunday, Lachlan's been sullen and pensive, like a scorned suitor from an effin' Victorian-era romance movie. Currently, he's brooding in another fashion brand's swanky photo shoot studio.

It's inside a corporate building, and with its stark white walls and no windows, it almost resembles a horror movie escape room. I half expect a creepy little puppet to come riding in on a tricycle.

I watch from a remote corner as a short, plump photographer proudly shares the vision for the ad campaign before the boys change. One by one they emerge in unbelievably outrageous outfits that someone somewhere considers "fashion."

Will's in a velvety magenta suit; Calum wears a fuzzy red trench coat; Mateo dons a fluorescent green cropped hoodie and shorts combo; and Lachlan steps out in a CLUELESS-esque yellow plaid two-piece suit. I snort and take a mental snapshot of the group.

My amusement fades and pulse speeds up when Felix makes an appearance. Black boots, iridescent black pants that shimmer like fish scales, and a neon orange mesh top that leaves absolutely nothing to the imagination.

I try to calm myself the hell down as he walks over. Halfway across the room, he tucks hair behind his ear and wets his lips, and all my calming-the-hell-down progress is erased.

This boy is going to be the death of me.

"Whaddya think?" he asks after stopping in front of me. "Not my typical style but—"

"You look hot."

"—it's alright." After I interrupt, he cocks a brow and smirks. "Oh?"

"Um. You look good in orange. That's what I meant."

"Right. Easy mistake to make." He plays along. *"But . . . you're hot, too,"* he signs, then darts off, leaving me to murder the butterflies aggressively flapping inside my stomach.

The butterflies increase tenfold as Felix poses. One leg in front of the other, thumbs tucked into the belt loops of his reflective pants; chin down, eyes up.

For the entirety of Felix's solo shoot, I ogle him. Luckily, nobody notices. The members, save for Lachlan, are busy cheering and catcalling.

The photographer finishes after a few minutes. Felix is rushed to the changing area, and someone passes him a silky white suit.

Will has his shoot while Felix changes. Once Will's done, he also changes into a white suit. The pattern continues as each of the members do solo shots—their bandmates holler at and flirt with them like fans in the background, and then they change into white or black.

Finally, they're posed together. In their contrasting light and dark outfits, they look like chess pieces.

“Good!” the photographer booms. “Gorgeous! Beautiful! Lachlan, Felix, relax please.”

They stand together in the far back. Instead of relaxing, Lachlan’s forehead puckers and he works his jaw, and Felix’s shoulders hike up.

“You’re so tense,” the photographer tuts. “You need— —relax and— —okay?”

Lachlan forces a smile, and Felix loosens his shoulders. The photographer studies them and frowns. They squeeze past Will and Mateo, who crouch on the floor in front, and grab Lachlan’s arm. With annoyed movements, they place his arm around Felix’s shoulders, then scoot Felix closer to Lachlan, until their sides are pressed against each other.

The pair look wildly uneasy, their bodies stiff, but the shoot continues. After two minutes, they tailspin back into looking like mortal enemies. Lachlan’s light eyes clash with Felix’s dark ones, and it reminds me of the battle between Darth Maul and Qui-Gon Jinn.

The photographer finally loses their temper and storms over to Necktie, flailing their hands around while complaining.

Immediately, Lachlan wriggles out of the pose and runs fingers through his middle part. Felix takes a huge step away, creating an icy, palpable space between them.

Will and Calum engage mediator mode, but Lachlan stalks off before they can problem-solve. He heads for the directors’ chairs marked with each member’s name and slumps down in his.

Felix grabs a bottle of water, staring blankly at the wall while he chugs it. I walk over. He swallows another huge gulp, then signs, "*Why didn't you tell me until now?*" He inconspicuously gestures to Lachlan.

"Your relationship was already . . . complicated. I didn't want to make things worse," I explain.

"It's not your fault. I just dunno what to do. There's not exactly a 'How to Proceed After Learning Your Best Mate Fancies *Your Girlfriend*' handbook." Felix signs "your girlfriend" so nobody can understand him.

Except for Lachlan, of course. But he's preoccupied by hiding his head in his hands while Mateo gives him a consolatory side-hug.

"Yeah. It's not someth—wait, hold on, *your girlfriend?!*" I sign back to him.

The worry momentarily slides off his face, replaced with an impish smirk as he says, "I mean, if you're ready to admit you actually 'connect' with me."

I realize he's referencing what I told him about being demiromantic. I'm about to reply with something undoubtedly super clever and funny, but movement in my peripheral vision distracts me.

I turn to see Necktie dragging Lachlan toward us by the sleeve of his gaudy black suit. Calum, Will, and Mateo follow, grimacing.

When he reaches us, he shoves Lachlan next to Felix so he can look at both of them. The others maintain careful distance.

"What the hell is wrong with you two?!" Necktie bellows, then lowers his voice to an inaudible hiss.

I can only see the side of his mouth, making lipreading impossible. Judging from Lachlan's flared nostrils and Felix's teeth grinding, whatever he's saying is worse than usual.

Finally, Will steps in. "Andrew, we're just tired. This tour has been taxing." He glances at Felix and Lachlan.

"Yup. We're fine," Felix insists, voice hoarse.

Gears churn in Lachlan's head. He's been a wild card recently, so it's anyone's guess if he'll accept the nicely wrapped excuse Will concocted.

His rib cage slowly expands and shrinks again. "All good. Just exhausted," he replies persuasively, like a politician lying about a potentially career-ending scandal.

Necktie laughs bitterly. "I don't give a shit if— —tired, or homesick, or miss your mommies! I don't care if you two hate each other! As long as— —not obvious. Nobody— —going to pay to see ***this*** DAYDREAM. Pull your shit together. ***Now***."

Chapter Twenty-Nine

A Super-Duper Airtight, Very Legally Binding Contract

Minneapolis, July 26

Fri, July 26, 5:34 PM

Group chat started by Cal

[Cal]

some ppl are NOT passing the vibe check
(ahem. lix & lach) luckily you have super
genius einstien friends to help!!
everyone come to will's & my room

[Just Will]

FYI, I don't approve of this plan,
but I don't have an alternative. Also, Cal,
you spelled Einstein wrong.

[Cal]

NOT THE POINT SEYMOUR!!! 🖕

I look at Felix, who's at the foot of my bed. "Are we going?" I ask after swallowing a bite of an overpriced gluten-free burrito he brought me. I was hoping to talk about what he told Lachlan in the pizza parlor—about the guilt and fear he feels because we're dating, and how our relationship puts DAYDREAM at risk—but evidently, Calum and Will have other plans.

"I don't wanna but . . . things haven't exactly improved on their own."

That's a nice way of putting it. I mean, sure, to placate Necktie, Felix and Lachlan pulled their visible-to-the-public-eye shit together. But behind the scenes, it's all uncomfortable glances, physical distance, and walking on eggshells. One false move and their fragile friendship will shatter into a million irreparable pieces.

He gives me a quick kiss before we clean up and head to Will's and Calum's room.

Felix chews on his lower lip as he raps on the door. When it swings open, his nervousness is replaced with uncontrollable laughter. My jaw drops as I take in the disorienting sight before me.

"I told you I didn't approve." Will sighs. He's wearing one of Lachlan's beige sweater-vests, khakis, and a coily gray wig tucked underneath an Irish flat cap. The cherry on top is the FX makeup that covers his face with hyper-realistic age spots and wrinkles.

Felix swallows his laughter as we follow Will into the room but loses his goddamn mind when we spot Calum. He's perched on the edge of one of the beds, wearing Ninja Turtle boxers and a long gray wig, and shoving tissues into a lacy black bra. His face is also old-person-ified.

"Mateo, are my boobs too lumpy?" he asks, adjusting the bra.

"I'm not looking at your boobs!" Poor Mateo's face is beet red. He's sitting on the other bed while Bhavani styles his hair.

"Hi, Natalie, Felix," Bhavani chirps.

Calum looks up. "Oh, Natalie! You have boobs, you know what they're supposed to be like. Come feel mine."

Felix places an arm in front of me, blocking my path—not that I was going to help Calum with his tissue-boobs, because I was ***not***. "Don't talk about her boobs. That's weird, mate."

"What the hell is this?" Lachlan demands from the doorway.

Will drags him into the room, and he takes a hesitant seat next to Calum while Calum tugs a muumuu over his head.

"We need to do some team building." Will sends a pointed look to Felix and Lachlan. "So we're going to spend time together like the best friends we are. We're going to have ***fun***. You guys are going to ***like it***."

It sounds more like a threat than a suggestion.

"O-okay," Felix agrees.

I lipread Lachlan mumbling, "Fine."

Bhavani hands Mateo a pair of khaki shorts and a short-sleeve button-up to change into, then turns to Felix. "We've got some work to do."

After a painfully awkward Uber ride, we finally arrive at our undisclosed location. Colorful tents and rides decorate a fairground, hundreds of people roam around, and a band is performing on a small stage. A sign near the entrance reads: ROSEMOUNT MIDSUMMER FAIRE.

We file out of the car, and I chuckle to myself at our disguises. Calum and Will are an elderly couple; Felix is a leather-jacket-and-racoon-eyeliner-wearing Bad Boy trope; Mateo is a nerd stereotype; and Lachlan . . . well, honestly, he doesn't look that different. He's got brown spray-on hair dye and a Thrasher shirt. It's pretty effective, though, because unless you get close, he just looks like your run-of-the-mill TikToker with mommy issues who goes viral for mediocre dancing.

I'm in a blond wig and sunglasses. I'm not famous, after all.

Calum pays for six tickets with his ridiculous pin-number-1234 card, and we enter the fairground. I'm hit with memories of attending the Puyallup Fair with my family. Dad and I would go to the petting zoo, while Mom and Jo rode roller coasters. It was a win-win since Jo has an irrational fear of farm animals and I get nauseated on fast rides. It was one of the best parts of every summer.

Once Will determines the best route, we start exploring. Calum links arms with him, and their cute old couple status is solidified. We take pictures when they aren't looking. Even Lachlan can't refrain from documenting the absurdity.

The first twenty minutes are smooth sailing while we play rigged games . . . if you don't count the fact Lachlan and Felix haven't said a single word to each other, that is. But the tension is obvious while we're in line for Dippin' Dots. Mateo and I stand next to each other, Calum's and Will's arms are linked, and Felix and Lachlan are using all of us as a barrier between them.

Calum jokes around to keep it lighthearted, but Felix and Lachlan don't play along.

"What's this about? Seriously! You've never kept arguments going this long," Will says, frustration evident. "Let us help. Tell us."

They glance at each other—pain from a fractured friendship crackling between them—and for a split second, Lachlan seems ashamed. I dare to hope that they'll pull their friendship off the cliff's edge, that ***somehow*** they'll be okay.

"It doesn't involve you," Lachlan snaps, his cutting glare aimed at Calum and Will. There goes that hope.

"It ***does***, Lach. It's affecting the whole band," Will rebuts. "We're not expecting— —sunshine and rainbows— —cut the bullshit!" Some parents cover their children's ears. "Kids these days." He gestures toward us with a grandfatherly smile.

After we're handed our ice cream, I glance between Felix and Lachlan, their silent hostility building like a storm cloud. I can't let this fester, but I can't risk saying too much.

I look directly at Lachlan and sign, "*We all said hurtful things. I've not fully forgiven you, but I'm sorry for lashing out.*" I hope apologizing will trigger a chain reaction. Even though—***ahem***—someone has significantly more to apologize for.

For a second, I think he'll relent, but then his gaze briefly slips to Felix before his response lands like a carefully aimed dart. "***I'm*** not the one who caused this problem. Don't put this on me."

"Are you kidding?!" Felix scoffs. "You—"

"I'm done with this bullshit." Lachlan shoves his Dippin' Dots at Calum and marches toward the exit, shoulders hiked defensively.

Felix grimaces as he watches Lachlan's retreating figure.

Calum and Will exchange glances, clearly frustrated by the drama they can't understand. Mateo fidgets awkwardly, and anger twists in my stomach.

"Screw it," Will gripes. "I'm going back to the hotel. It's too hot for this." He motions to his sweater-vest and wig. Mateo nods.

"I'm staying. I've got fair food to eat," Calum says before dumping Lachlan's cookies-and-cream Dippin' Dots into his mouth.

"*Date night?*" I sign to Felix half-jokingly, half-hopeful tonight won't be a total failure. He offers a strained smile.

Calum wanders off, Will and Mateo walk the same direction as Lachlan, and Felix and I amble toward the Ferris wheel.

Felix takes full advantage of the privacy in our basket and takes my hand. I lean my head on his shoulder, and he presses a kiss into my hair.

"I trust you," he says out of nowhere.

I sit up, confused. "*What?*"

He tucks long blond hair behind my ears. "I was thinking about how hard it is to rely on people, y'know?" There's an unspoken sadness in his words, a darkness casting shadows on his light tone. "*But you . . .*" His eyes meet mine, and the somberness slips, replaced with sincerity. "I can tell you anything."

My heart stirs, and I cup his face. "*Same-same.*" He leans down to connect our lips. I relax into the kiss, and the weight of the evening momentarily lifts.

He leans back, wearing an impish grin. Uh-oh. I eye him suspiciously, and he laughs. He reaches into the front pocket on his leather jacket and brandishes a pad of purple sticky notes and a silver glitter pen. I chuckle at the fact he left his fanny pack at the hotel but still brought emergency Post-it notes.

"Can we promise to always be here for each other?" he asks, hope shining in his eyes. I instantly nod. I can't imagine not being here for my dazzling boy.

He starts writing, slow and arduously. "*Want me to do it?*" I ask.

"*Thanks.*"

I take the pad and transcribe as he speaks. When the note is written, I sign my name at the bottom and hand it to him. He signs below mine.

"You're stuck with me now. This is super-duper airtight."

I return his smile—reminded of our first Post-it note contract. As our basket starts lowering, I press a lingering kiss to his cheek. "You're the only person I'd want to be stuck with, baby," I whisper against his ear.

24/7
I PROMISE TO always be
there for you.
Rain or shine, up or down.
(Even when you're annoying)
Natalie Nielsen
F.SONG ♡

Chapter Thirty

The Girl Felix Song Loves

Denver, July 29

It's a little past midnight when Felix and I step inside a cozy 24-hour café nestled on 16th Street in Downtown Denver.

The rich smell of coffee swirls around us as an incognito mode Felix orders. We settle at a table in the far back, and he holds my hand underneath like we're in middle school.

"Whaddya reckon we should do?" He uses slightly choppy SimCom, but I appreciate his effort since there's background noise and he's wearing a mask.

"We could start by talking about how you're scared of ruining the band, or this whole Lachlan thi—"

"*No.* I wanna focus on us tonight."

I get why he's refusing to talk. However, watching him lose his best friend and be guilt-ridden for dating me is nearly unbearable. I can't force it, though. He'll talk when he's ready. So I drop it.

He Googles parks nearby, and I grab my own phone while we wait for our drinks. I double-check the ringer is off (I'm overly paranoid about that now) and snap a picture. With his hood pulled up, beanie hiding his hair, and black surgical mask covering half his face, the boy across from me could be anyone. I set the picture as my lockscreen, then text Jo.

Mon, July 29, 12:06 AM

[Natalie]

://image.attachment//:

I'm obsessed with him <3

[Jo]

KSKSKDKSKAJJSKSK CAN WE KEEP HIM

[Natalie]

I'm planning on it!

Seeing Felix is still preoccupied, I also open Google and set alerts for "Felix Song." I never cared about what articles were written about him before—I actually got annoyed whenever his name or face popped into my social media feeds—but things are different now. I want to know how he's being covered in the press, and I ***especially*** need to know if any rumors are swirling.

I add alerts for "DAYDREAM" and the other members' names, too. I didn't know anything about the other boys before the tour, but now I consider them—with one current exception—close friends.

Once we're outside, drinks in hand, Felix's GPS tells him to turn left. Supposedly, we'll arrive at our destination in ten minutes.

Felix slips his hand into mine, and I'm transported back to the gem hall—a similar mixture of hypervigilance and exhilaration sparks in me.

"I want to know more about you," I blurt.

"Like what?" He quirks a brow, amused.

"Random stuff. What's your favorite movie? Go-to karaoke song? Comfort food? What superpower would you want? Do you think hot dogs are sandwiches?"

A deep, hearty laugh escapes him. "Damn. Er . . . MAMMA MIA!; 'Disaster' by Conan Gray; doenjang-jjigae, which is a soybean stew; being fluent in every language; and absolutely not. I don't care— —technicalities."

I join his laughter. I wasn't expecting him to answer rapid fire.

"My turn," he says. "D'you sleep— —door open or closed?"

"Open, usually."

"What?! That's messed up. What if an axe murderer is creepin' around?"

"I'm pretty sure a closed door wouldn't deter them."

"Famous last words of someone who gets axe murdered," he tsks. "D'you believe in any conspiracy theories?"

"Quantum immortality. But it freaks me out to think about."

He squints. "You're freaked out by quantum immortality but not axe murderers? Interesting priorities." I jab him in the side, and he laughs. "Would you rather have hair for teeth or teeth for hair?"

"Teeth for hair, I guess. How would you eat with hair teeth? Also sounds like a sensory nightmare."

"D'you reckon you'd have to floss them?" he muses.

"Okay, you don't get any more questions, you weirdo!" I exclaim with a chuckle.

Thankfully, we soon arrive at the park. It has a walkway lined with trees and boundless sky that stretches to every corner of the city. Billions of stars contrast against navy blue, dotted around as if an artist flicked paint onto a canvas.

We settle on a bench, and a beautiful peacefulness surrounds us. We could fill the empty space with deep conversation or snarky banter, but instead we let the night embrace us with purposeful, affectionate silence.

He wraps an arm around me. As I snuggle against him, I realize how hopelessly and overwhelmingly strong my feelings are. I'd never be able to describe what it's like. There's not a word for these emotions. There's only Felix—a boy as infinite and radiant as the stars.

"Why're you looking at me like that?" Felix's silky voice grounds me in the moment. He takes off his mask to sip his hot chocolate.

I force myself off the cloud I was floating on. "Because you're fun to look at."

"I know tha—ow!" he exclaims as I jokingly flick his cheek. He releases me from under his arm and makes a show of rubbing the spot I hit, which is obviously horribly wounded. "Hey," he says after dropping the act, "look at me." He tucks his thumb under my chin and lifts my head.

My heart speeds up as he studies my face.

"Close your eyes," he requests. "You have a loose eyelash."

My eyes flutter shut, and when I open them, he extends two mascara-caked lashes toward me.

"Make a wish."

"What is it with you and wishes?" I laugh.

He stops to think about it, looking up while he contemplates. "I'd like to think the universe is rooting for us. It wants our dreams to come true, but we need to share what those dreams are."

"You can have my wish," I tell him. "For the first time, it seems like Jo and I can create the Deaf Center we planned with Dad. And then there's . . . well, you. I don't want to get greedy with the Wish Gods."

He beams at me and places a chaste kiss on my cheek. "You're an angel . . . But unfortunately, I don't think they're transferable."

There goes my cheesy moment! "Oh my god, blow on the damn eyelashes!"

He chuckles before squeezing his eyes shut, really thinking it through, then blows. They float into the darkness, along with whatever hopes and dreams he sent with them.

"Can I ask what you wished for, or is that against the privacy policy?" I joke. He stares into the night with a deep frown and, without looking, laces our fingers together.

"I wished I could tell the girl I love that I love her, without worrying about any consequences."

The confession steals the air from my lungs.

"The girl I love."

Is that what all these beautiful, messy, indescribable feelings are? Emotions knotted together so tightly you can't possibly untangle them. Ones that make your head spin, body burn, and leave your thoughts muddled. A love with no limits.

I search for a reply, but nothing comes close to how I feel about him. In this moment, words and signs fail me. Losing track of everything else, I lurch forward and kiss him. It strips away everything—a vulnerable, heart-bared, every-possible-string-attached kiss.

It's unlike anything I've ever felt. Real, raw, perfect, with a touch of danger. It heals the wounds we've gotten and gives us strength for anything to come.

His hand slips into my pulled-up hood and onto my jaw, his cold fingers brushing through my hair, sending a shiver through me as they ghost over the skin behind my ear. I slip mine beneath his hood, grip the back of his neck, and pull him closer because I can't bear to be far from him, even for a second.

For a few precious minutes, the whole world fades away, but the spell is broken when he suddenly jerks away and scrambles to pull his hood back over his head, which must've fallen in the heat of the moment. A drunk group stumbling through the park, raucously singing sea shanties, reminds me all too suddenly that we're in public.

He grips my hand as they amble away. I nervously scan the park, but nobody else is in sight.

"I'm sorry," I breathe once they're gone. "I shouldn't have kissed you in public."

"Don't be sorry, darling. But . . . maybe we should head back to the hotel."

I chuckle. "Yeah."

He plugs the address into his GPS, gets up, and pulls me to my feet with a tugging grin.

His phone feeds us directions, and my boy and I set off into the night, affection and desire crackling between us like a lightning storm.

☆ ☆ ☆

THUMP! THUMP! THUMP!

I sit bolt upright in bed, clutching the sheet to my body. I've almost convinced myself it was an axe murder–inspired dream—because who would knock so thunderously it wakes the Deaf girl from a dead sleep?—when Felix flicks the bedside lamp on, and his wild, fearful expression confirms it was real.

Another set of booming knocks rings out.

He slides out of bed and tracks down his sweatpants. I grab the clothes nearest to me, which turn out to be his purple-and-white sweater and my jeans.

THUMP! THUMP! THUMP!

He heads for the door and hunches over to look through the peephole. The color drains from his face. "Get back." Felix points to the bed since it's not visible from the entryway.

I don't move. It's not fair to make him face whatever's happening alone. "Go. Please!" The desperation in his voice is enough to convince me, and I rush to the bed, barely sitting on the edge, my heart racing.

From where I'm perched, I see light from the hallway flood into the room as the door opens. "How fucking stupid are you?!" a familiar, furious voice screams.

Chapter Thirty-One

Caught in 4K

Denver, July 29

The panic pumping through my veins barely registers before Felix stumbles backward into the room.

"Do you know how much trouble you're in?!" Necktie screams while bursting in, iron-hot fury emanating from him.

Felix stays silent. He balls his fists so tightly his knuckles turn white.

"ANSWER ME!" Necktie's next words blur together in a mixture of yelling and cursing. I feel myself slowly starting to shut down when a loud voice suddenly cuts through the shouting.

"Hey!" Will calls as he walks in, concern and a hint of dread painted on his features. The other members, all dressed in pajamas, step inside.

"What's going on?" Calum hazards, brows tugged into a heavy frown.

Necktie bares his teeth in a snarl. In a swift, forceful movement, he unlocks his phone and slams it against Felix's chest. "See for yourself."

The corners of his brows knit as his eyes float across the screen. While Felix reads, Necktie's attention snaps to me, his face burning bright red and veins on his neck popping. "And you . . . I warned you not to mess with my band!" he growls. "You little—"

"Enough!" Felix speaks for the first time. "This is my fault. Don't blame Nat." Calum snatches the phone from Felix; the other boys crowd around him to read.

"I blame both of you!" Necktie shoots back. He continues shouting, but it fades into little more than a buzzing in my ear as I grab my own phone off the nightstand and find multiple Google Alerts on my lockscreen:

Teen Sensation Felix Song's Disturbing Sexcapades!

"America's Sweetheart" Has a SALACIOUS Double Life!

Sorry, Girls: Felix is TAKEN!

I click on the first article, and my stomach drops when I'm met with a photo of two shadowy figures in an empty Denver park.

The picture could be of anyone . . . if it weren't for Felix's fallen hood. Exposing soft, tan skin with a mole on his cheek and long, frosty blond hair poking out from a beanie.

Though it's impossible, it feels like the only sound I can hear is my heart hurtling around my rib cage. It beats so violently it seems it'll crawl up my throat. My blood runs ice cold, and the world around me starts spinning.

I sway on my feet, seasick and panicked, as sound filters back in.

"Pack your bags!" Necktie shouts at me. "You're going home!"

"The hell she is," Felix interjects.

"No. I'm done with— —bullshit! Choose. The girl or the band."

"You don't have the authority to fire anyone!" Will exclaims.

Necktie shoots him daggers. "You think— —label won't agree? They made the rules!" he spits before turning back to Felix.

"P-please," his voice breaks. He looks between his bandmates and me, tears shining in his eyes.

"But remember, because of your non-compete clause, you can't record music for six years. You wouldn't only be out of— —band; you'd be out— —the music industry. And do you think DAYDREAM will survive with— —frontman gone? One Direction only lasted five months after Zayn left, and— —wasn't even— —most important member! Choose carefully."

The words hang in the air, crushing every ounce of hope in the room.

Felix opens his mouth, but before any words escape, I bolt.

My feet move on autopilot as I run down the hall. My vision blurs as I slide to the floor, my back scraping against the cold wall. I draw my knees to my chest, and my breath comes in ragged bursts, as if the weight of everything—Felix, the band, the consequences—has stolen the air from my lungs.

The gravity of it settles in the pit of my stomach, an unmovable stone.

"Natalie, hey," a gentle voice soothes as I'm brought into a comforting hug. My body trembles, my thoughts a chaotic swirl, every fear, every doubt crashing into me like an avalanche.

I squeeze my eyes shut and force a breath, desperate for control. My hands are clammy and I'm lightheaded, but I center myself. It's not easy. It's not quick. But I have to.

I lean away from the figure crouching beside me. A boy with

dark brown bed head, a pajama shirt with a drum graphic that reads WHAT ARE YOU SNARING AT?, and a soothing pair of olive eyes meets my gaze.

"Mateo . . ." His name catches in my throat. "What's going to happen now?"

He considers me for a long moment. He grows grim as he finally says, "Andrew's not going to let you stay together—not while Lix is in DAYDREAM . . . I don't think this has a happy ending, either way."

My heart sinks. Why can't we be together ***and*** he can stay in DAYDREAM?

The words seep into me like a toxin, flowing through my body and invading every blood vessel. As much as I want to dismiss his perspective, deep down, in the furthest corner of my soul, I know he's right.

My chest heaves once more, and I lean against Mateo. He wraps me in another hug as I come to the bitter realization that happily-ever-afters only exist in fiction. There's no such thing as a perfect, mess-free ending in real life.

Felix Song may act like Prince Charming, but life isn't a fairy tale.

☆ ☆ ☆

When we re-enter Felix's room, the sun is peeking above the horizon and tints the walls pink.

Felix is hunched over on the edge of the bed, tears streaking down his face. He doesn't look up when we enter, lost in his thoughts, like he's not fully here. Lachlan silently observes, and

Calum and Will stand in front of Necktie, defending us, faces hard with determination.

When he notices me, Felix approaches Necktie with a locked jaw. His lips move, but I can't tell what he says.

"Fine." Necktie scowls and checks his watch. "You can have five minutes to talk."

He storms off, and Mateo shuffles toward the door. "Good luck," he says awkwardly. The boys follow him into the hall, and Calum shuts the door.

Immediately, Felix yanks me into a tight hug. I count the seconds as they pass, and when we reach twenty, I force myself away from him. We're on borrowed time.

I planned a speech in the hallway, but now that we're alone with nothing but our could-have-been love story and tears threatening to spill, everything I wanted to say evaporates.

Unable to conjure up anything else, I apologetically circle a fist on my chest.

He shakes his head rapidly, messy hair swaying. "***I'm*** the one who's sorry. If I was a normal teenager, Felix from Seattle, not 'America's Sweetheart,' we wouldn't be dealing with this."

He tries to hide his pain, but it's written all over his face: eyes shimmering with tears and lips twisted in agonizing guilt. It's woven into the way he speaks, voice thin and quivering.

I clamp down on the inside of my cheek. ***You can't cry, Natalie. You can't.*** I square my shoulders and steady my wobbly chin.

"You ***are*** Felix from Seattle," I emphasize. "No matter who your label tries to make you be, you are—and always will be—Felix from Seattle. They can't take that away from you."

"They can take everything! But I won't let them take you," he says. I read his lips, hanging on to every word. "You're the only person who helps me remember who I was. Who I ***am*** underneath all the lies."

I throw my arms around his waist and bury my head in his chest. My heart is breaking, but I force myself to hold it together. I blink away tears before stepping back. "The boys know who you are, probably even better than I do. They love you, and I know you love them. Don't make a rash decision, okay?" My voice is steady, measured, though inside I'm crumbling.

"It's not rash. I can't lose you—"

Worried I won't be able to calm his racing thoughts, I cut him off with a kiss.

Our lips meet in a clash of emotions. Fear, longing, relief. I reach up, and my fingers brush his soft skin and his hair, committing each sensation to memory. Painting a mental picture of this beautiful, devastating boy.

Felix loves me in a way I've never been loved, and I'm not sure I will be again. Dazzling, bold, and breathtaking. He would fight for me. For us. He would set aside his own aspirations and dreams to keep us together.

In this moment, I give him everything I have, the love I held back, the feelings I locked away. My fingers in his hair and the fabric of his hoodie in my clenched fist are the only things anchoring me. I pour my heart into the delicate dance of our tongues, the tenderness of our embrace, as if they can convey everything I can't say.

When he pulls away, it's a gut-wrenching sting. The breaking of something beautiful that I never wanted to lose. But, somehow, it's a relief, too. Part of me knows I wouldn't be strong enough to do it. He brushes hair out of my face and caresses my cheek.

"I'll stay here instead of coming to the concert. It'll allow everything to cool down," I blurt, afraid if I don't say it now, I never will.

"Alright. How 'bout you go to your room before Andrew comes back. I'll handle him, and we'll talk about next steps tonight, yeah?" I hate how relieved he seems.

I briefly debate hugging him, but it's a very real possibility I'd never let go. I gather last night's clothes off the floor and head for the hall; my heart aches with each beat, and my lungs feel depleted of air the closer I get to the door.

One hand on the knob, I freeze. I don't know what possesses me to spin around, but suddenly I'm staring at him from across the room. I take a long, lingering look, drinking in every minuscule detail, from the way his skin glows golden in the early-morning sun to the way his tangled bed head falls on his shoulders. He smiles at me—a bittersweet blend of affection and yearning. My heart splits in two.

Because even though he doesn't know it yet, ***I*** know this is the last time I'll see him. Not as the Felix Song the world knows—from billboards, talk shows, and sold-out stadiums.

This is the last time I'll see him as Felix from Seattle. As ***mine***.

☆ ☆ ☆

My Felix,

I'm sorry I left like this, but I can't be the thing that drags you down. I won't let you put me before yourself, your future, or the band.

Promise me something, would you? Don't let

others tell you who you are. You're so much more than what they think. You're funny, selfless, and one of the best people I know.

I'm sorry you never got to tell the girl you love that you love her... But trust me, she knows. She feels the same way.

I've thought of a million ways to say goodbye, but I don't want this to be "goodbye." I want it to be "see you later." Maybe your wish will come true and someday that'll be possible. Let's hope the universe is rooting for us.

Thank you for giving me something—no, someone to daydream about.

See you later, Pretty Boy,
Your Nat

Sadness and guilt wash over me like a tidal wave, destroying everything in its wake as I stare at the envelope that contains all the words I couldn't say to Felix in person, along with the Post-it note IOU that started this journey, a red X across it to void our "contract."

I'll worry about finances when I get home. The $40,000 was supposed to be "no strings attached," but I don't want his money.

I want ***him***.

Teary-eyed and brokenhearted, I press a kiss to the front of the envelope, whisper a final goodbye, and slide it under his door.

@SongHype2014 2h ago

I KNEW that slimeball was gunna use Felix for clout! He's an angel & she took advantage of him! She is pure evil!! Esp since she was his TEACHER. That's a gross betrayal of trust! Idk how he'll ever trust anyone again. **#SaveFelix #WeLoveYouFelix**

@FelixSongUpdates 1h ago

He's *19* . . . he's not in middle school or something. And if she wanted clout wouldn't she step forward as the girl in the pic?? I beg y'all to get some media literacy and leave this poor girl alone

@WillsLovelyGirl 49m ago

POOR GIRL!?!!? Felix was manipulated and exploited yet she's a POOR GIRL? This is a masterclass in victim blaming

@Dreamer02752 24m ago

jfc that bitch better stay FAR away from my baby boy & hope nobody finds her name+address bc i'll literally hunt her down 🤬 never ever have i wished harm upon someone more than rn

»»»

@FelixSongUpdates 14s ago

I'm the first person to rant about thinking you "know" celebs/ parasocial relationships but I'm 110% POSITIVE Felix and the other boys are disgusted by y'all. What the fuck is wrong with you?? He deserves a private life. Keyword: PRIVATE. If you "love" him as much as you say, you'd be happy he's happy! LOG OFF AND GO TO THERAPY

Chapter Thirty-Two

Not in a Sexy Way

Seattle, July 29–August 11

Outside SeaTac Airport that evening, late July humidity clings to my skin. I carefully scan the pickup zone until I spot Jo sitting on the hood of my ancient TOYOTA Corolla. Ginger and I dart over to her.

She jumps down, and her expression morphs into abject horror. "*You look terrible!*" She drags her thumb under my puffy eyes, scrubbing away smudged mascara. Even the best waterproof mascara is no match for post-breakup tears.

"*I'll kill him!*" she signs angrily. "*Nobody hurts my sister!*"

"*You saw the picture? I kissed him first. It's my fault*," I sign lifelessly.

"*Everyone's seen the picture*," she replies.

Of course they have. Why wouldn't the whole world be gossiping about Felix Song's mystery lover? It's such a tantalizing story—forget how the brutal online name-calling and demoralizing headlines will affect anyone involved! Who cares about people's emotions when there's a chance to exploit them for profit?

It's only when she starts massaging one of my shoulders that I realize how tense I am. "*I'm really sorry.*" She gives me a hug, then loads my suitcase and backpack into the trunk while I strap Ginger into her doggy seat belt.

Arriving home is bittersweet. The chipped white paint and key lime–green front door of our Ballard home only emphasizes the painful realization that I'm really ***here***. Back in Washington, 1,330 miles away from Felix.

Jo gets out, unbuckles Ginger, grabs my bags, and heads for the door. Ginger bounces around the overgrown front yard like a lamb, ecstatic to be home. I peel myself out of the car, and Ginger follows as I walk inside.

From the doorway, I catch a glimpse of my mom's graying pixie cut, her glasses perched on her sharp nose while she reads in the living room. She glances up from the novel; her brows curve downward, and her lips press into a line.

I can't deal with her right now.

Breaking eye contact, I snatch my bags from Jo, dash into my room, and slam the door. Then, like a raccoon with delicious trash, I drop to the floor and furiously dig through my backpack and suitcase, tossing flannels, underwear, and dog toys aside, until I uncover the oversized, purple-and-white-striped sweater I flagrantly stole; the Felix-branded pink blanket; the charcoal drawing of him canoeing; and the collection of sticky notes.

Each note is salt in the wound, and a fresh round of tears threatens my eyes. His awful jokes and sweet messages are an agonizing reminder of all I left behind. Tears run down my cheeks as I drape the blanket over my lap and hug the sweater and inhale deeply, breathing in Felix's god-awful cologne. With my eyes closed, it's almost like he's here. Strong arms wrapped around me, fingers grazing through my hair.

I'm startled when a hand touches my shoulder. I rip my face out of the sweater and see Mom leaning over me. My muscles instinctively tighten, and I shy away from her touch. She lowers herself to the ground, across from me.

Her steel-gray eyes study me before she delicately wipes one of my tears; I freeze, stunned by the intimacy. The last time she was this gentle with me was when Dad was diagnosed. For a second, I'm a child again, desperate for comfort from a mother who rarely gave it.

"I . . . tried my best to raise you girls after your dad died, but I made mistakes. I tried to protect you, but I hurt you instead." She hesitates, as if deciding whether to add the next part. *"I don't always agree with you, but I admire you. I love you."*

The world tilts on its axis. This isn't the mom I've had all my life, a constant critic who meets vulnerability with walls of ice. My mother doesn't apologize. She doesn't admit fault. But here she is, offering something foreign and fragile.

My heart unexpectedly aches as I attempt to reconcile the woman in front of me with the one I've known. This is the closest she's ever come to being the mother I've longed for. And for once, I let myself lean into it. Just for a moment.

Because—as recently evidenced by me ***completely*** misjudging Felix—I realize maybe I've been wrong about her, too. Maybe I've been so focused on what she's failed to give me, I haven't seen what she's been trying to offer in her own, flawed way.

"I love you, too." I sniffle.

"I'm sorry about you two. Do you want to talk?"

I'm not surprised she knows about us. Either Jo blabbed or Mom saw the news articles and drew assumptions.

"*No.*" I've had too much for one day.

Mom tucks faded pink hair behind my ears. "*OK. Leftovers are in the fridge if you're hungry.*"

I lower a hand from my chin, and she disappears into the hall.

When the morning sun peeks through my window, I stretch out on my floor and stare at Felix's sweater in my grasp.

I justified stealing it because I needed something to prove everything was real and I wasn't having some elaborate coma dream. But in the spirit of moving on, I fold it and stow it—along with his other things—on the top shelf of my closet, behind a box of Dad's things. Out of sight, out of mind, right?

Then I grab my phone and pace, trying to convince myself to turn it on. I powered it off yesterday. I couldn't bear to witness his live reaction to my departure. My flight touched down right as DAYDREAM's concert ended, and by the time we got home, he must've returned to the hotel and read my letter.

Taking the plunge, I power it on, and notifications instantly obscure the picture of Felix set as my lockscreen. They stack on top of one another in an endless stream. When the surge stops, I have 129 unread texts, 22 missed video calls, and 77 Google Alerts.

Opening the Messages app would be a lose-lose. If I don't open it, not knowing what he said will eat away at me. But if I read his messages, I'll be tempted to reply, and that's something I absolutely ***cannot*** do. No matter how much it feels like ripping my heart out, I need to maintain this distance. I can't rob him of his dream.

I take a forceful inhale, and on the exhale, I launch the app.

Mon, July 29, 8:43 PM

[Pretty Boy 🙃]

Nat don't go!! Where are u rn?? I'll come get u & we can talk

Tues, July 30, 12:02 AM

[Pretty Boy 🙃]

Pls anwser my calls! We'll work this out!!

I keep scrolling through his dozens of texts, stopping when a message tugs at my heart especially hard.

Tues, July 30, 7:02 AM

[Pretty Boy 🙃]

Nat you don't have to talk to me ok? Text one of the boys if you want. Just pls let me know your safe. That's all I care abt. I love you. I'm sorry.

Tears prickling my eyes, I perch myself on the edge of my twin-size bed, my hands shaking uncontrollably as I click on his contact and scroll to the bottom. My finger hovers over the Block Number button.

A fiery, visceral pain seizes me, nearly causing me to double over when my finger finally hits the button and I watch his contact Thanos Snap out of existence.

"Out of sight, out of mind" is a load of crap.

It's been five days. An entire 117 hours since I left. Since I last saw, touched, or talked to Felix Song. He's extremely out of sight, yet I can't stop thinking about him.

I stay busy every second of every day, yet my mind always wanders back to the frosty-haired, warmhearted boy. Teaching ASL lessons, I think about how his eyes lit up while I signed stories. Painting fluffy clouds on the ceiling of the K–5 room reminds me of DAYDREAM's tour poster. Making coffee, I remember how unbelievably sarcastic he gets if he consumes caffeine. During nights I lie awake, I reminisce about late-night study sessions that morphed into so much more.

Even now, I ***should*** be preoccupied with writing a blog post, but instead, I'm standing behind the front desk, scrolling through DAYDREAM's Instagram like a Stage Five Clinger. It's counterproductive to "moving on" and "healing," but I can't help it.

Unsurprisingly, Felix has been radio silent. The only post-scandal activity on DAYDREAM's account is a carousel post with a photo of the sea of fans at their Dallas concert two nights ago, followed by a selfie of Calum and Will ZOOLANDER smizing while backstage.

It hits me how much I miss the rest of the guys. I never expected it, but they became the coolest friends I've ever had. Losing them in all this makes everything exponentially harder.

A hand flapping in my face rips me out of phone world and back into real life. "*Mrs. S and* A-V-A *keep asking about you. They want to know when you'll teach them again now that the tour's almost over*," Jo tells me.

I cringe. I've resumed private lessons with my other clients, freeing Jo of her substitute teacher role, but I can't bring myself to tell the Songs I'm back. It's too much. Too raw.

"*I'm not ready*," I answer, hands trembling at the thought of facing anyone remotely associated with Felix.

She huffs. "*I know. But I'm caught in the middle! It's annoying!*"

"*Sorry my misery is inconvenient for you.*"

I can tell she's fighting the urge to roll her eyes as she steps behind the front desk and gives me another suffocating hug. Then she rifles through her backpack and pulls out two sack lunches before sitting on the ground. "*You're* H-A-N-G-R-Y."

I sit beside her and turn an apple over and over in my hand, lost in thought.

Jo snags my attention by poking my leg. "*Have you talked to him?*" she asks while biting into her bologna sandwich.

My appetite vanishes into thin air. I set the apple down. "*I blocked him.*"

Her jaw drops. "*He's so sad! Why would you do that?!*"

"*Me too! We're both sad!*"

"*I know. Sorry. But I feel bad for him.*" She juts her lower lip with a frown. "*Also . . . you didn't get me a signed album or poster.*"

"*I don't want to talk about Felix.*" Jo reluctantly drops the subject and starts filling me in on Ava's progress. I shove Felix into the far corners of my mind, ignoring the heaviness weighing on me.

☆ ☆ ☆

After nearly two weeks of being glued to my phone, I finally turn off my Google Alerts and DAYDREAM's post notifications and set a personal rule that I can only check their Instagram twice a day. (I think that is a perfectly acceptable ***and*** healthy coping mechanism.)

As soon as I get home from a day full of renovations at the Center, I flop onto my bed. I put the fuzzy pink Felix blanket over my shoulders like a cape while Ginger snuggles next to me and falls into a peaceful sleep. I press a gentle kiss to her snout before plucking my phone off the nightstand—where I left it this morning in order to adhere to my twice-a-day cyberstalking rule. If I don't have my phone, I can't check it. Work smarter, not harder.

I immediately go to the band's Instagram account. No new posts, but their story has four recent additions.

First, the boys posing outside their LA venue with enthusiastic grins, save Felix, who looks checked out and exhausted; second, Mateo making a goofy face while Bhavani does his makeup; third, a short clip of Lachlan doing an onstage mic check; last, a video of all of them in their subtle-but-flashy, boyish-yet-sexy stage outfits as they perform.

A hairline fracture threatens to split the two pieces of my heart into three. In every clip or picture with Felix, he looks like a vampire. And ***not*** in a sexy way. He's paler, with bloodshot eyes and lifeless expressions. He looks sick of being tried in the court of public opinion.

It takes me a dozen tries to swallow the lump in my throat. I close out of Instagram and doomscroll on other apps. My pulse quickens when I discover #FelixSong and #DAYDREAM are trending at number one and two.

I click the first hashtag, and my feed is flooded with posts from worried fans and tabloids sharing links to the newest articles they've written.

Posts discussing the picture of us are interspersed, and I nearly heave at what more zealous "fans" are saying. Everything from insults to slut shaming, all the way to attempted doxing and graphic death threats.

The vitriolic hate is seared into my mind, even as I click out of #FelixSong and into #DAYDREAM. My disgust (and fear) is slowly joined by concern for Felix as I read posts from different fans. Some share their own vampiresque pictures and videos of him; others discuss their concern for his mental health or DAYDREAM's lackluster performances. Apparently, in Austin he sang off-key; during their Phoenix show, he zoned out the whole time and missed cues; and tonight he teared up while singing "Lovely Girl."

Tears cloud my vision as I close the app and click Mateo's contact. I video call him, but it goes unanswered. I try Calum next, since there's no way in hell I'm calling Lachlan, and Will is more likely to give me shit than Calum. Silently praying he'll be in his typical chill Bro-Dude headspace, I press the Call button and sit up.

Anxiety builds as it rings, but finally, his face appears. His unicorn horn hair, lack of shirt, and big brown eyes would probably bring me comfort if he didn't have a cutting scowl.

"So your phone ***does*** work," he bites. "We texted you a bajillion times. You could've let us know you were safe. It's been two weeks! What the hell, bro?"

Ouch. I exhale sharply as his iciness hits me.

I repeatedly open and close my mouth, searching for a reply. Why did I call? What was I going to say? I can't remember anything now.

"I'm really worried about Felix," I squeak out.

"Join the club."

"I just want to make sure he's okay. Or that he will be okay. I've seen stuff online, and I'm concerned."

"If you— —worried, talk to— —yourself." His speech cuts out, but I understand the gist.

"Leaving was the best thing I could do, Cal, for the band and for Felix. I have to stay away, or it'll ruin your careers!"

He scoffs. "He's miserable! He's ruining his career anyway." His eyes bore into me, harsher and darker than ever. "You dumping him like that, giving him the silent treatment . . . it broke him. None of us know how to help him, and it's made— —rest of the tour pretty shitty. Andrew's threatening— —anyway. Don't be delusional, ***this*** isn't 'best for the band.'"

Chapter Thirty-Three

Some Strings Attached

Seattle, August 17

This isn't best for the band is permanently etched into my psyche.

I've tried everything short of hypnotism to make myself believe leaving was the right move. But is anything ***really*** right if you have to convince yourself it was?

The question ricochets around my brain like a pinball and exacerbates my little I-can't-stop-thinking-about-Felix's-annoyingly-attractive-perfectly-symmetrical-face-and-how-much-I-want-to-smash-my-lips-into-his problem.

I look at the list of ASL sentences on the whiteboard in the front of the classroom, reconnecting myself to the world around me. I turn toward the students, hoping I wasn't zoned out for too long.

While they sign flawlessly, my mind drifts again because, as if this situation couldn't be any messier, DAYDREAM's in Seattle for their grand finale concert tonight. In fact, thanks to social media—which has thankfully moved on from posting death threats, though I still see the occasional theory about Felix's mystery lover—I know which hotel they're staying at, the license plates of the SUVs they're driven around in, and even what Calum DoorDashed last night.

The internet is a scary place, but Felix being twenty minutes away is scarier.

At the end of class, I reach under the desk and boop Ginger's nose before grabbing the eraser and wiping the board. My cleanup is interrupted when Jo pops her head into the room.

"*Someone's here for you,*" she signs, waggling her brows. "*In the office.*"

The eraser clatters to the floor and startles a sleepy Ginger. Someone randomly dropping by the Center to visit me, the day after DAYDREAM arrived, is too much of a coincidence for it to ***not*** be Felix. Right?

Shit, shit, ***shit***.

Did he come all this way to pull an UNO Reverse Card and break ***my*** heart? Does he want to tell me I'm the literal spawn of Satan and he loathes my very existence? Either way, I'd probably deserve it.

I take a beat to center myself before heading for the office. My pulse pounds, nerves alight with anxiety. I stop outside, hand floating above the doorknob, and my thoughts run wild.

If he's behind this door—strands of long hair framing the face some deity hand-sculpted, wearing his obnoxious BURBERRY trench coat—***what do I do? What do I say?***

Should I apologize? Kick him out? Superglue our hands together so he never leaves my sight again?

I steel myself and twist the handle. A familiar face sits at my desk, his arms neatly folded on the desktop, blond hair shining underneath the fluorescent lights.

A surge of distress, shock, and irritation hits me, and I scoff. He has a herculean amount of audacity to show up here after everything he did.

"Hey . . ." Lachlan greets.

"I have nothing to say to you," I spit, harsher than intended.

I turn to leave, but he pops up and blocks my path. He grabs my hand and uses SimCom with the other. "He's going to quit after our Seattle show."

I yank my hand away. "W-what?! He can't! I left so he can stay in the band!"

"I know. But he won't listen to anyone. Especially not me—"

"No shit," I murmur, but he ignores me.

"—and you're the only person who has a chance to get through to him." He grabs his phone and flips the screen toward me. He shows me a VIP ticket in his Apple Wallet for tonight's concert. "You have to come and talk— —him."

"Don't tell me what I 'have' to do!" I huff. "This is real rich coming from you. So, what, you see the value in our relationship now?" I bite down on my cheek. "I can't go. Have his family talk to him, maybe, but I'll ruin everything."

"Everything is already fucking ruined!" he snaps.

"And whose fault is that?!"

Dirty blond hair falls in his eyes as he hangs his head. He scrubs hands over his face before looking at me. "Natalie . . ." he starts, wetness forming in his ocean eyes, emotion bleeding through the calculated calmness I've come to expect from him.

"*I'm sorry*. I'm so sorry. There's no excuse for how I acted or treated you, and— —don't expect you to forgive me. Actually, you ***shouldn't*** forgive me, but seeing Lix absolutely head over heels for someone hurt more than— —thought, and I snapped. I never should have gone behind your backs. You make him so happy, in— —way I"—he falters, voice breaking—"in a way ***I*** never could. I love Felix, but that's not his problem. Or yours."

My jaw hits the ground. What the ***hell***?!

"Lachlan . . . you're . . . in love with ***Felix***?" I stammer, unable to comprehend the bombshell he just dropped.

Lachlan wasn't being a shithead because he had a crush on ***me*** . . . He was in love with ***Felix*** and wanted me out of the way?! (As if that isn't the I-need-to-stop-making-assumptions-about-others icing on the cake. Good lord.)

He rubs his eyes, nodding. "I didn't want to lose him, so— —tried to keep you apart. But I'm going— —lose him anyway. We all are. There's no DAYDREAM without Felix, and it seems that there's no Felix without Natalie."

"Lachlan . . ." I shake my head in disbelief. "I appreciate the apology, but you or the boys or his family will have to convince him. I'm not going."

"Please! You're the only one he might actually listen to." I gulp. He works his jaw but ultimately backs down. "*OK. Fine.*" His hands are weak as he signs. "But I'll email you the ticket anyway. Think about it." He plucks my business card off the desk and leaves.

I double over and squeeze my eyes shut, lip pressed between my teeth, willing myself not to cry as memories are thrust to the forefront of my mind.

Felix's heat shielding me from biting nighttime wind, the stolen moments where we escaped and explored, the arsenal of supplies in his PRADA fanny pack. Memories of the tour and the feeling of loving and being loved are seared into the depths of my soul.

No, I tell myself. I can't.

The thought cuts through me like an order, a command I repeat in my mind. I have to stay away. For Felix's own good. Memories can't rewrite the rules, and my feelings—dangerous, complicated feelings—can't cloud my judgment.

Time on the lobby's wall clock passes with ruthless precision. 5:28 p.m. By now, the boys are backstage, reconnecting with their families, while fans buzz with anticipation outside the venue.

This is torture.

I try to distract myself by going through mail. My mindless, zombielike sorting halts when I come across a white envelope hand-addressed to me. There's no return address.

I swallow a clump of nerves as I slice into it with the letter opener. ***Please don't be another huge bill.*** I take the letter out and unfold it; a smaller slip of paper and a USB drive fall out. I snatch the paper before it floats to the ground, and my eyes widen in disbelief. It's a cashier's check for $23,500.

Picking my jaw off the floor, I lean down and grab the USB drive, which has a pink sticky note attached to it. It's impossible to tell if my heartbeat speeds up or stops completely as I read the familiar and charmingly messy handwriting.

WATCH THIS AFTER READING
THE LETTER.
THANK YOU FOR EVRYTHING.

XXX

With shaky hands, I turn my attention to the longer letter.

NAT,
I'M NOT SURE WHERE TO START. YOUR BETTER WITH WORDS THEN ME.

1—I TRIED FOLLOWING MY DREAMS & IT DIDN'T WORK VERY WELL. WHAT I'M DOING NOW ISN'T WHAT MY DREAM WAS. ITS NOTHING COMPARED TO THE DIFFERANCE YOUR MAKING. YOUR GONNA CHANGE THE ~~WOLRD~~ WORLD.

2—DON'T GET WIERD ABOUT THE MONEY. $23,500 IS WHAT I OWED YOU. YOU EARNED IT, YEAH?? NO REFUNDS!!!

3—BASED ON YOUR IDEA, I'D LIKE TO START A NON-PROFIT TO FUND DEAF CENTRES AROUND THE CONTRY, STARTING WITH YOURS. I RESEARCHED IT BUT THERE'S A LOT OF LEGAL JARGON & WE BOTH KNOW WHAT HAPPNED LAST TIME I DID CONTRACT STUFF . . . CAN YOU HELP? NO STRINGS ATACHED

4—I LOVE YOU. & I'LL NEVER SAY IT AGAIN IF YOU DON'T WANT ME TOO. BUT I HOPE YOU'LL LET ME SAY IT AGAIN. EVRY DAY OF MY LIFE.

XXX
YOUR FELIX

P.S: YOU CAN KEEP THE SWEATER YOU TOOK . . . BUT IF YOU DON'T WANT IT, LEMME KNOW. ITS MY FAVOURITE :(

P.S. #2: OH HEADS UP THAT THIS 100% LEGALLY BINDING CONTRACT IS STILL IN PLACE. WHAT YOU DO WITH IT NOW IS UP TO YOU . . . BUT IT'LL DEF HOLD UP IN COURT. SUPER OFICIAL. IRONCLAD. (I KNOW I SAID NO STRINGS ATACHED . . . MAYBE SOME STRINGS? THE STRING LEVEL IS UP TO YOU. NO PRESSURE)

P.S. #3: OK NOW WATCH THE VIDEO. IT'S GONNA BE POSTED IN A WEEK BUT I WANT YOU TO SEE IT 1ST. OK THAT'S ALL!!!

I peel off the purple sticky note attached to P.S. #2 and hug it to my chest. It's the contract we scrawled on the Ferris wheel in Minnesota. A tiny, ridiculous promise that meant the world.

That still does.

Clutching everything, I bolt to the office and whip the door open. Jo looks up from where she's typing on our prehistoric desktop. "*I need the computer!*" I urge, pulling out the chair she's in and nudging her.

"*Did Mom do something else?!*" she asks after standing.

I don't reply. I jam the USB drive into the computer, minimize the window Jo was using, and press Play. The circle of death spins for a few minutes while the video loads. Jo loses interest and plops down on the floor to rub Ginger's belly.

Finally, guitar strumming flows through the monitor speakers; I crank the volume. Bold text on a black screen appears.

Story of Our Love

Written by Felix Song

Shot and edited by DAYDREAM

My breath catches in my throat as Felix appears on-screen. He's standing on a surfboard on a beach while Calum steadies him. I recognize it from LA.

Subtitles at the bottom of the screen appear as the song starts. The scenes in the video keep changing, and I remember nearly every one. I even filmed some. From Will being sprayed by water guns and Mateo's alligator-induced meltdown in Miami, to Calum and Felix holding hands at the National Mall, to footage from various concerts and them holding up state flags onstage.

Tears well in my eyes as footage from Rockefeller Center plays. Felix's ruby-red cheeks as he accidentally does a split, his dark eyes clearly focused on someone off-camera, his impossibly wide smile as I'm telling awful jokes triggers agonizing pain straight into my heart.

It's like I can physically feel my heart crumbling into dust, every suppressed emotion suddenly raw and bleeding again. More clips play—Calum throwing the first pitch at Fenway Park, Lachlan and Felix laughing in the gem hall, and clips from cities I wasn't there for. San Antonio, Phoenix, Portland. I try to focus on the subtitles through watery eyes.

(Verse 1) Oh, our love was like the summer breeze
Gone too fast, wild and free
Hand in hand, we found our way
You were a risk I loved to take

(Bridge) Underneath the stars, we talked 'til dawn
Silence and sound, the difference in our lives
Walking in the wind, hidden in the shadow
of doubt
You and I came together in the haze of
fleeting summer days

(Chorus) Did I not hold on tight? How did
I go and lose my light?

In the story of our love, this chapter ended far too soon
The story of our love was an honor to write

(Outro) So here's to us, the love we shared
Though seasons change, my heart stays true
In the story of our love, I'll always choose you

As the video ends, tears cascade down my face. I furiously wipe them away, but my chest heaves, and shocks of regret and guilt shoot through me. But after watching it again to make sure it isn't some lovesick hallucination, I burst into a fit of hysterical laughter.

I'm so desperately in love with Felix Song I feel it in my very core. My love for him is woven into the fabric of who I've become over these past few months. I love him so much I don't even balk at the fact he sent a $23,500 cashier's check in the mail as nonchalantly as my grandma sends birthday cards with five bucks.

This letter and song and video, beyond a shadow of a doubt, solidify my choice: I'm going to the concert. I'm going to say everything I never got to. I'm never going to leave his side again.

Jo watches in perplexed alarm as I launch out of the chair and scramble for my keys. "*Where are you going?!*"

One foot out the door, I hurriedly reply, "*I'm getting my boy back.*"

Chapter Thirty-Four

The Boy Natalie Nielsen Loves

Seattle, August 17

Unfortunately, Downtown Seattle traffic doesn't care if you have a time-sensitive love declaration to make. Rush hour serves no one.

Ironically, as if the universe is laughing at me, I get stuck next to a DAYDREAM—LIVE IN CONCERT! 8/17! billboard and stare at an enormous picture of the boys for forty minutes.

When I move past the cluster of traffic, I speed toward Climate Pledge Arena a little faster than what's legal. The clock on my dashboard becomes a ticking time bomb, and whenever the number changes, I nearly break into a cold sweat.

Finally, I arrive. Unable to find parking, I have no choice but to park in front of a fire hydrant. I peer at the bomb-slash-dashboard and grimace. 6:27 p.m. Only thirty-three minutes until showtime. Thirty-three minutes to find Felix.

I make a mad dash for an entrance. ***Please don't get a parking ticket. Please***, I beg any and all divine beings.

Thankfully, most fans are already inside, and the lines aren't unbearably long. Once I'm through security, a tough-looking person stops me. "Scan your ticket."

I grab my phone to present the ticket Lachlan sent, but it isn't in my inbox. I check my junk folder, but it isn't there, either. ***Shit.***

"Um. Hi"—I look at the security guard's name tag—"Glenn Fitzgerald. This is really hard to explain, and you look like a busy person, so I'll spare you the details, but ***super*** funny story . . . I don't currently possess a ticket."

Glenn Fitzgerald blinks at me.

"I'm guessing you're not going to believe me if I tell you I'm with the band?"

"Correct."

Double shit. I move to the side and check the time. 6:38 p.m. Twenty-two minutes.

I open Contacts and scroll to Lachlan. He's my final chance at getting past Glenn Fitzgerald. (No shade; they're very good at their job. If I were them, I wouldn't let me inside, either.) I hit the Video Call button and continue pacing as it rings, but it times out.

I call again. Thankfully, he answers. He's in a dark area. The light from his phone barely illuminates him enough for me to see the collar of his sweater-vest and middle part.

"I'm here!" I exclaim, in disbelief he actually answered. "Your email didn't come through!" I rush to explain the situation and where I am.

"We're about to perform!" He pinches the bridge of his nose while he thinks. "Okay," he says, "I'm coming."

He hangs up, and I pace, trying to expel nervous energy while I stare at the time on my phone and wait. My anxiety skyrockets when two minutes turn into five, and there's now only seventeen minutes left before showtime.

Worst-case scenarios run through my head. What if Lachlan tripped and broke his ankle? Or Necktie forced him to stay? Or he wanted to get the last laugh, so he lied about emailing the ticket and isn't coming to my rescue after all?

Just as I've convinced myself Lachlan won't have a redemption arc, he barrels into the atrium. The few fans left in line squeal or yell his name, and he waves hurriedly before rushing to security and flashing his Artist Pass. "That one's with me."

Glenn Fitzgerald eyes me suspiciously but doesn't fight it.

"Thank you!" I rush, glancing at the time. Alarms go off in my head. 6:47 p.m. Thirteen minutes.

Lachlan's eyes widen as he peers at my screen. "Damn it. Follow me."

He grabs my hand and we take off running through the building, a long hallway, and down a flight of stairs. We go through a door labeled UNDER STAGE ACCESS and enter a dark corridor. Dozens of cords run along the ground, and it's jam-packed with stressed stagehands.

"***Shit***," Lachlan hisses, looking past me. "Natalie, go! Go!" He shoves me, which causes me to headbutt a metal beam.

"Ow! Jesus, we're in a rush, but a concussion isn't going to help—" I shut up when I spot Necktie storming toward us.

"Go!" he repeats.

I elbow past staff members and stagehands as I search for Felix. I stop when my path is blocked by a boy in a familiar pink cropped sweater and jeans. "Mateo, move!"

Mateo jumps out of his skin and whips around. "N-Natalie?!" he stutters. I feel bad for startling him, but when he moves and I have a clear view of who's in front of him, the emotion vanishes.

Hunched because of the low ceiling, Felix is a ghost of himself. Gauntness sharpens his cheekbones, and his silky V-neck button-up hangs looser on his frame. His dangly gold earrings seem out of place—a glimmer of gold on someone who's been dimmed.

My stomach twists, a painful mix of guilt and helplessness claws at me. I creep forward until the tips of our shoes touch, overwhelmed by the urge to reach out and breathe life back into the broken, fragile boy.

"I'm sorry," I choke out. My throat closes, trapping every unspoken emotion inside.

How do people in romance novels do this? How do characters find the perfect words to slice through chaos and lay everything bare?

I meet his eyes, praying that somehow he'll see in my tear-filled gaze the words I can't find. I can feel the vibrations as my heart pounds.

When he only blinks at me, expression unreadable under the low lights, my brain scrambles for the right words. "I never meant to hurt you. I was trying to p-protect you, but I fucked up. I only wanted . . . I just . . . if you tell me to leave, I will, but please don't," I urge.

My fingers tremble as I pull our Post-it note promise from my pocket, smooth it between my fingers, and offer it to him. He doesn't move.

"Rain or shine," I breathe, quoting the contract, "up or down. Hold me to it, baby. Please."

He still doesn't take it.

With a huff, I stand on my tiptoes and smack it onto his

forehead—like he's done to me dozens of times. His lips part in surprise and he peels it off, eyes roving over it.

Time stands still.

I'm on a cliff's edge.

But then, in one fluid motion, his arms circle my waist and haul me close. Before I can even breathe, his lips capture mine.

The kiss is fierce and electric. My fingers curl into the collar of his shirt, anchoring me to him so letting go isn't an option. The boys cheer, but they seem a thousand miles away. There's nothing but Felix—lips hot against mine, our love blazing bright.

We smile into the kiss, and I step back. His forehead rests against mine, and the air between us is charged, humming with everything we've said and everything we haven't.

"I love you, Felix Song." The words tumble out, and they feel right. So right. "I love you, I love you, I love you. And I'll say it every day of my life if you'll let me."

His face softens into something achingly tender. He cups my cheeks like I'm the most precious thing in the world. "*I love you, too,*" he signs. "I want nothing more than to hear that every day."

I drag him into another deep, dreamlike kiss, my hands sliding into his hair as his arms tighten around me. Kissing under a dark, cramped stage, surrounded by confused staffers and hollering bandmates, seconds before Felix will be presented to thousands of adoring fans may not sound like a fairy tale ending . . . but I don't want a fairy tale.

I just want the boy with stars in his eyes.

Chapter Thirty-Five

Dreams Come True

Six Months Later

Seattle, February 16

"You're late!" I gripe as DAYDREAM comes bowling through the doors of the new and improved Nielsen Family Deaf Center.

Mateo is the first to hug me, followed by Calum. Will greets Ginger first—after obtaining permission and assuring me he took Zyrtec—then quickly side-hugs me.

Lachlan embraces me last, then rubs an apologetic fist around his chest and side-eyes Felix. "We're late because, surprise, surprise, Lix got lost."

My focus shifts to Felix, and I cock a brow. "Seriously? You've driven here dozens of times and you still don't know the way?"

He shrugs while shuffling toward me. He pecks my forehead. "*You look beautiful,*" he signs, lower lip jutted, his "you can't possibly be mad at me" face. And damn it, I ***can't*** be mad at that cute face.

On the other end of the lobby, Jo circles a claw-shaped hand on her sternum, "*Make-me-disgusted.*" Beside her, Ava beams ear to ear and clasps a hand over her heart.

I sigh, but my frustration is gone. "*You're beautiful, too,*" I return Felix's compliment.

Though we're already behind schedule, I pause to take him in. His natural, healthy black hair that's styled in a shorter, shaggy wolf cut and light BB cream that gently emphasizes his features make him look more human. Like Felix from Seattle—a nineteen-year-old guy who happens to be in a famous boy band.

Like my boyfriend, who happens to be America's Sweetheart.

All the boys look ***real*** now, but they still have a splash of teenage superstar glamour. They can't completely abandon their brand.

After the tour ended—and after hearing my genius advice—the boys met with their corporate overlords and served an ultimatum: Make changes or lose DAYDREAM. It was a huge risk, considering their six-year non-compete clause, but a good lawyer of their own plus their recent success had the label agreeing to the majority of their demands.

Most changes were minor: They can wear the clothes they want as long as they're not too Sk8er Boi, emo-kid chic; record some original songs; and play their instruments. Lachlan even got permission to wear his eyebrow piercing in public!

But the biggest, and best, change was Necktie being fired and replaced by Layla, a Black woman with long purple locs, who is a strategic yet compassionate manager that actually listens to the band. That's karma.

I'm incredibly biased, but I like them better this way. These are the boys I know and love.

"You ready?" Felix asks. He looks past me with a hopeful yet cautious smile.

I turn as Mom re-enters the lobby after quadruple-checking everything is ready to be unveiled. Even after months of revamping, she's paranoid something will be out of place or unfinished. But the rooms are perfect. Everything is perfect.

"We've been ready for ten minutes," Mom replies. *"That's a bad color on you,"* she changes the subject, pointing to the Shrek-green sweater underneath Felix's BURBERRY trench coat. She pats his cheek as she walks off.

Felix and I exchange pleased looks. She's warming up to all the changes in our lives one blunt comment at a time.

She flicks the lobby lights to get everyone's attention. *"The event's starting soon!"* I interpret for her, and the boys gather in front of the doors.

Before we head outside, Jo snags my wrist and leads Ginger and me behind the front desk. She hands me a gift-wrapped box. I tear through the paper, and my breath catches. A wooden frame encases one of Dad's and my drawings for what we wanted the Center's lobby to look like.

It's the last sketch we ever did together.

I run my fingers over the glass, landing on our signatures scrawled in the bottom corner.

"You made it a reality. Look." She motions between the lobby and the sketch. They're nearly identical.

"We did it together," I correct, then wrap my not-so-little sister in a hug.

Eventually, she frees herself and turns to the wall behind the desk. She hangs the drawing on two nails she ***insisted*** we put there yesterday.

I beam at her, and against my will, wetness forms in my eyes. "*KissFist. Thank you.*"

"*Don't cry. You'll ruin your makeup!*" she warns, then links our arms, leading Ginger and me into the cold February air.

Outside, a large crowd has gathered: D/deaf folks and their families and friends, volunteers and sponsors, local ASL teachers and interpreters, some disability advocates, reporters, and one of my favorite Deaf-Hard of Hearing authors. Cameras roll and photographers snap pictures as the band members organize themselves behind the red ribbon in front of the building.

Ava heads for where Mr. and Mrs. Song are mixed in with the crowd, but Felix snags her hand and positions her in front of him, keeping her close during this big moment. Jo, Ginger, and I stand in the front, and Mom's behind us.

"Thank you for coming to the Nielsen Family Deaf Center's Grand Reopening!" I use SimCom so everyone can understand me. "My family always dreamed of making a difference in the Deaf community. To teach sign, push for inclusivity and accommodation, and show people, Deaf and Hearing, our beautiful world.

"And thanks to our generous sponsors, and the help of the Daydream Foundation"—I gesture toward the band, who flash genuine, toothy smiles—"we've taken a huge step toward accomplishing that!"

Pure joy overwhelms me as the crowd erupts in applause.

Jo steps forward with a pair of comically oversized scissors. I hold one side of the handle, and she takes the other. Together, we cut through the ribbon and ring in a new era of community, diversity, and joy.

My heart threatens to explode as my beloved Deaf Center fills with people for the first time in years.

Children crowd around a volunteer who's conducting an ASL storytime, Ava mingles with other D/deaf teens, and parents tour remodeled rooms and learn about our after-school programs and weekend day camps.

Mr. and Mrs. Song and Mom sign with one another in the main classroom. Jo hands out pamphlets, and Will follows her and takes photos for our social media.

The Center my parents built from the ground up, my second home, is finally what Dad envisioned. I wish he could see it.

After an hour of giving interviews, socializing, and personally thanking sponsors, I station myself by the front desk. It provides a vantage point to observe everything and greet people coming and going.

"*Have a great night!*" I tell Sabrina, Frank, and Frank's girlfriend Janet as they leave.

"*Goodnight!*" Frank signs, then, turning to Janet, he yells: "NATALIE SAID GOODNIGHT, HONEY!" He resumes pushing Janet's wheelchair, and Sabrina apologizes as they step outside.

"*I love Frank,*" Ethan, one of our volunteers, signs with a chuckle. "*You told me you wanted to introduce me to someone, right?*"

I grin mischievously and lead him down the hall, accompanied by Ginger.

We enter the K–5 room, and I spot Lachlan and Felix in the corner. Lachlan chats with a young couple while Felix entertains a baby with cochlear implants. The baby has their chubby fists wrapped in his hair and giggles as he makes funny faces.

I wait for a pause in the conversation. Eventually, the parents reclaim their baby. The baby flaps their little hand at me as the family leaves, and I melt.

"Hey," Lachlan greets using SimCom. He glances between Ethan and me.

"This is E-T-H-A-N, sign name Ethan. He's nice, cute, and smart!" Then I turn toward Ethan and gesture to Lachlan. *"Ethan, this is L-A-C-H-L-A-N. He's above average."*

Lachlan scoffs, and I stifle a chuckle. The pair blink at each other for a second. *"Nice to meet you,"* Ethan signs with red cheeks.

A similar blush creeps onto Lachlan's face. *"You . . . come here often?"*

Felix snorts at his best friend's clunky flirting. I take him to the lobby. "So you're a matchmaker now?" he teases. "Might wanna help Mateo. He's floundering."

I crane my neck and peer into the community room, where Mateo's doing ***something*** with his hands, but definitely not signing, to Jo. Will awkwardly teeters near them. Poor guy must be cursed to always be a third wheel. "It's great immersive practice," I joke. I doubt Jo minds being his teacher.

Felix spins me around to face him, his grip on my hand tightens as he leans against the wall. *"I'm proud of you."* His signs are steady and genuine, and the depth of emotion is clear in his eyes.

I glance at the new framed picture of Dad's and my sketch.

"He's proud, too, love," he signs.

Triumph laced with heartache materializes as tears. Like Frank can't stop yelling, or Felix can't stop being annoying and hot, I can't stop tearing up whenever I think about Dad. But tonight, it's mostly happy. Because we did it. We made his dreams—***our*** dreams—come true.

"How do you feel?"

"Good," I reply, though it doesn't nearly encapsulate my emotions. *"I really think the Center will change a lot of lives."*

Felix nods, strands of black hair falling in his eyes. *"I agree."*

I inch closer and brush the wisps away, running my free hand through his hair. *"Thank you for everything, baby."* I stand on my tiptoes and kiss him.

He leans into it. I let him push the boundaries but quickly break away since this is a family-friendly event.

He pulls back with a dangerously radiant grin. *"We should celebrate!"* He pretends to think deeply about what this "special celebration" could be, tapping fingers on his chin. "Ah! *How would you feel about going on a trip with me?"* A glimmer of mischievousness dances in his eyes.

I quirk a suspicious brow. *"What does 'a trip' mean?"*

"Our first world tour is this summer . . . And I want you to come," he signs, then adds, "Tokyo and Berlin have some great gluten-free bakeries!"

I freeze, letting the news sink in. I knew this was coming. America's hottest boy band can't become the ***world's*** hottest boy band without, you know, traveling the world.

After processing, I laugh. "Loving you is never going to be easy, is it?"

The corners of his eyes crinkle. "Yeah, nah, I don't reckon it will be. But y'know what?"

"*What?*"

"*It'll never be boring.*" He winks.

DAYDREAM Wiki Member Partner Profile

FULL NAME: Natalie Elanna Nielsen

AGE: 19

HEIGHT: 5'5" (165 cm)

HOMETOWN: Ballard, Washington, USA

PARTNER: Felix

NATALIE FACTS:

- Her hobbies include playing with her dog, grassroots activism, drawing, beating people at board games, and critiquing book-to-movie adaptations
- Her role model is her dad
- She loves horror movies and finds it funny how much of a scaredy-cat Felix is
- She's a huge bookworm, and some of her favorite books are CEMETERY BOYS, SO LET THEM BURN, THE HUNGER GAMES, and THE LOUDEST SILENCE
- Her life motto is "Risk is better than regret"
- When asked what three things she couldn't live without, she said pastries, bodily autonomy, and Felix

Author's Note

Dear Reader,

Ever since I started writing, I dreamed of creating a feel-good, YA rom-com that featured unabashed Disabled joy. Now, don't get me wrong, SOMEONE TO DAYDREAM ABOUT is a book that was also born out my love for boy bands, Disney Channel Original Movies, sarcastic main characters, and fanfiction—but above all else, it was created out of my passion for books that take well-loved tropes and put a fresh, Disabled twist on them, and my desire to share some of my own experiences being Deaf.

My dreams came true with STDA. A book where Natalie—a girl who takes great pride in her identities, as well as sign language and Deaf culture—gets to have her main character moment and fall in love; where Felix, a Hearing love interest, isn't celebrated or seen as "charitable" simply because he likes a Deaf girl; where disabilities aren't treated like a bad thing, something that needs to be "cured" or "overcome."

I wrote SOMEONE TO DAYDREAM ABOUT for readers, like me, who long to see more love stories highlighting marginalized characters—but also for readers who wish to get a glimpse into a different perspective. Perhaps most importantly, I wrote STDA to show readers from all backgrounds that Disabled characters are not only allowed to get but ***deserve*** to get the "happily-ever-afters" that able-bodied characters have received time and time again.

Thank you for letting me share it with you.

—Sydney Langford (they/them)

Acknowledgments

They say publishing a book is like running a race. Well . . . getting SOMEONE TO DAYDREAM ABOUT on shelves was like an ultramarathon up a 90-degree mountain. I wouldn't have reached the finish line without incredible cheerleaders.

While One Direction isn't ***technically*** responsible for this book, let's be real—they definitely inspired it. Thank you for being the soundtrack of my youth and for teaching me to dream unapologetically big.

To Asia Harden, my guiding light during the darkest moment of this book's journey: Your brilliant notes, encouragement to embrace the goofy chaos, and belief in me means the world. You're an editor who makes writers feel like superheroes. The offer of a forehead kiss is on the table.

Emily Forney is not only my superstar agent: She's a friend, cheerleader, and occasionally my therapist. You fought for STDA like it's the next HAMILTON (and honestly, it kind of is, right?) and stuck with me through every unhinged spiral. You're so good at your job that it makes the rest of us look bad.

Heartfelt gratitude to the awesome team at FSG and MacKids: Julia Bianchi, Allyson Floridia, Tracy Koontz, Allison Verost, Alexa Blanco, Gabriella Salpeter, and Chantal Gersch. And

Betsy Cola for creating a cover that captures everything I love about Natalie and Felix—and STDA itself.

Mom, you're a saint for proofing every iteration of this book (and for not disowning me during our lively "debates" about some of your suggestions). You deserve a co-author credit—or at least a nap. Cam, you've been a great sounding board and best friend. My service dog, Boss, and regular dog, Rusty; and my incredible friends, Nona, Toby, Hailey, Taylor, Briana, Guanting: I love y'all!

Shout-out to my bookish buddies who make this industry less lonely! Aiden Thomas, Cass Biehn, Kamilah Cole, Clare Edge, Sujin Witherspoon, Anna Sortino, Victoria Wlosok, Sarah Street, Taylor Epperson, Christina Li, Amparo Ortiz, Meredith Tate, Autumn Kohler, Brenna Jones, Sophie Gonzales, Lilly Lu, Gabriel Torres, Layla Noor, Birdie Schae, Famke Kim-Thy Halma, Taylor Grothe, Wenyi Lee, Elba Luz, Tiara Blue, Camille Simkin, Kalie Holford, Matthew Hubbard, Christen Randall, Hanna Kim, Justine Pucella Winans, Nicoletta Poungias, Isa Agajanian, Steph Barros, Katherine Morgan, Ann Zhao.

To my amazing street team: Thank you for the endless support!

I'm grateful for the feedback from my Korean American authenticity reader, Kim Stoker, and my Kiwi consultants, Nikki, Elly, and Sarah, who all helped ensure accurate representation.

Thank you to some of my fellow members of Signed Ink—a coalition of D/deaf/HOH authors and illustrators—and trusted friends/mentors in the D/deaf community who provided such valuable feedback and cheerleading.

Elanna Heda. You were the very first person to believe in this story and gave it wings to soar. I will never forget the once-in-a-lifetime opportunity you gave me. Thank you for setting this journey in motion and for your immeasurable impact on my career and this book.

Finally, YOU, dear reader! You're the magic that brings stories to life. Thank you for reading, dreaming, and making this adventure unforgettable.